© Bruce Christianson/Photologic.com

ABOUT THE AUTHOR

HEATHER MCELHATTON is the author of *Pretty Little Mistakes* and *Jennifer Johnson Is Sick of Being Single*. Her commentaries and stories have been heard nationally on *This American Life*, *Marketplace*, *Weekend America*, *Sound Money*, and *The Savvy Traveler*.

She and her pug, Walter, split their time between Minneapolis and Key West.

MILLION LITTLE MISTAKES

Also by Heather McElhatton

Pretty Little Mistakes

Jennifer Johnson Is Sick of Being Single

MILLION LIT

MILLION LITTLE

LE MISTAKES

MISTAKES

HEATHER MCELHATTON

HARPER

NEW YORK ● LONDON ● TORONTO ● SYDNEY

HARPER

MILLION LITTLE MISTAKES. Copyright © 2010 by Heather McElhatton. All rights reserved. Printed in the United States of America. No part of this book may be used or reproduced in any manner whatsoever without written permission except in the case of brief quotations embodied in critical articles and reviews. For information address HarperCollins Publishers, 10 East 53rd Street, New York, NY 10022.

HarperCollins books may be purchased for educational, business, or sales promotional use. For information, please write: Special Markets Department, HarperCollins Publishers, 10 East 53rd Street, New York, NY 10022.

FIRST EDITION

Designed by Justin Dodd

Library of Congress Cataloging-in-Publication Data is available upon request.

ISBN 978-0-06-113326-8

10 11 12 13 14   OV/RRD   10 9 8 7 6 5 4 3 2 1

FOR COLIN

HOW TO READ THIS BOOK

Don't read this book straight through, as you would a "normal" book. If you did, it would seem like a collage of many different stories, none of them making any sense. Instead, start on page one, and at the end of that section you'll have a choice to make. Make it, and turn directly to the corresponding section. In this way you'll control the story and the outcome of your chosen life.

As in real life, good behavior is not always rewarded and bad decisions can sometimes lead to wonderful (and not-so-wonderful) results. When you reach the end of your journey, return to the beginning or anywhere else along the way where you'd like a second chance. The trick is to never turn back and always follow your gut. You never know what life may bring, or what miracles are up ahead, speeding toward you as fast as they possibly can.

MILLION LITTLE MISTAKES

1

You win twenty-two million dollars in the Big Money Sucka! lottery. You've been playing the same numbers for years, always knowing nothing would happen, always cursing your *bad luck, dumb luck, tough luck, no luck*, wondering why nothing good ever happens and then *Crack!* Luck lands like knuckles across your jaw.

There's a phone call, thumping on the door, news cameras, TV lights, a lottery man handing you an oversized check, cameras flashing, and your whole world is forevermore changed. Twenty-two million little green song-birds are now singing in your bank account.

Big money and you've been hungry. Not for food, but for something else. Something you always wanted to do, or get, or see and thought you would've by now—if only things had been different. If you'd had more money, more time. Fewer detours. Better passengers. Fewer accidents. That thing you dream about that sits aching ice-bright in the greasy little waiting room of your heart. Your dream deferred and almost dead . . . but not quite.

You know the one.

Now you can do it. Pay off bills, get out of debt, help friends and family with various disasters. You can finally afford to dream. You're set. You're stable. You're free. So, should you quit your day job? You like what you do, it pays well and you've advanced far, but you can leave now. You're financially secure. Money is a lullaby. Small soothing words whisper in your head, a chorus repeating: *You're safe. You're safe. You're safe.*

If you quit your job, go to section 2 (p. 2).
If you keep your job, go to section 3 (p. 4).

2

From section 1

You knew quitting would feel good, but you had no idea *how* good. When you go into work and officially tender your resignation, ten years peel away from your posture, twenty pounds lift off your body, and you look every penny of fifteen million dollars richer. (Your lump-sum payment of twenty-two million got corn-holed by *applicable taxes*, cutting the winnings to fourteen million nine hundred and five thousand dollars [$14,905,000.00]. But hey, almost fifteen million is a lot more than you had before, right?)

The receptionist, who's never even said *good morning* before, gives you a quick little beauty-queen wave and all your coworkers say, "Congratulations!" or "Hey, Rockefeller!" and there's backslapping and hugging but there's also something strange in their faces. Micro sneers, quizzical glances, flashes of envy. Sharp shadows darting across their faces so quickly you wonder if it's real.

It's real.

They hate you. They hate you because you were the *lucky one* and if you didn't exist then the whole universe would shift one soul over and they might have won the lottery, and don't they deserve it more? Don't you know how many kids they have? College tuitions? Medical bills, leaking roofs, crumbling foundations, divorce lawyers? They've worked here longer, suffered more, and are far more deserving than *you*. Who the hell are you, anyway? According to these faces, you *personally* have deprived everyone of a windfall and are keeping them from sending their children to private schools and taking dream vacations and retiring early.

Your boyfriend, Aidan, reminds you that you've worked hard and you deserve a break. Ignore anyone who thinks you don't deserve it! Some people just can't be happy for other people's success; they think there's a limited supply of luck in the world and your gain is their loss.

Screw them. You can't help it if you're lucky. You should enjoy yourself!

He's right. You deserve a silver Mercedes convertible. So you buy one and drive it right off the lot. Then you drive it into a tree. The whole front fender is crunched, your coccyx is sprained, and you're confined to the couch for a few days, where you stay up late eating chocolate ice cream and pepperoni Bagel Bites while trying to keep the cat off the remote control and ordering stuff off the Home Shopping Network. You purchase a Stadium Gal (a mobile urinary station so you don't have to get up from the couch), an Apple MacBook, a matching set of Prada life accessories, a plasma flat-screen TV (size: insane), a king-sized memory foam mattress with enough silk bedding to swaddle a baby elephant, a Kenmore washer/dryer with antimicrobial misting cycle, a Segway scooter, a George Foreman grill with a year's supply of hoagie meat, a motorized armpit razor with ionizing magnets, and a twenty-four-week sex-therapy video series with free "vibrating walnut"—a remote-controlled device that stays "in place" and can be turned on and off from a nifty device in your purse.

Not that you've been doing anything sexy recently—your love life (as Aidan likes to continually point out) has been nonexistent since the accident, and before that it wasn't much to brag about either. You've been with Aidan for quite a while now, so long that the initial white-hot thunderstorm of attraction and romance has faded into more of a comfortable, lukewarm bath. There was a lot of passion at first and maybe there still could be; it's hard to say. You're grateful he's been so dependable all this time, and you don't fight much, so there's really nothing to complain about—but sometimes you see other couples and you think, *Is this it? Is this all I get?*

You're about to embark on a brand-new chapter of your life. A time to start fresh and take chances. Do you want to stay with Aidan and work things out, or brave this new world with your trusty vibrating walnut?

If you end your relationship, go to section 4 (p. 6).
If you keep your relationship, go to section 5 (p. 8).

3

You keep your job. You like the security, especially since your lump-sum lottery payment got shredded by taxes. More like *amputated*. After the government takes what "they're owed," you're left with a measly $14,905,000.00. You're angry. Disillusioned. But your boyfriend, Aidan, points out that while "almost fifteen million" dollars sounds like a lot *less* than twenty-two million, it's a lot *more* than you had before, and by keeping your job you're just adding equity into life, a chance to gild, to enhance while keeping your foundation solid.

That Aidan. He always knows what to say.

When you tell your boss that you're staying, however, he stares at you for a minute and then asks if you're crazy. Why aren't you quitting? Why not take all that money and do something amazing or at least amazingly stupid? It's almost like he and your coworkers resent you. You make their worlds just a little bleaker, reminding them of what they don't have, of what didn't happen, of who they can't be.

Aidan tells you to ignore them. The monkeys shriek, but the circus rolls on! He suggests hiring a financial advisor—someone to help you with your finances and investments. It's not a terrible idea and the lottery board has a list of advisors they recommend, but you're not sure. You've heard horror stories about some of those consultants. One lottery winner in Ash Flats, Arkansas, hired a financial advisor who ended up murdering him and running off with every penny. Authorities found him living in Mexico with a harem of pubescent concubines.

Another firm advised a Powerball winner in Chickasaw, Oklahoma, to invest in a well-respected slow-growth mutual fund. Nine months later it was exposed as a Ponzi scheme and all the lottery money was gone, along with every penny of her life savings. The upshot is, there are good money managers and bad. Hire the right one and you have an ally for life; hire the wrong one and they'll rob you blind. Plus, you can always manage this newfound money circus by yourself.

If you hire a financial consultant, go to section 6 (p. 10).
If you manage your own money, go to section 7 (p. 12).

4

You kill the relationship softly. First, you start ignoring Aidan's calls and pick random days when you just don't answer the phone. When he asks what's wrong, you say he sounds like a crazy stalker. You also sigh frequently, so he knows something bad is coming. When you're finally ready to lower the boom, you write him a short but earnest letter, which you'll present at the perfect moment, outlining the various reasons you're leaving.

You take Aidan out for a fancy dinner and wait for that crucial window of time when the dinner plates have been cleared but the dessert plates have not yet been set down. Then bombs away. You give him the letter and he reads it while you entertain yourself with text messaging. Despite your carefully chosen words, however, he gets redder and redder in the face. He's furious. He jumps up and bursts out of the dining room, forcing you to stay there and eat an entire chocolate fondue by yourself. Terrifically thoughtless. Well, that's Aidan for you. Always being negative.

Now that you're a free agent in this world, sponsored by fat cash and unhindered by people who bum you out, you really want to change things up. But where do you go? One idea might be to book passage on one of those around-the-world luxury cruises. A voyage of epic proportions that navigates the globe with grace and style. Not to mention an all-night shrimp bar. It would not only be a good way to see the world, it would be a good way to see millionaires. How do they live? Where do they go? What do they eat? Who do they marry? After all, you have no idea, and why would you? Up until now, your idea of luxury was pretty much relegated to double-ply toilet paper and occasionally getting a bikini wax.

Another idea presents itself on eBay. Apparently, some well-heeled blue-blooded socialite in New Orleans has decided to sell her life. All of it. At first it sounds strange, but the aristocrat's life offers you a rare opportunity to step into shoes that simply cannot be bought. Shoes that would otherwise take a lifetime to put on. A staffed antebellum mansion filled with heirloom antiques, family jewels, a full-service limo with driver, a vintage yacht harbored at the New Orleans Yacht Club. (Usually someone has to die before one of these coveted slips opens up.) A country club membership, plus social introductions, political connections, and power lunches with the mayor. It's a meticulously built life of elegance and ease, and you can have it all for a cool ten million.

If you go on a luxury cruise around the world, go to section 8 (p. 13).
If you buy the aristocrat's life on eBay, go to section 9 (p. 20).

5

You don't break up with Aidan. The relationship isn't perfect, but what relationship is? Besides, everything is different now. You have enough money to start your life over. You can do anything you want.

First of all, you'll get out of debt. Completely and totally. All your credit card balances will be *zero*, and just thinking about those bloodsucking leeches at the credit card companies losing your carcass as a feed bag makes you giddy with joy. Those life-killing, muck-dwelling, pus-producing parasites would gladly turn this entire society into a blank-faced tribe of debt zombies who must endlessly work at jobs they hate so much it makes their eyes bleed just so they can pay their minimum credit card balances.

Imagine when the overlords discover they lost a zombie! *Sirens sound! Shouts are heard!* They were going to use your initial credit card purchase of seventy-dollar Rollerblades over ten years ago as a seed fund for at least two of their CEO retreats in Aspen!

You could pay off all your family's bills, too. I mean, it's your family! Family sticks together, and haven't they always stuck by you? They need things! They have medical bills and missed mortgage payments and children with crooked teeth! They have broken water heaters and dogs with hip dysplasia!

They'd like you to take care of them, just like they took care of you. After all, you made it safely to adulthood, didn't you? Nobody drowned you, did they?

You are *family* and family takes care of each other, right? Now it's time for you to take care of them. The lists of requests pour in. One cousin needs money so she can open a miniatures store at the strip mall. It's her lifelong dream. Your mother has always wanted a state-of-the-art houseboat, the kind with a GPS navigation system and a whirlpool bathtub. Your dad, who put you through college, would also like a state-of-the-art houseboat, so he can go fishing with grandpa. Your uncle says he needs an emergency loan to pay his property taxes and his three daughters need college educations or they'll end up giving twenty-dollar Hanoi Hannahs at the truck stop.

To cover everyone's mortgages, credit cards, medical bills, and school loans—it'll cost a lot. Then, if you give everyone some money for all the things they want/need/will die without, like new houses/new cars/better vacations/college funds for the kids, it would eat up a lot of your money. You couldn't buy anything wild and crazy for yourself, no fleet of mono-grammed Bentleys or luxury safaris, but there'd probably be enough cash left over to buy a nice house, and you could have everyone over for big dinners—and if no one had any debts, no credit card bills or looming mort-gage payments, your mother's withering dream of having a family dinner where everyone got along might actually come true.

Then again, how many people get this opportunity? Here the unbeliev-able has happened, you won the freaking lottery, and for the first time in your life you can do *anything* you want. No budgeting, no scrimping, no pussy "five-year plan" to get something cool started. The engines are rum-bling and the thrusters are ready. Buy yourself something ridiculous! So what if you break your mother's heart? She's used to it! The angel on your shoulder says you should help your family, but the devil says it's time to tell everyone to go to hell and make your weird-ass dreams come true.

If you buy yourself something ridiculous, go to section 10 (p. 26.)
If you pay all your family's bills, go to section 11 (p. 28).

6

You meet with two highly recommended financial consultants. First, there's Mr. Cook, from the lottery board. He looks like a nervous woodland creature with a shy, bright pink face and ears like soup bowl handles. He's from a respectable law firm that specializes in wealth management, and even though he can't reveal the names of his clients due to confidentiality laws, he assures you he works for the very wealthiest families.

His plan for your millions is conservative. He thinks you should keep your job for now, refrain from making any major purchases, tell as few family members about your new fortune as possible, decline all media appearances, invest mostly in blue-chip slow-growth mutual funds, and live off a modest monthly income. Sounds smart . . . but not very fun.

He says smart is better than fun in the long run. Otherwise you may suffer from Sudden Windfall Syndrome, which happens to people without proper financial boundaries. Instead of saving their money and planning wisely, they buy big-ticket items, rack up debts, spin out their credit, and wind up bankrupting themselves. "Sudden money can become overwhelming," he says. "Fifty-one percent of all lottery winners commit suicide. I've lost several clients myself."

Fifty-one percent? That means it's not only *possible* you'll commit suicide, but *probable*. He says most people expect money to fix their lives, to make them happy, to make them beautiful and well-liked and to repair their marriages. When it doesn't, some despair. They think that since being a millionaire didn't make them happy, nothing ever will. They drink and turn to substances. They forget who their friends are. Nobody lasts long after that.

Next you meet with Mr. Bossrock, a big refrigerator of a man with a barrel chest and a deep laugh. He has a thick gold chain around his sunburned neck and a tight knot of chest hair peeking out of his open silk shirt. He just got back from the Caribbean, where he was checking out some offshore investments and spear-fishing for shark. He caught two and has the digital images on his phone to prove it. Everything about him seems exciting and alive. He manages the estates of many Hollywood celebrities, European rock stars, celebrity chefs, enterprising millionaires, playboy billionaires, and reclusive trillionaires. He explains his *aggressive capital gain* philosophy, which is to go where the crowds aren't, to take big risks for big reward. He says Sudden Windfall Syndrome is a myth. Something conservatives made up. "If that guy's had clients commit suicide," he says, "maybe you'll be next." Bossrock thinks you should take a couple million and buy something fun. Cars, trips, a Rolex like his, whatever you want. Then you'll buy up some real estate—namely, a new house to live in—and then you'll start investing in some very hot deals. Hot deals only he knows about. "Think big," he says with a wink, "and be big."

Two men, two totally different financial styles, and you have to choose one to help you manage your money. It's not that big of a deal, really, it's only the rest of your life.

If you hire Bossrock, go to section 12 (p. 31).
If you hire Cook, go to section 13 (p. 33).

7

You decide against hiring a financial advisor. Your family thinks it's best and even Grandpa Joe approves. He looks you right in the eye (like only an ex–marine drill sergeant can), and says, "Darlin', always trust your gut and nobody else's. Come hell or high water, all right? Promise me that." You nod and promise him you'll manage your own money and life will be good. After all, life is short and this pile of money is tall. Think how many things you can do and what you can buy!

Your family knows what you should buy. A kidney. Doctors say your cousin Lanie doesn't have much time left without a transplant and the donor waiting list is miles long. Someone has to buy this girl a new organ or she'll die. Your uncle's having heart trouble from the stress and your aunt is all puffed up from crying. Everyone looks to you, the family's only millionaire, to save the day.

Buying a kidney is expensive however, and so is the aftercare and the ongoing treatments, which you'll also be expected to fund. The doctors also warn you that her other kidney might fail, too. If you become Lanie's medical benefactor, it may be a long haul and cost a big chunk of money. Possibly into the millions.

If you pay for Lanie's kidney, go to section 14 (p. 34).
If you don't pay for Lanie's kidney, go to section 15 (p. 36).

8

From section 4

You take your girlfriend, Sam, along with you on your three-month luxury cruise aboard the *Asylum of the Sea*. At a quarter billion dollars, it's the biggest, most expensive cruise ship ever built, boasting a length of six hundred and fifty feet, a weight of forty thousand tons, and a virtual guidance system that communicates with satellites in space.

The ship has a retractable stern, an amphitheater, a rock-climbing wall, a white-water rapids simulator, an indoor ice-skating rink, a simulation Central Park, an actual grass putting green, a vintage merry-go-round, a tattoo parlor, a fortune-teller, its own radio and television stations, and a clear Lucite swimming pool that cantilevers over the sea.

The ship departs from Los Angeles and heads to the Panama Canal, Santiago, Antarctica, Cape Town, the Seychelles, Mumbai, Singapore, Hong Kong, and Osaka. After the spectacular departure with fireworks and synchronized jets flying overhead releasing smoky ribbons of color in the sky, there's a champagne toast and now all you have to do is soak up the luxury. Relax, read, sleep, eat, have sex, sleep. Repeat.

Your staterooms are the grandest on the entire ship. The penthouse suite provides butler service, a personal chef, a master bedroom with small refrigerated nightstands so champagne is always in reach, a small but formal dining room with an endlessly replenished fruit bowl, and a private terrace with its own hot tub. The hot tub has a light show you can activate at night, which changes the simmering water from azure blue to bright pink to quartz yellow, only you think the quartz yellow looks more like hot pee, as if for some reason it was advantageous to bathe in a cauldron of boiling urine, so you don't turn on the hot tub light show that much.

The crew goes out of their way to make sure every experience is excellent.

Stewards fly around the ship in little white jackets like startled doves and it's said there's one crew member for every two passengers on board, but that doesn't seem mathematically possible. Where do they sleep? No matter what you do, from sitting down to dinner or setting down your towel, everything is whisked away or served up or replaced with nearly alarming speed, as though your every action has been anticipated and prepared for.

Even with all this pampering and solicitous servitude, you and Sam do find some flaws in the service, actually. Every night the maids leave a towel on your bed folded into the shape of a swan or an elephant or a teddy bear or a monkey, but that's it. Four animals only? After the monkey, they start up with the swan all over again and it gets boring. Also, you've noticed at dinner sometimes the pats of butter are carved into rosebuds, but other times they're just plain squares. You hate the plain squares. These things could be fixed with the smallest of advance planning and you should probably write a letter.

You begin to see little problems everywhere. Your stateroom, for instance. The complimentary bathrobes are knee-length instead of full-length. If you want a full-length bathrobe you have to buy one at the spa. Also the fruit basket, which is replenished daily, stops containing kiwis, even though you expressly asked your steward for kiwis. He says the ship *is low on them* but they still somehow show up every morning at the breakfast buffet garnishing the watermelon fruit bowls. You then notice an irritating hum coming from the ventilation system that keeps you awake at night, until between the robes, the kiwis, and the humming you can't even stand to be in your stateroom.

Then you meet a tall man with green eyes. Edward. He's onboard with his family to celebrate his parents' fiftieth wedding anniversary. He's witty, charming, and polite. The perfect gentleman. He escorts you to your room at night and never asks to come in. He invites you to eat with his family and the captain of the ship. (This ticks Sam off a little, as you leave her to dine alone across the room at one of the lesser tables closer to the kitchen, but whatever, you're trying to start a shipboard romance here.)

Finally, you can't stand his genteel ways and attack him one night. You wind up making passionate (albeit slightly awkward) love in one of the fiberglass rowboats lashed to the side of the deck. At first you try to keep your budding romance secret, but soon enough everyone can tell you two are in love, even your still-slightly-annoyed friend. You're perfect together! You play tennis, get side-by-side massages, take long walks at twilight. You like all the same movies, all the same music, and he kisses you eagerly, hungrily, like he may never see you again.

There are mishaps. You take a face plant on the lido deck while cruising around on a speedy little Segway trying to catch up to Edward, and when you're trying out the very popular (but freezing!) wave machine while learning to surf, you fall and get caught up in the jets, spinning around like a frozen shrimp in an aqua blue skillet.

Still, looking past these few minor bumps and bruises, you must admit it's a breathtaking way to see the world, to sit in idle luxury as the purple mountains of Patagonia drift by, or to get a detoxifying aromatherapy massage on the lower deck at sunset, or to admire the pod of bottlenose dolphins following the ship as you chip biodegradable golf balls into the sea. (This is actually not as enjoyable as the other activities because you worry that [a] the balls are not biodegradable, that's just something they tell passengers to get them to shut up and remain entertained for five minutes, and [b] one of these golf balls, biodegradable or not, is going to crack a dolphin right on the skullcap and kill him dead.)

The cruise delivers some of the most visually opulent destinations you've ever seen. The Panama Canal is an engineering miracle. Imagine something as soft and secret as water lifting hundreds of thousands of tons of rusting steel, the locks delivering the ships one by one from the Atlantic to the Pacific Ocean.

After Tierra del Fuego, the ship sails down the Drake Passage, through a maze of small icebergs to the Antarctic Peninsula, where it looks as though you've left the planet. In the Neumayer Channel, and the Gerlache Strait, mountains of turquoise ice floats on black water as penguins dive off flat cakes of snow. It's all gorgeous and eerie and you sleep deeply in Edward's arms that night.

The voyage from Antarctica to South Africa is rough, as you were told it would be, but when you finally depart Cape Town, and steam northward, the water calms and you can relax again. Then, when the ship is just off the coast of Somalia, you suddenly spot a small motorboat approaching.

You point it out to Edward.

Other passengers gather around, wondering how such a small boat could be *this far* out at sea. You all stay quiet and watch with great interest as the strange and surreal events unfold. The small boat is loaded with thirty-odd Somalian boys, all thin and none of whom could be over nineteen years old. They pull up alongside your ship, which seems mammoth next to them, and toss grappling hooks onto the lowest railings, which two boys scamper up without effort. They throw rope ladders down to their comrades, who cheer, adding to the sensation that something amusing is happening. It's only when the rest of the boys start pulling themselves hurriedly up the ladders that someone asks, "Are they pirates?"

They *are* in fact pirates and they not only have guns, they have grenades, automatic weapons, and an extremely ominous surface-to-air missile launcher. An ear-shattering alarm starts to pierce the air and the captain comes on, ordering all passengers to the Poseidon Dining Room. He says to go as quietly and quickly as possible.

Edward has vanished. You're hustled along with the rest of the group like cattle into the Poseidon Dining Room, which is designated as the de facto meeting place for all emergencies because it's the only dining room that can hold all the passengers at once. As you pass through the glass doors to the dining room it's the silence that scares you the most. Everyone is waiting for instruction, some already with their luggage and wearing bright yellow lifejackets. Edward is not among them.

The chief security officer calmly explains the boat is being hijacked and a collective gasp sounds around the room. You feel sick. Blessedly, Sam shows up beside you, linking her arm in yours while somewhere onboard the captain negotiates with the pirates.

The security officer, a tall man with a thick shock of white hair and a refined chin, continues, "We are safe, ladies and gentlemen. This room is the hardest part of the ship to penetrate, aside from the engine room and the bridge. It's specifically designed as a 'passenger safe hold' and can repel attack while supporting life. As you see, it extends the entire width of the vessel, leaving only two entrances. One in front, which you all came through, and one back through the kitchen, both of which my crew are now securing."

Everyone turns toward the front entrance of the dining room as a security engineer finishes punching in a set of codes and two metal doors slide over the glass.

"These doors are now unbreakable," the officer says. "Airtight and blast-proof."

"What about the windows?" someone asks.

"The windows are unbreakable and bulletproof as well. I urge you now to stay calm, make yourselves comfortable, and let the stewards know if you need anything. Besides the convenience of bathrooms located directly to my left, the kitchen will remain open and there are enough provisions in the galley to last a week. Of course, once we explain to our new friends they've accidentally pulled over a passenger ship, we hope to have you back enjoying your cruise in a matter of hours."

He steps down as the whine of an electric screw gun starts up and the engineers rivet the blast doors in place. Then they set iron bars across them. Despite all these security measures and the officer's assuring words, you don't know what frightens you more, the fact that it's happening or that they were so prepared for it. Then the engines stop. That constant, almost inaudible sound that's always in the background ceases, leaving a queer silence magnified by all absence of motion. "Well, they made it into the engine room," someone says, "or maybe into the bridge."

The security officer assures you it's protocol to stop engines in this situation, so the ship is easier for the navy to track. Then he leaves, aided by two armed engineers. The next twelve hours are spent getting comfortable. Staking out little mini immigrant camps inside the great hall, people band-ing together with their families and friends. Thank God Sam's here, especially since there's still no sign of Edward. Someone says he and his family escaped on a private lifeboat. What on earth is a *private* lifeboat? Do people bring their own lifeboats on cruise ships?

The chef who runs the carving station turns on his glowy red heat lamp and starts carving roast beef. By midnight almost everyone is sitting at a table or eating, telling every disaster-at-sea story they've ever heard. It's a pretty decent waiting room considering the situation, and the waiters and stewards keep on like nothing is different, offering to bring ice water to tables and clearing away dishes.

Another twelve hours pass and nobody knows what's happening. Even the security officers who are locked in with you are clueless. The captain hasn't issued new orders, and neither has their commanding security officer. The radio was cut. His last message was, "Hold at all cost," which does not sound good.

Nor does it sound good the next day, when the glass doors of the dining room begin to rattle violently and then shatter. Shouting outside starts and everyone clutches tighter into one big group as the crew stands guard, guns drawn. Popping sounds can be heard and louder banging. "They're shooting at the doors!" Everyone runs to the far side of the room.

Then a massive booming sound ricochets around the room and a big cloud of smoke pours into the hall as the doors blow open. The explosion knocks several passengers down. People are hurt, cut and bleeding from flying debris. The pirates unarm the security officers within seconds of entering.

There will be no more roast beef carving stations from this point on.

The pirates round everyone up in the center of the room and say they've taken the ship. The captain and his crew are dead. They need everyone to hand over their wallets, purses, cash, and jewelry. When people start claiming to not have their wallets or purses with them, escorted trips are organized, two pirates taking five passengers each to their staterooms to retrieve these items while the rest of the passengers stay guarded in the Poseidon Dining Room.

The food runs out, the toilets start to overflow. People who don't have their heart medication or insulin or allergy medicine start dropping. All this and there is still no sign of the coast guard. Nobody but you and these maniacs. And no Edward, of course.

Finally the pirates say they're going to trade 90 percent of the ship's passengers for their own safe transport back to Somalia. They need ten hostages to remain, ten people willing to stay on board so that everyone else can go.

Then they ask for volunteers.

If you decide to get off the ship, go to section 16 (p. 38).
If you volunteer to stay on board and remain a hostage,
go to section 17 (p. 40).

9

You purchase the aristocrat's life and the marvels roll in. An estate lawyer descends with a giant stack of deeds, titles, contracts, and other pertinent information. He explains you will be taking over the extraordinary life of a *true* Southern belle. He can't say where she is or why she left, but rest assured, you're about to have an adventure that only a few people in this world will ever experience.

The LaLaurie House in New Orleans is now your home, a French Empire mansion on Royal Street in the French Quarter. As advertised, the estate comes fully furnished with pristine French Empire antiques, a full-service staff, a black stretch limo with driver, and a Bugatti Veyron with red and chocolate interior hand-stitched by Hermès parked in the driveway. (Only a few hundred will ever be made and the car can accelerate from 0 to 60 in 2.4 seconds with a top speed of 253 miles per hour.)

You now own the *Well-Deserved*, a beautiful mahogany boat that debuted at the Monaco Yacht Show in 1934 and was heralded as "a boat for discerning pirates." It's made from the finest wood lacquered eighteen times over, every detail meticulously hand-finished. Also as promised there's a membership at the prestigious New Orleans Country Club waiting for you. The estate lawyer blots his head with a handkerchief and admits this was the hardest part to pull off, as the club doesn't hand out memberships to just anyone with money. You have to *be* somebody. It's frequented by blue-blooded ladies of society as well as retired senators and seated governors, and, of course, all their wives and mistresses, so discretion is of the *utmost*.

When you fly down to the vibrant, incredible city of New Orleans, you meet your new staff. They wear crisp uniforms and have all worked here a long time. The cook, Thalie, is tiny and shriveled, her rough, wrinkled skin looking older than the branches of a live oak tree. Thalie makes huge dinners fit for a Confederate army. She-crab soup, barbecued shrimp, pork shoulder, red beans and rice, corn bread with butter, pecan pie, tea cookies, sweet tea, and Sazerac cocktails afterward. She serves you silently, always eyeing you with curiosity, but like everyone else, she doesn't ask questions. You know what they're all thinking, though.

They're thinking you don't look like a millionaire. You didn't even bring any of your own furniture and the only clothes you have fit in a small bag. That's because you're leaving your old life behind. Nothing of yours would look right here, even your *family* wouldn't look right here. The staff looks more elegant than your fat old uncles in their black socks and stained track suits.

You start making appointments with the city's top personal shoppers, hairstylists, and cosmetologists. You get a new wardrobe, dermabrasion, Botox, tattooed eyeliner, and liposuction. You're ecstatic with the results, except the Botox renders you unable to raise an eyebrow or look annoyed, which causes more problems than you'd think. Every time you want to let someone know you're displeased you have to say so out loud because your face won't.

Your aristocrat's life even comes with a best friend. Your wealthy neighbor, Maribelle St. John, has agreed to show you around New Orleans. She's a force of nature, Maribelle, you can hardly keep up with her. Cherry redheaded, positively aggressive, endlessly gregarious, and skinny as a stir stick, even though she drinks double gin and tonics at noon. She says, "Every woman should redecorate a house when she steps foot in it, whether it needs it or not." She knows which decorators to hire and which auctions to attend, even though you hate those auctions, with all that nerve-wracking shouting and competitive tension. You always end up going home with something strange, like a stone gargoyle or an antique writing desk that came over on the *Mayflower.*

She introduces you to her friends at the country club, takes you to cocktail parties, theater openings, charity balls, and most important, she gives you all the pertinent social gossip you need to navigate the deep social waters of the South. She tells you "Bless her heart" is what Southerners say instead of "Fuck you." As in, "She was never good with children, *bless her heart*," or "You forgot to bring wine again? *Bless your heart!*"

You're having such a good time going to parties and buying anything you want, it's a total shock when the bank calls and Mr. Deloit, the head of private accounts, asks if everything's *all right*. What does he mean? Of course everything's all right!

He's noticed some high-volume spending on your account and suggests you come in sometime and sit down with a financial planner, who can help you budget for your ongoing financial needs. What does he mean, *budget?*

You promise to set up an appointment and thank him for calling. Okay, sure, maybe you got a little crazy with the spending at first, but it's not going to stay that way. Once you get everything you need, you won't have to keep spending so much, right? It always takes extra engine power to get a ship up to speed, but then it can coast, and coast is what you do, right into the heart of the social scene.

Your new life comes with invitations from the crème de la crème of New Orleans society and everyone wants to know who the new belle of the ball is. They're charmed by your social naiveté and newfound resources. Everyone loves you when you're rich! You've never been more thrilled or exhausted in your life. The laughter gets louder and life couldn't be better.

Then things start happening.

The first event was during a party at your house. You're speaking with the lieutenant governor and his wife when you spot a very strangely dressed woman standing in the corner. She's staring at you. You excuse yourself from the conversation so you can go introduce yourself, but when you look her way again, she's disappeared. A week later, you're in the kitchen and you see what you guess is a new maid in the butler's pantry. When you ask her what her name is, she's gone.

There are sounds. Usually at night. It's a series of knocks at first. Tiny ones, as though someone was tapping on your door with a pencil. Then doors slamming, and then you exit your bedroom one morning to find five pennies facedown on the floor, all lined up in an orderly row. No chance it's an accident; as much as you try to convince yourself it is—it isn't. Then there are the shadows that rearrange themselves along the floorboards, as though a long creeping mist branched along with your steps, evaporating whenever looked at directly.

Mind games! Tricks!

The city has such a haunted history; surely this is your overactive imagination. Maybe your jangled nerves? Your doctor prescribes earplugs and sedatives so you can sleep at night, and sleep you do, so soundly, in fact, you wake up one morning with something heavy and wet on your stomach, soaking through your T-shirt. You're aware of it before you look, your breath quickens, and your heart cracks up into your throat. You look down and there is a monstrous dead toad on your stomach, his eyes sewn shut with thick white twine.

The maids come running when they hear your screams and they swear they haven't seen anyone in the house. No doors are unlocked, no windows broken, everyone is accounted for. When you call the police, they won't even come to the house, because dead toads rank a notch or two under dead citizens, of which they got a lot. Thanks for calling.

You don't dare tell Maribelle what's happening, you don't dare tell anyone outside the house. It's only when you get the idea to visit the library at the historical society that you start to find some answers. Bad answers. LaLaurie has a horrific past. It turns out it was originally built in 1832 for Dr. Louis LaLaurie and his French-Creole wife, Delphine. Delphine LaLaurie wasn't just known for her lavish parties; she was also known for her well-behaved slaves and what she did to them. It's all right there in the newspaper stories, eyewitness accounts, and court documents.

Apparently, on one particular evening in the spring of 1833, Delphine was having a grand dinner. The newspaper says she'd purchased two hundred Spode place settings just for the evening and the dinner menu included poached salmon with mousseline and roast duckling marrow. Guests who arrived early claimed the house looked especially grand that evening, every detail perfect. They enjoyed champagne cocktails while waiting for Madame to come downstairs—she had a habit of waiting for all her guests to arrive before she made her entrance. Nothing unusual about it at all.

Delphine was in fact getting ready in her bedroom and a young slave girl, Leah, was combing out her hair. As the story goes, the girl accidentally snagged Madame's hair, sending her into a rage. Guests were still pulling up in carriages, dressed in their finest, as Madame LaLaurie chased Leah around the bedroom and out onto the balcony, where the twelve-year-old toppled over the balustrade and fell to her death on the front stoop.

Unable to conceal the crime, Madame LaLaurie was brought up on charges of abuse, but received only a minor fine from the judge, a frequent guest at their house. She was made to sell her slaves, but, through a relative, purchased them all back later. Life gradually returned to normal for the LaLauries, the parties and balls began again, the grisly death poured out from general memory as fast as champagne poured into crystal glasses.

Then, on April 10, 1834, during another party, a fire broke out in the kitchen, which was in a building set back from the main house. (It's now the garage.) The New Orleans fire brigade responded immediately, as they always did for the finer homes, only to find the LaLauries' slaves shackled to the oven. They themselves had set the fire in an attempt to bring light onto what was happening inside the house.

They directed the firefighters to a small room above them, where screams could be heard inside. The heavy door was bolted and locked; the firefighters had to use a battering ram to enter, and when they did, they stepped into a putrid house of horrors. Before them, locked in cages big enough for a dog and chained to the walls and floor, were disfigured, dismembered slaves, the victims of Madame LaLaurie and her physician husband, who had been conducting crude medical experiments.

One man looked as if he'd been given a primitive sex-change operation. Another man had a hole drilled in his skull so his brain could be probed with a stick. A woman inside a cage that restricted any movement had all her joints broken and reset at odd angles so she resembled a human crab.

Another woman had her arms amputated and her skin was peeled off in a circular pattern, making her look like a human caterpillar.

As the police were removing these poor souls and dispatching them into ambulances, the LaLauries' angry guests formed a mob outside and threatened to ransack the house and burn it down. They had no idea their hosts had been running a Grand Guignol theater in their community, a dread stage of gruesome entertainment. Before they could get hold of the LaLauries, however, the family escaped in a carriage and fled to the river. They were never seen again and their fortune, which was hidden somewhere in the house, was never found.

This is your home now. The bloody LaLaurie mansion. Peering out to the back building, which was once the kitchen and now is the renovated five-car garage, a queer feeling passes through you. You can almost hear the wailing. You grill Thalie about the history of the house until she breaks down and tells you everything. She says there's a curse here: anyone who owns the LaLaurie mansion is destined to kill or commit suicide. It's already happened multiple times. She knows, she's seen it.

You ask her what to do, beg her for ideas, and she says there is one way, but it's dangerous. You can try and remove the curse. She knows a lady, a vodoun priestess who can lift curses even when they're heavy. If you want, she'll arrange a meeting. You thank her for being so open and honest with you and tell her you'll think about it. She says, "Yes, ma'am, just don't think too long."

That night you pace the floors all night long and by dawn conclude you really only have two options. Sell the house or face Madame LaLaurie and make her get the hell out.

If you stay in the house, go to section 18 (p. 42).
If you sell the house, go to section 19 (p. 47).

10

From section 5

You decide to buy yourself something stupid-cool, something only a millionaire could get, but what is that exactly? Every idea you have on your own seems a little insane, like throwing a pool party with all-midget bartenders dressed up like various children in history (Little Orphan Annie, Spanky, Lindbergh baby) or buying a flock of emperor penguins to live in your apartment. Aidan's no help, either; he's not thinking big enough. He wants to put money away for retirement and maybe buy a hunting cabin up north. Well, that's great, for him. Not for you, though. In need of inspiration, you leave Aidan home and jet off to the "Millionaire Fair" in Kortrijk, Belgium, where you shop around for something deliciously decadent, but the choices are staggering. Should you buy a thirty-thousand-dollar Swarovski crystal—encrusted toilet seat? Rent the private chateau in France where *The Da Vinci Code* was filmed? Buy cubic zirconium wheel rims for your car? Bid on a "discreet yet primal night" with the sexiest bullfighter in Spain? Commission a Japanese "helper" robot who does windows and performs seven different types of fellatio?

You can't make up your mind, afraid you'll do something stupid, like the lottery winner in Myrtle Beach who won five hundred million, bought himself a solid gold Lamborghini, and died three days later when he crashed it into a tree. Your decisions are made vastly easier by the goddamned Russians. They're in mass attendance at the Millionaire Fair and they're dangerous. They're overnight billionaires with easy-to-influence "new money" whims, and they spend money like Earth might explode into a fine atomized spray sometime tomorrow. In the two days you hang out together, your new friend Vitali buys his girlfriend, Nika, a full-length white mink coat and a helicopter. His pal, Oleg, who already owns the world's largest collection of Fabergé Imperial Easter eggs, decides to buy a new submarine. His *old* one isn't big enough to reach the *Titanic*, which he plans to visit so he can ram it. You don't ask for further clarification on this desire. Russians just like ramming things.

And how.

You actually have a fling with Oleg in his penthouse suite after drinking several shots of Stolichnaya Elit out of shot glasses made of solid ice. Then Oleg demanded you take a champagne bath, ordering the concierge to fill his tub with warm Dom Pérignon and white rose petals. You could have left, but why? Certainly, you didn't mean for things to get so out of hand. (After you soaked in the deliriously effervescent water while listening to Oleg recite Russian poetry, he lifted you out of the bath and turned you over, whereupon he Helsinkied your Vologda for such a duration that the next morning you walked as though you'd just gotten off a horse.)

By the end of your four-day sin-a-thon you're more than ready to go home. You can't bear to leave without completing your millionaire mission and picking up a ridiculous gift for yourself. (Maybe you're feeling a little guilty and you just want to get it over with.) The two standout purchases may be predictable, but they're classics and you think Aidan would enjoy them, too. You could buy a private island, a sanctuary from the cold cruel world, or you could get one of those deluxe megayachts, which is like a private island that moves. They both involve rest, relaxation, and each cost five million dollars on the nose.

If you buy a private island, go to section 41 (p. 133).
If you buy a megayacht and travel the world, go to section 43 (p. 147).

11

Paying off everyone's bills makes you like the mayor of your family. Everyone suddenly respects and loves you. They loved you *before* of course, they just love you more now. Bills and mortgages overflow your desk and you can hardly write checks fast enough to cover them. Aidan also seems to love you more now. His price? A Harley-Davidson. (Everyone has a price, whether they know it or not.)

You try to keep up and give everyone what they want; only the money is draining fast. Eventually you seek the help of a financial counselor at your bank, Mr. Jeremy Strothers. He's just a guy on the client services staff, but he isn't like the others. (Aidan insists on calling him "Germy Jeremy, the Boring Banker Boy," however.)

Jeremy puts you on a financial diet and offers to handle your family. From now on if anyone wants money, they have to call him. He also handles the rest of your financial affairs, suggesting insurance plans, retirement programs, retirement funds, and slow-growth investment strategies. You got really lucky running into this guy. He's always there to answer your questions, he's never confused or overwhelmed, and he knows exactly what you should do. Plus, he's funny and flirtatious. Very well dressed. Not to mention *quite* handsome. You have a crush on Banker Boy.

Jeremy keeps things professional, though. You have to ask four times before he'll agree to meet you "off campus" at a wine bar near the bank. Even then, he wants to talk about your long-range investment goals and starts suggesting various real estate opportunities he knows about. Try as you might, the only passionate response you can get out of him usually is when the topic of flipping houses or redeveloping high-traffic consumer corridors comes up. In the end, after listening to all he has to say about the merits of real estate investments, you buy a small, ten-unit apartment building. You're hoping it will be the foundation of a new, steady revenue stream (and also that it'll convince Jeremy to sleep with you).

Three more property purchases later, it works. You're celebrating the acquisition of a split-level duplex and you drink too much. You insist you can't go home until you sober up and he takes you back to his place, where you attack him in the most unladylike manner, releasing what appears to be the other side of this buttoned-up banker. He tears this book off the shelf, *100 Positions You've Never Tried Before*, and starts on page one, performing the "Bailout Feeding Frenzy" on you while you're pinned against the wall, the "Snack-Master" while you're draped over the couch, and the "Holy Mess" on the floor of the shower.

In the morning you have *100 Bruises in Places You've Never Seen Before*.

After that, you meet Jeremy almost every day at his place, explaining your lengthy absences to Aidan as necessary trips out "property hunting." Sometimes these hunts require days, if not weeks, in other cities. This part is actually true. You and Jeremy take clandestine trips not only to make progress on his *100 Positions* book, executing the "Sticky Igloo" and the "Angry Monkey" on rented hotel beds, but also to actually look at real estate—and you're not going to sexy places, like New York, Miami, or Aspen, either. Jeremy prefers smaller markets, like Dubuque, Naperville, and Wichita. ("Lopsided Catapult," "Broken Tacklebox," and "Funky Lunchmeat," respectively.)

You close deals all over the place and Jeremy hires construction crews to renovate the houses and buildings before putting them back on the market. Some pull quite a nice profit and others idle, so you turn them into rentals, which provide a nice, steady, ongoing income. You're so grateful for Jeremy's sound advice and hard work, which is considerable, taking into account how boring some of these destinations are and how difficult it is to get certain sexual props through the security line at the airport. (Try explaining to a TSA agent why you have a watermelon, a vibrating collar, and an aluminum rolling pin in your carry-on luggage.) He's done it all just for you—up until now. Finally, one night at the Indianapolis airport, after some gravy-drowned breaded steaks and a pitcher of Miller Lite at T.G.I. Friday's, Jeremy asks if you'd be willing to take this relationship to the next level.

He wants to move in together and also start investing together, sharing properties and profits fifty-fifty. With your combined incomes and his market savvy, you'll have twice the number of properties rolling over. It's something to think about. As the affair with Jeremy continues, you feel worse and worse about Aidan, who's a really nice guy. You hate to hurt him. You never meant your fling to turn into a "thing," but now that it has, you're also able to see how Jeremy makes a good partner. It's time to choose one guy or the other.

To keep doing this isn't fair.

If you run off with Jeremy, go to section 46 (p. 159).
If you stay with Aidan, go to section 47 (p. 162).

12

From section 6

You retain the services of Mr. Bossrock and he immediately shares his ideas on how to invest your money, none of which include giving it away. Not to friends or family. He says the best way to help those you love is to further solidify your own standing. Increase your fortune. The more stable you are, the stronger you can be for everyone else. First order of business is to quit your job. Splitting your attention will rob other endeavors, and the decisions you make now are critical.

You're so glad you hired this guy; you don't make a move without his approval. Aidan doesn't like him. He wants to know why Bossrock gets to run your life. Why do you listen to his every word like it was a commandment chiseled in stone? What if the guy is a crook? What if he's an idiot? He looks like an idiot! Aidan doesn't seem to understand how lucky you are to have sound advice to listen to in the first place. He's just threatened and insecure. And besides, it was his idea to even hire a financial planner.

As time goes on and Bossrock maintains control over your purse strings, the fights with Aidan get quite nasty. The coup d'état comes when Bossrock cancels Aidan's birthday trip to Jamaica because of some political unrest in the region. He says it's not safe at the moment, but Aidan thinks it's a great big "mind screw" and gives you an ultimatum. He says you have to choose between Bossrock and him. "There's not room for two leading men in this motherfucking movie!" Then, before you can even respond, he says, "Forget it!" and calls you a zombie, a robot, a mindless money-obsessed idiot.

Bossrock brushes it off, saying millionaires are never alone. To cheer you up, he proposes two *big* ideas. He's found a couple of different business opportunities that are sure to get your mind off the past and onto the future. One idea is buying your own private island, which you can develop into a deluxe hotel. The hot properties he found are amazing and only for those "on the inside."

The other idea he calls "more creative." A *once-in-a-lifetime opportunity* that was brought to him in secret and is "a bit unusual, but lucrative." There's a major A-list celebrity who wants to do a deal with you. It guarantees big financial returns and includes an amazing social life loaded with the most powerful deal makers, the most exclusive parties, and the sexiest people in Hollywood.

If you buy an island, go to section 24 (p. 69).

If you go for the Hollywood deal, go to section 25 (p. 70).

13

From section 6

You hire Mr. Cook. His conservative nature is comforting; it makes you feel safe—like he won't let you do anything stupid. He turns down your request for a new Mercedes, saying your current car is fine. Then, when your family clamors for cash, Mr. Cook politely shoos them all away. He just won't allow it. "Pay one and you have to pay them all!" He won't even give Aidan a Harley-Davidson until he passes an intensive state-trooper-approved motorcycle safety class. "Another money-saving device," he explains. "Better to pay for a safety class instead of a funeral. Not to mention the cost of an accident victim who doesn't have the decency to die, but insists on remaining a vegetable. It's the height of inconvenience."

Mr. Cook recommends you put your money in a handpicked investment fund. The Silverlock Trust is an upper-echelon titan based in New York and guarantees regular returns by placing instant trades with futures, currencies, and stocks, causing a 1 percent guaranteed, no-risk profit. "You do that twenty times a year," Mr. Cook says, "take away management fees and taxes and you've got a steady fifteen percent return." You have no idea what he's talking about. You don't know much about percentages and rates of return and all that mumbo jumbo. Maybe investing in real estate would be better? He frowns and says, "*Maybe*, but the housing market is unpredictable and a property you can't sell isn't an investment, it's just another expense." Still, the choice is yours. Investment company or real estate?

If you invest in Silverlock Trust, go to section 26 (p. 74).
If you invest in real estate, go to section 27 (p. 78).

14

You help Lanie—you'd be a monster not to. She gets her kidney, which arrives in a scuffed cooler and for all you know was hacked out of some unsuspecting frat boy in Tijuana the night before. Nevertheless, Lanie receives her lifesaving surgery and your family is so grateful. Without you, she might have died.

Now your aunt wants to know if you can give them a monthly allowance so she can quit her job and stay home with Lanie. It would mean so much to them. Well, *okay*. How can you say no? You give your aunt some money so she doesn't have to work. She's going to be Lanie's full-time nurse now, it's not like she's slacking off. But then your uncle gets ticked off because *he* still has to work and why should he be the only one getting up and going to a job he hates every day? How is that fair?

So you increase their allowance but this causes your mom to break down and weep. She can't believe you're playing favorites like this. Hurting your father. Don't you know how much he wants to retire? Now his own daughter is bankrolling his brother-in-law while he still has to slave away? Lord! You feel terrible! You didn't mean to hurt anyone! You set your parents up with a monthly allowance, too. In fact, everyone in the family gets one. Everyone except Grandpa Joe. He deserves financial aid the most, but he won't take it. He says the day he takes money from his own grandchild will be the day he puts a bullet in his head.

The crappy thing is *you* still have a job. The way you're hemorrhaging cash, there's no way you're giving up the only steady thing you have. Unfortunately, work suddenly really sucks. Ever since you got the money, people act weird around you, like you don't belong. Coworkers stop chatting with you and start acting professional and cold. You overhear people talking about barbecues and boating trips but you're never invited anymore. What is wrong with everybody? Your boss even turns you down for a promotion. "It isn't personal," he says. "We both know you don't really need it and there are people here who do."

Not personal?

Things at home are stressful too. Everyone seems to be fighting. Fighting or complaining they're not getting enough money. Aidan can't understand why you won't spend a dime of your lottery winnings on anything *fun* and you finally just snap. You tell him to back off. This is a *family* matter and he's not family, in case he forgot. Aidan leaves after that and spends a week at his friend's house. Then he says he wants to break up. You're not the person he thought you were.

Your uncle calls a month later and says Lanie's back in the hospital. She came down with a high fever and her body has inexplicably started to reject the transplant. She needs a new kidney, immediately. The donor bank has a match, but they'll need another hundred thousand dollars. That's just for the kidney. The hospital administrator will call you about the cost of surgery and aftercare, okay?

If you buy Lanie another new kidney, go to section 28 (p. 80).

If you don't buy Lanie another new kidney, go to section 29 (p. 83).

15

You turn down Lanie's request for a new kidney as nicely as you can. If you start handing money out to every aunt, uncle, and distant cousin there is in the world, you're going to go flat broke. Once you start hemorrhaging cash, when does it end? How do you decide who to help and who to refuse?

Your family is furious. They're stunned by your selfishness and just about to disown you, when you're saved by some guy at your aunt and uncle's church. He's decided to donate his kidney to Lanie. The Lord has led him to do so.

Amen, sucker!

Still, it's probably a good time to get out of town, just until your family forgets your "breathtaking narcissism." Aidan, who was the one person to totally support you through the Lanie ordeal, says you should do something extravagant. This money isn't supposed to be some big headachy nightmarish burden, it's a *gift*. It's okay to have some fun with it! Why not indulge yourself?

After some intensive daydreaming, you whip up a list of crazy ideas and take Aidan to dinner at the Lobster Barn. After reading through all your ideas, there are definitely two top contenders.

You and Aidan could attend the world's most expensive dinner in Bangkok. Ten ultimate courses each paired with the most exceptional and rarest wines in the world. Celebrities, dignitaries, and only the luckiest foodies will witness these six chefs, easily the world's most talented and sought-after and insane culinary geniuses, who will be brought together for one night only. You'll be one of a very few people who ever taste a meal that costs forty thousand dollars. This is the kind of dinner that Hemingway and Churchill and Mary, Queen of Scots would've enjoyed. Rich, rare, and refined. Decadent as hell, too.

The other idea is a Russian research ship that is taking passengers on a twelve-day sail out to sea off the stormy coast of Newfoundland. They're headed to the site of the *Titanic*, to the actual shipwreck on the ocean floor. You'll be one of a very few people ever to see this notorious icon with your own eyes. The trip also costs forty thousand dollars, and while meals are included, you're pretty sure the galley on board doesn't quite have their Michelin star yet.

If you attend the world's most expensive dinner in Bangkok, go to section 30 (p. 85).
If you take a ship to visit the *Titanic*, go to section 31 (p. 89).

16

From section 8

You and Sam jump up and get in line with all the other passengers who want to leave *now*. Your heart starts beating so loudly you can't hear anything else. Maybe they're taking you on deck to shoot you. Maybe you'll be tossed overboard as shark bait. What will happen to those left behind?

Suddenly a pirate grabs you out of the line and pulls you through a door, out into the painfully dazzling sunshine. Someone on a megaphone is shouting at you; there's the sound of helicopters, a siren, wind whipping against your face. Damn, it's loud *as hell* out here. The dining room must have been soundproof as well as bulletproof. Then you're lifted off your feet, rushed to the railing, and thrown overboard.

You land in the warm water with a deep plunge, choking and sputtering, waves slapping your face as your wet clothes threaten to pull you farther under. You kick hard, losing your shoes, flailing, trying to push to the surface. When you break out, there's a hard thump on your back as a U.S. Navy SEAL in the water grabs hold of you. The retrieval boat rushes alongside him and they haul you into the boat. Dear God, thank you for the U.S. armed forces.

You're saved.

Everyone is taken by shuttle boat to the shore, where an army convoy escorts your passenger van to a nearby military base. You're given dry clothes and a hot meal before being debriefed and loaded into a vacuous, noisy cargo plane. When you land hours later at yet another military base in Morocco, the group is told there's been a development. Apparently there was a rescue attempt on board the cruise ship that went bad, friendly fire was involved, and all the hostages who were left behind are now dead.

The whole thing is a disgraceful mess. Everyone gets very quiet and stares at the floor.

When you get home things are a little depressing. Edward never contacts you again. You have no idea what happened to him. At least you have money to cheer yourself up. You can abscond to a remote hideaway, a tranquil spot to think and heal, like a timber lodge on Lake Superior, or maybe a room on Sex Island. A modern-day Fantasy Island, it's a private island in the Caribbean where all your fantasies come true and your painful memories are forgotten.

If you buy a remote lodge on Lake Superior, go to section 32 (p. 98).
If you go to Sex Island in the Caribbean, go to section 34 (p. 106).

17

You decide to stay on board as a volunteer hostage. Sam does, too. Most everyone else, though, leaps up and files down the long, dark hallway, leaving you and Sam alone with eight other people, all of whom look like they just made the hugest mistake of their lives.

After a long, sleepless night waiting, startling at every sound and creak you hear, the morning finally comes and the pirates round the ten of you up. They bring you on deck and hold guns to your back. There, within swimming distance, is a U.S. Coast Guard battleship, anchored resolutely in the water.

There's no sign of the passengers who left, but then again, there wouldn't be. So much for the tall and gallant Edward. Wherever *he* is.

Love is dead. So is chivalry, romance, and the concept of a good man. That fucker left you here to die after you did things to him in bed at *his request* that the Vatican has declared mortal sins. Even if you weren't so angry, you're still utterly confused. It's so surreal standing on an empty, drifting cruise ship escorted by the U.S. Navy. Your captors seem relaxed; it's just another day at sea for them—you half expect them to open the margarita bar.

You ask if you and your fellow hostages could relax on the deck chairs, since it seems like it'll be awhile, and the pirates actually say okay. The sun sinks lower and a cool breeze kicks up. Finally the pirates put you back into the Poseidon Room, but they must not be too worried about security now that there are only ten of you, because they only leave two guys to guard you and they're both pretty young. Maybe fifteen. By midnight you're bedded down on the couches in the bar area and you can see the stars through the windows, each one crystal bright and blazing against the black silky sky.

You think about home. Your family. Your friends. If you make it off this ship there will be changes.

You must have dozed off because the next thing you know Sam shakes you gently awake. It's dark and quiet, everyone else in the room in some uncomfortable state of slumber, even the lone watchman by the door. The other guard must have left and this one sat down to rest. Now he breathes heavily and his hand lies limply on the butt of his rifle. The door beside him is shut and might be locked, but might not be.

This is it. Sam and you talk quickly. If you move with precision and stealth, you might be able to sneak through the door and make it outside to the railings, where you could both jump overboard before anyone caught you. You're *sure* you could swim to the rescue boats if they haven't drifted farther away. On the other hand, you could also lunge for the rifle resting loosely beneath the pirate's hand and shoot your way to freedom. Your grandfather taught you how to shoot a rifle once . . . when you were eleven.

If you sneak out, go to section 33 (p. 104).
If you grab the gun, go to section 35 (p. 109).

18

From section 9

You decide to keep LaLaurie. You call the vodoun priestess, Miss Edelle, who will try to purify the house, and this decision causes a good deal of your staff to suddenly quit. Those who remain act oddly. The upstairs maid starts wearing a giant gold crucifix around her waist, Thalie butchers a dozen chickens that she won't let anyone touch, and your driver pours a thick line of salt across the backseat floor of your car.

No point in arguing.

On the next new moon, Miss Edelle arrives at midnight. She has large eyes and long braids that swing like cedar roots as she sets down her scuffed silver briefcase and gives you a strange handshake. (Third-degree Masonic.) Her grip is strong even though her fingers are slender as smooth coral. Her thick Creole patois makes it hard to understand what she says, and she whispers softly through the house, careful not to disturb. She circles around and says, "Dis one big. Dis one strong."

She lights a milky-orange chunk of olibanum, which smokes and sends yellow vapor drifting down the dark hallways. Then she takes out a large rattle, which she calls her asson. Pieces of snake vertebrae inside a hollow calabash. She proceeds to shake it while lighting white candles, sprinkling salt around the perimeter of the property and making an ornate pattern on the marble floor in the foyer with a coarse yellow powder that smells like sulphur. She closes her eyes and chants. Her body jerks occasionally, as though someone was randomly touching her with a live electrical current.

Afterward, she looks at you and shakes her head. "You cheval for the loa now," she says, but you don't understand. "Cheval?" She nods. "*Cheval* is French for 'horse.' You de horse and Legba *monter la tête*. Gets on your head. The loa—he on your head. He ride you like a horse."

After she packs up her silver briefcase and leaves, Thalie comes out of her hiding spot in the pantry. "That's no mambo," she says of Edelle. "That's *boko*. Dark spirit. That's no blessing on this house, just black magic."

Black magic or *boko* or not, Miss Edelle says there's one crucial element left for the clearing. If you are truly to be the new master of the house, then you must face Madame LaLaurie. You must spend an entire night above the garage alone in Madame LaLaurie's old surgical suite. So, armed with an inflatable mattress, a down comforter, an oil lantern, and a forty-ounce plastic cup of red wine, you settle into the musty room. It's been used for storage up until now and old, anonymous boxes draped with spiderwebs line the walls. You center your air mattress in the very middle of the room, careful not to touch any of the walls, because even though the Madame LaLaurie curse is undoubtedly just overblown runaway rumor, there are in fact the strange dark holes in the floor, just the size of a meaty eyehook, and missing chunks of crumbling plaster from the walls, where it looks like sharp objects were pulled away.

Around three a.m. you wake up with a start, not even remembering when exactly you fell asleep. It's the heat that woke you, the strange, heavy heat in the room, as though there were a wood-burning stove in the corner going full blast. You try to open the door, but it's locked. There isn't even a lock on the door; did someone shove something heavy in front of it on the other side? You run to the window but it's stuck fast. You look around wildly and start to call out for help. No one hears you—or maybe just no one comes. The heat continues to increase, sweat beading on your forehead. Your cell phone won't work. There's no way out and you can't breathe, it's like a sauna, like an oven, like being pressed inside someone's mouth.

You use the heel of your shoe to break out the tiny panes in the attic window to get fresh air. Your body is so hot now it's cooking. You are literally roasting from the inside out. You lie on your back and by kicking hard with both feet you're able to kick the entire window out and crawl through, scraping your legs on the sharp glass and jagged wood. Outside you grab hold of the slimy copper gutter, slick with damp leaves, and try to pull yourself up higher onto the roof, but then something gives way, you slip, and it all goes black.

When you come to, you're in a hospital, a dark-haired nurse standing beside you, your family gathered around the foot of the bed. They tell you that you fell out the window and broke your leg and punctured your lung. You're lucky to be alive. One of the nurses gives you a lavender envelope that was left for you at the nurses' station. It smells faintly of olibanum and simply says: *She gone.*

You return home a day later and the house seems transformed. As though every wall got a fresh coat of paint and a cool spring breeze swept away any bad memories. Life can now continue and no one need ever know about this particular episode.

Continue it does, and a few weeks later Maribelle introduces you to a nice gentleman. Mr. John Harris Wadley Jr. He's a bit older, silver starting to show at his temples, but he's tall and dashing, with twinkling blue eyes. The great-grandson of an oil baron, "Jim-Junior" belongs to that rare class of old money where future generations of original titans don't become utter fuckups. Jim-Junior started life with every luxury a person could have: a wealthy, stable home, a loving mother, a strong father, a fine education, and a trust fund that would take care of his every need for the rest of his life. Most people in his situation would coast, spend their lives on fickle whims, spending, traveling, becoming tourists in their own lives, but not Jim-Junior. He worked hard. Prospected new land, drilled his own fields, and built his own refinery despite a treacherous and competitive market.

Now in his fifties, he's a widower twice over and known to be actively looking for the next Mrs. John Harris Wadley Jr. He's a little old for you, but you're charmed by his winsome smile and genteel Southern charm. You waltz across the dance floor, feeling very nervous about your sweaty hands and stepping on his toes. Not to worry—a real gentleman finds ways to smooth over all ruffles and your petty indiscretions on the dance floor float effortlessly away, as though they never happened.

Jim-Junior calls you. He sends white dahlias, an antique silver flask engraved with your initials, and an ermine stole, which shows both his age and his political affiliation. He pursues you with equal parts consistency and politeness, which is not easy to do. He takes you to the best places in town. Maribelle is ecstatic with your good fortune. "Honey, if you don't snag that man, I will!"

Everything comes to a head one evening at Arnaud's. All your friends are celebrating Maribelle's birthday and the whole restaurant's been rented out for the occasion. A lovely dinner of lobster and chilled gin gimlets is served and then rounds of toasts are offered around the cheerful table. That's when Jim-Junior suddenly stands up and claps his hands together. "Friends," he says, "it's time you knew the real reason for tonight's celebration." He puts his hand on your bare shoulder. "As I sit next to this beautiful creature I feel it is time to order Strawberries Arnaud."

The room gasps.

The waiters look thunderstruck. The sommelier begs the gentleman's pardon, but did he just order Strawberries Arnaud? "Yes, I did, man!" Jim-Junior says brightly. "Hurry it along!"

What the hell is Strawberries Arnaud? Jim-Junior pats your hand. Then white-gloved waiters appear and set down a rare Charles X crystal liqueur set and the sommelier pours you a glass of vintage port. Someone clears their throat and asks how thirty-thousand-dollar wine tastes. You almost choke. There's a smattering of polite laughs, but mostly the whole table stares at you, jaws open as you take another small sip. It's as though you're performing a feat too great to be believed.

Then the waiters set a crystal bowl of strawberries down in front of you. It's pretty, but if pressed, you'd have to say there's nothing particularly *fancy* about it. Maybe it tastes like gold bullion or is sprinkled with diamond dust. You pick up your spoon and are just about to take a big bite, when Jim-Junior stops you (spoon already midair). "I don't think you want to eat a two-million-dollar diamond, do you, kid?"

That's when you notice the pink four-point-seven-carat diamond ring resting pristinely on top of the top strawberry. "It's one of a kind," the head waiter says. "It belonged to Sir Ernest Cassel!"

Jim-Junior holds up his hand. "I can take it from here," he says and smiles at you. "Darling," he says, getting down on one knee, "marry me?"

If you say yes, go to section 36 (p. 112).

If you say no, go to section 87 (p. 274).

19

Life's too short to be feuding with a dead female serial killer, so you move out. Well, you plan to. A real estate agent is obtained and LaLaurie House goes on the market while you take a trip to Paris with Maribelle on a whirlwind shopping spree. Then you go to Spain and then to Saint-Tropez. When you come home, the real estate agent says it shouldn't be long before a buyer comes along, so you wait.

. . . and wait.

. . . and wait.

But nobody's interested in buying your house. Plenty of people come to look at LaLaurie House and the open houses are as popular as your old cocktail parties—it's a free tour of a notorious historic mansion! But no one makes an offer. The real estate agent blames the housing bubble, the bad economy, the lasting effects of Katrina and just about everything else, including the neighbor's dog, who barks too much. People don't like noisy neighbors. You jokingly offer to kill the dog and she ponders it before answering, "No, not yet."

Fourteen months go by.

No worries, you have your social life to entertain you. Nothing's changed there. You keep going to yacht parties and art openings and charity balls and you keep buying rich gowns and new jewelry and having your face sanded and resanded at the dermatologist's. You keep up appearances even though you're on pins and needles waiting for something else to happen at the house. You start sleeping in the downstairs guest room, where "things" don't seem to happen, but your headaches get worse. Advil, Tylenol with Codeine, Vicodin—nothing can touch them. You don't sleep well. There are nightmares and thrashing in the sheets. You wake up sweaty, with a strange fever that comes and goes. Over time, you become unable to go to the grand events and then even the informal get-togethers seem too exhausting to bear.

All the while, the bills keep coming. The mortgage, credit card bills, lawyers' fees, yacht club fees, country club fees, medical insurance, life insurance, doctors' bills (Valium, Xanax, Vicodin), house bills, staff salaries, electricity, gas, water, telephone, cable, wireless Internet, weekly flower delivery, and so on.

Another six months pass.

And another.

The bank calls. Your funds are seriously running low. You sell off your toys, the boat, the cars, the jewelry, the furniture. When there's nothing left to sell, the overdue notices come. First friendly reminders, then second notices, then warnings, and finally threats. You have to let the staff go, leaving you to wander the empty house alone. You sleep in the living room, closing off as many sections of the house as you can to save on utilities.

Your cousin calls and asks to use "your big mansion" for her wedding reception. You tell her it's a bad time, you're redoing the floors. No problem, she'll change the date to whenever's convenient, the money they'll save is worth it! She keeps at it, countering your every excuse with a solution until you tell her to stop being a leech. You're sick of everyone expecting things and taking you for granted. The truth is you don't want her trailer-trash boyfriend and his hillbilly family in your house because they'll probably pee in the sinks and throw cigarettes on the floor.

The bank calls every day and now Mr. Deloit finally leaves one last message. He regrets to inform you that since you've exhausted your lines of credit, failed to make any arrangements with the bank, and refused to respond to the many, *many* notices they sent, the bank is repossessing the house. He'll be around with an officer to make sure the property is vacated in three days.

In a fit of despair you finally run across the street and confess your bankruptcy to Maribelle. She can't believe it. You were hoping she might offer to put you up for a while, or at the very least be sympathetic to the situation. She didn't come from money after all—she came from a trailer park in Macon, Georgia. Her reaction, though, is stunning. She's angry and then stony cold. It's as though she just realized she'd been fraternizing with the help. She says she's very sorry for your change in "life circumstances" and she wishes you the best of luck. Now she has to go to a hair appointment.

So it goes with all your good buddies at the country club; the phone goes deathly silent, the invitations stop arriving, and it's as though you never existed at all. Such is the way of the wealthy—they fear the poor are catching.

What now? You can't go home; you're too ashamed. They think you disowned them and you basically did, you never even had them down to the house once. How can you go home broke and broken, expecting them to take care of you after the way you treated them? No. You can't. You'll pull yourself together, and when you go home, you'll never take them for granted again. You write your mother a cheerful letter and tell her you're going to Europe. The house doesn't amuse you anymore and you're looking for a new home in Paris or Spain. You'll be gone for months and you'll drop them a postcard when you can.

Using the last of your cash you check into the Peachtree Motel, supposedly for just one night. You buy a bottle of cheap Merlot from the corner Sip-n-Go and drink it in the bathtub. Then you send out for more wine. Bless the Sip-n-Go, they deliver. That's when things get fuzzy. A week later the manager uses his master key to unlock your door and finds you passed out and covered in dry vomit.

He's really nice about it, though, nicer than he had to be, possibly because in the cheap hotel business, this kind of scenario isn't altogether uncommon. He brings you coffee, waits for you to take a shower, and even lets you use the office phone. But you don't know who to call. He sighs and tells you there's a women's shelter nearby run by a nice church. It's basically a flophouse but you'd have somewhere to sleep tonight. This makes you cry and the manager says he also has a buddy with a dude ranch in Llano, Texas.

He always needs workers. He says it's nice country out there, good people, wide-open spaces. He offers to call his buddy and he'll even drive you to the bus depot and buy you the ticket because you remind him of his daughter and you look like you could use a little help. Should you trust him?

If you take the bus ticket to Texas, go to section 23 (p. 65).
If you go to the nearby homeless shelter, go to section 38 (p. 119).

20

You bid on the deceased collector's property, which turns out to be a rare wine collection. A Christie's representative informs you by phone that yours was the winning offer and suggests you come in person to collect the item, since the cost of insuring and transporting antique fluids is prohibitive. They once had a bottle of Montrachet break during transit, catalyzing a catastrophic lawsuit that bankrupted not only the shipping company but the wine enthusiast who'd bid on it.

So you go to New York City in person with a few dozen of your friends and family in tow and let Christie's make a big deal about the unveiling. After all, the lot was blind—no one had ever seen inside the dusty wooden crate of wine, which was still sealed with several unbroken ancient-looking wax stamps. Camera crews from as far away as Reykjavik and Taipei film the crate's opening, held right on Christie's main auction stage. You stand next to Henry Short, the head of Christie's wine department. He's a small, dignified man with big ears who wears wire spectacles and a sweetly old-fashioned pocket square. You notice his cheeks pink slightly as he speaks briefly before opening the crate.

"Robert Louis Stevenson called wine 'bottled poetry' and I for one am all too aware of this truth. So many tremendous bottles of wine have passed through Christie's. Wines with epic stories. How many times have I wondered what they tasted like? The fourteenth-century Cognac from Normandy, the Benedictine liqueur found deep in French catacombs, spiced mead uncovered on a shipwreck in the Aegean Sea. These bottles carry the stories inside them. They ferry poems through time. For this we honor them, because unlike stories written in a book, we cannot open them unless we mean to destroy them. In the end, these are poems we will never know."

Mr. Short speaks awhile longer, but you're lost in his words, thinking of how spectacular and fragile the world is. When he's done, a lab technician assists him in opening the crate with a small, ceremonial silver crowbar.

Inside your wooden mystery box is a single wine bottle. Funny-looking. Old. It's black and nestled in some mealy sawdust mixture. There's clumsy writing across the face in a thick white scrawl, as though someone labeled the bottle using Wite-Out. You can't read what it says, but you know it says something— Under his breath Mr. Short mutters, *"Oh, my."* After he lifts the dark glass bottle out and sets it on the table, a silence falls across the room. Then whispering. *"Chateau Lafite? Chateau Lafite!"*

It's a 1787 bottle of Chateau Lafite, an incredibly rare Bordeaux. Applause breaks out and cameras flash. Upon further inspection spidery initials are found etched into the glass.

Th. J.

Mr. Short looks visibly sick. He'd secretly considered bidding on the mystery crate himself but backed out at the last minute. Now his voice is deliberately steady as he announces the bottle appears to be from President Thomas Jefferson's personal wine collection. It's most likely the rarest and most expensive bottle of wine in the world.

That night the auction house throws a celebratory dinner at Masa, a venerated sushi restaurant located high atop the Time Warner Center. The crowded table is populated with some of the world's most glamorous citizens, who've paid to see the bottle of wine (which sits ceremoniously next to you at the table), and there are also reporters from the *New York Times*, *Wine Spectator*, and *Forbes*, all of whom will be doing stories on this fortuitous event. Jokes are made about uncorking it and everyone having a slug, but of course the wine's well past its drinkability. It would taste like putrid vinegar now. Instead the table decides to wash down their three-hundred-dollar omakase dinners with some cold Sapporo beer.

The conversation is lively, everyone guessing how much you could resell your bottle of wine for and whether this is the burgeoning beginning of your new career as an international wine czar. Then Mr. Masa Takayama, the restaurant owner and head chef himself, comes out to offer you a toast. He's just raising his small porcelain sake cup, when one of the waiters reaches in to clear away an empty, wasabi-smeared plate and knocks his elbow right into the bottle of Chateau Lafite, sending it crashing down onto the floor below.

Black glass splinters and ochre-red wine spills. People start yelling, chairs are pushed back, waiters dive in. Amidst the pandemonium one person stays still. Mr. Short is staring at the floor, his teacup-handle ears a brilliant pink. After some time he reaches down slowly and touches his index finger to a small red puddle on the floor. Then he closes his eyes and touches the drop of wine to his tongue. He winces and then smiles.

This poetry tastes like rusted iron and rainwater.

The event effectively, dramatically ends your days as a collector. From now on you spend less time remembering and more time looking. You spend money on experiences instead of things. No more hunting skeletons. No more housing the dead. You buy wine in order to drink it.

21

From section 86

You don't like the idea of losing all your money, even if it does mean falling in love. What good is love when you're hungry or need medicine or Louboutin shoes? Plus, you can always get a dog if you don't find a man. They're a statistically much healthier choice for women. You tell Niobe you're choosing financial security and she sighs. "Go to Trafalgar Square," she says, "and look up." Then, aided by her ivory walking cane, she hoists herself to stand and leaves you alone in the restaurant.

Looks like you're getting the check.

Okay. This seems bogus, but Trafalgar Square is nearby and it's a nice day. So you get a big caffe latte and go sit on the stone steps of the fountain and look up. You study the tops of buildings and the clouds passing by and anything that seems above you. While you're sitting there, Niobe's warning about the *Bête Noire* starts to bother you. What if she's right? Maybe she isn't, but if she is—you'd be responsible for, God, over a dozen lives being lost. She said to sell it, so you give yourself a challenge. Can you sell the *Bête Noire* before you find whatever it is here that's "up"?

This turns out to be easier than you thought. You call Captain Marquardt, who's on the bridge at this very moment cruising northward somewhere off the coast of Singapore. You ask his advice about selling the yacht and he offers to buy it. He and a few Dutch businessmen are looking to start a luxury charter company called Silverspun Charters. There's something about that name you like. On a sudden and somewhat reckless hunch, you make him an offer. You'll *give* him the *Bête Noire* for free in exchange for the financial equivalent in the Silverspun shares, and on these conditions: (1) Captain Marquardt must head into the Port of Singapore immediately and remain at anchor until you approve setting sail again. (2) While at anchor he'll draw up paperwork transferring ownership of the *Bête Noire* and incorporating you into his new company, and he'll have a complete set of stem-to-stern diagnostic tests done on the vessel—electrical, mechanical, hydraulic, everything. You don't care what it costs or how long it takes. (3) Upon completion of these tests, he will have the yacht painted white. Every inch. No color may be used except good old God-fearing navy, and only when absolutely necessary.

Captain Marquardt gets very quiet. "You know that could lay us up for three months, right?"

You say yes, you know, and ask, "So, how about it, do we have a deal?"

Captain Marquardt pauses. "Yes, ma'am," he says, "we absolutely do. Recharting our course to the Singapore harbor now."

Just then a scrawny Indian kid walks by wearing a black T-shirt with big bold white letters that say: LOOK UP.

Over heaping plates of cheap Chinese food, he says his name is Jagjeet Singh. He's a possibly brilliant architecture student who eats ravenously as you pepper him with questions. You ask him what his absolute *dream project* is, and he instantly takes a worn black notebook from his pocket. "I keep having this recurring dream," he says, "of a living building. It's off the grid, even though it's in the city. It provides its own utilities. Water, electricity, energy. There are no utility bills and the reserve energy it creates is sold back to the city." You ask him what he thought the dream meant and he looks at you funny. "I don't think it *meant* anything. I think that's what it was. A building that doesn't need outside utilities to operate, and you know where everything came from?"

You shake your head no.

He points to the ceiling. "Look up!" You look at the ceiling of the Chinese restaurant, which is remarkably grimy. "No, I mean the *sky*. Everything a building needs can be taken from the sky instead of the ground. No more using fossil fuels or chemically treated water. This building uses solar panels, wind power, rainwater collection, a condensation filtration system . . . all the technology is here."

You offer to build Jagjeet's dream. Only you'd like to make the building a combination residence and boutique hotel. More people would see it that way and you could pull in more press. Jagjeet smiles. He's a handsome devil.

For the next three weeks he works at your Grosvenor House suite and fires off blueprints as you hire all the crews who will do the actual work of building a hotel. The construction company, project foreman, site managers, and the project team, who'll be responsible for getting all the various zoning approvals, building permits, and construction licenses at various stages of the project. They'll hire a hotel management company when the time comes. Your goal is to get this sucker fully self-supporting so you don't ever have to show up, unless you want to.

Jagjeet goes over every detail of his design with Alistair, your lead contractor, who's not too happy about the plan to forgo standardized building practices and use only recycled, postconsumer, or repurposed materials. There'll be no neat bundles of new materials delivered from the lumberyard on this project and Alistair is already irritated. There might be a growing number of green architects, but not too many green contractors yet.

In order to help out, Jagjeet helps assemble recycled materials through every means possible. He buys up materials slated for the landfill from demolition crews and salvage yards all over the country. Sloppy stacks of mismatched wooden beams and odd iron girders arrive daily, as do pallets of broken tile and hundreds of rusty shipping containers. One day a decommissioned Royal Navy torpedo boat shows up, thirty feet of maritime steel, which Jagjeet plans to pirate when building hotel furniture. Alistair's livid. How's he supposed to build a hotel that's up to code with this garbage?

Jagjeet hires an impressive crew of fellow architecture students who sort the incoming materials into organized piles. They diligently comb through every garbage can, Dumpster, junkyard, and landfill in London looking for building materials. They hunt through secondhand shops, sewer tunnels, alleyways, and abandoned buildings, dragging all their little broken, rusty treasures back to the hotel. They all worship Jagjeet and call him "Starchitect." He's comfortable with praise as well as adulation and seems well-suited for monarchy.

Captain Marquardt calls in the middle of all this from Singapore to give you a status report and he sounds unwell. His voice is shaky. He says the marina was doing a routine system flush of the *Bête Noire* when engineers found fifty pounds of C-4 explosives in the hull alongside a remote-controlled incendiary device. They have no idea how it got there, but the bomb squad swept every inch of the ship with dogs. "That bomb would have blown a beluga-sized hole in us," the captain says gravely. "Whoever put it there could have scuttled us from a safe distance. We could have gone down anywhere in the Indian Ocean. Probably would've been over before a distress call even got out. I don't know why you wanted a full sweep of the boat, but we all owe you our lives."

Man. You can't take credit for anything, someone was just looking out for you. Dolly, Niobe, God, angels, gut instinct, who knows. Maybe it's all the same thing in the end. You call Interpol and report suspicious activity concerning your Russian friends. If you ever find out that those cossacks sabotaged your boat, you'll kill every one of them.

Jagjeet and Alistair manage to complete the hotel a month ahead of time. A big press conference is scheduled for the hotel's opening and your publicist can't fulfill all the requests for interviews with Jagjeet. He's been besieged. (Nobody flocks to *you*, of course, because nobody even knows who you are. Secretly, though, this is how you like it.)

On the day of the grand opening, you hang back with the TV cameras and news crews who wait around all day for Jagjeet to arrive. Anticipation is heightened by the unbelievable fact that Jagjeet managed to put a huge white fabric sheet over the building several months ago, forcing Alistair and company to work inside a virtual yurt so no one could see the building before its unveiling. Finally a long white limousine pulls up to the building and Jagjeet emerges wearing a crisp white linen suit with a bright red Sikh's turban. He strides up to the waiting podium and says he'll keep comments short, as one's work always speaks more eloquently by itself.

"Today I offer you a new concept in shelter," he says. "Not just a building, but a sanctuary. By using technologies from the past as well as the future, this building is able to get everything it needs from the sky. It can harness the sun, capture the wind, and collect the rain, providing its inhabitants with heat, air-conditioning, electricity, and clean drinking water. All for free. Ladies and gentlemen, I present you with London's newest, freshest, and greenest sanctuary. I give you . . . the *Skybox*."

The giant white curtain falls and the street stands transfixed. The building you're looking at is . . . bizarre. Elegant. Lovely. Impossible. The exterior is made from thousands of car windshields, which have been cut into irregular square shapes and sandblasted a smooth, milky green. Large triangles of brushed aluminum are patchworked across the façade and create a futuristic awning over the front doors. Jagjeet explains these are airplane wings salvaged from decommissioned military aircraft. Here they're able to continue doing what they were meant to. Protecting people.

The media loves him. He leads the cameras through the hotel slowly, referring to his interior design as "Décor-aste," decorating with waste. The aesthetic created is a visually mystifying amalgamation of elegant, odd, unexplainable, and grotesque. Everyday objects are transformed. The colorful chandeliers in the dining room, which look like forests of upside-down pastel popsicles, are actually tightly bound clusters of scuffed-up plastic buckets with halogen lights anchored inside. The hotel rooms are built from stacked shipping containers. The furniture inside is made from crazy found objects. Rugs made of woven six-pack rings, beds created from torpedo boat pieces and unclaimed government coffins. Chairs, desks, and lamps manufactured from old typewriters, wooden rowboats, old encyclopedias, chopped-up bowling balls. . . .

The Skybox is a runaway hit. It wins awards, gets featured in glossy travel magazines, praised by high-end architecture digests, and recommended by groovy eco-living publications with Drew Barrymore on the cover. *National Geographic* includes you in a documentary about sustainable architecture and the Lonely Planet gives you an entire section in their UK guidebook, the dog-eared bible for travelers everywhere. Jagjeet's career is launched into the stratosphere, and despite his ever-growing arrogance, he still calls to catch up and tells everyone that you were the one who first believed in him. Decades later, when his hair begins to turn gray, he'll tell reporters he never had a client before or since who gave so much, took so little, and opened their heart, trusting him completely. It was only because of your faith that Alpha Initiation was born. Who knows? Without you, maybe he'd still be designing residential garages.

You find yourself owning London's premiere boutique hotel and living a very glamorous life. You're invited to all the best parties, premieres, theater openings, gallery shows, poetry salons, and pretty much any other social or cultural event you like. Your favorite thing, though, is talking to strangers. You hold court in the Skybox tearoom and talk to travelers from all over the world. You're grateful to provide all of these wayward kittens safe shelter.

True to Niobe's prediction, you never really do fall in love. You love people, you have dear friends and close relationships, some of which are quite meaningful and some of which are large pains in the ass. On balance you don't know if you'd pick the same path again. It's hard to imagine your life without the hotel and the endless stream of vibrant, colorful travelers that flows through. You get to meet people from all over the world and every holiday season you throw a huge all-tradition-inclusive dinner where all your little wayward kittens are welcome.

When you pass away, after a long, wonderful life, you're greeted in heaven with honors. It's a butterfly sanctuary of sorts. A place where all souls arrive in their true, primal form on winged bits of color, flying free and ever-protected from the immense infinity beyond and all the many, many dark things waiting.

You're surprised by the number of rap stars and drug lords in heaven. The Furies explain that while on Earth, a soul's job is to create sanctuary, and anyone who does so is blessed. Sanctuaries come in many forms. Not just hospitals, homes, friendships, and families, but things as mundane as secure employment and as fleeting as sudden smiles at strangers. These are the emotional igloos that keep all heaven's souls safe, even if for only a moment, from the ever-howling storms around them.

This means, of course, that tight-knit roving gangs of thugs are more holy than the most sanctimonious priest, if he offers no protection to those in need. It turns out sweet Jesus prefers a well-aimed gun to the cold shoulder a full seven days a week.

22

Chip's disappointed when you tell him you can't go to Indonesia, but how can you leave now when you're just getting back on your feet and ready to move out of the shelter? It's hard to see him go. It feels like telling Indiana Jones you can't join his quest to unlock the mysteries of an Egyptian tomb because you have homework.

It's a comfort when you finally do move out of the shelter, though, and into your own tiny (roach-infested) apartment in the Marigny, a bohemian neighborhood next to the French Quarter. The floors of your place are wall-to-wall ancient yellow linoleum and there's no oven, only a hot plate and a microwave, but the neighborhood is better and you have a bathroom all to yourself now. Still, you get an ugly feeling in your stomach when you see the big houses in the Garden District through the smudgy streetcar windows on your way to work. It was so easy to be rich.

At the museum work drones on and sometimes you think you made a big mistake not going to Indonesia. Chip sends a postcard of an incredible ice blue ocean and a sunset that's stupidly perfect. He says he's having a great time. So great, in fact, it turns out he never comes back again, or calls, or writes, leaving you with a bruised heart to carry around in your tired rib cage.

Time passes. Some interesting things happen, like when a kid from the Morningside inner-city youth program somehow unlatches the fire ant exhibit, launching an emergency evacuation of the building. Then Hilda gets stung by a blister beetle, causing fried-egg-sized welts on her hands and arms. She's at the hospital for a week. A month later the Port of New Orleans Harbor Police call Mr. Nicholas with an odd donation. They caught bug smugglers from Peru trying to sneak eight thousand dead insects into the country. Exotic insect collecting is a very lucrative trade; however, it's illegal to take any bugs out of Peru, living or dead, so the creepy-crawly contraband was confiscated and is now donated, with permission from the Peruvian government, to the New Orleans Insectarium.

In the Bone Room, the arrivals are some fascinating, horrifying creatures. Rhinoceros beetles, red tarantulas, scorpion spiders, giant roaches, leafcutter ants, and the Amazonian giant centipede, which is a centipede big enough to eat bats. Mr. Nicholas is incredibly excited about the new cache and puts the whole team on categorizing and preparing the insects for display.

Your job is to rehydrate the dried-out beetles so they can be pinned on mounting blocks. You soften them up in soaking solutions of vinegar, detergent, and filtered water. Then you boil them for up to three minutes, depending on beetle size and how dried out they are. You're monitoring a large *Coleoptera* boiling away on a Bunsen burner, careful that the specimen doesn't macerate and lose antennae or tarsi, when you hear a horrid little screeching sound. On the floor right beside your foot is a large reddish black cockroach.

A Madagascar hissing cockroach.

The only hissing cockroach in the world, these cuddly critters force air through breathing pores to make a weird *ffffttttttt* sound. You scoop the little guy up, put him in a glass observation box, and name him Britney Spears. Mr. Nicholas has a strict "no pets" rule in the lab, but you say you're keeping him for scientific study. When Mr. Nicholas says he doesn't see any scientific study going on regarding the cockroach, you make sure he sees you put Britney into a glass specimen box and study him under a microscope. "Very interesting how the . . . abdomen has . . . segmented parts," you say, totally making up bullshit observations out loud, but then you actually see something weird. The cockroach has mites. Most cockroaches have mites, but these are different.

Mr. Nicholas decides to give Britney a temporary stay of execution and Hilda says Britney's lucky to have mites, because cockroaches with mites always have less fungus and some of those fungi are vicious. Bugs infected with *Cordyceps* fungi have an unstoppable compulsion to climb nearby plants, clamp their jaws tight at the very top, and let the fungus eat out their brain until spores erupt out of the insect's head.

Disgusting!

But it gets you thinking, if the mites eat fungus on roaches, would they eat fungus from anywhere? Would they eat household mold? You carefully transport ten of the twenty-five mites you find on Britney to glass slides with varying types of mold spores. (You want to leave some behind to keep Britney clean.) Then you get mold spores from the Louisiana swampland exhibit upstairs and from the drain in the women's bathroom sink.

Within three days, each mite has eaten every single species of mold, so you go find more types of mold. Bob Thompson, a helpful inspector at NOLA Mold, a New Orleans residential and commercial mold inspection company, agrees to send you virulent mold specimens to test. He gives you biohazard petri dishes with *Cladosporium*, *Penicillium*, and *Aspergillus*. He also gives you the granddaddy of molds, *Stachybotrys atra*, otherwise known as "black mold," frequently found in water-damaged homes and able to produce lethal toxins that cause serious health issues in humans. He tells you that if you found an organic substance that eats black mold, he'll make you a millionaire.

Ha.

Your unstoppable mites, however, are worth more than a million. They gobble up all the new mold samples, including *Stachybotrys atra*. You bring your findings to Mr. Nicholas and he thinks it's all very interesting, but doesn't see the value of your discovery. Bob Thompson, however, goes lulu beans *crazy* over the prospect of a new weapon in his unending, often losing battle against toxic mold. You ask if he wants to be your business partner and he says, "Damn hell yes, I do!"

He develops prototypes on a "mite delivery system," while you work on an incubator, a sort of romantic mite boudoir, that provides the little clear-legged, six-eyed darlings with a perfect humidity-controlled, temperature-controlled atmosphere for "doin' it." Soon you're able to hatch baby mites at an alarming rate and Bob has perfected his eco-friendly Mite Gun, which delivers a harmless mix of mites and biodegradable filler (sawdust).

Mitex, the world's first all-natural mold killer, is born.

He treats the first fifty houses for free and the word spreads fast. Soon Bob can't keep up with all the jobs coming in, everybody swearing that with *one treatment* their houses are mold-free within sixty days. With more than a thousand species of mold common in the United States, nobody has ever found one single product that kills every kind of mold, and not just the active spores, but the inactive spores, too. That's always been the problem—a house is treated for mold and everything's fine until the inactive spores hatch. Then the owners have to start all over again.

Bob hires more employees, moves to a bigger warehouse, and starts advertising on TV. Soon he's cleaning houses in Arkansas, Mississippi, and Florida. Then, during a "health tips from Hollywood" episode on *Oprah*, Julia Roberts says black mold is a national epidemic. She has all her houses treated with Mitex before she'll even set foot in them.

Mitex is an overnight worldwide sensation. Frantic customers call from Malibu to Maine. Hospitals, government centers, even Buckingham Palace need immediate assistance. That's when you and Bob decide to sell the patented Mitex "recipe" to an international chemical conglomerate for a cool sixty-two million dollars.

This time, you know exactly what you're doing with your money. No more extravagant crap, no more status seeking, no more false friends. You go home and buy a big piece of land, upon which you build a compound of eco-friendly houses for you, your parents, and all your family. Light, airy buildings with bamboo floors, vegetated roofs, solar panels, solar shingles, double-glazed glass, wind generators, and geothermal rainwater collection systems. Homes that are self-sustaining, taking everything they need from the air, not the earth. A bit more expensive to build but never another utility bill again in your life.

Imagine.

You put a large chunk of money in slow-growth mutual funds and only spend the dividends, never the principal, which means you have a lower annual income, but it's for life. Most important, it's enough. You have everything you need—your friends, family, security, and it's not going anywhere. You might have fallen down on your face in New Orleans, but you climbed on the back of roaches to get up again. Some say those insects are disgusting, but you think they're beautiful. Those polished amber wings were wide enough to fly you out of poverty and deliver you safely to the shores of enough. You will be forever grateful.

23

The hotel manager drives you to the bus station, which is nerve-wracking, because isn't this how slave traders work? They find down-and-out girls, offer to help, promise them a great job somewhere, and the next thing the girls know they're waking up underneath a guy named Vladimir in a brothel in Kiev? You stay pressed against the passenger door as he drives, your hand on the handle. You don't care if this Cadillac is going seventy miles an hour down the freeway: If he tries anything, you're opening this door, tucking, and rolling.

Poor guy. He doesn't do anything but take you to the Greyhound bus station, buy your ticket, and give you a little cash for the road. He writes down the address of the ranch and tells you to keep in touch. You thank him and try not to cry as you promise to pay him back one day. He just tells you to watch out for yourself and if you can help someone else out one day, someone in a jam, well then, do it and you two will be even.

The bus drops you off in Llano and you have to hitchhike ten miles north to reach the ranch. A farmer picks you up and drives you out. Every mile of the way you're not sure this is a good idea and wonder how a person can go from sipping Pimm's poolside to shoveling horseshit, or is it cowshit? Whatever shit they have on dude ranches.

By being a damn fool idiot, that's how.

At the ranch you meet the owner, Ralston, a wiry man with rusty-colored hair and a deep sunburn on the back of his neck. At first he doesn't understand you're the person his buddy sent. "You?" he says. "He thought you should be a field hand? Goddamn. Let me see your hands. Good Christ, all those hands are good for is stirring tea. You know how many cups a tea we drink around here?"

He doesn't wait for you to answer.

"None! That's how many!" He's angry. You're going to have to hitchhike back to New Orleans. You feel like crying again. "Oh, hell," he says. "Don't make that face! All right, look, wait up! *Don't cry.* If you need some work, we can put you . . . hell, I don't know, we'll put you somewhere. Ida Mae!" A big red-haired woman comes running and he tells her to find you a place to sleep and something for you to do because apparently he's responsible for every goddamn sob story out of New Orleans.

Ida Mae leads you away and tells you not to mind Ralston. "He's my baby brother and he was born cranky." She sets you up in a narrow back room with a sink in the corner and she says for now why don't you just help her in the kitchen.

The next day Ralston shows you the ranch. You ride along with him as he checks in with the hands. He talks a lot and points out local sights as the pickup truck bounces down the road. "That's Babyhead Mountain," he says, pointing to the pine-cloaked hill in the distance. "Got its name in 1873, when settlers found the head of a little baby girl there. Mary Elizabeth, Bill Bederman's daughter. It was stuck on a stick and people said Indians done it."

He turns the truck down a long gravel road and you stare at the mountain.

"Wasn't the Indians, though," he says. "It was longhorn ranchers. Lotta money in longhorn then. Still is. When the old fort got shut down, Comanches started stealing the longhorn right out of the pastures. Comanches can steal anything. Nab Custer's mustache at high noon if they wanted. Nobody could get the cavalry to come out, though, wasn't a big enough problem, I guess, so those ranchers thought they ought to make the problem look bigger. They kidnapped that little girl, cut her head off, and said it was the Comanches. Comanches, my ass. No Comanche would kill a child. Steal 'em, sure, but kill 'em? Never."

You smile.

As improbable as it seems, you suddenly like this feisty little rancher.

You work hard on the ranch and Ralston gives you more and more responsibility, even teaches you how to ride a horse. He says you have a natural ability. You ask if you can ride the wild horses penned up in the pasture.

He says no, they're not broke in yet. So who breaks them in? "Cowboys break 'em in, darling! You ever been to the Renegade Rodeo? Best wild horse riding in the state. Cowboys come from all over. You can see some real ridin' then." You don't want to watch them, you want to *ride* them. Ralston spits and says there's more chance of you finding a dude ranch in New Jersey. You beg and he says *no how, no way, not gonna happen*. You're enough trouble without needing an ambulance to come all the way out here and pick you up.

Fine. You wait and get Bobby, one of the younger ranch hands, to teach you. He takes you to a palomino trotting around the ring of a smaller, separate pen. "He's been wearing the saddle for three days now," Bobby says, "so he's used to that, but he's never had a rider." He shows you how to hold the reins and says if the horse bucks, just hang on. It's not the holding on that hurts you, it's the falling off. You get up easily enough and for a moment it's like some weird miracle is happening, like you're a horse whisperer or something, because the palomino just stands still. "He likes me!" you shout.

Then the horse goes batshit crazy. He wasn't digging your groovy vibe when you got in the saddle, he was just confused. He was like, "What the *hell* is on my back?" Then, when he heard your voice, he freaked. It's like riding a wild freight train as it derails from a track. The palomino bucks and pitches so hard you squeeze your eyes shut. It feels like your eyeballs might get slammed out of their sockets. You're hanging on pretty good until you're suddenly aware you're flying. You open your eyes and you see the sky, then you're looking at your own boots, then there's the ground, then it all goes black.

You wake up in bed and Ralston's there with his hat in his hand. Ida Mae leans in. "See? I told you she'd be all right. Oh, darlin', don't move. You got a fractured rib or two."

A flash of hot pain pulses on your left side.

"We don't know how many have snapped," Ralston barks. "'Cause nobody here remembered to pick up a medical degree! Isn't that right, Bobby?" Bobby stands sheepishly in the doorway. "Take yer hat off!" Ralston shouts at him. "How many times have I told you to take yer hat off in the house?" Bobby takes his hat off and Ralston glares at him. "Useless! Get outta here.

Go strap a newborn baby to a bull's head or whatever else you think is a fine idea!"

Bobby slinks off.

"Now, now." Ida Mae puts a lovely cold cloth on your head. "Let's not get worked up."

"Oh, I'm worked up," Ralston says. "Plenty worked up. She coulda been killed!"

Ida Mae smiles. "Let her rest now," she says. "Go on. Go."

"Damn women," Ralston mutters and stomps out the door.

"Sorry," you whisper to Ida, but it hurts when you talk.

"Hush now." Ida smoothes out your hair. "Don't fret. Don't you know my little brother only acts like that when he's keen on a girl? He wouldn't be so angry if he wasn't so worried, and he wouldn't be worried if he wasn't afraid to lose you. Sleep now." She leaves and closes the door. You fall back asleep. Silly Ida.

When you're back on your feet again, you've at least got a new nickname. Jockey. The ranch hands wave and say, "Hey, Jockey! They caught a wild bobcat up Babyhead Mountain, you gonna ride it?" Ida Mae says not to worry; it only means you're fitting in. They don't give nicknames to just anybody.

You get back to work, taking it easy on your left side, and by spring you've finally saved up enough money to head home if you want. You'll have to come clean with your family about what happened to the lottery money, but at least now you're not going home empty-handed. When you tell Ralston you're thinking about heading home, he gets real red in the face and looks down. "I wanted to talk to you about that," he says. "I don't know if you're busy or got plans up north or some such, but yer not as much trouble as I thought you'd be and I was wonderin' if you'd stay on awhile longer and marry me."

If you marry Ralston, go to section 40 (p. 128).

If you go home, go to section 79 (p. 251).

24

From section 12

Bossrock carefully lays out your island options, and after sorting through them, you narrow it down to two choices. One is a series of man-made islands off the coast of Dubai called "the World." Each island looks like an actual country or state. There's France Island, Iceland Island, California Island, and so on . . . and with the level of luxury and security provided by the government of Dubai, they're very popular with the superrich. Elton John owns England, the Hiltons got Florida, Bono has Switzerland, and Sarkozy bought Ireland, mostly to annoy the Irish. The islands are so in demand, there's actually only one left. Bossrock says it's prime for five-star hotel development.

The other island is in Costa Rica. A tiny emerald island off the southern coast of the Nicoya Peninsula, which is already home to an established eco-ranch. The ranch needs an investor, a silent partner to help fund its next stage of development. They've been doing brisk business with backpackers and local travelers, but they want to attract a more international class of ecotourist. Since the island has its own source of fresh water, it's the only one in the region that can become a true tropical oasis.

If you buy the island in Costa Rica, go to section 49 (p. 165).
If you buy the island off Dubai, go to section 63 (p. 204).

25

You decide to go for the Hollywood deal and Bossrock gets excited. Only the more he describes it, the stranger it seems. "George Clooney wants to marry you," he says. "He needs a bride and you're it." He tells you this sort of thing is done all the time when actors need extra cash or extra credibility or to prove they're not gay.

"George Clooney is gay?"

"Of course not!" Bossrock looks around wildly to see who might have heard. "Spread that shit and we won't get the deal!"

"He's not gay?"

"No. He's a Fabergé egg addict."

Bossrock explains George Clooney has a bad spending habit. Buying up extraordinary and rare Fabergé eggs has put him in the vicinity of the poor house. Also, the constant barrage of tabloid accusations on why exactly he's so dedicated to his potbellied pig, Max, but not to any one woman has earned him some rather unsavory accusations.

At first you don't believe Bossrock until he starts laying out the details in earnest. Sex is permissible but not obligatory. Residing together is mandatory but vacationing together is optional. No children are expected, none are especially wanted, but if they come, "he's amenable."

"Amenable?"

"Everything in Hollywood is for sale. Cloons is tired of getting nominated for Oscars and then losing them to men with children. He's tired of being portrayed as the consummate bachelor and the taxes are ballbusting."

"Cloons?"

"Plus, as I mentioned, he's broke. He's seen your photo and your bio, he likes that you're not an actress, that you're from a solid family. You're the perfect sudden girlfriend. If you agree to it, the two of you will meet at an ecotourism hotel while on coincidental tandem vacations in Hawaii."

You can hardly believe what you're hearing.

You marry George Clooney. This is not as fabulous as it sounds. Actually, it's sort of a rip-off from the get-go. No big fairy-tale wedding, no white dress, just three lawyers in a high-rise chrome office who ask for your signature in triplicate. Clooney's agent tells the press that the two of you absconded to Bali, where you partook of an ancient Balinese wedding ritual involving incense, virgins, and goats.

The agent even produces photographs of your nonexistent wedding, sold for a cool million each to *People* magazine, photographs that you and George took on a closed Paramount lot where they'd built a set that resembled a serene Balinese waterfall. The "children" who crowd around you are union midgets airbrushed with a tawny caramel color so they look like scampy Indonesian children (poor enough to be cute but not so poor they're bummers) who've come to see the big wedding.

Makeup artists airbrush your skin with an Ernie-and-Bert orange-colored vegetable dye so you look "less jaundiced" in your meringue-shaped wedding dress. When you later apologize to the wardrobe stylist for the orange streaks that cover the inside of the dress, she shrugs and tells you to forget it—they're giving all this stuff to the Goodwill.

That's just the beginning of the bizarre freak show that is your life. After your fake wedding comes news of a fake honeymoon in Beijing, where the two of you apparently opted to feed Chinese orphans rather than indulge yourself on a yacht or at an extravagant spa or hotel. After you return from your humanitarian holiday, you're given a list of intimate yet charming details you can recite to the talk show hosts when they interview you about your "dream wedding" and your "wonderful honeymoon."

"George knows I love fresh grapefruit in the morning," you say cheerfully into the unblinking camera lens, "so even though we were in ... *[struggle to remember, struggle to remember]* ... the Ningxia Hui region of Beijing, he managed to get a crate of them through so I'd start each day right." (Audience: *ohhhh!*)

What else about George? *Oh—he loves boxcar racing and deep-sea diving and collecting vintage cars.* (When in actuality he hates anything that goes too fast, even the *idea* of deep water sends him into fits, and anything old he's convinced is covered with germs.) *He eats like a horse at home, I can't grill him enough steak.* (Strict vegetarian.)

George Clooney is not the man he's made out to be. He's much better, actually. He's soft-spoken and likes gardening and tends to his indoor aviary. He likes astronomy and home-brewed beer and these weird Fabergé eggs, ornate porcelain ova he lines up on the mantel and watches closely as though they might hatch.

He never touches you, and while this initially relieves you—it begins to be a bit irritating. I mean, you're *his wife* for God's sake. And though he may be weird, he's still hot. You have needs, don't you? You're not allowed to have affairs with anyone else (it says so in the contract) in order to avoid any *Enquirer* magazine hoo-hah. So what? Why shouldn't he want to touch you? You go to the gym six days a week, you've been following the dietician's kale juice/quail egg diet. It begins to enrage you. "You could at least hold my hand," you suggest in his first editions library in the south wing of his Bel Air home. "You could give me a back rub. I don't have Ebola or anything."

He politely declines and goes back to reading his Fabergé egg catalogue. Those fucking eggs.

Something deep inside you starts to bubble and boil, like hot tar. You hate him. He should make love to you. The next thing you know you see a Fabergé egg flying through the air and smashing against the wall just behind George's head. Then you look down and realize not only did you throw it, but you have another one lined up, ready to go. You spend the next forty-five minutes chucking Fabergé eggs at George Clooney, trying to harass him into fucking you.

It's a situation you'll later look back on and think, "Did I really do that? Was that me?" because as the court case will show, George Clooney is an incredibly decent man with the mixed fortune of being a movie star, and therefore he's held to standards not attainable by mortals, but nevertheless, everything he does, says, eats, and thinks is under scrutiny. Then you came along and made it all worse. The man was just looking for a moment of peace and you handed him a burning three-ring circus with psychotic clowns.

You would be the psychotic clown.

The resulting media onslaught and terms of your iron-clad contract dictate you have to leave town. Fast and for a while. So where do you want to lay low while the media frenzy dies down?

If you choose an ancient monastery in Ireland,
go to section 51 (p. 174).
If you choose a small hideaway in the Seychelles,
go to section 54 (p. 179).

26

Just one month after investing in Silverlock, a big fat dividend check arrives in the mail. It's *amazing*, like hookers for nothing and blow for free. (You've been watching more pimp and gangster movies lately.) You'll get money every month now and your principal investment will never be touched. This is how rich people amass true wealth, just like Mr. Cook said. Well, hell. If you're going to be getting fatty-fat checks in the mail every month, why do you need to work?

Aidan says it's considered rude to quit in an e-mail, but you don't care, you're doing it because you're the new boss around here, or hasn't he seen your sweet big-ass bank account? He rolls his eyes and says, *yes*, he's seen your sweet big-ass bank account. Many times now.

After a few months pass, Mr. Cook agrees it's time for you to buy a new home. His real estate agent finds a lovely two-million-dollar house inside the esteemed gated community of Airedale Downs. It's an eight-bedroom, six-and-a-half-bath, seven-thousand-square-foot redbrick Colonial set on an acre of manicured land. In back of the house is a large white stone patio with a freestanding fire pit and a state-of-the-art hot tub complete with rotating seats and light shows. It's all designed to make you relax and unwind, like your own piece of heaven right here on Earth.

You let Aidan move into the new house with you, but no one else. When your family complains about their crappy homes and wants you to buy them houses, too, all you have to do is say, "Well, if Mr. Cook says okay, then let's do it!" and everyone gets all happy and says *thank you* and *they love you* and *they'll never forget this.*

Then they talk to Mr. Cook. He graciously and efficiently handles all their requests, ultimately always telling them *No*. Then he gives them a silver engraved Silverlock pen, to ease their pain. He must have given away a lot of silver pens by now.

Time passes and you and Aidan are happy as pimped-out clams. Monthly checks keep arriving and you're able to spend them quite efficiently as you decorate the house and invest in all manner of toys, like a sleek, stainless-steel pool table with black-satin lacquer finish, chilled beverage holders, and neon purple under lighting. Also, a big surround-sound movieplex system that makes all the windows in the basement rattle when you watch action movies.

Life is good, even though certain family members keep asking to stay with you, and you have to admit, some of them have pretty justifiable reasons. It starts with your mom and dad needing a place to stay while exterminators bug-bomb their house. They pretty much moved in and never moved out. Then you learn their house is for sale. The amount of luggage they brought with them should have been your first indication they were planning on staying longer than the weekend.

Then your cousins Beth and John get kicked out of their house, evicted without notice because of some court-ordered tax seizure issued against their landlord, so you let them and their three kids, Eliza, Caitlin, and Bailey, along with their three giant dogs named Paco, Luc, and Frances, stay with you until they can find a new place. That just never really happens. One month passes, then two, and then you notice they've used masking tape to put their names on the mailbox.

Mr. Cook says he warned you against letting anyone in your house, and you try to explain. These aren't handouts, they're emergencies. You're not a monster, and if you have blood relatives who are homeless, you surely can give them one small corner of the giant roof over your head. Right? What's money for, if not helping your family?

He just rolls his eyes and says to call him when you're fed up.

Next your aunt Phyllis and uncle Sydney show up on your doorstep. Grandpa Joe moving in was your idea. You always hated his senior care facility, it smells like fart. He's genuinely frail and needs attention, so he moves in with his longtime best friend, Ada, whom he says is his nurse, but they agree to share a room and sometimes strange sounds come from their bathroom. After that, there's no telling who moved in when. At some point, cousin Wes shows up with his three kids, Noah, Leah, and Abby, along with their three geriatric cats, Whiskers, Miss Boots, and Carmen Electra, two hamsters named Taco and Enchilada, and a freakishly large hermit crab named Grumbles, who uses a dented Diet Sprite can for a shell.

Then your little brother, the ex-marine, needs a place to crash and your second cousin, Mia, announces she's pregnant. The house may be a mansion, but it's as crowded as a New York tenement. The adults occupy all eight bedrooms on the second floor and the basement is turned into a sort of *Lord of the Flies*–themed "kids-only" zone, with beds and toys and cribs and couches occupying every inch of space. Aidan has to move his pool table to the garage. It's not so bad, though; at least you know you're not wasting your money. It's going to a good cause—namely, your flesh and blood. Plus, you sort of like having people around. Nineteen people to be exact, twenty after Mia gives birth to little baby Jason. You're happy to give your family a roof over their heads, but you don't hand out cash. You keep a firm grasp on the purse strings because the money only goes so far.

Besides your astronomical mortgage there's insurance, gas, water, electricity, and maintaining the grounds. Plus, keeping the refrigerator full is a constant challenge. The kids alone could strip a buffalo wing the size of an actual buffalo in ten minutes. So what? You have a good time with them. They play kick the can on the heated driveway, while your uncle Sydney prunes the rosebushes.

Aidan whines every so often about how cramped the house is, but since he lives off your dime, too, he can't really complain. You get married for the tax break. It's a nice little ceremony in the backyard, and you give him a Harley-Davidson for a wedding present. He gives you nice soap. A year later your first child is born, a baby girl named Sophie. She's perfect. Most babies are beautiful, but she is Gerber-baby perfect and she has a grip like a union steel worker.

Then a year later you have a little boy and name him Michael, a roly-poly exuberant little man with chunky cheeks and severe asthma. It could be worse; you had the misfortune of visiting the pediatric ward—all the kids with leukemia and spinal injuries, my God, you know you're lucky all he has is asthma. You try to remember this as you have a half-million-dollar air-purifying system put in and replace every pillow, comforter, and piece of fabric in your home with hypoallergenic alternatives, all of which seem expensive.

After Michael is born, you ask Mr. Cook if you couldn't buy a bigger house. You're splitting at the seams. Cousin Wes had to give up his room once your babies were born, so you could have a nursery. He lives in the basement now, and he doesn't look so well. You don't think he gets much sleep. But Mr. Cook doesn't like the idea of buying a bigger house. He says now isn't a good time to move money.

This annoys you. It's *your* money. You haven't done anything irresponsible with it, or even remotely outrageous. You have a nice house. That's it. You also house and feed an army, but that's it. No yachts or Humvees or gold-plated toilets, so why can't you get a bigger house? One with a laundry room big enough to service a city hospital?

You trust Mr. Cook, but maybe you should put your foot down and demand he release some money. He says you're in danger of doing what almost everybody does when they win the lottery—assume you have a limitless supply of money. "Even millionaires have to live within their means," he warns.

If you insist on a bigger house, go to section 104 (p. 332).
If you make do with the house you have, go to section 115 (p. 362).

27

From section 13

You decide to invest in real estate. You never trusted those slippery Wall Street types. What good are they except to lie and cause trouble? Find an honest broker and you'll find a scorpion that bakes lemon bars.

So Mr. Cook introduces you to a real estate agent who deals in big-ticket properties. Miss Sumpter is a no-nonsense grim-faced woman with one waxed eyebrow that sits slightly higher than the other one, giving her a permanent look of slight disapproval.

She offers you two properties that she considers airtight investments. The first one was brought to her by a friend in the Palm Beach county tax assessor's office and is a brand-new luxury condominium tower right on the ocean. The Coral Arms is for sale because the developer, Eli Esteban (known for his beautiful companions and opulent properties), had a sudden change of plans when the IRS hauled him away for tax evasion. The Coral Arms is his most magnificent creation, and he'd planned to live in the penthouse. All the other residential units in the building, which start around eight hundred thousand dollars, have been presold, as have all the retail spaces on the ground floor. It's one of those sweetheart deals that never goes public and is available only to those with the right connections. People like you.

There's also a piece of property available in Montana, a gorgeous twelve-thousand-acre cattle ranch just on the Yellowstone River. A contractor pal in Miles City tipped her off to this magnificent piece of land, which is being offered at a wildly low price—to the right buyer. The owner was recently diagnosed with emphysema and must move to Arizona; his ranching days are over and he's hoping someone will buy the Big Sky Six-Quarter Ranch (BS6Q) and keep it operational. You don't even need to know anything about ranching. The place is fully functional, completely staffed, and very profitable; you wouldn't have to do a thing. You can buy it and sell it to the next highest buyer, live there and become a Wild West cowboy, or even turn it into a dude ranch, allowing tourists to come and help with cattle drives. No matter what you do, it'll turn a profit.

Aidan is really excited about the Coral Arms in Palm Beach. Grandpa Joe likes the sound of the ranch. You're not sure. One place is posh penthouse living in a wealthy, stylish tropical city. The other is Wild West cowboy quarters on rugged, rolling wild acreage.

If you buy the property in Montana, go to section 50 (p. 172).
If you buy the Coral Arms, go to section 55 (p. 183).

28

You pay for Lanie's second kidney. Refusing would be her death sentence. The surgery doesn't go well, however, and eight hours later she slips into a coma, as her body rejects the new tissue. The whole family hovers around her as she hangs in the balance between life and death. The night passes, then the week.

Lanie refuses to wake up and she refuses to die. She stays in her coma for a month, then three months, then six. All the while you are paying all her hospital bills. Your family is distraught, worn out, exhausted, and weak. All anyone can do is wait and pray. As your bank accounts dwindle, you warn your family you don't know if you can afford to keep paying for Lanie's extended hospital stay and maybe it's time to pull the plug. They freak out. They call you selfish and thoughtless and awful. You apologize and the subject of pulling Lanie's life-support plug doesn't come up again.

Not for a year.

A year of waiting. Waiting for something to happen. For Lanie to live, for Lanie to die, for Aidan to just freaking call you. *Just once.* You've tried to call him and you can't do it. First, not enough time had gone by, and then too much time had gone by. You didn't know what to say, you didn't want to make things worse, you couldn't fathom how to make things better. You've written letters and e-mails but they're all inept. Useless. Unable to say the one thing that's true. *Aidan, I love you and I always have. I'll never stop, either. You're the only one I want. Please come back, Aidan. Please.*

But Aidan never called and the depression came slowly—so slowly, in fact, almost no one, including you, even noticed. In the beginning, you just started going to bed a little bit earlier each night. Then you began sleeping in. Your voice mail got full. People started asking if you were out of town. You turned invitations down with more and more frequency, saying you had to be at the hospital, which just isn't an excuse that anyone's going to question or complain about. Even your best friend, Sam, who can usually detect your bullshit, says it's good you're taking more time off to be there for your family.

Of course you're *not* being there for your family, you're not being anywhere except your bed, the toilet, and sometimes on a wild spree you'll shuffle to the kitchen for a handful of oyster crackers. You tell your family you're pulling more hours at work so as to stay financially afloat. Not much they can argue with there.

Even your boss lets you coast for a while, knowing you have an unwell family member, but finally after weeks of coming in late or not coming in at all, the phone rings. You're in bed, staring at the ceiling, and you let it go to voice mail. He leaves a message and says he's assuming and *hoping* you finally bought a yacht and sailed off to Greece. "It's a good thing, too," he says, "because you're fired. Let's face it, things haven't been the same ever since your big lucky day. I'll have the paperwork sent over."

Then he hangs up.

Man, that is the *upside* to depression. The love of your life is gone, you're teetering on bankruptcy, your boss just fired you, and you can't even summon the energy to get upset. You just keep repeating that phrase in your head: *Ever since your big lucky day, ever since your big lucky day, ever since your big lucky day . . .*

Finally, when you run out of food, you realize you either have to kill yourself or get up and go do something, because the prospect of starving to death in your bed over the course of however long it actually takes a person to starve to death—a few weeks? a month? especially considering you have access to tap water in the bathroom, which will really drag things out—is terrifying. You could be lying there wasting away for quite some time. And there's absolutely nothing to watch on TV.

So, fine. Whatever. You need to make some money. You have a grand or so left, maybe a bit less. You could always go get a job, like people do when they need money. Or you could hit this Grandpa Joe–style, and take what's left of your money and your self-esteem to the horse track.

If you gamble, go to section 58 (p. 192).
If you get a job, go to section 60 (p. 198).

29

Enough is enough. You've lost half your money already taking care of *not* yourself. These people are going to bleed you dry, so you tell every last one of them that they're life-source-sucking leeches and to stop treating you like an ATM. No more medical funding and the stipends are ending in six months! They all have to return to functioning citizens with jobs! Oh, do they *hate* you for this.

You are cheap, selfish, self-centered, manipulative, immature, and will *never* understand the meaning of family! Your aunt disowns you, your father says he's never been so disappointed, and your mother is too heartbroken to speak.

Well, how d'ya like that? Here you've done everything for these people and they hate you, what does that mean? It means it's time to get the hell out of town, that's what! You don't care where, so long as your family doesn't come with you. Now is the time to follow some wild dream, some crazy plan. If not now, when? You're poring over travel brochures one night, trying to choose between a luxury African safari and a deluxe spa cruise, when you hear glass breaking. Then *Crack!* Something hits your head and everything goes black.

When you wake up, you're gagged with a damp dish towel and tied to your favorite easy chair in the living room. Two clowns are staring at you. *Actual clowns* with red noses and fright wigs. Damn, you should have put that security system in! *What is this?* One is pointing a gun at your chest. The other holds up a stack of poster boards, which are already written on. Good fuck. Cue cards. He shows you the first one:

> You are going to give us all your money, fuckhead!

Cue Card Clown tosses the card down, revealing the next one:

> If you don't give us what we want, we will kill you.

Then Gun Clown brings out your laptop. It's logged on to a banking account.

| Wire ten million dollars into this account or you die. |

You shift around in the chair, your hands bound painfully. Why are they doing this? And why are they doing this in such a queer way? No talking? Using posters? Through the piercing shriek of adrenaline whistling through your ears, you realize one of your hands is looser than the other. You start to work it free. Then it hits you—these clowns aren't talking to you because *you'd recognize their voices.* This immediately summons two opposing feelings: relief, because if they don't want you to recognize them, they may intend to let you live; and fear, because these clowns threatening your life are *people you know.*

You clear your throat and try to act calm, indicating if they remove the gag, you won't scream. Cue Card Clown loosens the towel and you spit dry bits. Gun Clown unbinds your right hand so you can type your password into the laptop. You ask for water, which Cue Card Clown brings you. You're trying to buy time here, trying to decide what to do next. If you send all your money to their account, maybe you'll get it back again and maybe you won't.

On the other hand, if you refuse to pay, these jokers might kill you. Then again, they might not. They certainly don't seem professional. Still, the big unknown is who they are and how far they are going to take this. You have one hand unbound and the other one ready to break free. There's a sliding glass door just steps away, and if you make it outside, you can jump over the railing and into the bushes below, which are right next to your car. The keys are above the visor.

If you authorize the transaction, go to section 56 (p. 187).
If you make a break for it, go to section 59 (p. 196).

30

The world's most expensive meal will be prepared by some of the most celebrated chefs in the world and served at the Dome restaurant in Bangkok, Thailand. Ten courses paired with their own rare wine will be offered. Each seat will cost forty thousand dollars. Tax and tip are not included. Aidan wears a tuxedo and you wear a long emerald gown for the occasion.

On the menu:

FIRST COURSE

Crème brûlée of foie gras with tonga beans
Paired with 1990 Louis Roederer Cristal
Chef Alain Solivérès

SECOND COURSE

Tartare of Kobe beef with Imperial Beluga caviar and Belon oyster
Paired with 1995 Krug Clos du Mesnil
Chef Antoine Westermann

THIRD COURSE

Mousseline of pattes rouges crayfish with morel mushroom infusion
Paired with 2000 Corton-Charlemagne, Domaine Jean François Coche-Dury
Chef Alain Solivérès

FOURTH COURSE

Tarte fine with scallops and black truffle
Paired with 1996 Le Montrachet, Domaine de la Romanée-Conti
Chef Antoine Westermann

FIFTH COURSE

Lobster osso bucco
Paired with 1985 Romanée-Conti, Domaine de la Romanée-Conti
Chef Jean-Michel Lorain

SIXTH COURSE

Ravioli with guinea fowl and burrata cheese in a veal reduction
Paired with 1961 Château Palmer
Chef Annie Feolde

SEVENTH COURSE

Saddle of lamb "Léonel"
Paired with 1959 Château Mouton Rothschild
Chef Marc Meneau

—PALATE CLEANSER—

Sorbet "Dom Pérignon"

EIGHTH COURSE

Supreme of pigeon en croute with cèpes mushroom sauce and cipollotti
Paired with 1961 Château Haut-Brion
Chef Heinz Winkler

NINTH COURSE

Veal cheeks with Périgord truffles
Paired with 1955 Château Latour
Chef Heinz Winkler

TENTH COURSE

Imperial gingerbread pyramid with caramel and salted butter ice cream
Paired with 1967 Château d'Yquem
Chef Jean-Michel Lorain

The dinner concludes with fireworks and champagne spilt everywhere as people hug and kiss good night. It's delightful! *Stupendous*, actually, which if you think about it is not a word that comes up often. Good food shows you what's possible in life. Ordinary ingredients like water, sugar, and salt change from elemental building blocks into exquisite works of art when prepared by loving hands. As Mozart said, this is the key to all genius. "Neither a lofty degree of intelligence nor imagination nor both together go to the making of genius. Love, love, love, that is the soul of genius."

The dinner gets you talking about art and passion and how nothing is worth doing unless the sum is greater than the parts. One way or another, everyone must struggle in life, it's a universal rule. No one knows *why* it's a rule, we might have gone with something different, but no matter how much health, wealth, talent, or luck a person has, everyone, absolutely everyone, struggles with something.

And yet.

And yet while everyone struggles, works hard, suffers setbacks, endures spells of mind-numbing monotony, bursts of sheer terror, and black pits of injustice, in the end some people *get* something for their efforts while others don't. Some struggles seem to pay you back, while others just make you keep paying. Struggle with childbirth and you'll be paid back with life; struggle with jealousy and you'll only be paid back with more pain. Unless of course childbirth results in your own death or jealousy inspires you to achieve greatness—these things can be tricky. One person's miracle is another's nightmare. Like loving Jesus or having children or buying timeshares in Florida, we have yet to find one single thing that's always good, all the time, for every person.

So if you're going to struggle, then why not struggle with something that's going to pay you back? What is it you really want to do? What would be a lot of work but give you something wonderful? Well, this trip has opened your eyes to the marvels of traveling, that's for sure, and it's opened your eyes to the institution of culinary art. You stay up all night brainstorming ideas, hatching plans, until the sun rises and you've narrowed your choices down to two ideas. Two choices that would be assloads of work and pay you back with oceans of love.

One idea is to incorporate traveling and food by starting a specialized touring company that caters to the very wealthy and discerning palates of that quirky group known as "the foodies," people who live for haute cuisine and will do anything/pay anything/go anywhere to find it. You'd travel the world with these select groups sampling the freshest, rarest, most exquisite foods all over the world. You'd host celebrity chef dinners, tour vineyards, eat mangoes in Thailand, sip hand-pressed rum in the Indies, throw candle-light dinners on glaciers in Iceland. It'd be a nonstop culinary world tour and you could even make money doing it.

The other idea is to buy some gorgeous piece of property abroad and start a vineyard. You've always wanted your own vineyard. Imagine making award-winning wines and sharing your love of excellence with others. It would be a little piece of paradise. A sanctuary of tranquility and excellence.

If you start a culinary world tour, go to section 57 (p. 189).
If you buy a vineyard, go to section 61 (p. 201).

From section 15

You and Aidan decide to see the *Titanic*. It's the experience of a lifetime! The journey lasts twelve days and costs forty thousand dollars each, but it's deluxe all the way. You fly to Newfoundland first class and check into the Hotel Fairmont, a grand seaside hotel that overlooks St. John's harbor, where the ship departs the next morning. That night you have dinner at the hotel with some of your shipmates: the Cassmans, the Steins, Dr. Pinkerton, Mr. Ed Peters, the Bellow sisters, and a jolly man who goes by Brewer—all fellow millionaires except for Ed, an electrical engineer who won the trip from a radio station in Ohio.

The next morning, you shop for last-minute supplies: Dramamine, Beemans spearmint gum, extra-strength Tylenol, first-class stamps, a green harmonica, and a shark-tooth necklace on a leather cord. Aidan gets a very expensive new pocketknife that can cut through titanium. *Typical.* Where does one even run across titanium? A space launch? Mid-afternoon you board the enormous research ship *RV Kelvik*, a Russian vessel licensed to research and explore the site of the *Titanic*. Right now they're looking for two of James Cameron's robotic camera bots that are still missing from his last film shoot. For the next two days while you're at sea, you'll enjoy sweeping views of the Atlantic, sleep in grand staterooms, eat gourmet meals, and meet the pilots, scientists, and researchers who're responsible for keeping you alive.

You're introduced to Captain Anatole Sagavitch, chief pilot of the "Pod," or small submersible taking you over two miles down to the ocean floor. He pilots *Alpha*, and another equally dashing captain pilots its sister submersible, *Omega*. The Pods look like enormous orange helmets with glass faces. The faces are framed with a tangle of metal instruments, halogen lights, hydraulic thrusters, robotic arms with rotating jaws, GPS sonar guns, pan and tilt cameras, and backup emergency life-support systems. They're serious pieces of machinery, able to withstand pressure up to twenty thousand feet. Seven feet of nickel steel separate passengers from the million pounds of water trying to get in.

During the safety drills on deck, you find the interior of *Alpha* to be surprisingly claustrophobic. You knew it would be small—it only takes six people at a time—but you didn't expect the walls, covered in instruments, to be so completely close all around you. One wrong move and you're afraid you might bump an oxygen ejection button or shut down some crucial navigational sensor. Captain Anatole assures you everything will be fine, and for two days you practice shimmying down the airlock manhole and wriggling over into your bucket seat without crashing a kneecap into any of the control panels. Aidan gives you a wink and says not to worry, he'll be there watching out for your enormous clumsy knees.

Finally the morning of the descent arrives; the weather is overcast but calm and you get the go-ahead from the weather control room. Everyone puts on their heroic astronaut-inspired dive suits. They are one-piece white Kevlar jumpsuits with big metal buckles that are stamped front and back with professional-looking logos that say TITANIC PIONEERS! You hold Aidan's hand and take your place in *Alpha*. Once all your safety harnesses are secured and the cross-checks completed, the cables and hoses are removed from the exteriors and a massive crane picks the Pods up one by one and sets them in the water. First *Alpha*, then *Omega*.

What's strange about all this—the crew shouting, the crane hoisting, the splash in the water—is that you can't hear any of it. It's all completely silent. The *Alpha* is soundproof and it's only after you descend a few hundred yards that the captain turns on the outside speakers, which let the sounds of the ocean rush in. You instinctively dig under your dive suit and tug up your shark-tooth necklace, as though it's an underwater ID badge. The air seems a little stale in the Pod; is it stale? Did it smell that way in the drills? But then they wouldn't have just fueled everything up; this is just what it's supposed to smell like now . . . and is it a little hot maybe? No. Stop. You look over at

Aidan and smile nervously. He gives you a little wink. Thank God. If the Pod gets stuck at the bottom of the ocean and you have to decide who to eat first, at least you have backup.

As the *Alpha* sinks down through the water and into the darkness, the inky abyss all around you makes you sit on your hands, clench your jaw, and physically will away a panic attack. While the captain is nattering on about depth ratios, winter tidal currents, and native species of coral, you're calculating, without the benefit of any actual math, just how much pressure this black ocean must be pressing on the tiny glass air bubble you now find yourself in. Rapid-fire unwanted thoughts scream through your head.

Why would you pay to put yourself in imminent peril?
Of all the adventures available, why did you pick the one without oxygen?
When will this end?
Will this end?

Finally someone says, "There it is!" and sure enough, the powerful Pod halogen lights illuminate the fossilized bow of the *Titanic*. As you strain to look, the captain is reciting a litany of facts. He says before the *Titanic* went down it was eight hundred and eighty-two feet long, had four electric elevators, two libraries, and two barbershops, as well as fifteen thousand bottles of beer, forty tons of potatoes, and seven thousand heads of lettuce on board.

Why he's telling you this, you have no idea. Are you supposed to look for fossilized potatoes rolling around the sea floor? Plus, it's not too comforting to hear all these eerie facts concerning one of the greatest maritime disasters when you yourself are not only at sea, you are *under* the sea, at the bottom, having willingly completed 95 percent of your own drowning. You shouldn't have thought that.

An alarm buzzer sounds, which sends the captain into frenzied action. He gets on the radio and starts barking orders. You have no idea what's going on and the Pod takes a violent turn to the left, as though something smacked its face.

You know from safety drills the Pod has two hundred and fifty hours of life support on board, which roughly equates to three and a half days of oxygen per person. That alone should comfort you; three and a half days is a long time when you have a support ship as big as an oil tanker equipped with every kind of rescue apparatus known to man floating directly above you. Out of the port window you see *Omega* hovering. It's come around the wreck and is whisking to your aid, although now *Alpha* is sinking faster than a nickel-plated anchor.

The interior lights of *Alpha* go out and the green emergency lights blink on. You hear a loud clanking sound as the sub hits the deck of the *Titanic* and everything loose is thrown forward, including Brewer, who's already unbuckled his safety harness. This is beyond ironic. As far as you can gather from frantic Captain Anatole, *Alpha* has lost a thruster and can go right and left, but not up or down. The captain thrusts hard port side, briefly lifting the vessel, and tries to catch the current. If the *Alpha* is sideways, the horizontal thrusters might act as vertical thrusters.

At first it looks positive, the Pod lifts and everyone gasps, but a split second later there's a thundering scraping sound as you hit an unseen foreign object. People are screaming, expecting to feel water rushing in, as the crack sounded so loud it must have split the sub in two, but there's no such sensation and the sub seems to be sitting innocently on the deck of the *Titanic*, just as it had sat aboard the *Kelvik*. The captain shouts, "All right, we have a situation, but there's no reason to—"

Screeeeeeeeeeeeeeeeeeeeeeeeeeeeeeeeeeeeee!

His voice is drowned out by the shrieking of shearing metal as the deck you're resting on wholly gives way. The Pod tumbles down into the rotten hull of the *Titanic*, crashing and crunching through honeycombed girders. When you finally come to rest, you are three floors below the deck, farther into the heart of the *Titanic* than any other expedition has gone. Despite being plunged into the guts, the Pod seems to be functioning. The interior lights come back on, you can still breathe, and the radio still seems to be connected to the outside world. The captain is yelling at someone on the mother ship and you actually catch a glimpse of *Omega* out a *Titanic* porthole. It's circling the ship trying to find you.

This is insane. You are in a submarine sunk inside a ship.

This is not happening.

This is not happening.

This is not happening.

The lights stutter out and green emergency lights blink back on.

This is happening.

Now pray. Ask God to save you. Swear you'll do anything and everything if he gets you out of this. You'll never buy anything impulsive or ridiculous again, you'll give all your money to charity.

The captain tells you that everything is going to be all right. They're devising a rescue plan on the surface and *Omega* will deposit its passengers on the *Kelvik* and return to stay below as long as possible. He says the *Alpha* is fully intact, all the systems and reserve systems are working. You're going to have one hell of a story to tell your kids. (He probably shouldn't have mentioned kids because right then everyone pictures their families and all the people back home who would be devastated by their death.) The captain reiterates everything is going to be fine. You'd really like to believe him, but his voice is shaking.

Your only comfort is the pressure of Aidan's hand. It's like your life-support line. You clutch at each other without pause and you decide if you ever get off this thing, you are getting goddamned married.

Six hours later the *Omega*, which has spotted you through a torn opening far on the *Titanic*'s starboard side and has loyally stayed there with its bright track beam on you, has to surface to resupply with oxygen. "If they have to resupply," Dr. Pinkerton asks softly, "don't we?" The captain clears his throat. "The reserve supply kicks in now," he says. "We're now on the emergency support system." Someone starts weeping and none of you say anything. You're all thinking the same thing—we have three and a half days to live.

Eighteen hours later you are in the dark. The dark of the dark. The *Omega* had to surface, bad weather is coming, and the captain gently explains you're going to half reserve, to save energy. So now only two small green lights are on at the head of the sub, above the window. They look like two green eyes staring at you. The one thing you wish the captain would turn off is the outside stereo. You can hear strange faraway booming sounds and random clicking as fish communicating with each other whisk past in flashes of silver and white against the ink.

The *Omega* returns around nine in the morning, so it says on the clock; all you know is you're surrounded by perpetual night. Your inner circadian system starts to become disoriented—it should be light by now but it isn't. Still, you feel better when the captain turns on the entire emergency light system again; it seems practically bright now. Imagine being in a pitch-dark room for twelve hours and then someone turns on a nightlight. It's blinding.

When the *Omega* arrived you had just finished a breakfast of bottled water and PowerBars, part of the emergency stash on board. You're impressed by all this preparedness; it's as if they expected it to happen, which also makes you sick with anger. They even have a "waste container," a soft plastic bladder with a biohazard symbol on it and an elongated mouth. This, combined with the privacy of a thin blanket drawn over your lap, is your bathroom. Luckily, fear or adrenaline or perhaps not eating much for twenty-four hours prevents anyone from needing to expel anything but liquid.

The *Omega* brings news of the new plan, which is that the *Kelvik* has sent for dive rescue crews and deep-sea welders who can hopefully cut you out of your metal coffin. The *Omega*'s new position, outside the starboard windows, which you can see through fallen beams, illuminates a new section of your craft and you can see for the first time some of the barnacle-encrusted fixtures around you. Judging by the chair-shaped chunks of coral and wall lamps (one is shiny silver, the others are completely black and covered in mollusks, you have no idea why; it is beyond your somewhat limited knowledge of underwater mineral reactions), it looks as though you have landed in a ballroom. A series of smooth black squares with ornate ridges tumbled into a heap in the corner looks like mirrors and the banquet tables; they are so covered with sea life they now look like coral tables.

The *Omega* uses its robotic arm to drop off a steel box, supposedly loaded with food and supplies, but the *Alpha*'s robotic arm can't reach it, leaving everyone on board just staring at the unrecovered box, which sits there in the gloom. At about ten p.m. the captain says an industrial sub is coming, an underwater vessel specializing in metal cutting, but at midnight it comes across the radio that the surface water is too rough to attempt a dive.

The next morning there's a clanking on the roof and the captain gets the robotic camera aimed at a long metal arm coming straight down. It's attached to the welding sub, whose captain radios down and says they're going to poke a hole in the roof.

They're going to poke a hole in the roof? Tears bead in the corners of your eyes and your sweetie squeezes your hand tighter.

Everyone waits.

People make an attempt at singing meek little songs until the captain says maybe it's time to stop and points out the low oxygen needle. Deep breathing and singing use more oxygen and you'll need every cubic inch there is left. That shuts everyone up for good.

People start crying again.

At nine p.m. the welding sub says a critical supporting beam is in the way. If they cut it, the rest of the *Titanic*'s deck will crash down and crush the *Alpha* flat as a manhole cover.

Someone starts crying.

At ten p.m. the captain passes out the last of the PowerBars. Aidan refuses to take one, insisting you have it. Definite marriage material. Why did you ever think he wasn't? This is classic hero stuff! It's too bad it doesn't matter as the *Titanic*'s list of victims is about to get longer, but if that wasn't the case, this would be a movie!

On the third day, the *Alpha* begins to list slowly and gently, like setting down a sleeping baby. Then there are groaning sounds and strange vibrations. The captain says it's coming from the welding sub above, but everyone can tell the sounds are coming from below. The floor is about to give out.

At this point everyone goes into their own private hell. By noon people dig around in their camera bags and pockets for scraps of paper so they can write out last wishes and good-bye letters. People name their loved ones out loud. You turn to your sweetheart, the one who's stuck by you through all this, and ask, "Wanna get married?"

The answer is a very definite yes. At ten in the morning there's a loud crashing sound and people scream. The welder sub has made contact with the *Alpha* again and this time it's anchored something to the roof. The captain says they're welding an air lock onto the sub, a sort of long metal tube that will act like a chute. Once it's welded on, the water will get sucked out, air will be pumped in, and they'll lower a rescue rope down. One by one you will be hoisted up. That would be awesome if there was any oxygen left.

People start to lose consciousness. You try to stay awake, but you just need to sleep a little. You rest your head against Aidan's shoulder and go to sleep, possibly for the last time ever. At least you're together. At least you weren't alone.

You wake up to screaming. Smoke. Blackness. You are choking on something and then something hits your head. There's a burst of billowing air, like inhaling after breaking the surface of the water after a deep dive. Your lungs burn with the sharp edges of the oxygen, your eyes fly open and you try to sit up, but you can't. You're tied down and everything is white. So white. A hot pain comes at you from your left-hand side. It's as if it notices you and then rushes in. Voices and beeping. Something tightens and releases. You sleep.

Five days later you wake up at Mercy Hospital in Newfoundland. You've been unconscious ever since they rescued you in a dramatic scenario the likes of which are worthy of a blockbuster action film. The welders finally secured the tube and got it filled with air, but the cutters had the race of their lives, or rather the race of *your* life, trying to cut through seven feet of nickel steel. Then, when they broke through, the sparks hit the blast of oxygen rushing out of the compromised sub, causing an explosion that nearly broke the weld. Evacuation was a panic, stuffing two people at a time into a tube designed for one. People were yanked, bruised, cut, and banged as they were forced up and out of the failing *Alpha*. You were unconscious for most of it; they cracked three of your ribs and cut your scalp deeply trying to save you when your harness caught on the damn instrument panel on the ceiling.

Know what saved you? Aidan and his titanium pocketknife. Your sweetie cut you free and saved your life. Now you're safe and sound and they expect a full recovery. At home your family is a mess. Your coworkers throw you a big welcome home party at the office and your boss gives you a promotion. The sobbing and crying and worrying is nothing compared to the hive of reporters who want your story. All you know is it took going to the bottom of the sea to find out what's really important: everything that isn't on the bottom of the sea. Your family, your sweetheart, and your own sweet life are what's important. Nothing else. In fact, as long as you have each other, you could see taking or leaving the money at this point. Part of you would like to be a roaming philanthropist. A person who goes out into the world and helps others in need. Not through some big fund or trust, but by getting out there and seeing what needs to be done and getting dirty. We need miracles in this world; think how good it would feel to know you're out there making them happen.

On the other hand, you could raise one hell of a family. You certainly have all the resources you need to raise healthy kids. Stable relationship, healthy family dynamics, the ability to give children a good thing. The bottom line is you want to make the world a better place. So you either get busy helping the people who are already here or you get busy building a family dynasty filled with people for whom the world is grateful.

If you have a big family, go to section 48 (p. 164).
If you give the money away, go to section 62 (p. 203).

32

From section 16

Dirk Clayhill is a handsome, successful real estate agent and for the time being your part-time personal driver, as he spends hours showing you properties all along the North Shore of Lake Superior, driving up and down the coast of Minnesota and Michigan until you finally spot your piece of paradise.

It almost seems too good to be true, a vintage lodge named Oziyapi, which is Dakota for "Restful." Wraparound porches, wide plank floors, stone fireplaces, moose heads, Navajo rugs, overstuffed leather chairs. The modern updates don't hurt, either. Whirlpool baths, an ionized sauna, and a gourmet kitchen provide an extra level of luxury. You buy the majestic lodge on Lake Superior, a stunning combination of modern engineering, Swedish Cope craftsmanship, and classic log cabin design.

It's a relief to breathe fresh air and get away from the bad memories. It's hard to be anything but happy. You don't even mind being alone so much out here, in part because you're not alone very much. You invite Dirk over for supper one night and then almost every night after. He's funny and smart and very successful. One of the top realtors in the area. More than anything you like how you feel when he's around.

You laugh a lot when you're together. He lets you be strong, make decisions, but he never seems submissive or weak. From the first kiss over grilled salmon at sunset to the deep thrusts on the kitchen table at midnight, you're never unaware of his masculinity. It's what makes you feel safe exploring your sexuality. You let him do things.

He also cooks for you, brings amazing bottles of wine, and tells hysterical realtor stories. Like the time he locked his clients out of their car or when he had to have a house's "aura" cleaned before the buyers would sign, or the couple from St. Paul who were looking at vacant land with their little dog when a hawk dive-bombed and *whoosh!* flew off with little Snowball. That one's actually not very funny. The rest of them are, though, and you could listen to him for hours.

If you had one concern, it might be that you drink too much. An easy thing to do when you're savoring three-hour dinners and talking till dawn. You call Sam and confess you're falling for this guy. She says that's fine, just don't do anything stupid, and if you do something stupid, don't videotape it. Good advice, duly noted and then scrapped without notice when Dirk takes you up Gunflint Trail and serenades you in a canoe. That night you allow the little Sony camcorder to blink its red light while you let Dirk do things. He's really been getting into restraints.

Nothing can pierce the bliss of this tranquil place. You redecorate the guest rooms and your friends come up for the Fourth of July; you put in a new dock and your family comes for Labor Day. Everyone thinks Dirk is delightful, although Sam thinks he's "creepy." She's just jealous and you don't blame her. Dirk is a catch. He says you need a bigger boat, one with a cabin so you can make love all night at sea. He wants to make you scream so loud that Canada hears.

You buy *Against All Odds,* a thirty-five-foot vintage yacht with polished teak cabins and brass fittings. The 1930 Elco Cruisette is delivered dockside by the Duluth harbormaster himself, Captain Bernard White. He calls the yacht "a fine girl" and points out the detailed work on the brass binnacle compass, the French ormolu clock, which is still ticking under watertight casing, and the old telegraph instruments that say *Ray & Co., Liverpool,* and remain at the ready on their brass pedestals.

You take the yacht out with Dirk under the full moon, and just as he promised, make love all night as the boat rocks gently. You take her over to the Duluth harbor and have steaks at Fitzger's, then go up to Grand Marais for sugary cinnamon apple fritters at World's Best Donuts. Dirk buys a new fly-fishing reel at the Beaver House, a big old tackle shop with a giant bass coming out of the building. Well, you buy the reel for him, but you don't mind; it's a gift and you love making him as happy as he makes you.

Then you steer *Against All Odds* into Thunder Bay on the Canadian border and decide to stay overnight at the False Creek Casino, which has an excellent chophouse and a semi-attached water park, Tomahawk Thunder. The clerk at the reception desk is just handing you a room key when a little waiter comes up with a bottle of Dom Pérignon and two flutes on a big poker chip tray. Dirk grins; he ordered a bottle of champagne before you even got to the room! The corks keep popping the rest of the night and you swill bubbly while playing slots, craps, keno, pontoon, and blackjack. Then you have a bottle of red wine during dinner, mostly to disguise the taste of the fish.

You might have made it to your room intact if the manager hadn't given you a Free Wampum card, meaning all your drinks are now free. He gave everyone in the Blackhawk Show Lounge a card after two very mentally handicapped children wandered out onstage during the magician act. The obese girl stood onstage wearing a dripping wet lime green bathing suit and emitted shrill screeches as the boy, also in swim trunks, sprang into an impromptu dance. The magician looked ill. The boy went on bounding across the stage until he crashed right into the dove stand, releasing birds into the audience.

The manager apologized extravagantly, explaining the two had gotten away from their group, the Special Olympics Upper Midwest chapter, who were having their Champions Weekend Retreat next door at the semi-attached water park.

That's when the drinking really starts. Which makes no sense, because you're a bloody millionaire, you can drink anything you want anytime you want, but there's something about a free drinking coupon that makes a person embrace filthy excess. It's Dirk's idea to order "one of everything" from the casino's "Claim to Fame" cocktail menu. Bubblegum Martinis, Canadian Cherry Cosmos, Dirty Cheerleaders, Frangipani Daiquiris, Chocolate-Coconut Mudslides, and a tasty, minty green drink called a Dead Carp.

By the time you stagger out of the bar and walk barefoot through the casino, you're drunk. Possibly blackout drunk, but you do remember snapshots. There was Dirk realizing he'd left his coat back at the restaurant and you telling him to leave it, you'd buy him another one. Then at some point you were at the beach and Dirk asked you to marry him and you said something like, "Whaddya fuckin' think?!" which must have been a *yes*, because then you're back at the casino in the exotic shop atrium, where the little cone-shaped chapel that looks like a teepee is open twenty-four hours a day. (*Why?*) Then you wake up in bed naked save for one shoe on your right foot. The mattress beneath you is damp and red; the bottle of Pinot Noir on the nightstand tipped over. It's when you stagger out of bed and peel back the wet sheets that you find a signed, sealed, half-soaked wedding certificate.

You and Dirk got married.

After the initial shock and embarrassment, you both laugh till it hurts. He confesses he'd been planning to propose to you next month, had an elaborate scheme all laid out, and was assuming you'd want a big fancy wedding. Now look! *It's already done!* Back at Oziyapi, you plan a big party, a proper reception so family and friends can share in your amazing, giving, boundless love. When you tell your family they're so happy for you; your friends are thrilled you found your soul mate. Only Sam wrinkles her nose and says, "He's weird." Dirk toasts you, his new bride, and says you are everything to him. Without you, he doesn't know what he'd do.

Six months later, everything goes to hell. It's always the same story. You fall in love with a person, only to discover they're not that person, they're somebody else and so are you. In this case, Mr. Dirk Clayhill turns out to be quite the actor. You catch him on board the *Against All Odds* with an Asian teenager, some banjo-playing slut who works at Dixieland's Good-Time Jamboree at the mall. He says this girl is like a niece to him, as though that would make it better. What were you doing with your niece, Dirk? Whispering into her mouth?

Then the bank calls you and asks if you want the direct deposits on your *new account* to occur on the first or the fifteenth of each month. Ummm . . . what new account? Why, Dirk's new account, of course! You find money missing everywhere. Strange credit cards start arriving in the mail. Receipts for hotels, bars, strip clubs, and lingerie stores, but Dirk has never once bought you any lingerie—he said he was *turned off* by lingerie. He's got an excuse for everything. The hotels are for his clients, potential buyers in from out of town. He puts them up sometimes. The bars and strip clubs are for clients, too. Some guys are into that. Not him, but he has to take clients wherever they want to go. The lingerie? That, um . . . was for his sister. No, *his niece*! Not that niece! Not the banjo-slut niece, another one you haven't met yet.

You file for divorce. Your lawyer said it would be quick and dirty, an easy case of a gold digger taking advantage of a—he chooses his words carefully—of a *trusting* person. When you get to mediation, however, Dirk's lawyers produce a stack of documents you've never seen before. Letters from you. Letters you apparently wrote to him that say things like, *I love you, I want to take care of you, I want to make sure you never have to worry about money again, even if we split up I want you to know I'll always provide for you. . . .*

What?

The letters are printed and signed by you, but you didn't write them. You tell the court it's not your signature, but a cold feeling of dread spreads across your stomach because the signatures look *just* like yours. The court allows the letters into evidence. A handwriting analyst confirms your signature. The phony love letters are as good as contracts and they claim you'll provide for Dirk indefinitely. The absolute worst part is the letter that claims you bought *Against All Odds* for Dirk. It was a gift. Afterward, your lawyer confesses your case is no longer quick, but it's definitely dirty.

You bring in character witnesses. All your friends and family are glad to help, but their testimonies are shot to hell on cross-examination when his lawyers ask for clarification. "Did the defendant say Dirk was the love of her life?"

Your family squirms and meekly replies something like, "Um . . . I guess."
The lawyers lean in. "Yes or no?"

"Yes."

In the end, the judge awards Dirk a generous monthly stipend and *Against All Odds* is now his. You seethe with anger. You yell and scream at your lawyers but nobody can help. You throw anything he ever gave you (not much!) into the lake. You smash silver-framed photographs, drive by his office and spit. But what really gets you, what wakes you up at night and makes you head for the refrigerator to anger-eat until you've gained fifteen pounds, is him getting the *Against All Odds*. The money you'll never see again, but the boat? You love that boat! It's yours! If he thinks he can have your boat, he's got another thing coming. You'd rather see her sink than see him on board.

If you sink the yacht, go to section 64 (p. 208).
If you let Dirk have the yacht, go to section 65 (p. 212).

33

From section 17

You silently gather yourself up into a crouching position, hold your breath, count to three, and then together you and Sam spring like bounding wildcats for the door. It's anything but graceful though, and you knock something over in your scramble. The clatter wakes everyone up, including the pirate, who grabs his gun and chases you outside.

Heart hammering, people shouting, gunfire blasting . . . there's the railing! You can do this! In one breathless pole-vaulting leap, you dash for the railing, catapulting yourself over the side, and screeeeeeeeeeeeeeeeeeeeeeeee eeeeeeeeeeeeeeeeeeeeeeeeeeeeeeeeam as you drop two stories straight into the water. . . . *Keep your arms to your sides, keep your arms to your sides, slice the water feetfirst, don't break your back, don't break your back.* . . .

You knife into the warm water, the suctioning force ripping off your shirt. You kick hard and try to stay underwater as long as you can, taking awkward froglike kicks toward the rescue boats. You surface gasping for air and find yourself halfway to the rescue boat! They see you! They were waiting for jumpers! Brave souls who refused to give up! You can see Navy SEALs already suited and preparing to jump in for you. There's screaming everywhere, a commotion behind you. It starts raining. Hailing. Sharp pelting all around you, then a quick pain and blackness.

A damn pirate shot you—right through the lung.

You gasp and sink, water rushing in over your head and a deep, strong current pulling you underwater. The divers seem so far away; the world above you darkens and bleeds out as you descend to the ocean floor.

In the end they can't even manage to retrieve your body. You were too far away, sank too fast, and had on nothing bright or buoyant.

They can't find you.

Down, down, down you go—a bone anchor through the quiet blue—coming to rest in a quiet place of big sleep where little green fishes come up kissing shyly. You come to rest between canyons of sea rock that are as deep as the Grand Canyon. It would take a submarine not yet invented to retrieve your body. Worry not! You're on the move. Your skeleton will never stay put for long, dancing instead with the warm ribbons of water that curl around and cruise past every continent, taking you easily everywhere you ever wanted to go.

It turns out anyone who dies at sea without a proper burial becomes a bank of red coral. *Precious coral* it's called by some, because it is the most protected and expensive coral there is. Artisans harvest long spindly fingers and polish the matte finish to a glassy shine before turning the brilliant red bits into stunning jewelry for wealthy women all over the world. Dead? You are not dead. You are going to the opera; you are going into the halls of government. You are out and about in little pretty pieces all over the world.

34

Sex Island looks just like its brochures. White sand beaches, thatched huts on the water, and a room-service menu filled with sexual perversions. You can pick up your bamboo-handled phone any time of the night or day and order any service you can think of. Erotic massage, exotic dances, sexual partners offering oral, anal, couples, multiples, invisibles, BDSM, or dominatrix, and the list goes on, including things you've never heard of before. What exactly is a *Louisiana Steamboat*?

The selection of sex partners, or "hospitality companions," as they're called, is vast. You can ask for your male companions to be "classically educated" or "delightfully naive." They'll wear anything you want: leather studded collars, business suits, pilot uniforms, thong-style Speedos, prison guard uniforms . . . and do whatever you want, in order to better facilitate whatever fantasy you desire.

Certain companions specialize in original characters, like Thunderbuns, the Peruvian love lord, and Orgbot, the horny robot from the future. There're plenty of famous characters to choose from: Captain Kirk will come dock his shuttle in your *Enterprise* and Indiana Jones will storm your room and catch you with his whip. Under the "New Characters" category is Teen Vampire Boy, Dan Rather, and Alvin the Chipmunk.

Prices and fees next to the services range from a thirty-dollar "Texarkana hand job" all the way to a ten-thousand-dollar all-inclusive "harem party," where your choice of up to ten hospitality companions will stay with you for an entire seventy-two hours, doing anything you want. Role-playing is encouraged. The guidebook's list of OTR (off the rack) fantasies is three pages long. Affair with coworker, affair with best friend's spouse, convert a lesbian, get kidnapped/swept away, lose your virginity, peeping Tom, relapsed priest, and celebrity sex with George Clooney, Harrison Ford, Elijah Wood, LeAnn Rimes, Meg Ryan, Barbra Streisand, et cetera. . .

The island has all kinds of themed areas for these specific fantasies. Waterfalls, rose gardens, balconies overlooking the ocean, gazebos on the verdant hillsides, crystal-clear rivers flowing through the lush jungle, private beaches and public beaches (where actors dressed as everyday citizens at the beach pretend to be horrified/amused/disgusted so guests can have sex in public).

Large air-conditioned Quonset huts house a large variety of indoor fantasy sets. There's an executive office suite, airplane bathroom, prison cell, doctor's office, parents' bedroom, grocery store fruit section, porn video soundstage, Eskimo igloo, caveman lair, troll grotto, vampire altar, Thai brothel, Martha Stewart's kitchen, and a lifelike re-creation of the U.N. General Assembly, where actors wear suits and sheiks' garb and sit stoically at their desks as guests hump away. (Some hump secretly, while others do it right on the speaker's podium. Preferences vary.)

So many people request religious-themed fantasies that an entire church was built, complete with an entire bank of confessionals, which are the most popular spot for sinning. Likewise a firehouse was constructed nearby with an adjacent police department for emergency-response-team fantasies. Firefighters and cops are big. So are fire trucks. You're told during peak season the ladder of Engine 39 has to be hosed down hourly.

Your tastes at the moment run a little more classical. You'd like a companion in your thatched hut. Someone to talk to. You request a tall, good-looking, intelligent man who likes poetry, gives foot rubs, and cooks. And who loves oral. The reservations desk says they have two candidates for your pleasuring.

Boy A is a tall, blond, blue-eyed snowboarder who loves romantic comedies, baking cupcakes, and "going down on sexy ladies."

Boy B is a tall, dark, green-eyed Pilates instructor who loves Shakespeare, French cuisine, and "the high art of cunnilingus."

"And they both know massage?" you ask.

"Yes," the hospitality coordinator says. "It's a prerequisite for working on the island. I'll send their measurements now." She hangs up and the little fax on the kitchen counter starts to whir. Out comes the boys' bios, complete with height, weight, penis length, and best of all, penis girth. Let's just say that either of them will do fine.

If you choose Boy A, go to section 66 (p. 213).
If you choose Boy B, go to section 70 (p. 226).

35

You decide to grab the gun. Why? Because you are one of those people who rise to the occasion, who act fearlessly in the face of danger. There is no school for this, no genetic code, some people just possess the ability to act. This can come early or later in life, descending like a thunderbolt on the unsuspecting head of someone who never felt like a hero before. The point being, heroes are made in split seconds, when a *decision* hangs like a scythe separating those who would step forward from those who would not.

You step forward.

Sam counts to three and you spring toward the sleeping pirate, plucking up his gun, and jumping back before he's even fully awake. He grasps helplessly at the ground where his rifle should have been. The other passengers quickly circle behind you, everyone finding makeshift weapons. Table legs become blackjacks, chafing dish lids are shields, a hot plate dangling by its cord is now a heated ball and chain.

"Okay," you say to the startled pirate, trying to keep your voice steady. (God, your hands are trembling.) "Stand up!" The kid stands, eyes crazy with fear and his tense body language indicating he's fighting the urge to bolt. "Here's what we're going to do," you tell him, "everybody's just going to stay calm."

He nods and then the gun goes off in your hands. It just explodes without warning.

"You shot him!" someone shouts, as though it wasn't obvious as the kid slumps over onto the floor. You look at the gun. It seems alive now. Like a dark, oily, panting animal, which you thought was on its leash, but had planned an attack all on its own.

Sam shouts, "Let's go!" and the group of passengers charges out on deck, overtaking the startled boys who are supposed to be on guard. They immediately drop their guns and hold up their hands, but you notice neither drops his cigarette. Two of your fellow passengers, husky men in khakis who you later learn are reservists who've waited a lifetime to do something useful with boot camp, disarm the pirates quickly. Now you're three guns strong. When the other pirates come running, you're already in V formation, guns drawn and ready.

Big spotlights from surrounding rescue boats illuminate the deck as Navy SEALs start appearing over the railings. They come from all directions, all at once, and you've never seen a more heroic sight. When they've neutralized all targets and secured all passengers, they load you onto a military escort ship and you look around for Sam. Where is she? She was right behind you the whole time. *You saw her* . . . Didn't you?

An annoying woman with a military badge escorts you into a room and starts talking at you. She says there was friendly fire. Bullets. Ricochet. Then she takes a deep breath and says, "Sam's dead. She was hit by a stray bullet. Nobody knows whose. Either way, it was an incredibly daring rescue. Only two lost. One of theirs and one of ours. It could have been so much worse. The nation owes you a debt of gratitude. You're a hero."

Sam's *what?*

After that things get blurry. At home you're miserable. People won't leave you alone, constantly wanting you to talk and calling you a "hero." They credit you with saving lives. Your brave act led to the capture of ten international terrorists, who in turn gave up more names and information in exchange for lesser sentences. The whole dust-up gets you on a Wikipedia page about "Cruise Ships That Became War Ships." The story circles the globe, inspiring citizens everywhere to tell you that *you're awesome.*

And every time you hear it you want to die, like Sam did. Like you should have. It was *your fault* she was even on that boat and it very well may have been your bullet that killed her, no one can say, or maybe they just *won't* say, which is what you're starting to suspect, which makes the blood running through your veins feel like oozing black toxic tar. You sleep all day and all night. You don't eat. You won't see anyone. In fact, the only thought that runs through your head is that this lottery money is cursed and anything you do with it is cursed and as long as you have it, bad things will happen.

If you keep the money, go to section 67 (p. 220).
If you give the money away, go to section 71 (p. 228).

36

From section 18

You say *Yes!* and the table erupts with applause and cheering. You agree to become Mrs. John Harris Wadley Jr.

There's a big opulent wedding at the country club and Jim-Junior pays for everything, including rooms for your whole family at the Windsor Court Hotel. They're generally well-behaved, even though your cousin gets drunk at the reception and your mother is horrified by the age of the groom (who's only five years her junior).

You keep LaLaurie but move into the Wadley rural riverside plantation, Nutwood, so named for the rare pecan trees that grow all around the property. It's an absolutely picture-perfect place, with bucolic vistas and shaded Corinthian columns. You are going to be so happy. Jim-Junior is the perfect companion; he's someone you respect and he can make you laugh. What else is there?

There's sex. Sex is a problem. Well, a *challenge*. It's a challenging area, a part of your marriage that could use some work and possibly a blindfold. Jim-Junior insisted you wait until after the marriage for your first time together. He didn't want to ruin the tenderness between you or move too quickly. Now you're pretty sure it's because he didn't want you to run screaming before all the paperwork was signed. Everything on Jim-Junior is wrinkled and dappled with age spots.

Everything.

When flaccid, his penis looks like a bleached parsnip. To make matters worse, Jim-Junior, *bless his heart*, has obtained a prescription for Viagra from some maniacal backwoods doctor, so instead of being the kindly, impotent, grandfather type you hoped he'd be, he's hornier than a merchant marine on shore leave and able to stay hard for hours.

There isn't enough swamp liquor in all of Louisiana to get you through it. Especially if you remember his mother is downstairs. She moved in a week after you did, *bless her heart.* Apparently upon hearing of her only son's nuptials, Miss Meridian Vivcott Rae demanded to move back into her ancestral home. She hated you at first sight and asked Jim-Junior, "Why can't you ever pick a skinny one?" Now she lives in the east wing. The thought of her rocking away in her junior suite makes it all but impossible to perform. You could slap motor oil down there, but the thought of her instantly makes you dry as needlepoint yarn.

Being Mrs. John Harris Wadley Jr. turns out to be different than you pictured. You thought your days as a plantation owner's wife would be spent leisurely touring the rose gardens or browsing Frontgate catalogues and ordering whatever you wanted, but this is far from your daily itinerary. As lady of the house, you're expected to host *all* the events at Nutwood. Cocktail parties, champagne receptions, black-tie dinners, white-tie galas, semiformal teas, ladies' luncheons, holiday open houses, Easter Sunday brunches, auxiliary lunches, charitable auctions, political fund-raisers, and yacht club clambakes.

You don't know how to do half of what's required. You spend all your time researching things like *How to throw a cotillion. Acceptable menus when having a district court judge over for dinner. Paper napkins at traditional Southern pig roast?*

Even Maribelle is stumped by some of your new duties, and Miss Meridian Vivcott Rae, who can hear a maid open the liquor cabinet from upstairs, becomes mysteriously deaf when you ask her questions. Jim-Junior is useless; he hasn't got a clue and thinks women should just know these things. It starts to make you really resentful—like he didn't want a wife so much as needed a chief of staff for his precious family plantation.

Well, the joke's on him, because you run the place "like a donkey drives a car," according to Miss Meridian Vivcott Rae, which is what you have to call her *every* time you address her. "Would you like some tea, Miss Meridian Vivcott Rae? What a lovely ring, Miss Meridian Vivcott Rae. No, of *course* I don't hope you die so I can get my hands on the family jewels, Miss Meridian Vivcott Rae!" She acts nice whenever Jim-Junior's around, but when he travels, which is increasingly more often, she turns into a shrieking harpy. She shouts so loud sometimes you half expect eels to come out of her mouth.

The events, the friction, the exhaustion, it's too much. Things go from bad to worse until you decide you have to leave. What good is being a millionaire if you don't have a single hour of peace? You resolve to tell Jim-Junior you want a divorce right when he gets home from his big fishing trip. Hopefully he caught something nice out there on the ocean with his buddies, because when he comes home, all he's landing is divorce papers.

The day before he comes home, you're at the doctor's because your acid reflux has kicked up again from all the cocktails you need to get through a damn day. The doctor, however, says you're pregnant. *Pregnant?* Jim-Junior told you he was sterile, which you had no problem believing because he never managed to impregnate either of his other wives despite desperately trying. The doctor says you're actually fairly far along. Didn't you have symptoms? Queasiness? Tiredness? Of *course you did!* You just thought it was from running a plantation and taking care of that Confederate crone! "Not to worry," he says. "You're in good health, and think how happy Miss Meridian Vivcott Rae will be to finally have an heir!"

Oh brother. It's true, the Wadleys would be hysterical with joy if you produced an heir, but you'd also be tied to them forever. If you terminate the pregnancy, the doctor assures you of strict confidentiality, no one ever needs to know. You'd be free to go, but go where?

If you terminate the pregnancy, go to section 72 (p. 229).
If you continue the pregnancy, go to section 76 (p. 240).

37

You decide to join the Luxiste Club. It sounds intriguing and possibly ne-farious. Dolly's happy. "You're going to love the initiation ceremony!" she squeals. "All I can tell you is it involves a full moon and a two-thousand-year-old olivewood forest. Plus, you get your own monogrammed sword." She writes down a contact number and says there's plenty of time before the group heads out on their trip to Atlantis. You should be able to sail over in time if you want to.

"Atlantis? As in Atlantis, the lost city of Atlantis?"

"Well, I don't believe the residents of Atlantis consider themselves *lost*," she sniffs. "They worked rather hard to relocate their city and enjoy the solitude of living underwater. Plus the seafood! You can imagine."

"Atlantis *exists* and people live there?"

"Well, of course, darling! My, you're dark today."

"Didn't Atlantis topple over in some earthquake or something?"

Dolly rolls her eyes and starts to brush her hair, which means she's ready to end the conversation. "Darling," she says, "it was one of the wealthiest cities that ever *existed*. Do you think they actually fell victim to some natu-ral disaster? They didn't live in Ecuador, for heaven's sake. They've just got the best gated community on Earth, that's all! You'll see. Send me a picture of the new baby giraffe at the Bioparc if you can."

You give Dolly a kiss good-bye. She really has been lovely. You're even sorry to see little Bikte go, but let's face it, Dolly adores him and how many Pomeranians get to live with an heiress on her superyacht? (Actually, that's probably a fairly decent number.)

Back on board the *Bête Noire* you call the number for the Luxiste Club and a pleasant woman with a posh British accent answers. "Luxiste Club. Identity, please."

"Yes, um, I'm . . ."

"Identity, if you please."

You give your name and can hear typing. "Yes," she says, "I have you here. Sponsor D. Dupont. Your Luxiste identity is Jericho-Leeds, how may I assist?"

You give her your name again.

"We use Luxiste identities here," she says. "Please do not repeat your name. Your Luxiste identity is Jericho-Leeds. How may I assist?"

You stumble around and say you heard people were um . . . going to . . . Atlantis?

"Indeed," she says and starts typing.

Sheesh, this is hard. Dolly might have given you a few pointers on how the club works. You feel like a newly created vampire without a coffin.

"I see you're currently at the Royal Phuket Marina," she says. "Your initiation ceremony will be six o'clock next Sunday, the Castle Lizard in Cornwall. After initiation, transportation to Atlantis will be arranged directly."

"*What?*"

"Six o'clock next Sunday, Castle Lizard in Cornwall."

Then she hangs up.

You have no idea what just happened. Frankly, you're too scared to call back. Instead you ask the captain where Cornwall is and he says it's the southernmost tip of England. Can you get there by next Sunday? He checks a map and says yes. The engines power up, the anchors are hauled in. Off to Cornwall you go.

On the way you research "Castle Lizard" and find one castle in Cornwall, one and only one, so hell, that must be where you're supposed to go.

You really hope this isn't some freaky Druid thing.

There is no harbor in Cornwall big enough to accommodate the *Bête Noire* and you haven't arranged for a slip in any of the crowded busy British ports, so the captain drops you off at the Port of London. You'll fly back later.

You hire a car to Cornwall, and you're just passing through the outskirts of London when the vehicle is suddenly rammed from the side. You spin. Hit something hard. The air bags are hissing and you can taste blood in your mouth. *What happened?*

The driver is slumped over the wheel and unconscious. Suddenly two masked men are at your window banging, yelling something in another language. For a second you think you're dreaming. *This is Dolly's kidnapping story.* It's not real.

Wake up!

The men get the door open and grab you, dragging you roughly out on the road.

This is real. It is happening.

Authorities find you two months later half buried in Mucking Marshes, a landfill outside London. It's been a municipal and commercial dumping ground for decades. Barges float waste down the Thames and the landfill has grown over the years, covering hundreds of acres with swarming mountains of refuse and sewage, making this one of the largest landfills in Western Europe and your murder investigation nearly impossible.

When Dolly Dupont learns of your murder, she picks up the phone and dials her man for these jobs. Within the week every one of your assailants is quietly located, abducted, and being held on a ship headed for a lonely island north of the Shetlands. The island has no name and is listed as "uninhabited," despite having over two hundred residents. It's Dolly's private island and it's where she deposits "rehabilitation-immune criminals."

Surrounded by a roiling, inhospitable ocean, cut off from civilization, and without proper food, shelter, or medical care, these "naughty ones" live very bleak and short lives.

After your assailants are delivered, Dolly's man calls the *Noblesse Oblige* to give her the report. He asks if it wouldn't be easier to toss people into the ocean.

Dolly laughs as she lightly kisses the little bird perched on her finger. *No*, she says, he shouldn't toss anyone in the ocean. She could never have him kill anyone. Doesn't he know that? Life is *precious*. Hasn't she told him before? "Our job is just to separate the bad apples from the bunch," she says. "What God does with them once they're chucked out of the orchard—well, that's up to him."

3 8

From section 19

You move to Calvary House, a Baptist women's shelter in the Ninth Ward. It's actually an old church with the main sanctuary converted into a dry-walled honeycomb of small living cubicles with chicken-wire ceilings. When you lie in bed and look up, you can see through to the vaulted ceiling and dirty stained glass windows above. It would be tranquil, but the noise in this place is unbearable. The narrow hallways are teeming with children running wild and women arguing while bouncing a screaming baby or two in their arms.

The church ladies who run the center are tough. They don't ask questions, they don't want excuses, they tell you the rules. If you don't follow them—you're out. There's no swearing allowed at Calvary House, no drinking, no drugs, no substance abuse of any kind. TV is not allowed, but you can listen to preapproved religious radio stations. Each day at 5:00 a.m., everyone gets up and trudges to early-morning prayers. Then you have ten minutes to retrieve toiletries from your locker and clothes from your room, so you can wait in line for a shower, which is timed. Five and a half minutes for each person. Not a second more. Once, when you accidentally went over and didn't even hear the egg timer going off, a staff member barged in and told you to get out.

At 8:00 a.m., breakfast is served in the basement and there's another long line for food. No pushing, no shoving, no cutting in line. If the room gets too noisy, a counselor flashes the overhead lights and says, "Stop serving!" until everyone quiets down. By 9:00 a.m., most of the building empties out. Women in training go to the Counseling Center, women with jobs go to work, kids in school go to class, kids not in school go to the Childcare Center. Everyone else waits around outside until the shelter opens again at 4:00

p.m. Dinner is at 5:00 p.m., and if you miss it, you don't eat. After dinner there's another mandatory church service.

They say all these rules are necessary to keep order, to teach discipline, and they help women in their rehabilitation, but almost every day someone breaks a rule and their locker is cleaned out that night. The hardest rule for you by far is *no swearing.*

You had no idea how often you swore, or wanted to, until now.

You can't stand being here much longer. You start looking for work anywhere you can find it. Anything to get yourself out of this place. Someone says there's a bar on Bourbon Street hiring and there's also a posting in the Career Center, which says, *"Wanted:* Lab Assistant." It doesn't say anything more.

If you work at the bar, go to section 73 (p. 232).

If you work at the lab, go to section 77 (p. 245).

39

From section 86

Your session with Niobe leaves you completely uncertain of her psychic skills. Go to Ireland if you want to be lucky in love? A little abstract and easy, no? Plus, *where* in Ireland? Should you plan some random cross-country train trip, look for signs that point you to . . . *Whump!* An old man bumps into you. He's wearing dark glasses and carrying a white cane. He's blind. *"Liss-doon-var-nah,"* he whispers, teeth dark as cinnamon bark. He repeats the word, hissing like wind through a window grate. "Lissss-doon-var-nahh!" Then he presses a dark red flower into your palm. He doesn't say anything more.

Back at the bed-and-breakfast you twirl the little red flower between your fingers and try to remember the word. The innkeeper's just been wiping up a spill behind the counter and blots her damp hands on her apron while listening to you repeating the word in multiple fucked-up variations. *"Lisbon-dar-dah? Lime-on-vard-ah?"*

"Right!" she says. *"Lisdoonvarna!* Old town on the west coast of Ireland. Lovely town. Just lovely." She goes back to wringing her mop. "Hope you're not headed over there, though! Tremendous crowds this time of year." She picks up the bucket of water beside her and starts to lug it into the back, adding, "The big matchmaking festival is going on now. Very popular. No hotel rooms for two towns in each direction."

You stop twirling.

She squints at you hard. "If you did go, though, I might know of a place. My nephew's wife runs the Black Horse. She keeps a spare room in back."

You're on the next flight to the tiny coastal town of Lisdoonvarna, famous for its beautiful scenery, active mineral baths, and annual matchmaking festival. The hookup festivities are already in full swing. Irish marching bands, gypsy horse riders, meandering pub crawls, clattering clog dancers, hysterical limerick contests, and, of course, a *lot* of public drinking. You check into the Black Horse, freshen up, and step out, only to be nearly run down by a man on a bicycle. "Oy!" he says. He's tall and has dark curly hair, bottle green eyes, and a deep dimple on his chin, which you have the immediate and overwhelming desire to lick. He gets off his bike. "You're feckin' gorgeous!" he says, letting the bike roll into some garbage cans. "Where's yer husband?" He looks around. "Can I take him, or is he a big fucker?"

You nod, staring. "You could take him."

He bows and extends his arm, which you take. Just like that. You're walking down the street arm in arm, as though keeping a preset appointment. His name is Liam. He's a mechanic with an accent so thick there's no hope of understanding him. "How are you?" sounds like "Hawareya?" and a half pint of Guinness is three pounds forty, which sounds like "treepounds-torty."

At the bar you nurse a beer for hours. Liam's got more bawdy stories than anyone you've ever known, but they're all so funny you can't get annoyed; you just keep laughing till it hurts. "Let me tell you about bad luck," Liam says. "There was a bird once, Rosalinda. She went to my school. She had hair like black silk ribbons and a little mouth sweet as a cherry. I worked like the devil himself to get her in bed. Spent all me money, wrote love songs, made an outright arse of meself, and you know what she did? She broke me *feckin'* heart!" You ask what happened. He shakes his head sadly and sighs. "She had a vagina like a badly packed kebab! Can ye imagine? Her parts looked like a Chinese butcher window. Me heart broke in two! Her sister was worse. Hers was so loose it might've been a wizard sleeve."

You stay at the bar drinking till it closes. He's quite open about his checkered past; had plenty of women, committed plenty of petty crimes, spent a fair amount of time in the local precinct. A regular rogue. All thug. Pure trouble and you adore him.

You don't let him into your bed, though. Not right away. Instead you play coy, which is *murder*, especially the next day when he puts you on the back of his motorcycle and drives like a bat out of almighty hell to some castle ruins alongside a sleepy creek, where he unpacks a "picnic" from his trouser pockets. Warm beer and cold pork chops wrapped in paper towel. He says he stopped at the bakery, but couldn't decide what kind of donut you'd like, and there were so many different kinds, he panicked and left. That's when you break down, kiss him, and say, "Glazed are my favorite."

Holding out on sex takes all your strength. Even with your best effort and sternest self-reprimands, you can only resist Liam's utterly unfair magnetic charm for sixty-two hours and forty-three minutes. Then you push him down hard on your bed, hungrily covering his mouth with kisses. Within moments your clothes are torn off and he's going down on you, making you squirm delightfully. Then he lifts his head. "Oy!" He grins. "Glazey donut!"

You extend your visit for another two weeks and Liam takes you to his ramshackle house, which is in the nearby coastal town of Doolin and strewn with bike parts and heaps of dirty laundry. You meet his sweet mum and beautiful sister before taking off all over Ireland, where Liam makes ferocious love to you in various hotel beds with his truly remarkable penis, which he calls "the widget." He often sings to you afterward, usually an old Hank Williams song or a Delta blues ballad about terrible heartaches and true love gone horribly awry.

It's incredibly romantic.

This whole time you've managed to keep Liam from knowing you have money. You don't talk about your family, or your home, about winning the lottery or buying the boat or cheating on Aidan. You've kept your cell phone off this whole time. Haven't called home once. You just want this to be what this is. Nothing else.

Then, when you're finally headed back to Lisdoonvarna, Liam asks if you ever had a pint in the Dark Beast Bar. That's what people call the little bar inside the Black Horse. You stare at him and reach into your jacket, pulling out the blind man's little red flower from your pocket. It's crumbling, brittle bits missing, but you realize it's the exact color of the *Bête Noire*. Niobe's words come roaring back into your head. *It's going to sink and take all souls on board with her.* You run like hell for your phone and try to contact the ship, frantically calling Captain Marquardt's cell phone and the bridge's satellite phone and the emergency radio—but no one answers. There's a lump in your throat that you can't swallow.

The *Bête Noire* went down two weeks ago somewhere off the southern tip of Sri Lanka in the Indian Ocean. There was a sudden storm and a single distress signal went out. Then nothing. Debris was found. Apparently there was an explosion, but no one knows why. A complete investigation is still under way. The only thing certain is there were no survivors. Up until the moment you called home they were starting to think you were dead, too. Since Dolly bought your plane ticket to London, no one knew to look for you there. Your mother's hysterical and several law firms immediately manage to serve you papers right there at the Black Horse Inn. The families of the *Bête Noire* crew lost at sea have already begun a suit. Quite a few people plan to cash in on this tragedy, and in the end quite a few people do.

Right then, though, you fall to pieces, weep uncontrollably in Liam's arms, and it takes hours to get the whole story out. The lottery, the money, the boat, the psychic, the disaster. After you've said everything there is to say, you just sit there as Liam stares at you, green eyes unblinking, until he finally blinks and lets out the most uproarious belly laugh you've ever heard. It takes him a good five minutes to get hold of himself. Utterly inappropriate. There is nothing to laugh at! Then he gets on his knees, makes the sign of the holy cross, and thanks the Good Lord out loud. "Aye, take it all back, Lord!" he shouts. "You're not a weary bastard set on making me life shite! Ye made her poor, Lord! Ye made her poor!" Then he picks you up and swings you around, kissing you and laughing until you manage to punch him enough times to get him to let go.

He's happy because he was already set "on losin' yer sweet ass." He could tell by your shoes and your "ridiculous coffee drinks" that you had money. He was "shite-scared about it too" because he's tried being with girls who have more money than he does, but it doesn't work. Ever. He makes a good living and he wants to provide for the woman he loves, not the other way round. His pride won't take it. Call him a sexist bastard or a dumb culchie but that's the way he is. If he isn't the provider it all eventually goes to hell.

Did he just say for the woman he *loves?*

You move into Liam's little raggedy cottage. He's impossible to live with, barely house-trained. He can seemingly pee anywhere *except* in a toilet. He drinks too much, swears enough to earn the ire of every mother in the neighborhood, and stays out till all hours, toting back his chums at all times of the day and night. Once you woke up at four in the morning and there he was in the kitchen cooking dinner for twelve drunk friends. He was making a curry.

Anything that makes you crazy is because he's *feckin' Oirish*.

"Liam! Why can't you use a coaster!"

"I'm *feckin' Oirish*!"

He breaks dishes, loses wallets, credit cards, car keys, and cars. More than once he's been out drinking and called you in a panic, insisting his car was stolen, only to find it the next day parked a few blocks from where he *swears* he left it. He'll keep insisting someone else moved his car despite any and all empirical evidence to the contrary. Liam also has this uncanny inability to walk through any room without knocking furniture over.

That said, your little life here in Doolin is heaven. You start to fix up the house and cart out the garbage all over the yard. As all the *Bête Noire* legal battles continue and your fortune is dismantled piece by piece as the lawsuits and settlements and insurance companies do their worst, you're oddly removed from it. Safe overseas in your little seaside cottage. Your family and friends come to visit and they all think Liam is nice, but a bit too rough around the edges. Your girlfriends particularly don't understand how you put up with the urine stains. They think he's probably a passing fancy and will be replaced when you get bored. But they're wrong.

All of them.

Well, not about the urine stains. Those are hellish. What they don't understand is that this man delights you. Seriously. The drinking, swearing, bawdy stories, it lights you up inside. You can't help grinning, laughing, shaking your head. Even when you make a fist and curse the heavens while shouting, *"Liam!"* because once again you've found jam-covered toast smeared inside the bedsheets or your toothbrush goes missing and is mysteriously relocated out in the garage, where someone has used it to clean carburetors—even then, everything he does on a certain level delights you.

He's like a little boy who doesn't know better and, *okay, okay,* that's not ideal, but what is? What man is perfect? More to the point, what man isn't a mere two steps or less from being a total disaster one way or another? Face it. The nice guys don't really challenge you. The challenging ones aren't nice to you. The stern ones can't lighten up, the fun ones forget to mail electricity bills. The passionate ones get jealous, the smart ones aren't funny, the successful ones spend too much time at the office, and the steady, reliable ones make love like tax auditors. So, if none of them are perfect, isn't it a good idea to pick your favorite imperfection? Liam screws up but he's always sorry and his sins are misdemeanors, never felonies. He's never been unfaithful, doesn't even look at other women. He's never once been verbally abusive and it doesn't matter what you're wearing, you could be hunkered down for the third day in a pair of flannel camouflage sweatpants and that man would stop upon seeing you and grin. "Aye, lass," he'd say, "ye take my breath away." Then he plays R. L. Burnside songs in his underwear.

Decades later, on your thirtieth anniversary, Liam takes you back to the castle where you first drank warm beer and ate cold pork chops, as he does every year. It's the only day he's allowed to drive his motorcycle. This year the menu is the same, with an added bonus of a thin blanket to sit on and a small handpicked bouquet of daisies.

Liam kisses you and raises his glass for a toast. "Oi want to thank ye, love, for makin' me lifelong dream come true. I fell into terrible-true love with ye, as ye know. Nothin' could send me away, so it's with real fondness I say *thank ye* for never havin' parts that fell into a kebab state. I woulda loved ye, but kebab parts break me feckin' heart." Then he takes a slug of Guinness and asks if he ever told you about the O'Malley twins, Cocktrough and Slapper, girls in his grade school who promised to show him their tits, but used the promise of those tits to lure him to the river, where they beat him to a raw pulp instead. He still thinks of them fondly.

Liam loves to tell the O'Malley story at his favorite watering hole in heaven. The Trinity Pub isn't the *biggest* bar in heaven, but it's one of the most popular. The free-topping potato bar has real bacon bits and Jesus bartends every Saturday. (You and Liam lived the rest of your wonderful lives together, and then, at the age of eighty-two, a motorcyclist cut you off and you both died in a car crash. You were chewing Liam's ear all the way up to heaven. Didn't you always tell him how dangerous those damn bikes were?)

He's a real joker, Jesus. It's always good to catch up with him and find out what religion he's embarrassing this week, or where he's sending the next typhoon and which island nation will be demoted to a coral reef, but frankly you prefer the drinks the angels pour. They bartend weekdays and they're a lot less stingy with the whiskey.

Naturally all the bars are closed on Sundays, since folks still get into a lot of trouble in heaven. Black eyes, bar brawls, illegal bets on monkey fights. (All the animals from Noah's Ark are notorious hustlers.) One woman even fed her husband's favorite sweatpants to the seraphim, claiming they were covered in so much barbecue sauce, any intelligent angel would know to eat them and not wear them. Yes, there's a lot to atone for on Sundays. That's when everybody goes to God's house and says they're sorry for whatever it was they were doing on the weekdays.

40

From section 23

You have a big ranch wedding. All your family is in attendance and Reverend Holcombe from Pontotoc presides. Ida Mae makes you a bouquet of bluebonnets, which you nervously grasp, while standing beside Ralston in the little wood atrium he built under the ancient hacienda.

The ceremony is tough. You can't hear a word the preacher says. It's hellfire hot and everyone in the sweltering audience fans themselves as sweat drips down your back and your face aches from your perma-terrified grin. At some point you say, "I do," and Reverend Holcombe pronounces you man and wife. The ranch hands fire off Civil War cannons, which are loud and nearly kill Snowbell, the quarter horse Ralston mounts as you toss the bridal bouquet over your shoulder. Your new husband swoops his strong arm around your waist and hoists you up on the back of the horse, then gallops off across the meadow as the crowd cheers.

Damn it's nice to be with a man.

After the ceremony, there's barbecue, beer, and bluegrass. Grandparents dance and kids run around in their crisp plaid shirts and little cowboy hats. As the moon rises, the big bonfires are lit and the band stays well past midnight, when they were supposed to go home. "I never thought I could be this happy," you whisper to Ralston. He kisses your forehead and winks. "You can't know nothing for sure."

So begins life as a rancher's wife. Well, rancher's wife *light*, since Ida Mae snatches most of the work away from you and says you should just be concentrating on having a baby. You'd need Ralston to do that, though, and he's working long hours now that it's summer. He's usually gone all day and into the evening and you learn not to expect him home till "dark-thirty."

Ralston's out of town at the Houston Livestock Show one weekend when Ida Mae comes running into the living room and tells you to turn on the news. Someone's killed little Ella Cutter, the youngest daughter of the Cutter family, who live just a few miles away, south of Babyhead Mountain. Someone snatched the little girl while she was playing outside and strangled her. Then they left her body on the porch and wrote TIME TO GO on her little forehead in dark green permanent marker. The reporter says police have no leads and authorities are asking for anyone with any information to call their tip line.

"Goddamn sons of bitches," Ida Mae sneers. "Who would do such a thing? Who would kill an innocent child and write on her face with permanent marker?"

You don't think you've ever heard her swear before.

"There's a time and a place for just about anything," she says with authority. "I could kill whoever done this. I grew up on a cattle ranch. I'm capable of quite a lot."

Ralston returns with a load of new livestock the next evening but doesn't want to drive down to the Cutter house. "You ought to go pay your respects," Ida Mae says. "They're neighbors."

Ralston says he's tired. "Hell, Cutter's a stubborn son of a bitch," he says. "Got enemies all over. Probably had it coming." Then he goes to the kitchen and asks if there's any pie.

So you pay your respects without him. You sit next to Ida Mae in silence as the truck bounces down the road toward the Cutter farm. What did Ralston mean, "Probably had it coming"? Someone strangled his nine-year-old girl! You want to ask Ida Mae if Ralston has some stone-cold crazy side you don't know about, but you know better than to be critical of him, because she'll defend him to the end. So you ask her, "Do they have enemies? The Cutters?"

She snorts and says the Cutters are as nice as they are poor. You ride along in silence. You can see the Cutter farm up ahead, a long line of cars parked on either side of the road. "Maybe they had a land dispute with somebody," you say.

Ida Mae makes a face. "A what?"

"Ralston's always telling me about fights over water tables and property lines."

"They don't fight with anybody; they don't do business with anybody. They're poor! I think Mr. Cutter catches most of their dinners in the Pecum River—" She stops talking.

"What?"

"I forgot the damn pie."

The Cutter house is swarming with neighbors and people from town. The men mill around the driveway, talking among themselves with their hands shoved deep in their pockets. They seem like overgrown schoolboys unsure of their manners. The women bustle in with casseroles and baskets of bread. You're not able to talk to Mr. or Mrs. Cutter; they're sequestered in a back room, surrounded by relatives. Ida Mae finds a big jar of peach preserves in the truck. You leave it on the dining room table, which is already heaping with baked goods and hot dishes. "Mrs. Smith brought five pies," Ida Mae hisses. "Show-off."

Back home Ralston's missing again and you go look for him, but the ranch is big and you need a damn bullhorn to find someone. You check his office, but he's not there. You notice the side drawer of his desk is slightly open though. The little one he never uses because it's "not big enough to piss in." You open it gently with one finger. Empty. You smile with relief and start closing the drawer, causing a permanent marker to roll forward.

It's dark green.

You shut the drawer, go upstairs, run a hot bath, take two Percocets left over from your fractured rib, and knock yourself out. It's time for this day to be over.

The next week is a blur.

Then Ralston leaves for a Limousin bull auction in Atlanta and you feel like you can exhale again.

You're in the kitchen canning peaches with Ida Mae when the sheriff pulls up. He comes inside and takes off his hat, setting it on the table. You pour coffee and Ida Mae gets cream. Ida Mae takes out the coffee cake and asks what brings the sheriff out today. He nods. "Does Ralston know the Cutter family real well?"

Ida Mae's hand freezes, but only for a split second, then she starts cutting coffee cake again. "He knows 'em," she says.

"You know about that business with the Pecum River?" the sheriff asks.

Ida Mae narrows her eyes. "I know it."

The sheriff sips his coffee. "Bad business."

She says nothing. The sheriff takes his hat to leave. Says he'll stop back to talk to Ralston later. When he's gone, Ida Mae flies up the stairs into your bedroom. You ask her what she's doing, but she can't even hear you for how fast she's ripping open drawers, cabinets, and nightstands. Whatever she needs isn't there, so she flies down the stairs, wisps of red hair coming undone, and she storms his office, assaulting the closet first, then the bookshelves, then the desk. She's on her knees pulling out a bottom drawer. It must be a nightmare because nothing seems real. *Is she looking for the marker?* You reach out to show her, but she stops, sits back, finally exhales.

She found it. A thick red folder stuffed with papers. Sketches. Blueprints. You can't make out what she's looking through, but you know not to stop her. She pulls a single sheet of paper and reads it, which takes time, because she's shaking.

"It was water," she whispers, holding out the paper. "It's a bid for the Cutters' land. He wanted their *water*. The Cutters live on the Pecum River, only access for miles, and Ralston's pastures have been drying up for a decade. He told me last year he was going to make the Cutters sell their land. If he didn't, he'd have to sell half the herd." She starts to get wild-eyed. "He said he'd make them sell! He must have hired somebody to . . . he wouldn't hurt anyone!" That's when you open the side drawer and show her the dark green marker. She stares at it, shoulders slowly dropping. "What now?" you whisper, cold prickling the back of your arms. "Now *nothing*," she says, eyes dark.

"We don't tell *anybody*?"

She takes a step closer to you, setting her muscular, beef-slaughtering fists on her hips. "No," she says. "Not anybody." Then she tells you to take the Cadillac and run errands in town until six, when Ralston gets back. "And make sure people see you," she says.

It takes all your strength to go. Your heart is pounding, pulse surging, thoughts racing. *He did it. He couldn't have done it! Tell someone. Don't tell anyone! If he killed the girl, he'll kill the boy. He is not a murderer! Yes, he is. No, he isn't!* You pull into the parking lot of the grocery store and take out your cell phone. You can't call the police, not until you know for sure. You have to either confront Ralston or somehow warn the Cutters.

It's the only choice left.

If you confront Ralston, go to section 78 (p. 248).
If you warn the Cutter family, go to section 132 (p. 426).

41

From section 10

You buy Navassa Island. Three square miles of emerald green paradise located in the Caribbean about seventy miles east of Jamaica. Right at the southwest entrance to the Windward Passage. It's mostly made of raised coral reefs and limestone plateaus, which are ringed by a steep rocky shoreline housing large seabird colonies. The grassy interior is wide and flat with thick stands of fig trees that support a small herd of wild goats and two species of reptiles found nowhere else in the world: an iguana and a tiny curly-tailed lizard.

You spend months building a new dock. None existed before and a demolition crew brought in from Kingston uses C-4 to blast into the rocky shoreline. Next you widen the north beach and build a spectacular Haitian plantation–style villa on the cliffs above. You tell the architects and decorators you want the house to look like the summer home of traveling Panamanian dignitaries, summoning the construction of generous, open-air rooms with tall ceilings and terrazzo floors and long, hand-tailored white linen curtains that blow in the gentle, tropical breeze.

The island is spectacular. Everyone should have one. The sun is warm, the breeze is cool, and your staff keeps all worries away. The house is always spotless, and anything you could ever want is shipped in, olives from Greece, wine from Burgundy, bed linens from Egypt, and fragrant bath salts from Penhaligon's in London. Cook prepares delicious meals with freshly caught ingredients.

Every night you and Aidan sit on the tiki-torch-lit deck and sip chilled champagne while dining on cracked lobster, grilled mahi-mahi, sautéed plantains with mango-mint chutney. After dinner you take a long stroll on the beach and look up at the stars, thanking heaven and any other celestial beings that happen to be listening for all your good luck. Finally you have the life you've always wanted. Then you usually make hot, dirty, smelly raccoon love on the beach.

It's after one of these gritty seaside clinches that you see running lights out on the water. It's a boat and it's coming closer. Wait. Nothing should be coming close to Navassa, what is that? You both hurry to put on your clothes and follow the boat as it cuts sharply along the coast, but you lose it when you're blocked by a patch of thorny cactus plants and a sheer drop in the craggy coastline. Aidan says not to worry. It's probably someone who lives nearby. Nearby where? Haiti? There's nothing out here. No other islands. Just the inky night and the brilliant stars. Looking back at your magnificent home sitting proudly on the hill, all the windows and doors wide open, it seems too vulnerable.

The phantom boat zips past your island twice more; both times it's at night and you can't follow it farther than the east beach. You have a security system installed, which is a little odd, but you sleep better, which is good— since you haven't been sleeping well at all lately, and not because of the phantom ships offshore. No. You've been getting your bank account statements online and you can't believe how much money you've spent.

At first you actually thought there was a mistake, but after reviewing your withdrawals and purchases, you find no error in accounting—you've just been burning through money faster than an incinerator. Buying the island, building the house, hiring the staff, not to mention drilling the artesian wells and importing every single beer and pat of butter from across the ocean—it all costs money. Big money. If something doesn't change, you might lose this island and this life forever, and the only thing worse than never having money is having it and then losing it. Before, you were blissfully all right with vacationing at chain hotels with attached water parks. You had no idea what you were missing.

One evening Aidan comes running up from the beach yelling. The phantom boat is back, and you're both finally able to follow it by jogging along the upper cliff and cutting across the goat path through the interior of the island. The boat slows and anchors on the south side, near the old light-house. You and Aidan crouch down and watch as men start jumping out of the boat and splashing into the water as they unload boxes. They're all carrying machine guns.

You stay hidden, hardly breathing, careful not to make a sound—when all of a sudden someone taps you on the shoulder and you shriek. A young man stands there with a machine gun slung over his shoulder. He's wearing a dirty T-shirt that says I ♥ STEM CELLS. You expect to be raped, killed, left for dead, but instead he grins and introduces himself. "I am Sexy Star," he says. "That is my stage name. I will be very famous singer one day." Then another boy walks up, no older than sixteen, and he shakes your hand heart-ily, careful to keep one hand on his machine gun so it doesn't slide down his arm. "I am Dumas!" he says.

Aidan asks them what they're doing here, and Sexy Star looks at the boat. "Business." He says they often leave *azucar* here for their friends. *Azucar?* That means sugar, but you're a bit doubtful these kids are running sugar. He explains in bits and pieces that they come from Haiti, which is close by, and that they'd like to continue using your dock. They only come twice a month. "We'll pay you for the privilege. We are businessmen," Sexy Star says. He hands you a dirty envelope with some wadded-up cash inside.

Aidan quickly pulls you aside and whispers hotly in your ear. He says there's no way you should agree to letting them use Navassa. There's no telling what these kids are up to. They could be trafficking heroin or cocaine or even children! You could do time for aiding and abetting felons—is any of this getting through to you?

Well, yes, *of course it is*, but Aidan doesn't know about your financial concerns. He doesn't worry about money. No, he just orders up a jet ski or a box of porterhouse steaks from Manny's in New York anytime he wants to. Having pirates who pay you rent might be the one way to stay here, and even if you kick Sexy Star off your property, he'll just use another drop-off point nearby, and if you can't stop it, why not profit from it? You don't even know if it's bad.

On the other hand, Haitian jails probably aren't that fun. Medical care is most likely provided by a witch doctor and most inmates probably never leave, unless it's in a coffin.

If you do not allow the Haitians to use your dock,
go to section 80 (p. 252).
If you allow the Haitians to use your dock, go to section 83 (p. 259).

42

From section 73

You start working at Big Easy Guns on Dauphine, just down the road from the Tom-Tom Club. They sell antique weapons there, dueling pistols, World War II rifles, Civil War cannons, flintlock muskets, gunpowder flasks, medieval broadswords, even executioners' axes. They also sell some antique jewelry, fractional currency, and antique coins. There's even a gold coin in one case that Al says is from ancient Rome.

Al and Elbert are the owners. Big jolly guys. They're both funny and friendly, and even though they're a little rednecky, a little racist, and quite a bit sexist, you like them anyway. Al lives outside the city and says you're more than welcome to stay with him until you get a place of your own. You think maybe your luck is changing, but then they tell you about your job. They want you to walk up and down Bourbon Street passing out pink flyers that have valuable coupons on them, while wearing an inflatable grenade costume.

Wonderful.

You put on the white full-length unitard, which has plastic hooks sewn in the front and back. Then the guys help you put on the grenade costume, which clips into the unitard hooks and hangs limply until Elbert turns on the little built-in fan in back. Then there's a loud whirring sound as it balloons up, turning you into a giant camouflage green grenade.

They both have to push to get you through the front door, and when you pop out the other side, you almost flop over on the sidewalk and drop all the flyers. Some guy shouts, "Watch the fuck out, motherfucking hand grenade!"

So begins your new career.

You spend all afternoon walking up and down the street handing out flyers while getting hotter and hotter. The suit is like a convection oven and beads of sweat roll down your temples. Nobody wants the flyers. They step away without looking at you or tell you to get lost, and not one but *two* people punch you. You can't feel it, the blows land on your soft inflatable stomach, but still. Not cool. You quickly learn to identify who's a tourist and who's a New Orleans native and you only give flyers to the tourists. The natives are the ones who punch you.

You adopt a two-hour visual-target routine. Every two hours you stride past the shop handing out flyers so Al and Elbert can see you, then you go sit down somewhere shady, like the House of Voodoo loading dock, where there's an abandoned floral couch next to the Dumpsters. Or you hang out in front of the Sho Bar because the bouncer, Thompat, who's also an artist who paints portraits of rubber duckies with venereal diseases, gives you free Pepsis and good advice. "There's a cop," he says, nodding at a tourist holding a map. You tell him he's full of shit, that's a car salesman from Dubuque, but sure enough a minute later the "tourist" looks quickly over his shoulder and surreptitiously whispers into the sleeve of his Windbreaker, where his police radio is tucked.

Mostly you try to stay away from people. Sometimes you walk way down Bourbon, past all the shops to where the residential houses start. A few of them are boarded up, empty or for sale, and one little house with green shutters and pink trim has an unlocked backyard with a hammock slung between two shade trees. You like to sit your big grenade butt down in the hammock and swing while the rest of the world goes on by all around you.

One day when you're rounding the corner of the little house with green shutters, you find a group of people standing in the backyard. A big woman in a purple dress beams at you and says, "You here for rehearsal, sweet thing?"

You shrug.

Why not? You don't have anything better to do. Yesterday you swung in the hammock with a bag of gummi bears and thought up different ways to kill them (bite their heads off, impale them on sticks, launch them over the fence). Plus, these people seem pretty nice, no one even seems to mind you're wearing a deflated hand grenade costume. Purple dress lady says, "You stand right over there. All right. Let's begin before the Lord turns off all our light. Have mercy! Amen?"

"Amen!" everyone in the backyard shouts.

Sheet music is passed around. Everyone has to share. It's a choral group! You sing "Closer Mine Eyes to Thee" and "Jesus Carry Me Over" while a guy with a saxophone belts out soulful notes. Purple dress lady rearranges everybody, grouping the altos and tenors together, "so Jesus can hear you, children! You want Jesus to hear you? Yes, you do! There is not one sweet day that goes by sweet Jesus doesn't watch over you! Amen?"

"Amen!" everyone shouts.

You sing eight or nine more songs, including hymns like "Amazing Grace," popular standards like Billie Holiday's "Them There Eyes," and unusual choir pieces, like David Bowie's "China Girl." After you sing, purple dress lady says everyone did a wonderful job and sweet Jesus will sleep *so good* tonight. "And, babies," she says, "you know tomorrow we're back in the church, right? Don't nobody forget now. We had to come out into God's fresh air today so they could exterminate those roaches, but we back in God's house tomorrow. Amen?"

"Amen!" everyone shouts.

The group breaks up, people retrieve their bags and backpacks, and then they thread out the gate and across the street to where a small church stands. There's a small banner tacked below the windows that says TRINITY TABERNACLE REFUGEE CHOIR.

The next day at the appointed time you shimmy out of your grenade costume in the restroom of a karaoke club and put on street clothes before dashing over to the church. You take your place on the risers just as they're starting. This time there's an organ and a piano accompanying the saxophonist and you sing a mixed selection of hymns and secular tunes, including "Glory, Glory Hallelujah," "My Lord Is Coming," and "We All Live in a Yellow Submarine." Afterward the purple dress lady, whose name is Miss Camilla Allbright Day, asks "all you precious baby lambs" to pick up your travel packets if you haven't already. "And Lord, please," she says, "fill out your choir ID cards! Honey-children, I will have to lie down for *two weeks* come Sunday if someone gets left behind! Don't *do* that to me now, children. I know you all want to sing for sweet Jesus in Atlanta next week! And sleep in a four-star hotel! A-men?"

"Amen!" everyone shouts.

You go ahead and take a travel packet. Why not? You're like a refugee and the last time you stayed at a four-star hotel was around the time you lived in a mansion and never bought caviar under a hundred dollars an ounce. The papers inside your packet include a blank ID card, a housing preference card, a medical history questionnaire, and an informational brochure about TTRC that says, *Every year hundreds of immigrants from countries all over the world—Afghanistan, Ecuador, Somalia, Cambodia and others—arrive not speaking the language and having no community to call their own. The Trinity Tabernacle Refugee Choir (TTRC) was formed to provide spiritual communion for these newcomers, bringing diverse voices together.*

So it's like a Benetton ad, but with singing.

You fill out your forms carefully and try to pick a name and a country of origin that seem plausible, so you become Pilar Deux, from France. You have no known allergies and you'd prefer a nonsmoking room with wheelchair access. You turn your completed packet in, pick up a copy of the rehearsal schedule, and go back to the gun store, where Elbert asks you where the hell you go every day. He's not paying you to shoot craps with the meter maids—you better be handing out those damn flyers.

You make it to every single choir rehearsal before the big trip to Atlanta and you even attend the going-away potluck party. In that time you've befriended Chong Ju Hwi from North Korea, Esteban from La Morita, My Cho from Laos, and Lucky Luciano from Somalia. Her real name is Fawzia Malag Noor or something, but she never uses it. She says her people have too many customs, and the one she hates most is wearing a head scarf.

"Then why do you wear it?" My Cho asks.

Lucky just says, *"Because."*

When the Atlanta trip comes up, you pack a bag and tell the boys you're visiting friends for the weekend and you hurry to the church, where everyone loads up their walkers and backpacks and wheeling suitcases and picnic baskets onto the big blue school bus that'll take the choir to Atlanta.

Everybody sings as you're rolling down the highway. Miss Camilla says, "Sing louder, children, so the angels can hear!" And up go the voices, even louder, causing some hysterical, infectiously goofy, primal sense of good cheer to permeate your core. Here you all are, outcasts, old, orphaned, relocated, lost—every color skin, jumbled-up languages; the only thing in common is everybody's different. You try to fight it, but you can't. It's beautiful. Country club be damned, this is motherfucking fun.

You make it to the Hilton in Atlanta late that night and everybody stays up even later singing by the pool until the manager comes and tells you to stop. Who knows what he thought was going on, with senior citizens all the way down to teenagers from every nation singing "Jumpin' Jack Flash" by the pool, but he says people are complaining and everyone needs to go to bed. Miss Camilla descends on him like a wet hen. She says, "No, sir, Mr. Manager Man! Not today, sir. You turn around. Nobody is sending my babies to bed! These children have come from all over the *world* to sing for our Lord and Savior and it's too early for bed! The Lord is awake and this choir is awake! You got to be awake to see what God is bringing! You got to sing *loud* so the angels can hear! Amen?"

"Amen!" everyone shouts.

The performance goes perfectly, except a Guatemalan kid named Bert throws up backstage, but the audience gets to hear a perfect rendition of "Amazing Grace" and an a capella version of "Look at Me, I'm Sandra Dee," from the *Grease* soundtrack. After a standing ovation the governor's wife gets onstage with tears in her eyes because she thought the music was so beautiful.

Back home the program ends for summer break and Miss Camilla Allbright Day hugs everyone grizzly bear–style, crying and blotting her eyes with tissue. She says every day without her sweet choir is a dark day and she'll be counting the hours till she gets all you sweet lambs back in her corral. She's one classy lady, that Miss Camilla. Everybody cries and goes out for fried chicken and milk shakes and promises to come back next fall, but when they get up to leave, you have this sudden sense of terrible loss, like once they go, something important will be over. You suddenly hear yourself say, "Hey, anybody ever shoot an AK-47?"

That stops them.

You invite them all to Al's place to shoot guns. He's deer hunting for the weekend, and as long as you put everything back, he won't mind. Well, he might mind. Nevertheless, everyone from choir comes over and shoots shit to pieces, blasting up bottles, tin cans, ripe pumpkins, and anything else you can find that feels good to hit. They're all better than you, except Lucky, who's never held a gun in her life. You think she likes it, though; she gets a funny look when she lowers her smoking barrel and touches the edge of her head scarf. "In Somalia women aren't allowed to handle weapons," she says. "They can't even dance."

Chong says his father was North Korean military and made him fire a gun when he was eight. "It exploded in my hand so loud! He told me to shoot again and I tried but my hand shook until my father hit me. I never shook holding a gun again." Esteban, who's by far the superior shot, doesn't say much about his skill or where he got it. The big surprise is My Cho, who won't touch any of the guns, but when she spots a bow and arrow leaning against the shed, she swoops it up and merrily starts planting arrows deep in any tree she chooses, even ones across the highway.

The five of you hang out a lot; you go to movies and drink beer. They make a surprise visit to Big Easy Guns one day while you're working behind the counter. You never told them the name of the store where you worked, but they knew it was "the gun shop" and there's only one in the French Quarter, so they must have narrowed it down.

The bell on the door sounds as they walk in and wave. One look at Al's face when he spots your colorful clan makes you realize it was *not* cool you let them shoot his guns. "Hey, guys!" you say, "gimme a minute!" and Al pulls you behind the curtain.

"Who the hell are those people? They can't be in here! They could be terrorists! Worse! I can't sell them no guns! I won't!"

You tell him not to worry. They would be best friends if he got to know them. Chong had military training in North Korea and Esteban can hit a hardboiled egg a half mile away with his Glock. Al goes white.

The bell rings again and Al says, "I am not a bigot, I am a patriot, and it is every goddamned patriot's duty to protect this country and not hand out ammunition to any towel head who walks through the door!" You smile and shout, "Guys? Do you have any towels?"

Al smacks his forehead.

"Guys?" There's no answer, which is weird because My Cho has a snappy comeback for everything. You pull back the curtains and there in the store with your friends are four men in black ski masks. One's at the door, another is holding a shotgun on Esteban and Lucky, and the other two are pointing shotguns right at you and Al. Chong and My Cho are missing. Your heart starts hammering. The room is so quiet.

No one speaks.

"Hey there, fellers!" Al says. "Need to buy some ammo? We got a good deal on—"

"Shut the fuck up!" the closest gunman says. "Open the register or I blow you away!" The gunman's blue eyes are red-rimmed and dilated. "You gonna open the drawer?" he shouts, wagging his gun. You're frozen where you stand. Unable to move.

Esteban seems to think this is funny. He rolls a toothpick between his teeth. "You in a gang?" he asks, grinning at the gunman next to him. The gunman pokes his rifle in Esteban's face and says, "Fuck off, cholo!"

"Cool it, Danny!" Blue-eyes shouts, then he cocks the gun and moves in closer on Al. "I know you're supposed to be some war hero, but do the math, old man. You got four hostages and four guns on them. Nobody's a hero today. Right?" When Al doesn't move, Blue-eyes goes hysterical. "I said open the *motherfucking* drawer, *bitch*!"

"All right! Okay, don't get all shooty now, just, just give me a minute." Al starts hitting random register keys and getting all flustered. The guy by the door says, "Yep, that's how they do it in the marines. Pansy!" The other guys laugh.

"So, *Danny boy*," Esteban says, "you're a mick, huh? Eat your mom's potatoes?" Danny looks incredulous, even with a ski mask on.

"What did you just say?" he asks.

There's a horrible feeling rising in your chest, hot and powerful, like it could lift you to the ceiling. It's a sauna in here, everybody's sweating. *Oh God, why isn't it over yet?* You see a tiny smirk crawl up Esteban's lip. "*Non comprende boʒo loco?*" he says. "You didn't hear me, ese? Hey, *ese chango* here didn't hear me."

"You better fucking shut up!" Danny says.

Al can't open the register. "I can't remember the . . . I can't remember the code."

"You better remember the code, motherfucker!" Blue-eyes says.

"Okay!" Al says, resuming at the keys. "I got it. I got it."

Esteban leans into Danny's gun, like it was a microphone, and says, "I call you a . . . *mick*. Shit, *vato*, aren't you s'pose to shoot me now? Huh, *padre?*"

"Shut up! I ain't your fucking wetback daddy!" Danny presses the gun right against Esteban's forehead. Any second he'll shoot and you'll see Esteban's head vaporize into red mist. *This is all your fault.* Why did you decide to work at a gun shop? What good could come from it? *How will it all end?* This is when the anxiety rising in your chest bursts out of your mouth in wild, uncontrollable nervous laughter.

Everyone in the room turns to look at you.

You clamp your hands over your mouth but burst out laughing again. You can't hold it. Some nervous condition, Tourette's syndrome maybe. But it's like your freakish laughter is what everyone was waiting for. The green light they needed. The bizarre distraction they wanted. In that next moment, which hung breathless and outside the natural properties of time, what happens looks completely rehearsed, but it wasn't. It was just the poetry of instinct.

As you stand with your hands over your horrified mouth, Al pitches a self-activating land mine over the counter and then a dark gray canister that starts smoking as he pulls you down. Simultaneously, Esteban snatches the rifle pressed to his head by the barrel with both hands. He yanks it back and pops the heel of the gun into Danny's nose, which bursts with blood. Then he flips the gun over in one motion so the business end is now facing Danny. "My fucking daddy's *Nuestra Familia* from Folsom, bitch!" and Esteban shoots Danny in the stomach three times, plastering him back across the glass counter, which shatters. Meanwhile, My Cho rises like a dragon from her crouched position in back. She's holding a hunting crossbow and kneels forward, aiming at the gunman by the door. *Schwiiiing!* She shoots an arrow through his right eye. The gunman staggers back as she reloads, but before he can drop to his knees, she sends another arrow slicing through his left eye.

The yellow smoke billowing from the gray canister effectively blinds Blue-eyes and his remaining pal, but they're badasses, of course, so they throw down Texas-style and just shoot at everything. Bullets slice the air and zing off the metal shelves. The sound is deafening. That's when Chong Ju Hwi, disgraced son of a North Korean officer, who has climbed up a water pipe and shimmied his way across the drop ceiling, lifts the corner of a ceiling tile and noses his gun through the opening. He pauses. Waits for the space between the space. Then he rapid-fires two Smith & Wessons, one in each hand. The gunmen still standing drop over. No one even knew what hit them or where it came from.

Al springs around the counter to disarm the dead as Chong Ju Hwi drops like a spider from the ceiling. He stands momentarily as though listening for music, then he shoots all the men again. Then silence. Everyone comes out slowly, stepping carefully. "Everyone alive?" Al whispers. "Everyone all right?" Then you have a heart attack as the door bursts open and Elbert crashes in, sunlight flooding in behind him. "What in the *hell* do you people get into when I'm not here?" Al is laughing and out of the corner of your eye you catch movement on the floor. Blue-eyes's hand rises shakily, holding a pistol.

Al, watch out!

But Blue-eyes squeezes the trigger, and even after the explosion your ears won't stop ringing. You open your eyes and there's Al. He's looking down at the floor with great curiosity at Blue-eyes, who just got his arm blown off. It's a fleshy stump now that turns into a pulpy smear of jelly. All eyes turn to Lucky, who is standing by an open gun case, her bare head unwrapped, revealing a Mohawk on her otherwise bald skull. Her eyes are wide open and she's frozen, staring as she holds the pearl-handled Derringer .38 that killed Blue-eyes. Sirens.

The event becomes legend. A cautionary tale cops tell criminals. The lesson is, if you're going to rob a gun store, pick one without customers. Because if you get a deserter from the North Korean army, a survivor of Hmong internment camps, a runaway Somali bride, the son of Mexico's worst drug lord, a bullheaded ex-marine, and a cashier girl with lungs like Pavarotti, it doesn't matter what you come in with, it won't be enough.

It also becomes a favorite story down at the Trinity Tabernacle Refugee Choir, where Miss Camilla Allbright Day loves to tell the new choir members about her brave babies who took down those criminals, and certainly God was watching over them that day, just as he is watching over everyone now. *A-men!* she says. *Don't you know any of us together is better than all of us alone?* When they load up on the blue bus and roll down the highway to Atlanta and those children *sing sing sing*, the bus driver says he's sure sorry they didn't get a new bus for Miss Camilla this year. She says, *No sir,* not that. Not on this bus. On this bus it's not what you ride, sweet baby, it's all how you roll.

43

From section 10

You buy a megayacht on the last day of the Millionaire Fair and in a hung-over, woozy, possibly ill-advised rush of farewell camaraderie, you invite all your new Russian millionaire friends to come along for its maiden voyage. It's only fair. After all, Vitali *gave you* the diamond-encrusted Vacheron Constantin watch Nika decided she didn't want (not enough diamonds) and Oleg paid for a private jet to fly you home. The least you could do is take them sailing, right?

Well, Aidan doesn't like it. How could you just *buy* a five-million-dollar megayacht? You promise him everything's going to be fine after you're on board and setting sail for parts unknown. The boat is named the *Bête Noire*, or "Dark Beast," and is the height of luxury. She's one hundred and eighteen feet long and painted a glossy bloodred, which caused quite a sensation at her unveiling. Boats are supposed to be *white*. Red is unlucky, a slap to tradition, and that's why you like it. Well, that's why Oleg liked it actually, and you were a little drunk when you wrote the check.

At the marina in Miami, however, you love how she looks in the water; people have never seen anything like it. A crowd gathers to gawk and you feel like a regular celebrity going up the gangplank in your big black sunglasses. Inside Aidan can't help but admire the teak woodwork and crystal chandeliers, as well as the white marble inlay floors, wraparound Lucite bar, and of course the master suite, which has a remote-controlled retractable ceiling so you can watch the stars from the bedroom's heated Jacuzzi.

You discuss the itinerary as you leave the port. Monaco, Nice, Cannes, Saint-Tropez, Capri, Portofino, Mallorca, Barcelona, Corfu, and Mykonos, just to name a few. You spend the next hour or so relaxing by the pool reading travel guides, and at sunset you have cocktails surrounded by supernovas in the sky of orange and fiery apocalypse red.

Captain Marquardt sends a steward to give you a message received over the radio, which says, "The Russians are coming." Your heart freezes and you hear the ominous chop of an approaching helicopter as it beats across the open water. You turn to see Nika's metal wasp buzzing your way.

Aidan looks at you. "*Who's* coming?"

You try to act natural. "The Russians! No big deal. Just some fun people from the Millionaire Fair." Meanwhile, you're praying Oleg isn't on board and thinking: *Shit, shit, shit, shit, shit, shit, shit, shit, shit.* . . . You thought those guys would be too busy jet-setting around to ever remember your piddly little invitation! Did you even tell them what marina you were in? Did they use some mob connections to find you? Can you tell the captain to gun the engine and outrun them? Does this boat have guns?

You force yourself to stop spinning and think positive. It'll be all right. They *are* fun. You're sure their stay will be short. They probably have to get to some art auction or black market human-trafficking deal somewhere. The chopper sets down on your virgin helipad unevenly, causing panic on the bridge. The pilot, Vitali's sixteen-year-old brother Sasha, nearly diverts before he manages to avoid toppling. Finally everyone gets out as the *Bête Noire* crew rushes to secure the aircraft.

Vitali, Nika, and Oleg disembark loudly, drunk, unaware of their close call, followed by Nika's yappy Pomeranian, Bikte, who promptly bites Aidan and then disappears belowdeck. Right away there's trouble: Vitali and Nika are fighting and Oleg starts making rude comments to Aidan, dropping hints about how much money he has and saying something about Russian men statistically having the world's biggest cocks.

By dinner Aidan has had enough and tells Oleg to go fuck himself. Oleg in turn tells Aidan to stop complaining. After all, he's got a good life freeloading off a woman, a woman who gives a very good blow job.

Swearing. Shoving. Punches are thrown.

When Aidan confronts you and asks if this *motherfucking Cossack* is lying or not, you don't even get a chance to answer—Nika starts laughing and says she's seen the videotape of you and Oleg fucking, and she didn't think there was anything special about it *at all*.

Aidan leaves the *Bête Noire* in Phuket. He catches a plane home and never speaks to you again. The Russians take their sweet time departing, waiting another two days to get in their helicopter. You just stay in your cabin staring out at the Andaman Sea until they're gone. When you finally hear the chopper blades, you reemerge depressed and humiliated, barely able to make it an hour without crying. Then Bikte appears on deck. Apparently Nika left without him. Unbelievable. The whole situation seems terribly funny all of a sudden and you start laughing until the little Pomeranian, who's undoubtedly freaked out by having *you* for a new owner, comes and bites your ankle.

Things could be worse. Probably.

You decide to stay here for a while. You landed a choice slip in the Royal Phuket Marina, favored by megayachts and rife with plenty of other platinum world travelers who like to drink fine liqueurs and tell their unremarkable stories. Dolly Dupont, though, is different. She's got good stories and then some. The sole heiress to a titan pharmaceutical company, she more or less roams the globe on the *Noblesse Oblige*, her two-hundred-and-fifty-foot superyacht, which is packed chockablock with exotic antiquities, rare flora, and dozens of rescued animals. Someone said she even has an endangered pygmy deer on board, but you never saw it, which of course doesn't mean it wasn't there.

Dolly's private. She anchors just outside the marina and takes her sleek cigarette boat into town when she wants cigarettes, which is what she was doing when you met. She invites you over for dinner, where you bond over bottles of Leflaive Chassagne-Montrachet and sad relationship stories. She's terribly sorry about Aidan leaving. "He's no good, darling! You never abandon someone out at sea. It's just not done! But you know what my father said? You can paint the hull but you can't recut the jib. It's true, too. A bad egg is just a bad egg."

She's sworn off dating, claiming it's too complicated. Plus, she's never lonely. "If I had a slip in the marina, darling, people would drop by *night and day*. My nerves would *shatter*. Out here I can just raise the ladders, batten down the hatches, and people can come calling all they want. If anyone tries to board there's an excellent sniper in my crow's nest. Tong Lee. He's Hmong." She takes a long sip of wine and her eyes wander up to the stars. "They really are the best shots." You laugh, but look nervously up when you notice that she isn't.

Dolly doesn't think she's ever really been in love anyway. She's not wired for it. She lost her mother when she was eight, and then a year later her father died of a massive coronary, leaving her alone in the world with only an estate estimated at around five billion dollars for company. The *New York Times* called her the world's richest orphan, and two days later the kidnapping attempts started. Her nanny, Françoise, loaded her up into the car and said they were going on a picnic. Next thing a fleet of speeding police cars were running them off the road. Turned out there weren't sandwiches in the picnic basket. Just duct tape and a shovel.

After that, Dolly's guardians never left her alone. Armed bodyguards escorted her everywhere. "I got to see Santa only once," she says, "and I didn't ask for anything. I asked him to take all my money away and give it to poor children, only I didn't really care about poor children, I just thought if I was poor, maybe I'd be safe again."

You look over at her, caught by the tone in her voice. You start to say something and then just burst into tears. Dolly's so startled she knocks over the wine bottle, and just like that stewards come scurrying out from all four corners of the deck. *They must have been watching you the whole time*, waiting to meet your slightest need. Dolly shouts at them to get the hell back and it's positively creepy. The venom in her voice is piercing. Of course she resents being watched and yet she must be watched. Even she knows that. She's too recognizable and wealthy to ever be alone ever again. You realize Dolly Dupont is a prisoner, by any definition. She's serving a life sentence, and her one consolation is a cage called the *Noblesse Oblige*.

After that night, you spend most of your time with her, as does Bikte, whom Dolly loves. Dolly loves all animals. She shows you the enormous domed aviary in the ship's greenhouse, which is filled with chirping, happy little birds that she's rescued. When one stops eating, Dolly sends for an ornithologist from the Singapore Institute of Biology. After treating the bird, the vet makes an innocent, offhand comment about spending so much money on one little kingfisher and Dolly's eyes blaze.

She walks toward him slowly in her red kimono. "Well, then, I'm sorry for you, Dr. Chan," she says. "Because if you don't know a kingfisher's heart is just as important as your own, then you don't know much. The only things that matter in this life have beating hearts. Everything else is landfill."

Dolly decides to leave shortly after that. You're heartbroken. Not just because you'll miss her, but because you have no idea where to go now. Dolly seems to sense your anxiety and has a going-away present for you. You get to choose between a session with a very powerful psychic in London named Niobe, or a membership in the Luxiste Club, a secret society of people who seek unique experiences.

If you join the Luxiste Club, go to section 37 (p. 115).
If you meet with Niobe, go to section 86 (p. 272).

44

From section 98

You push on the bigger door, which sticks, so you push harder. The floor inside is old and looks too risky to walk on. There're a few objects on the far side of the room, a little dusty pouch, and a clump of what looks like metal chains. Desperate to find anything that might help you out of this place, you find a stick in the debris around you and fish about the floor to drag the objects over.

You manage to retrieve the pouch first, which is filled with little misshapen dice. Quite old and curious. You put them in your bag and then set about pulling the metal chains over. Halfway across, there's a cracking sound and the entire floor gives way, sending the chains plummeting down into an abyss of blackness. You throw the glow stick down, which reveals a large pit of skeletons impaled on bamboo sticks.

Actual freaking *skeletons*.

And these aren't nice and bleached-white skeletons, like the ones in science classrooms on TV; these are weird, crusty, and have dried leathery gunk in the eye sockets. You want to vomit, cry, scream, and run all at once. Instead you do none of those things and just stare at the wall. Either Santiago is trying to kill you and you need to figure your own way out, or he's not trying to kill you and he'll be here at dawn.

You take the matches from your bag and gather up some old wooden planks to make a fire. It sparks up easily and you get warmer as time passes. You drink your water and eat your chocolate. For the next six hours you stay huddled next to the fire, flinching at every creak, click, and noise. You become acutely aware of how cold the cement floor is, how stale the air. The fire illuminates the walls around you, some of which have graffiti on them.

Crude drawings of prostitutes and Jesus, along with faint brittle handwriting, probably prayers.

You try to keep track of how long you've been here and how long you have left to wait, but after a while your mind stumbles and you lose track. It's hard not to think about the skeletons. Without knowing exactly what happened here, you know exactly what happened here. Awful things. Men become less than human in places like this, capable of unspeakable cruelty to others. Their minds revert to a pack mentality, to animalistic survival, to doing whatever it is they have to do to survive.

You wake up unaware you had fallen asleep. The fire is out and your body aches. You get up brittle and sore, feeling for the flashlight and making your way back to the main vault. This time you wear your jacket over your nose and mouth, so you won't have to smell Mr. Sunderland. When you round the corner to the vault, there is the aluminum ladder shrouded in the heavenly light of the outside world. Santiago wasn't trying to kill you after all.

The authorities come to retrieve Mr. Sunderland. Then they begin to pull up all the skeletons from the room of spikes. (You wish people would call it something more original . . . but "Room of Spikes" sticks.) It turns out this was one of the torture rooms in the notorious San Lucas Prison, home to thousands of criminals and convicts, to ruthless, lawless men, and to the often sadistic guards who watched them.

Criminal analysts find hundreds of complete or partial shoulder stocks, bullwhips, machetes, chopping blocks, cannons, and thousands of leg irons. They find split wooden plates, decomposed fabric that was once soaked in arsenic, in blood, in every bodily fluid there is. They find journals, notebooks hidden behind toilet tanks and wired under metal beds that detail abuse and punishments of such an acute, profound nature as to be close to unbelievable.

The stories about San Lucas Prison are out of a horror movie. It was the Alcatraz of South America, worse than Devil's Island. Men lived in filthy, disease-ridden conditions and were only given new uniforms when a prisoner died. Then those (often typhoid-ridden) clothes were handed out, a death sentence for the next host. The prisoners starved. They wore balls and chains, shackles they carried according to their crime, and all weighing fifty pounds or more. They never came off; they were welded on, and the men learned to walk with them, sleep with them, carry them like babies.

When a prisoner was disobedient, he was taken to the end of the pier and tipped backward, so he lost his balance and fell into the deep water, where nothing more would ever be seen of him, except a brief line of air bubbles and a thrashing roil of red water when the sharks got to him.

The prison had a slaughterhouse by the kitchen, which dumped blood and offal from the pier, keeping a vicious and hungry mob of hammerheads patrolling the area constantly. They were always there, waiting for a prisoner or a piece of cow intestine to hit the water. Enough of them remain today that you install a shark net in the water just off the beach, a chain-link barrier in the shape of a goalie's net. Still, you rarely go in the water.

After the forensic teams locate every last skull and shard of bone on your island (over five hundred unique sets of DNA in all), the story is met with international shock as worldwide press coverage explodes. Reservations start pouring in, people from around the globe want to stay on Murder Island. That's what people call it despite your attempts to keep it a bit more dignified, but who cares—your room rates double. You even cheat a little and say the Mango Cabana is haunted by a prisoner, and that one goes for triple. You do try to keep things dignified. After a priest comes to bless the island, you have a memorial built with every known prisoner's name.

One night, Santiago asks if he could see the dice you found. He confesses that he lived on this island when the prison was open. Those dice are his. They're made from prisoners' teeth. You ask if he was a prisoner here and he says no, he was a prison guard. You give him the dice.

Time moves on. You marry a wonderful Chilean chef who starts as a new staff member and becomes a new family member. After a spectacular island "eco-wedding" with paperless invitations, organic catering, and rowboats picking up all the guests so no fuel is used on the ferry, you go on a honeymoon to your own backyard, because anywhere else wouldn't be as nice.

As the gracious owners of the Eco Ranch, the two of you greet thousands of tourists from all over the world—Sydney, Reykjavik, Cape Town, and Kazakhstan—everyone wanting to walk through the hallowed ground and leave a small gift at the large stone memorial, as has become the custom. You've found prayer beads, a Bible, a Koran, a carved jade elephant, a lock of blonde hair, and long, tear-stained letters in Spanish. You collect these offerings and add them to the small museum you built on the island, a museum for the lost men.

Your hope is that for all the thousands of souls who suffered on this island, over time there will be thousands more who visit to comfort them. This hope is realized threefold when you have three children of your own, all born right here. There's Alejandro the acrobat, who swings like a monkey in a tree; Daniela the artist, who plays cello and studies watercolor by the age of eight; and Eduardo the dreamer, who likes to just look at things, which is fine by you because all your children are perfect.

Maurizio asked to be bought out of the business around the time your first child was born. It was a financial hit to have to buy him out, but "hit" is a relative term. You're wealthy by just about anybody's standards. You and your family (and your extended family, who one by one come down as they retire) all live on Isla San Lucas for many decades, building a strange kind of serenity in a place that was once soaked in anguish and is now an enlightened oasis of tranquility.

45

From section 142

Sometimes to get out, you have to go down deeper. You crawl into the jagged tunnel, pulling with your arms and pushing with your good leg. It takes every ounce of energy you have; the pain is almost unbearable. Snowmelt and crusts of broken snow give way underneath your hands and your face becomes numb with ice. There's no going back now. You have to hope that faint blue glow you see is the outside world.

Time passes. A minute, ten, twenty, thirty. The tunnel has gotten narrower, the light dimmer. Your gloves are starting to soak through, your hands are getting frostbitten, and your breath is quick and shallow. You don't remember all the stages, but you know those are on the list of hypothermia symptoms. Okay, maybe that's a good sign. Your brain is still functioning. You have memories. What do you remember now? The house where you grew up, the carpet in your room, the dog. Can you remember the names of all the planets? Your head aches, your eyes burn, and everything around you seems like the inside of a glassy coffin.

There's a sound like rushing water, but faster. No, it's wind. You can hear the wind! You must be close to the outside world. You crawl faster, forcing your near-dead fingers to grip the ice rubble ahead of you as you drag yourself onward. The slope lessens by degrees, until you're crawling horizontally again. The ceiling soars up, and when you break through a crusty ridge of snow, you find yourself in a peculiar dome, a bubble pod of ice.

This is it! The world is just on the other side of the ice, you just have to break through. Lying on your back, you kick at the wall with all your strength. Nothing happens. You kick again, realizing how cold you are, and tired. A feeling of peace and calm comes over you and you start dreaming of blankets. You die quietly, skin paling, cells bursting from the inside out as they freeze.

Vos es hic, vos es non. You are here, you are not.

Everyone else in the group dies, too. You actually lasted the longest; they were carried down the mountain by the torrent of snow and smashed on rocks and things. The search crews find all of them but you.

In heaven, you have questions and plenty of them. You attend an open forum with God where everyone gets to shout at him and demand answers. It's like a grouchy neighborhood town hall with a busy councilman. "All right, all right!" God shouts at the boisterous crowd. "We've covered this! Cancer was just a bad idea and I shouldn't have put it in table salt."

"And?" a woman in the crowd shouts, planting both hands on her hips.

God's shoulders slump. "And . . . I'm *sorry.*"

"And?" she shouts again.

God rolls his eyes. "And I'll introduce a cure sometime next century."

The crowd boos.

"All right, *this* century! That should be easy. Do you know how hard it is to introduce a new cure with all your little scientists running around testing everything six ways to Sunday?" The crowd boos louder. *"All right!"* God shouts. "I'll put it in freaking rain-forest bark! Do they still have any?" He shoots a quick look at the angel, who's already thumbed through a pile of thick, smudgy folders. He gives our Lord and Savior the slightest flare of angelic nostrils. God smacks his hand on his forehead. "Fine! I'll put it in vitamin C! Must I put *everything* in vitamin C?"

You raise your hand timidly, almost hoping not to get called on, but God's eager to change the subject and picks you out right away. "Um," you stammer, "why is man so . . . flawed?" God looks amused. "Because I made him in my image, of course! It does say that right in the book." A round of nods and agreement ripples around the room.

"Aren't you holy and pure? Filled with light, maybe?"

The room explodes with laughter. God seems to get a kick out of it, too.

"Like I said, I made him in *my* image. I get jealous, lose my temper, cheat at cards. I nearly belted this one right in the mouth last week!" He winks at the angel, who good-naturedly winks back.

Is God crazy? It doesn't make sense. "But, you could have wired us to feel only unconditional love! Or made us immune to greed! Why did you make us like this?"

God shrugs. "You know what you know. Does a grizzly bear give birth to a sunflower? It's in the DNA, you can only give what you got. That's how it works. No way around it."

There's an awkward pause and the room falls silent until the angel pipes up. "We did good on the camel, though."

"Yes." God brightens. "I agree. We did very good on the camel."

46

From section 11

It's always a bit deflating when you're about to drop a bomb on someone and they drop one on you instead. You tell Aidan you're leaving him and he says *he already knew*. He's known about you and Jeremy for weeks, he just didn't know when you were going to grow a pair and tell him. You ask him why he didn't say something if he already knew and you can't believe his response. He admits he was hoping you'd marry him so he could take you for every penny. He was going to get revenge on you by taking away the one thing you love. Your money.

You move in with Jeremy. The first house you flip together is Miss Dottie Lully's house. Miss Dottie was a little old lady who lived in her home in Germantown, Ohio, until she was one hundred and two. (On the wall of her bedroom hangs a signed certificate from the president commemorating her hundredth birthday.) She had already outlived her friends and family, including her only son, who died a few years back. When she finally passed over, she had no heirs, no one to leave the house to, so her house went on the market "as is," the realtor hoping to get some extra money for the furniture left behind.

Jeremy convinces you to buy her house sight unseen, because the neighborhood is so good and the asking price is so reasonable. Of course, nobody explained to you that Miss Dottie kept every item she ever came across, no matter how small or insignificant. The first tour through her house reveals crowded countertops thick with dust, overflowing bookcases, cluttered tables, tall stacks of vintage magazines piled like paper skyscrapers, stout walls built from wooden milk crates which are neatly labeled. Old maps, broken dolls, ticket stubs, restaurant menus, empty perfume bottles, theater playbills, TV Guides. She kept wax paper, tinfoil, and gum wrappers, smoothing them out flat and bundling them into neat little bricks. She saved string and twine, wrapping them into globe-sized spheres and keeping them in old bowling ball bags.

Every wall is as filled as the floors around them, crammed with pictures, newspaper articles, and big circus posters from the 1920s depicting a young girl riding around a ring bareback on a colorfully plumed horse. DORALINDA, THE BAREBACK BEAUTY! Framed black-and-white photographs show a milk-fed fresh-faced Miss Dottie in her satin riding costume with thick white leggings and shiny silk-ribbon ballet flats. She stands in each picture ringside with a different horse. Hanging beneath these pictures is a large ornate riding crop inside a shadowbox. It's quite old, the handle wrapped in a faded red silk cord and studded along the base with large yellowing rhinestones.

The whole house is like a time capsule. The kitchen is very retro, mint green Formica counters and a baby's-breath-pink Electrolux stove. The pantry's packed with ancient foodstuffs, old oatmeal tins, glass Ball jars with rusty caps, and a deep freezer that's thankfully still plugged in and contains a dozen frosty packages of unidentifiable meat and a brown cardboard box labeled MIMI 1997–2008.

It's Miss Dottie's dead cat, Mimi.

Jeremy wants to get busy dismantling Miss Dottie's house, but the more you investigate the house, the more treasures you find. Vintage photo albums, first-edition books, collectible china figurines, kitschy glamour girl calendars, endless boxes of personal letters and photo albums. You sift through the layers of detritus and discover this woman had an amazing life. Journal entries recall her childhood home, which was lit with oil lamps because there was no electricity. The garage out back was once a little stable for their pony, Annabelle, who pulled the family buggy.

Jeremy suggests selling everything online. You're not sure. Separating all these treasures one person took a lifetime to collect seems wrong.

What if you turned this little house into a museum? Cleaned it up and built proper displays for all the stuff? You might even get the city to declare it a Historical Place, which would mean no property taxes and more money to fix things up.

He laughs and reminds you that all this work, flipping houses and buying real estate, it's all supposed to be temporary, so you can retire early and never have to work again. The problem with opening a museum is that then you'd have a museum.

Is that what you want to do with your golden years?

If you sell Miss Dottie's house for a profit, go to section 93 (p. 293).
If you keep Miss Dottie's house for a museum, go to section 95 (p. 304).

47

From section 11

You can't leave Aidan for someone you just met. Besides, how could you ever be sure Jeremy loves you for you and not your money? No, it's time to call off the affair and settle down with a sure thing. You take Aidan on a romantic vacation to St. Lucia, where you stay in a deluxe penthouse suite in a treetop hotel with a hot tub that cantilevers out over the emerald green waters. It's fun to spit at the monkeys.

The trip confirms your faith in Aidan. He's the one for you. The vacation seems to bring him around, too. He's more loving and attentive than ever. You both feel lucky. On your last night at the hotel he hides a pink coral ring in your mango sorbet and asks you to marry him. He says he'll get you a diamond ring back home, but he couldn't wait another minute to ask you so he got this ring at a roadside stand that morning.

What a guy.

Three months later you and Aidan are married in a small rose garden. Your family and friends all cheer as you walk down the petal-strewn path and everyone wishes you much happiness. You don't blame them for not suspecting—after all, you never suspected anything, so how could anyone else have predicted what this great guy who just pledged his eternal love to you was really up to?

Six months later, you discover Aidan's bankrupted you. Spent every penny. The bank says he sent it to Darfur.

Sent it . . . where?

Darfur. The bank confirms the transaction with Unicef. All your money went to the purchase of 888,000 antimalarial bed nets. The Unicef representative you speak with is very kind. She offers to send you a T-shirt.

Aidan apparently found out about your affair with Jeremy a long time ago and decided to rob you blind. You ask him *how could he do this to you?* Easily. People who've been betrayed can do just about anything. Good people go bad if you push them hard enough.

There's nothing you can do. No legal recourse. After you were married, he had legal access to your money and could make any asinine tax-deductible contributions he wanted to.

Now you're broke. Serious financial trouble. You have to stop payments to your family, sell off everything you own, and move in with your parents, who now treat you like a mildly handicapped four-year-old. You have to find a job, any job, fast.

If you work at the Living Museum, go to section 92 (p. 290).
If you work at the Pancake Ranch, go to section 94 (p. 300).

48

From section 31

You start your big family with a big outdoor wedding. Then you buy a huge adobe house on three acres of land just outside Durango, Colorado. It's a gorgeous place to raise a family; the town is framed by majestic snow-capped mountains, and has plenty of fresh air and wide-open spaces. You're not too far from Lake Powell and your land butts up against the far northern boundary of the Great Navajo Nation.

Your new home is loaded with southwestern charm. High ceilings, exposed beams, pine staircase, gourmet kitchen, eight bedrooms, each with its own stone fireplace, and the house has radiant-heated terrazzo floors throughout. There's a beautiful courtyard with a fountain out front and a large recreational backyard with a horse barn and a swimming pool out back. The only thing you don't have is kids, despite doing everything the books say. You eat healthy, avoid alcohol and caffeine, and take folic acid, zinc, and selenium. Aidan wears loose boxers, no tighty-whitey underwear. You keep a temperature chart, track when you're ovulating, and have sex at least three times a day. Unless you're exhausted, and then it's just once a day. Still, no babies. You wish you could buy pregnancy tests in bulk, even though they all say the same thing: *not pregnant*.

It makes you feel damaged and worthless. Aidan holds you when you cry and says he doesn't care if you have a baby, he just wants you to be happy.

If you go to a fertility specialist, go to section 125 (p. 386).
If you adopt a child, go to section 127 (p. 397).

49

From section 24

You decide to buy Isla San Lucas, off the Nicoya Peninsula in Costa Rica. Bossrock books a flight to San José, where a jeep picks you up at the sweltering airport and drives you two hours west to the bustling coastal town of Puntarenas. There, a chartered boat speeds you across the brilliant blue water. An hour and a half later the captain points out a thin strip of land shimmering through the blurry heat waves in the distance. There it is. Your own private island.

You step off the boat and make your way down the long cement pier, which leads to a steep stone staircase cut into the hill. Even though there's a hive of busy porters zipping about, hauling your luggage piece by piece up the steps, you take your time, walk slowly. A hard day's traveling and the thick, wet heat presses down on you, making your thoughts blurry like heat vapors. You make your way up the steps carefully, feeling twice your age, the sun pounding your shoulders and your eyes straining even behind these dark UV sunglasses. You'd trade your kingdom for a glass of ice water.

Then the dark arms of the jungle reach you, sweeping cool shade across your arms and pouring green into your irises and pupils and eyes and mouth.

You take off your sunglasses.

Your eyes adjust gradually to the dense, tangled wilderness, which contains more shades of green than you knew existed. Emerald, apple, aquamarine, algae, kelly, lime, pine, malachite, moss, sage, ochre, spinach. A lizard darts out from the undergrowth, a quick messenger that stops within kissing distance of your big toe and licks his lips before darting away again.

A golf cart with a striped canvas cover pulls up and the lodge transportation coordinator, Juan, drives you to the lodge. As the two of you bounce along the narrow green corridors and Juan lists the creatures that live here—iguanas, parrots, armadillos, monkeys, sea turtles, and saltwater crocodiles, just to name a few—your smile gets bigger and bigger. You probably look ridiculous, but you don't care because buying this island was not just a *good* choice, it was an *incredible* choice.

One thousand one hundred and fifty-six acres of paradise is now in your possession. A sprawling virgin rain forest, three beaches, two mangrove forests, eight pre-Columbian archaeological sites, a veritable metropolis of exotic inhabitants, and you get to live here for free. Well, not for *free*—after all, you had to pay millions to get in on the deal, but there'll be no room charges or cocktail tabs for you because you're *El Jefe*, *Le Patron*, *de Werkgiver*. You are the *owner*. (Well, co-owner.)

At the lodge your new business partner, a tall, slender man in a white suit named Maurizio, introduces himself. He's a warm, friendly faced *Tico*, or native Costa Rican, and a longtime client of Bossrock's. He opened his ranch, Paraíso Olvidado ("Forgotten Paradise") three years ago, but due to the terrible economy and a lack of investors with "eco-vision," he needs a new partner to help him take this piece of forgotten paradise "all the way."

He wants to upgrade amenities, market to an upscale clientele, put in a holistic spa and a man-made coral reef to protect the area's endangered species. Maurizio is a stickler for keeping every little thing on his eco-ranch organic and natural. From the teak beams in the main lodge, to the delicately framed blue butterflies in the guest suites, to the bamboo walkways leading to all the outbuildings, everything here is natural and local.

Solar panels run the electricity, all the fruits and vegetables are farmed right here on the island, using chemical-free pest control (which is just another way to say: forcibly relocated spiders). He keeps cows and goats for milk and cheese, chickens for meat and eggs. Natural yeast and bacteria break down animal manure, keeping the watershed and artesian spring clean. He pays local fishermen to bring him fresh daily catches and has even cultured a small oyster bed in the nearby shallow waters.

You stay in the Wild Orchid cabana, a posh little suite nestled in a grove of lemon trees close to the beach. The house is filled with locally quarried stone floors, mango wood furniture, and big bridal dresses of mosquito netting over the windows and bed. Your first night is marked with wild torrents of rain pounding down around you, thunderous and loud, resembling the sound of a mortar attack on the beach.

Usually, however, days on San Lucas are spent relaxing, reading, or napping in a hammock while Maurizio whips the ranch into shape. Your job is simply to fork over money and keep quiet. Hence your title, silent partner, which suits you fine because life here is best enjoyed with your mouth shut. In the morning you have your *desayuno* (breakfast) delivered on a bamboo tray and by *almuerzo* (lunch) you've usually had a dip in the ocean and/or a massage in your room from the very cute on-staff masseur. All your needs are met. The bartenders know your favorite drink, the hot tub is kept at just the right temperature, the maids *do not* tuck your bedsheets into hospital corners, and the fruit bowl in your kitchen is replenished twice daily. (There's a family of large red macaws on the island, brilliant thieves who pirate little green *mamones* from the fruit basket in the kitchen.)

While Maurizio gets the new holistic spa under way and designs new guest suites to be built on connected walkways out over the water, you fly your entire family down for an extended vacation. They go nuts. They of course absolutely love the island and they say you're the *luckiest person on Earth*, toasting you at festive dinners and presenting you with a handmade bamboo plaque that says MVFM: MOST VALUABLE FAMILY MEMBER. When it's time for them all to leave, the staff cooks up a special farewell langosto dinner and sings them a song about being sorry to see them go.

The oldest employee, both in actual age and in number of years working at Paraíso Olvidado, is the head groundskeeper, Santiago. People treat him with great respect. He lived on the island before the resort was even built and some even say he was born here. He takes you on the occasional tour, telling you old stories and showing you secret shortcuts to overgrown artifacts in the jungle.

You love these little journeys together, not just because they're fascinating, but because you're scared to walk in the jungle alone. There are some *serious* creatures in here. Some are beautiful, some are poisonous, some are both. You'll never forget the day you were following Santiago down a small path and you stopped to study the unusual petals of a pale pink orchid growing out of a dead tree stump. You were bent over, leaning into the flower, when the palm thicket beside you started to rustle, and rather than running you leaned in closer just as a black crocodile nosed her snout through the fronds, eyes locked on you, and started to emit a low guttural hiss. You froze. Any previous tutorials you might have had about handling a wild crocodile vanished. You stood there bone-still as the hissing creature advanced slowly, putting one meaty reptilian arm in front of the other, staring. The one clear thought in your head at that moment was, "So *this* is how I die." Then Santiago brought his machete down on her neck, splitting it open into a wide, grinning slit of ropy pink meat.

After that episode, you stick to the wooden walkways unless you have an armed escort, and there are no more incidents. Well, that is until the first accident.

The ranch had just reopened and a young German girl named Anja was found washed up on the beach. Drowned. Her eyes were still open, her tongue pale and protruding from her lips. There were bloody, seeping welts all over her torso and the official cause of death was cardiorespiratory arrest, but Santiago said sea wasps got her. Must be a pod nearby, and sure enough they started washing up the next day, bright purple, poisonous, gelatinous jellyfish. A single sting could be fatal and Anja was covered with hundreds. Santiago shakes his head. The pain must have been unimaginable.

Just a freak accident, right?

Then Eduardo, the young man who looked after the ranch's cows and goats, felt ill one day, so he went back to his cabin early and lay down. He died that night in his bed. The doctor said it was Query Fever, a bacterial infection contracted from animals and certainly just a coincidence. (Some say you can only get Query Fever by having sex with sheep, so it might not have been unlucky so much as imprudent, but still.)

Then an American tourist disappears. Mr. David Sunderland from New Orleans goes out for a walk after dinner and never comes back. Vanishes. Twenty-four hours go by, then forty-eight. Search parties on the ground comb every inch of the island. Military helicopters buzz through the tropical heat using infrared sensors to scan the jungle. The Costa Rican police are brought in along with cadaver-sniffing dogs and divers. Two weeks later there is no trace, no trail, no evidence whatsoever Mr. Sunderland ever came to the island except for his passport and wallet, which rest safely in his guest room alongside his bereft, silent wife.

An uneasy breeze blows through your piece of paradise and bookings start to drop.

Then there's the ghost.

Of course there's no ghost, but the few guests who remain start complaining about strange sounds at night, voices outside their windows, a low groaning, the silhouette of a large man watching them from the shadows at the edge of the forest. Before you know it the only human souls to be found on Isla San Lucas are on your payroll.

Insomnia sets in. The frogs at night make a biblical racket. It never bothered you before, but now the croaking is deafening, maddening. The money left in your accounts is draining rapidly. A quick call to Bossrock confirms what you feared. This is that crucial time when all the money has been spent and all you can do is wait for your profits to roll in, but you need guests to get profits and there are none. People talk and rumors spread fast. Chat rooms have sprung up and your ranch is now listed on certain nefarious and undesirable "most dangerous places to travel" Web sites.

You've got to turn this thing around. You can't go back to life the way it was, living nine to five in a cubicle with the seething, silent hatred of your coworkers—not that your old boss would take you back. No, there's no going back, only forward.

Then early one dawn, after a night of wakeful sleeping, your groggy eyes open to the figure of a man. He's standing there in your doorway with a machete in his hand. You jump out of bed, too scared to scream, and you realize it's Santiago, motioning with his hand for you to be quiet. He wants you to follow him, which you do, and he takes you away from the lodge down a path you've rarely been on because you thought it ended at the Dumpsters, but it does not. Instead it snakes along the Dumpsters and then veers off into thick trees and follows a little clear stream for about a mile. Then another quick turn and Santiago pulls a large pile of brush off the trail, revealing a small iron gate.

Through the gate the path widens and turns to mossy stone. Incredible. You were told there were no paved roads on the island whatsoever, but what you see next will shock you even more. It's a building, a low, crumbling stucco and brick structure that's very old, but not ancient. Too modern to be ruins, too dilapidated to have been used this decade; you have no idea what you're looking at. Santiago waves you onward and you follow him farther to another building, and this one has a sign above the door. It says HOMBRES PERDIDOS.

"Lost men."

Santiago starts telling you the story of the island. The real story. He says for over a hundred years, from 1873 to 1991, Isla San Lucas was a penal colony, a violent prison housing some of the worst criminals in all South America. How could you not have known this? Why didn't anyone tell you? Because you wouldn't have invested, that's why. The police and your own staff were probably paid by Maurizio not to tell you. There are no paths here, none that you knew of; you thought this whole area was just dense, snake-riddled jungle. Santiago kicks at a crumbling clump of concrete and says the ground is still honeycombed with crumbling jail cells. Wanna see one?

You do. He takes you around a mossy hill and down a short flight of steps into a dank, dingy concrete room that has graffiti all over the walls of naked women and religious icons. There are some old rusty metal beds scattered around and rat droppings pebbled all over the floor. Santiago says the island was used as an agricultural penal colony, where inmates slaughtered cattle. Then the blood and offal were dumped in the ocean, so as not to attract animals on the island, but the blood attracted plenty of animals, most of them underwater. That's why the warm waters around San Lucas now teem with hammerhead sharks.

He shows you another cell and then takes you up top again, where the air is fresh and you can breathe. Besides the cells there's the chapel and the torture chamber. He shows you the exercise yard, which is braided with crawling vines. At the very center of the yard he kicks back some overgrowth, revealing a manhole cover, which he drags off with great effort. You peer down into the hole, but the darkness reveals nothing.

"Oubliette," Santiago whispers.

"Wobble-what?"

"Pit. *Dungeon*. This is the only way in or out. They put the worst men down there. They never came up. No light, no sky, nothing. They stayed in the pit."

"What's down there now?"

"The answer."

He says the island is cursed because of all the violent deaths that happened here. It can only be undone one way. You have to sleep overnight in the pit. Just you, alone. That is the legend. If the owner of the island is willing to endure just one night of what these men went through, then the curse will lift. "What about Maurizio?" you ask him. "Why can't he go down there?" Santiago says he could, but he won't. He's already tried and couldn't bear it for more than an hour. Then he brushed off the curse and decided it was fiction. Fantasy. Now there's only one person who can stay overnight in the pit and break the curse. You.

If you do not stay overnight in the pit, go to section 96 (p. 306).
If you stay overnight in the pit, go to section 98 (p. 310).

50

From section 27

You buy the Big Sky Six-Quarter Ranch in Montana, which annoys Aidan in the *worst* way. He storms around shouting *just how in the hell is he going to work in Montana? He hates wide-open spaces! He's allergic to horses!* (You forgot that.) His mood gets worse. He says you made the decision even though he *begged you* not to. He told you what he wanted and you ignored it. You ignore everything he wants these days. He doesn't have a vote in anything.

Well, now you're getting angry. Are you supposed to do every little thing he demands? Whose money is it, anyway? The fight escalates until Aidan leaves.

After a few weeks of awkward silence and utterly failed attempts at reconciliation, you both decide to break up. It's mutual, only you would have tried to work on it if he'd said he wanted to, but he didn't, so fine. Let him be that way. You're not going to get all emotional, you're just going to take some vacation time off work and go visit the BS6Q. (That's the brand on all your cattle. All two thousand of them.)

Montana is amazing. So are the people. They drink whiskey here, not wine. They wear cowboy hats and cowboy boots and that's everywhere, including movies and weddings. They listen to country music and nothing else; they watch rodeos, not golf tournaments. They call liquor shops "package stores" and eat boiled peanuts. They smoke, drive without seat belts, and think sunscreen is crazy. They go to church and don't like logging trucks. They love the land. They *are* the land. Any time a road closes for a tourist's second home or a fishing stream is cut off for private use, there's trouble. Lots of things burn down suddenly, and at night.

You love being here, but it's a little lonely and there are never any new people around. You want to liven things up, while still making money.

One idea is to turn the place into a dude ranch, providing tourists with lodging and the thrilling opportunity of running cattle. Folks from the city pay good money just for the chance to experience a working ranch. They'll even shovel shit if you ask them to. Another idea is to turn your property into a Wild West amusement park. Whisky-barrel roller coasters, saloon-style restaurants, petting zoo, coal-mine rides. It's crazy, but haven't you—at one time or another—wished you could have your very own amusement park? This is your chance.

If you turn your property into a dude ranch, go to section 101 (p. 318).

If you turn your property into an amusement park, go to section 109 (p. 344).

51

From section 25

You arrange to stay on Skellig Michael, or Michael's Rock, as the locals call it—a small craggy island jutting up out of the sea, nine miles off the coast of western Ireland. Monks built beehive-shaped stone huts on the precipice, clearing off a plateau for a garden and cemetery. Then they ringed their little village with thick stone walls, so the island looks like it's wearing a stone crown on its head.

The architecture of these strange beehive dwellings is remarkable. They've survived for centuries due to quality and craftsmanship. No mortar was used; each rock was hand-chosen and then carefully fit into the over-all structure. The walls are Herculean—centuries of gale storms haven't knocked them down.

A boat drops you off on the little stone dock with two weeks of supplies. You just hope you didn't forget anything. The boat will come back in two weeks to deliver the new lighthouse keeper.

You move into the old monastery, which has been converted into simple living quarters. The first night you make dinner on the cast-iron stove, go-ing through two dozen matches before the pilot lights. The place is small and cozy, and there are ancient artifacts lying around, like a medieval-looking cast-iron teapot and an old broom made of bound witch hazel branches.

You spend hours watching the waves crash down on the rocks below. Around midnight a storm blows in; ferocious, howling wind wraps around the house and rattles the shutters so hard one upstairs flies right off like a dark green bird. What if something happened to you out here? Who would help you? What if you slipped and fell? Would anyone even find you before the seagulls pecked your eyeballs out? You can't sleep a wink all night as you stay up listening to the storm screaming around the house and vow you'll leave this island as soon as possible.

In the morning dawn creeps across the sky, reds and lavenders washing over any trace that something dark passed this way. Seagulls sun themselves on the ancient moss-covered walls; it's like another world. You spend the day reading and enjoying life without a single newspaper or tabloid popping up and ruining everything. Heavenly. You spend the first week catching up on sleep and stargazing. You're sitting at breakfast one morning when about a hundred yards from the dock, the water explodes and a whale as big as a black-and-white school bus breaks the surface, its body wholly suspended in midair for just a breathless second, before he dives down and vanishes.

The second week you begin weeding the garden and pruning the rose-bushes, winding the clippings into tight bundles for kindling. At the end of the two weeks, the boat comes back as promised and you have all your things packed. You told the captain that depending on how your visit to Skellig Michael went, you'd either return to the mainland with him or you'd stay on another two weeks. Then the new lighthouse keeper gets off the boat, a stunningly handsome man with glacier-blue eyes and a smile that could melt an ice cap. "Ye stayin' on?" the captain asks.

If you stay on Skellig Michael, go to section 102 (p. 325).
If you leave Skellig Michael, go to section 103 (p. 327).

52

From section 79

You get on the bus. Your mother would be heartbroken if you didn't show up. The hills roll past your window as the bus gets on the highway. Bye-bye, Babyhead Mountain, thanks for everything. But at home no one is happy to see you. *Why would they be?* You left them, lied to them, refused to help them when you could have. Now you want a big homecoming? Grandpa Joe says he'll help you get back on your feet. Just don't screw up this time.

He lends you some money to open your own bar. A seedy little honky-tonk on the edge of town called the Dew Drop Inn. It's the kind of place where women show off their muffin tops, men cash in their welfare checks, and the only way to get kicked out is to draw blood. You install a mechanical bull and start competitions. People love it. Your little dive bar turns into a Texas-sized success.

Not that you're rich, you actually run pretty close to the line, profits often just barely outweighing expenses. Still, you have a good life surrounded by friends, family, and a large tract of acreage, where you live until you're one hundred and two. You give everyone the same piece of advice someone once gave you. *It's not the holding on that hurts, it's the falling off.* Hold on long enough and see where the ride wants to take you.

53

You tell Gabe to leave without you. You can't leave these people behind.

"Fine!" he shouts. "Your funeral!" and speeds off.

Just as you're opening the heavy glass hotel door, something down the street explodes. There's a streak of light and then you're being pressed down, like rocks are being piled up on you. Something hot strikes your forehead and you go dark.

When you wake up, you're at the Emirates Hospital with your head bandaged. The nurse tells you a piece of shrapnel from an exploding munitions truck hit you. You're very lucky you didn't lose an eye. When you ask her what happened to the insurgent uprising, she says Sheik Nahyan now owns Iran and has renamed it New Dubai.

The cyclone did more damage than the Iranians; behemoth waves washed away most of the structures on every World Island. So sad for those who didn't evacuate, and so sad for people who weren't properly insured. Everything on your island is gone. Every building, statue, rose bush, and cruddy piece of Ohio bric-a-brac. It's all been washed away by the tides. Then another disaster strikes. It turns out Gabe got you everything you needed except flood insurance, since the Islands were thought to be flood-proof.

Well, they weren't.

Now all you have is a chunk of debris-strewn land. Nothing else. You don't care, you're glad you have your own island. It's where you'll live now, all by yourself. Let the world do what it wants to do, you're out. One thing the flood taught you was that time is all we have and it's running out. Despite your family's protests and everybody begging you to come home, you refuse. You'll live on the island alone, without the pressures of the world on you.

You do it, too. Move to Ohio Island and pitch a big army tent, where you live like an Amazonian in the jungle. A garden provides fresh fruit and you go fishing every day. You're like Tom Hanks in that movie, *Castaway*, only you don't want anyone to find you—and they don't. Not even after you step on a rusty nail, which is sticking up out of a weather-beaten plank, a leftover from the large piles of storm debris. You treat the wound right away, but it gets infected. Turns all kinds of colors. Seeps pus. Makes you sleepy and take long naps, until your leg feels heavy, waterlogged, and you can't even walk. Having no radio and unable to climb into the boat, you crawl to the shore, where maybe a passing pleasure craft will see you. They don't.

You die on your luxury island, alone.

54

You fly to the Seychelles, a chain of granite islands off the eastern coast of Africa. Only a hundred and fifty thousand tourists are allowed to visit each year, which helps protect the rare and endangered wildlife. There are three main developed islands; the rest are private or too small to populate. You'll be staying on La Digue Island, population two thousand, in a private bungalow made of takamaka and bois noir. There's also a swimming pool, tennis court, yacht, and, of course, a full staff on duty twenty-four hours a day.

It's expensive.

Which isn't the only remarkable thing about this place. The house decor is classic West Indies, a throwback to colonial Britain, with dark teak ceilings and gauzy white drapes tied to bamboo poles; the furniture is mostly wicker and upholstered with khaki ticking or a curious print with embroidered monkeys. The enormous bed reminds you of a breezy white sailboat, piled high with feather pillows and backed by a kite of canvas on the headboard. Cobwebs of mosquito netting are spun generously around the bed despite the fact there are few insects.

The owner of the house, an absent expat from London, must be an inveterate collector. Chinese vases, Persian rugs, and mute African heads populate the room alongside great glass display boxes of dead insects—butterflies, and flying beetles long gone but still with traces of remarkable color, their wings fragile green glass, their eyes dead bottleneck blue.

There's something about this place that lets you rest. A suspended element, as though the whole world has been put on pause so you can collect your thoughts. There's time here. Time for anything and everything; there's time for leisurely pursuits like collecting smooth, bone-colored shells from the shore, for unscheduled napping, for lengthy letter writing, and for sipping delicately blended cocktails at sunset.

Each evening as you sit under your avocado tree overlooking the ocean, the silent, solemn-faced houseman serves you gin and tonics with thinly sliced lime carefully arranged on bone china. You sip your drink and toast the blue sharks that cruise constantly in the turquoise water beneath you. Sharks are about the only danger on the island. There are few animals, mostly curious reptiles, colorful birds, and the occasional slow tortoise moving like an ancient steamship across the lawn.

The gardens are spectacular, festooned with brilliant yellow gingers, fire red heliconia, pink hibiscus, wild orchids of every imaginable shape and color, and a thick grove of aubergines, which drop their heavy purple fruit until they become a sticky mash on the ground. The groundskeeper said bees were the secret. When no bees come around, he sticks brightly painted oil cans on the branches, because bees love color, and even though they may not stop to fertilize a garden, they'll travel from far and wide to fertilize brightly colored oil cans.

You usually eat alone, outside on your terrace flanked by lit torches and waitstaff, silent rum-skinned Seychellois who must live somewhere on the island. Where? Why don't they talk more? You've tried to befriend some of them, but they remain determined in their silence. The elderly cook is cheerful; she often makes a cumin-and-turmeric-scented rice dish with red snapper called *bourẓwa*, or sometimes she grills fresh line-caught tuna or king steaks with octopus. Your favorite, however, is called Millionaire's Salad, because a whole palm tree has to be cut down so the palm tree's heart can be harvested, which is a slightly sweet, cool, crunchy vegetable and the salad's primary ingredient. You asked her not to prepare the curried fruit bat again, which tastes a lot like rabbit and has so many small bones you felt like the giant from Jack and the Beanstalk.

Bossrock says the heat isn't off you yet; the *Star Enquirer* has found many of your old high school "buddies" who sell them stories about your "secrets," which range from cheating on your sophomore social studies test to being a transgendered occult-worshiping witch. Clooney is being portrayed as a generous romantic who tried to give a "woman with a lot of problems" a chance. You better plan on staying in the Seychelles a little longer.

Months go by. Half a year. Two years. You buy a little bungalow of your own and spend your days happily exploring the islands, discovering one utterly astonishing geological anomoly after another. One beach, Anse Source d' Argent on La Digue Island, has soft, sugar white beaches broken up by giant pink stones, some larger than office buildings, creating a chain of small coves. They're perfect for secluded sunbathing, clandestine meetings, and erotic encounters.

Life here is incredible. It isn't completely perfect; if you want anything at all it has to be ferried in, and depending on the item, that can take weeks. If you run out of ketchup, you have to go to Mahe Island to get more. (Well, your cook goes.) Electronics, fashion, and medicine have to be flown in. Some things can never make the trip, like a McDonald's cheeseburger. The electricity on the whole island goes out sometimes and your backup generators are dicey. There is no hospital on the island, no dentist, no doctor. Even though you live in a grand home, you are as vulnerable as anyone to the fierce storms that can erupt.

Plus, there's the encroaching, echoing loneliness.

One day in La Passe you start talking to some freshly arrived backpackers named Auguste and Philippe. They're young vibrant people with Nalgene bottles and hemp shoes. They're visiting the island for the first time and they tell you with rushed excitement all about their adventures and travails, leaving you nodding and smiling for so long your teeth hurt. After they leave, you have a distinct pang of loneliness. Yes, you live in paradise, but you don't have anyone here. No one to eat dinner with or tell stories to. Forget romance—the only romance you can cobble together is the occasional fling with a tourist. The locals are too smart to get involved. You've been alone for a very long time now. You think of your family and friends back home.

Then, a few days later, you run into the couple again, who seem disturbed and upset. They tell you they had the stupidest luck on the beach. Philippe put their passports in a dry bag attached to his swim trunks when they went snorkeling at Anse Source d'Argent, and when they emerged hours later, sunburned and happy, they realized it was gone. They say it'll take two weeks for the French consulate to replace them, and while they have some money, they don't have near enough to stay for two weeks. You feel immediate concern for these kids. You wouldn't want to be on the other side of the world with no money. You could offer them a place to stay, but you never know these days, they might be serial killers. Maybe you should give them money for a hotel? That would be safest, but it would be nice to have some new hearts beating in your lonely house.

If you invite them to stay in your home, go to section 100 (p. 313).
If you give them money for a hotel, go to section 108 (p. 342).

55

From section 27

You go for it. Plunge right in and buy the gorgeous, gleaming Coral Arms. Your hand trembles ever so slightly as you sit in the lawyer's office and sign a stack of paperwork thicker than a phone book. Miss Sumpter and Mr. Cook are there to reassure you; they're both very pleased with your decision and say you'll have no more hassles after you're done signing these papers. After you sign the paperwork, a full-service property management company will take over and run the building itself. They'll take care of *everything*. The complete "life cycle" of the property is in their hands, everything from the remaining construction to the ongoing maintenance to transitioning incoming tenants. They'll act as manager, landlord, security detail, maintenance crew, and groundskeeper all in one.

Meanwhile, you get to lounge by the pool and host fabulous dinner parties and saunter around the complex enjoying your title(s). "Condominium Kingpin" and "The Tower Tycoon," or maybe "Queen of the Coral Arms." You probably won't hear these names for a while, though, since no one else moves in until construction is done, but that shouldn't take more than a couple of months. They're just tweaking little things, like finishing the outdoor tennis courts and surfacing the parking garage.

When you finally tell your family about your plans to pull up stakes and move to Florida, they all want to come, too. Well, sure, why wouldn't they? But you explain the narrow profit margin, which is based on 100 percent occupancy and how, with you living in the penthouse, you need every other unit to be paid for. *Penthouse? What penthouse? You're moving into a penthouse and we get stuck here?* Now they think your idea is crappy. Poorly thought out. *Stupid!* Don't you know about real estate bubbles and housing crashes and the horrible record-breaking hurricane season they've predicted?

When you tell your boss that you're quitting, he congratulates you with a grimace (also the vein in his forehead bulging). At your rinky-dink going-away party (held in the small conference room at 4:45 p.m. on a Friday), your coworkers smile tightly, barely suppressing their jealousy. Even when you try being humble and shrugging off your good fortune, it only makes the room feel smaller and hotter. Finally, when your boss's secretary starts reciting horrific crime statistics for cities without winters, you decide you've had enough of this little tempest in a teacup.

Enough! The story of your life awaits. Miss Sumpter has made your move a breezy dream by booking you and Aidan into an exclusive spa in Miami while she handles logistics. As you're being massaged, exfoliated, and rehydrated to the sound of prerecorded crickets, movers lug all your belongings across the country to the penthouse suite of the Coral Arms. They not only deliver your stuff, but put it all away.

When you arrive at the penthouse a week later, you're stunned. The sheik of Dubai could live here, or at least one of his more popular wives. Stepping off the elevator, you almost lose your balance as the doors open directly into your living room, a vaulted glass room with white marble floors, looking out over the vast ocean below. The glass walls create the sensation of hovering inside a clear bubble twenty stories above the sea, providing spectacular views and a thrilling kiss of vertigo.

The glass room opens up onto a brushed-aluminum terrace, which circles the building and connects all the rooms, each beautifully designed with Esteban's éclat aesthetic. Miss Sumpter has an inventoried list of all his "surrendered belongings," which furnish the apartment and are both opulent and odd.

The living room is dominated by a huge, electric-blue Lucite coffee table and a pair of dramatic red leather sofas. The bedroom hosts a mysterious ten-thousand-dollar mattress, which lies on the floor with no frame. The chandelier above the dining room table is your favorite. The inventory calls it a "Floating Fire System, handcrafted in Germany." When it's off, it just looks like a long, empty aquarium hanging over the table. At the flip of a switch, however, fuel jets inside the glass case ignite and an elegant fireball dances to life. It's an aerial fireplace. When turned low, the flames flicker down into small individual flames, like a sleepy chorus line of apricot ballerinas. When turned high, the flames leap up, roaring into an impressive blaze. Aidan says it's the coolest fucking thing he's ever seen and the only thing that could make it better would be an open slot for roasting marshmallows.

That first night at the penthouse is one of the most romantic nights of your life. The ever-helpful Miss Sumpter has an incredible dinner delivered. Carts filled with sumptuous foods are wheeled in—shrimp cups, filet mignon, double-stuffed potatoes, chocolate éclairs—and copious amounts of red wine, which you drink on the terrace while watching the distant lights of ships as they cross the ocean.

At midnight, Aidan leads you to the balcony. He kisses you and looks up at the stars, turns around this way and that like he's looking for one star in particular. "Just be patient," he says under his breath, and his foot starts tapping, which is something he does when he's nervous. "What is it?" you ask, afraid he has something bad to tell you. Then there's a brilliant flash of light across the sky. *Fireworks!* People on the boardwalk below start cheering and cars honk their horns as the sky lights up. Aidan's shaking so hard while rooting out a black velvet box from his pocket, he almost jettisons the thing over the balcony.

"It's this," Aidan says, and gets down on one knee.

He asks you to marry him.

"Come here!" you say, pulling him up. "Are you telling me you planned fireworks for tonight?"

He shrugs. "Sumpter might have helped," he says. "So what about it? Will you?"

You smile, lean close to his ear, and whisper, "You know I will, big guy, just sign a prenup!"

You nuzzle his neck and reach up to kiss him, but he pulls back. "What did you just say?"

You smile. "It's no big deal! Bossrock says every millionaire has one."

Aidan marches off to the bedroom. You follow, your voice getting louder and more shrill. You ask him *what's wrong, what's the big deal, why is he so upset?* He spins around, angry. He never thought you'd be so selfish and disloyal. You tell him you love him, but you have to protect your assets. He should want to protect them, too!

"I do!" he says. "I didn't know I was the one you needed protecting from!"

You argue for hours, until you've both cried, you're both hurt, neither of you can believe how horrible the other person is, and it becomes perfectly clear that if you want to marry this man, there will be no prenup. Either marry him with no strings attached or let him go.

If you insist on having a prenup before you'll get married, go to section 111 (p. 351).
If you marry him without a prenup, go to section 128 (p. 401).

56

From section 29

You type in your password and authorize the transaction. These idiots just want their money and then they'll go. After you click the ACCEPT button, they copy the authentication code and then Gun Clown shoots you point-blank in the chest.

It turns out the attack was paid for by *your uncle*. He paid an old military buddy to get that money for Lanie's surgery one way or another. Either through your willing cooperation or through your death. (Your mother apparently told your uncle that you'd drawn up a new will and left a medical fund for Lanie in the event of your death.) So Lanie gets a new kidney, and you get a coffin. (Then Lanie's new kidney fails and she gets a coffin, too.) Your medical fund buys her one hell of a nice reception, though, with a commemorative booklet about her amazing life and an opera soloist who sings "Ave Maria."

In heaven, it's like a crowded train terminal. You walk around dazed on a busy platform. People rush past, announcements blare overhead, steam engines hiss, everyone seems panicked to catch their trains. "Where do we go?" you ask someone racing by. They point up to a big automated destination board, displaying arrivals and departures.

NEXT LIFE	TRACK	LEAVING	OCCUPANCY
Egypt, cotton fields	2125	Imminently	33 percent full
Calais, waitresses	854	Eventually	15 percent full
Global, motherhood	4197	Indefinitely	82 percent full
Thunder Bay, taconite mine	7264	Usually	2 percent full
Qatar, zealots	757	Late	51 percent full
Vatican, priesthood	665½	Endlessly	SUSPENDED

NEXT LIFE	TRACK	LEAVING	OCCUPANCY
Global, the meek	0928	Whenever	79 percent full
London, Sotheby's	2214	Momentarily	N/A—waiting
San Francisco, vegans	963	Hourly	46 percent full
Jerusalem, Christians	756	Unexpectedly	1 percent full
Beloit, soy farmers	5719	Sunup	19 percent full
Venice, Hells Angels	8163	Sundown	23 percent full
Anchorage, strippers	7564	Midnight	92 percent full
Delhi, holy men	7564	Midnight	92 percent full
Global, pets	76	First light	Overbooked

People load on and off trains. Everyone's on their way somewhere else. Overhead, a woman with a British accent repeats herself in different languages.

You have thirty seconds to board your next life.
Vous avez trente secondes pour embarquer la votre vie prochaine.
You have thirty seconds to board your next life.
Avete trenta secondi per imbarcarti sulla vostra vita prossima.
You have thirty seconds to board your next life.
Sie haben dreißig Sekunden . . .

Thirty seconds?

Why thirty seconds? What's the rush? Then you look down and the corporeal essence of your arm is slowly turning to mist, vaporizing in long tendrils up into the air as you stand on the platform. What's happening? Is this what happens? Do you turn to smoke if you don't board a train?

You search wildly for the life you want and run breakneck for track 5542. As you board your arm resolidifies. No wonder people pick crappy lives; they hardly have time to pick at all. You got lucky, though, even though it'll be a bit of a wait till this train pulls out; you got what you wanted. You picked the "Rarely" train to Capistrano. You always wanted to be a sparrow. Or is it a swallow? Either way, you want to be a small winged thing. You're done being a human. Humans suck.

57

From section 30

So begins your first small business venture, Bacchanalian Tours, specializing in exclusive trips all around the world. Bacchus was the Roman god of wine and revelry, known for his love of excess and luxury. (When not capitalized, *bacchanalia* refers to a riotous, drunken festivity, but that works, too.) On your first tour, you and Aidan take six tourists, who pay three hundred thousand dollars each, to visit the culinary mecca of Spain.

Your group stays in deluxe hotels and eats at Michelin-starred restaurants, where they enjoy specially prepared meals from award-winning chefs. In San Sebastian you eat at Mugaritz, where the chef creates individual works of art almost too exquisite to eat. Smoked scallops with foie gras and mustard seed, cheese gnocchi in Iberian salted pork bouillon, wild turbot with borage reduction sauce, seared cheeks of sole with acacia honey, chocolate cake bites with cold almond cream and cocoa bubbles.

In Madrid, you dine in the stark white dining room of La Broche, where you drink 1996 Arzuaga Ribera del Duero Gran Reserva while the chef prepares purée of boletus mushrooms with *jamón ibérico*, lentils on planks of duck liver, confit of cockscomb, lamb sweetbreads with squid ink and champagne foam, roasted escargot with miniature violet potatoes, seared skate with gazpacho-filled pot stickers. For dessert there's pistachio sponge cake, cocoa sorbet, and an aioli of licorice with gin foam and black-beer ice cream.

The trip is a big success. Besides the excellent restaurants, you visit vineyards in La Rioja and Penedés, take cooking classes in Andalusia, sample olive oil in Granada, and shop for exotic food stuffs in Toledo, Ávila, Salamanca, Burgos, and Laguardia. All your clients give you rave reviews and promise to recommend you to their friends.

The second tour you take is bigger. Twelve people join your patented personalized "Spice Tour," wherein you lead clients around the world in search of the freshest, rarest, richest spices. At the beginning you present each tourist with a handmade wooden box that holds two dozen glass jars inside. These jars will hold the spices they buy. After the trip, it's a beautiful keepsake/spice box and the airtight containers keep the bus from smelling like a curry house.

The original Spice Tour covers India, where clients pour into the colorful rivers of the open-air markets to buy delicate, pink-petaled ginger flower, tangy betel nut, lime pastes, and dried red chilies that lie shiny red in turquoise boxes on the market tables. Ground fine as chalk or rough as rubble, the spices are every color of the earth and forest and flower and sky. Every flavor connects to unattached memory. Vanilla bean/dried witch's finger, paprika/walls of Siena, mustard seed/goldenrod field, cinnamon sticks/rusty pipes, cloves/little railroad ties, lentils/lime green ticks, lima beans/baby buttons, cumin/Egyptian clay, masala/sunset in Oia, rosewater/melted pink ice cream, saffron/spilled blood, cardamom seed/parking meter head.

In Goa your tour rolls down a long red clay road flanked by towering palm trees, where you get a private tour of the Sahakari Spice Farm, which employs hundreds of workers and a stable of speckled gray elephants to work the plantation. They grow chilies, curry leaves, turmeric, cinnamon, nutmeg, vanilla, cardamom, peppercorns, cloves, betel nut, cashews, and jackfruit. The popular thatched restaurant on the grounds serves a banquet of traditional Goan cuisine including *feni*, the local cashew fruit liquor; *ambot tik*, a slightly sour curry dish; *surmai*, a delectable fried kingfish; and *bebinca*, sweet layers of thin coconut pancakes.

The Spice Tour is so popular you book up tours for the next year and expand your touring areas to Thailand and Japan. Amazing! You and Aidan love the prospect of traveling together nonstop. How lucky are you? You spend the next three years showing people around the world, always moving onto another amazing location, endlessly eating phenomenal food, and it's all so incredible and awe-inspiring you become quite sick of it.

Traveling wears on you. You and Aidan are both sick of suitcases and customs officials, and you're especially sick of your clients. Foodies can be the pickiest, most demanding tourists on earth. Sometimes you'd rather shepherd goats through the streets. You've tried to hire other people to lead the tours, but things always go wrong when you're not there. They frequently go wrong even when you are.

You're at a cheese tasting at Le Sirenuse in Positano when one particular group pushes you to the brink. According to them, nothing has been right all week. They didn't like the hotel rooms, they pooh-poohed the restaurants and private dinners you arranged, and they have now spent hours, possibly days, one-upping each other in an unending game of "better than this." As in, "I had a foie gras in Toulouse that was better than this," or "The grappa at Satsko in New York is better than this."

It's exhausting.

You realize you don't want to do this anymore. You hate this. It's killing you. You don't want to spend one more minute with these people. In fact, when the group loads up for Rome, their final destination, you consider staying in Positano. You really should go with them, but you feel like you'll explode if you do.

If you go back to Rome, go to section 120 (p. 376).
If you stay in Positano, go to section 150 (p. 487).

58

From section 28

You gamble. It takes you the better part of two days to get dressed, and by the time you arrive at the track, it's late and half the races are over. It's also cold and the mostly empty stands are strewn with damp garbage.

This is *such* a bad idea.

Still, you're here, so you get a program and try to smell the winner, like Grandpa Joe used to, but it doesn't work. The overpowering stench of your own abject failure out-stinks everything. You choose a horse at random, just like you used to do on multiple choice tests, when you knew any attempt at actually solving the problem would only hurt your odds. You pick number seven and put all your money down, a thousand bucks, which you barely scraped together by rummaging through all your coat pockets and cleaning out your car for quarters.

You take a seat in the stands and stare at nothing. So here it is. The grand finale. At least when your horse loses, you can go home. A scruffy-looking guy in an old trench coat makes his way up the aisle right in front of you and says, "Mind if I sit here?"

You shrug.

"Sorry, kid," he says. "I'm not a creep. This is just my lucky seat."

He plunks down and unfolds his racing program, which relieves any anxieties you had. It's covered with the frantic notes and scribbles of a gambling addict. He's here to bet on horses. Nothing else.

"You got action?" he asks.

You nod. "All to win in the ninth on lucky number seven."

He checks his card. "Seven, huh? Who's that?"

You shrug and he looks up with a mildly amused, somewhat disgusted face. "You bet everything you got on a horse and you don't even know his damn name?" The guy shakes his head. "Well, kid, whether you're really smart or just reckless as hell, you're still damn good-looking, so I think everything's gonna work out for you all right."

Oddly, that makes you feel a whole lot better. Then the warning bell sounds, and the guy's riveted to the track. As the starting bell goes off and the horses fly out of the gates, your cell phone rings. *It's Aidan.*

"Aidan? Can you hear me? *Hello?*" Nobody's on the other end of the line. You can hear a rustling, though, and a door slamming. Then a car starts and your stomach sinks. This does *not* sound like a planned phone call. This definitely sounds like one of Aidan's notorious pocket-dials. Now you can hear a female in the background. Feminine voice. Pretty. Aidan says something, and just hearing the familiar resonance of his deep voice simultaneously soothes you and makes you sick. Something's wrong. You can almost hear what they're saying . . . but it's too damn loud. You sprint up the steep stadium steps and dash across the long concessions hall into the women's bathroom. "I really think you should," Aidan says.

"You do?" The girl giggles and you hear more rustling, like the phone rubbing up against fabric. "I just want the wedding to be perfect," she says.

"And that's why I love you," Aidan tells her. "That's why I can't wait to marry you."

The phone drops from your hand and splits open on the cement floor, the battery skittering under the sink and the back panel shooting under a stall. The room tilts violently and you catch yourself on the hand dryer.

"You all right, sweetie?" Two women in matching blue Windbreakers have walked into the bathroom and somehow surmised your phone is in pieces all over the floor and you yourself aren't feeling well. They pick it all up and help you reassemble everything. Nice of them. Although you weren't planning on touching that phone ever again. Outside, in the concessions hallway, you just stand there. No telling for how long. Time stops, everything stops. Your heart is hammering and you can't breathe. "Kid!" the trench-coat guy suddenly shouts. "Where'd you go? Did you see it?" He's smiling big at you but it's like he's not really here, but on a TV show. The whole place seems somewhere else. None of it is real.

"Your damn horse!" he shouts. "Number seven! She won, kid! Don't you get it? It was her maiden race. Hey, look, it's my buddy Glue Bucket, the Lucky Horse!" A teenager wearing a fuzzy horse costume comes over and fake whinnies at you as he hands over a complimentary T-shirt. He grins. "I told him you won, kid! What's wrong with you? You have a stroke or something?" You shake your head no. "You need a drink then?"

You nod and he tugs you over to the cocktail bar, where the bartender says, "Hey, Rick," and sets down two shots of whiskey. You don't drink whiskey. "Well, you drink it today, kid. Here. Down it. One shot. Let's go. You're killin' me. Drink the damn shot!" You down the warm amber liquid in one gulp, and by God if your new friend Rick isn't a damned genius. All the color, which had drained out of the room, comes filling back in. You can feel your feet now and your fingertips.

"Okay, look," Rick says, "a maiden race means the horse never won before. Nobody expected her to tonight, either, so the odds were stacked high against her."

"They were?"

"You know what that does to guys like me? I study the stats and research the jockeys and then you come in here and make a bet so blind it could've been an ostrich running around out there, and then you *win?* This could set me back for a long time. I might as well start picking horses based on their frickin' horoscopes or something."

"How much did I win?"

"How should I know, kid? Am I your bookie? How much did you bet?"

"A grand. All I had."

"Well"—he smiles—"then the next round's on you. The odds on good old number seven were . . . twenty to one." You start screaming and grab him, hugging him, jumping up and down. Who cares if you had to listen to Aidan and his slut-bride. None of that stings nearly so bad when you're suddenly twenty grand richer. You punch Rick in the arm and tell him how happy you are. "Kid," he says, "welcome to the best feeling in the world. Hang on to it. Now let's get drinks and head back. Only two races left."

"Are the windows closed? I wanna make another bet. I can do it again."

Rick says those are some pretty damn dangerous words. Everyone's sure they can do it again. He recommends enjoying your big win and not risking it. You guess he's right. You just had this feeling you could pick the next winner . . . but it's probably adrenaline. "I forgot to tell you the best part about your horse," Rick says, ordering two more whiskeys for the road. "Number seven's name."

"Let me guess. *Fat Chance?*"

"Nope," he says. "Come Hell or High Water."

He keeps on talking and it takes him nearly fifty yards to realize you're not walking beside him anymore. You're over at the betting windows, staring hard at the tote board, where they list all the horses and their odds.

"C'mon, kid," Rick says. "I don't want you to do anything crazy."

"Sorry," you say, "I'm going again. All I have is crazy."

You get to the window just in time. You're considering a dangerous idea . . . placing the granddaddy of all bets—*the superfecta*. It's the toughest bet in all horse racing, where you pick the top four finishing horses *in exact order*. If you bet on the next race and win, you'll have four hundred thousand dollars in your pocket. Of course, if you bet on it and lose, you'll have nothing. Rick points to a Gamblers Anonymous hotline number up on the wall. He begs you to take the money you already won and go home.

If you place a superfecta bet on the next race,
go to section 147 (p. 480).
If you take your money and go home, go to section 149 (p. 486).

59

From section 29

You decide to make a break for it. When Gun Clown looks down for a split second, you use your free hand to grab the edge of the laptop and crack Cue Card Clown in the side of the head as he bends over to check your foot ties. Then, with superhuman strength available only to animals on the brink of their own demise, you rip your still-tied hand free and chuck an end table at Gun Clown while simultaneously hurling yourself through the sliding door and sailing over the balcony into the shrubs below.

The police say it's a *miracle* you're alive, and while they would *never* recommend someone take on assailants like that, it's the only reason you survived. It turns out the attack was paid for by your uncle. He paid his old military buddy, Bruce, to get that money for Lanie's surgery one way or another. Either through your willing cooperation or through your death. Your mother apparently mentioned to your uncle at some point that you'd drawn up a new will and left a medical fund for Lanie in the event of your death.

Wasn't that nice?

Yep! *So nice* that your uncle wasn't going to wait for you to die of natural causes! They did in fact plan on killing you if you didn't hand over the money, and maybe even if you had. The irony is Lanie has some miracle recovery after one of her new doctors did some test no one had thought of doing before, and they realized that another kidney transplant probably would have killed her. Nevertheless, her father's going to jail and the rest of them can go to hell.

That's when Gun Clown's sister calls. She actually calls your lawyer, who relays her sincere regret at her younger brother's actions and she apologizes for his behavior. Something happened to him in the war, and no one knows what, but he's never been the same and basically has been going out of his way to fuck up the world ever since.

Long story short, she wants to give you something to try and right her brother's wrongdoing. Their family business is a fresh seafood grill on Orcas Island, the largest of the four islands that make up the San Juan Islands off the coast of Washington State. It's in a small mellow village with a few restaurants and hotels, a big health food store, and a community of mostly artists. The only thing guaranteed about Orcas Island is that it's far away. It could be peaceful and quiet, a great place to start a new life, or it could be a huge fuckup.

Hard to say.

Part of you just wants to buy a big mansion right here near your parents and hunker down until you feel safe. That was one hell of a situation, and to find out members of your own family were behind it—well, you don't know if you'll ever see the world the same way again.

If you buy a mansion, go to section 105 (p. 334).
If you move to Orcas Island, go to section 136 (p. 438).

60

You take the first job you can find, selling magazine subscriptions door-to-door and it's as dangerous as it is unprofitable. The company, Integrated Inc., is run out of a cheap highway hotel room and hires runaways, hobos, and ex-cons. They send these bedraggled fleets out onto the sidewalks to sell every kind of periodical—sports, beauty, science, news, fashion, teen beat, senior, architecture, travel, food, wine, auto traders, livestock, and so on—but nobody, absolutely nobody wants to buy magazines from some stranger who just unexpectedly rang their doorbell.

The few people who are even willing to open their doors wrinkle their noses at your magazine selection. You're not offering them the *New York Times* or *People* magazine, but strange-sounding knockoffs instead, like the *New York Magnet* and *People's* magazine. One particularly sour woman in a pink housecoat crosses her arms and says, "I wouldn't read any of those damn magazines! Not one!" Out of irritation or maybe plain exhaustion, you say, "Fine. God knows what you'd read."

She furrows her brow and answers your question. "A Christian sex magazine!" she says. "Never seen one of those. I'm a good Catholic, been married thirty-five years and I never cheated once. Same man this whole time and not one new idea between us in the same thirty-five years, either. I want someone to tell me how to make it fun in there. And cat calendars!" she shouts. "I want a goddamn Christian cat calendar!"

You walk home, wondering if you've just had the worst day ever . . . or been given the best untapped niche market idea of all time.

Christian porn.

You take the last of your money and start *Practical Procreation*, a marital-aid magazine geared toward Catholics and their Anglo counterparts—

Lutherans, Episcopalians, Protestants, Baptists, conservative Unitarians, liberal Mormons, and all the rest. Inside the semi-glossy pages are tightly focused images of married couples having sex in the missionary position only. The expressions on the women's faces are of grim acceptance while the men show ambitious apology.

Popular feature articles include frank conversations about timing procreation, whether "it" should take five minutes or ten, and acceptable bedside manners (for example, shouting out "Mercy!" is acceptable, while "Oh God!" is not). The magazine gathers a wide readership and many dedicated sponsors, who advertise everything from personalized family Bibles to God-friendly marital aids. *Lambskin of God condoms—ribbed for your rapture! Eucharist panties, edible and wafer-thin.*

The magazine fills a much-needed hole, so to speak, and your fortune begins to build. You start a publishing conglomerate, which is bought out by a Japanese holding company. You become a Big ol' Fat Mega Millionaire. (You're not fat, *your money is.* You're stinky rich. You're like *take a bath in gold bullion* or *buy a German tank for kicks* rich.)

So, whatcha gonna do with your big money?

First you buy your way out of the Lanie mess, by giving each family member a million dollars. Let them spend it on their potato of a daughter if they want to.

Then you change your phone number and move to Paris, where no one can find you. You need to focus on yourself. You've been granted a second chance, and you want to make the right choice this time.

You could simply become a bon vivant, a French term meaning "good at living." (It's actually French for "good liver," but that sounds gross.) Bon vivants are jet-setting world travelers. They're intelligent, educated, entertaining, popular, and pretty. They attend opening nights at the theater, get invited to all the best parties, date B-list celebrities, relax in tranquil Spanish villas, coast about in big luxury yachts, invest in artistic pet projects, all the while buying whatever they want, whenever they want, carefully cultivating a never-ending life of style and ease.

Some people, however, feel that no matter how much money you have, you could always have *more*. No matter how big empires become, they could be bigger. Certain people find this ideology greedy and ugly, while others insist it's the only responsible course of action for someone to whom much has been given. Some people are here to be empire builders. Captains of industry who aren't just *rich*, they have real power. The ability to move mountains. They can implement major changes and have lasting effects on society. Empire builders haven't much time for rest and relaxation, though, nor for parties and dating. If you travel, it's for business, not pleasure. Empire builders are all work and no play. They also own megayachts, however, and go to the White House for dinner.

If you become a bon vivant, go to section 106 (p. 338).
If you become an empire builder, go to section 114 (p. 361).

61

From section 30

You and Aidan decide to buy a vineyard. You were nervous about finding the right property, but fortune strikes and you're able to acquire two hectares in the Vosne-Romanée commune in Burgundy, France, at the northern end of the Côte d'Or, that great limestone ridge that produces some of the world's finest wines. Neighboring vineyards include some of the very best—Les Malconsorts, Cros Parantoux, Les Chaumes, and Clos des Réas. You know you'll never compete with them, but you do hope perhaps you can learn from them.

Your luck finding such a coveted piece of land rides the back of misfortune. The village lost more than forty growers recently due to economic turns and fickle Pinot Noir crops. Maybe that's one reason you get such a chilly reception. People in this village don't like outsiders and you struggle to fit in.

It doesn't take you long to learn tranquility and excellence aren't natural-born friends. Excellence of any manner requires blood, sweat, and tears, which are not native ingredients to tranquility. You pretty much have to pick one or the other. A neighboring farmer works the land since you don't know a thing about growing crops, but there's still so much to do. The vineyard is hard work, even with staff. Celeste Scott is your winemaker, Alex Galet your vineyard manager, and Vincenzo your handyman/landscaper and sometimes personal chef. What that young man can do with an omelet is not to be believed.

You open up to tourists and it's like an invading army of fat, demanding ants marching all over your property. They want tours of every aspect of the vineyard—the fields, the storage caves, the tanks, the warehouses; they ask to see your private house and would gladly snap a picture of your toilet if you let them.

Rumors start in the village. The wine giant Mondavi is making bids to purchase land in this area and the prices they're offering have convinced at least two vineyards to sell.

Sure enough, Mondavi representatives get around to contacting you and they offer you double what you paid for your property. If you want to get out of the vineyard business, now is the time.

If you sell the vineyard to Mondavi, go to section 122 (p. 378).
If you keep the vineyard, go to section 124 (p. 385).

62

From section 31

All right, you want to give this money away and do something good for your fellow man, but how? You could travel all over, handing it out to strangers like a Guerrilla Miracle Machine. Or you could build some type of sanctuary right where you are, where people from all over can come for help.

If you become a traveling Guerrilla Miracle Machine,
go to section 123 (p. 380).
If you build a sanctuary right where you are,
go to section 126 (p. 395).

63

From section 24

You decide to buy the island in Dubai. Just in time, too. There's only one island left for sale. Ohio. "No one wanted it," Bossrock says. "I don't know if it's because people haven't heard of Ohio or because they have."

You decide to turn Ohio Island into a big five-star hotel. Something amazing that people will come from far and wide to see. It will be your own slice of specific paradise, a unique experience that inoculates the weary patient from any prior conditions of boredom. Think of the beauty, the tranquility, the perfection of having your own blank canvas of an island to do with whatever you like. It will be fantasy incarnate—and fun!

Bossrock finds you a fancy New York hotel developer named Gabe Stone, a chubby little man (whose pants are too short and look painfully tight in the crotch) who's known for his "blockbuster hotels" all the way from Daytona to Miami. Gabe sees inherent problems built into your new property. "I don't like how Mid-East-y it is," he says, squinting his tiny eyes into the hot sky. "Can we get the sun less bright? It's a little much, isn't it? And who wants to be out here a million miles away from civilization surrounded by the towel heads? We gotta make this island feel like America. That's the only way to get people to come."

Bossrock convinces you Gabe is right. You've already dumped half your money into the purchase of the island and his services have been prepaid. So Gabe spends two years and basically the rest of your money building a giant Victorian hotel called:

ALWAYS OHIO!

ALWAYS AMERICA. ALWAYS OHIO.

Always Ohio? You stare up at the enormous sign over the ornate trellised veranda. Gabe says to trust him, so the ALWAYS OHIO! sign is bolted in place over the double-wide saloon doors (which lead inside to a cowboy-themed lobby). The rooms are furnished with bright white wicker furniture and carpeted with a repeating pattern of the American flag. There are barber poles on the front desk and racks of teddy bears and Civil War memorabilia on the walls. It looks like a T.G.I. Friday's, but not as good.

A chugging yellow crane has already finished anchoring a huge plaster facsimile of the Statue of Liberty on the pitched roof. On a clear day her lit torch (red liquid crystal and orange neon) can be seen from as far away as Abu Dhabi. Gabe Americanizes everything; he landscapes the gardens with oak trees and even sprinkles dandelions around the walkways, named "Columbus" and "Toledo" so no matter where you go, there's the reassuring sense of being in America. "But isn't it good we're in this exotic place?" you ask. "Why not use the tropical lushness instead of hiding it? Have a spa with sea salt and mango treatments and a restaurant with fresh coconut cocktails?"

"Been done," Gabe barks. "Been done a thousand times! And you want to see a person who's allergic to coconut? This guy. I'm allergic to coconut. A coconut rash is the most god-awful fuckin' rash there is. Oozes and itches like you got coconut coming out of your pores. Besides, maybe you've heard of a little place called *Branson*?"

You nod. Yes, you've heard of Branson. The place entertainment goes to die.

Gabe snorts. "Branson's the biggest moneymaking vacation destination west of the Mississippi. I built the whole city, practically. I know what I'm doing." So whatever. You let Gabe do what he does, which is apparently look up every single thing Ohio is famous for and replicate it. He litters the lobby saloon with Buckeyes memorabilia and mounts a display of lightbulbs, since Ohio is where the incandescent lightbulb was born. Outside he grows various species of corn in a "soil exhibit," located inside the atrium on the east lawn, which is right next to the manicured "mounds," so landscaped because Native Americans known as Mound Builders inhabited the state at one time.

While all this creativity is going on, you stay in Jumeirah, which is the nearest metropolitan city to your watery island world. You shop during the day, and in Dubai there is a lot of shopping to be done. The Dubai Mall is over nine million square feet and has a ski park, where you can snowboard, tube, or go downhill skiing, which is a nice break because it's hot in the city; sand is always blowing up from the baked streets, stinging your eyes, and the sounds of endless construction pound around you night and day.

Some of the most terrifyingly modern and magnificent structures are being built in this city right next to ancient stone mosques and roads originally created by the Byzantine Empire. Some have said Dubai is like a clever child with overly indulgent parents.

Anything it wants, it gets.

Even though the city is located in the middle of the Arabian Desert, emerald green lawns, massive fountains, and verdant gardens run like rivers through it, despite centuries of drought. They strive to have the biggest, the best, and/or the first of everything and anything.

Dubailand is twice the size of Disneyland, making it the biggest amusement park in the world. The Dubai Waterfront development is the largest in the world. Palm Island is the first and largest man-made island that can be seen from space. The world's tallest hotel is located here, as well as the world's first underwater hotel, and the Al Burj, the centerpiece luxury hotel of the Dubai Waterfront holds the title for tallest man-made structure in the entire world. It exists within multiple weather zones simultaneously, the ground floor enjoying the desert climate while the top floor is chilly and well above cloud cover. The coup de grace is the Dubai Space Port, which is still under construction. It will offer luxury intergalactic travel, when intergalactic travel is available. They like to be ready.

When your hotel is finally ready for the grand opening, you want everything to be perfect. The New York–style hot dog buffet, the Confederate flag decorations, the imported swans gliding elegantly across a simulation Lake Erie. The hotel is filled to capacity; even Bossrock and his wife are there. You arranged for a grand picnic with a giant fireworks display, even though the forecast is for clouds and a chance of rain. There's always a little rain at every memorable picnic.

The guests are good-natured about the tents and umbrellas; they enjoy the old-timey banjo quartet and the bugler brigade. But then the rain knocks down the awning over the shrimp bar and the wind picks up. Everyone hurries inside and weather forecasters warn of a tropical cyclone forming thirty miles out at sea.

The storm is a fantastic vortex of chaos, a class-six cyclone, which crashes onto the southern tip of the island, carrying a surge of water taller than the boats moored in the bay. The younger trees lie almost flat against the ground as the wind howls down against them; fronds of the larger trees are ripped right off. Tiles on the roof start peeling away; the torrential rain plasters down and turns the manicured lawns into moving rivers of mud. The storm is getting worse. Officials say everyone should get to the mainland, but the water is swelling and some boats aren't making it. You must either evacuate your guests or ride out the storm here.

If you stay on Ohio Island, go to section 97 (p. 308).

If you evacuate the guests, go to section 99 (p. 312).

64

From section 32

If you can't have that boat, no one can. Fueled by three bottles of red wine and a belief that the American Indian ancestors native to this area would approve, you row out to the marina to sink the white man's boat. Under the cover of darkness and armed with a fully charged cordless drill, you tie your skiff to the dock next to *Against All Odds* and drill two-inch holes in the yacht's hull until she scuttles. You can hear water blurbing up in her belly as you row away. She'll be down by dawn. You're near giddy imagining Dirk's face when he hears the news. His party barge is now a freshwater reef.

Your lawyer calls in the morning, he's coming right over. The marina security cameras caught everything: your face, the skiff, the drill, the yacht going down, the electrical lines going with it, half the harbor grid shorting out. The harbormaster watches the security tape and tells the reporter interviewing him that only the *worst sort* of criminal would scuttle her. He shakes his noble head sadly and says, "A true sacrilege."

You're sued blind.

County prosecutors, Dirk's lawyers, the Duluth Port Authority, they all file suits against you. Even the Environmental Protection Agency is suing because the boat had hazardous, flammable something-or-other on board.

Then, a month later, the insurance company says they're suing you for fraud. What fraud? You didn't file an insurance claim. Well, they have a claim and it has your signature on it. If you didn't send it in, who did?

Dirk, the human skin tag, that's who.

He reported the vessel sinking to the insurance company, claiming *Against All Odds* went down in an accident. He figured it was worth a shot, since the yacht and the insurance policy are in your name and it's *your* signature on the claim form. (His practice really did pay off!) When all the mediations, negotiations, trials, and deals are done, you're lucky to walk away broke and not in jail. Dirk gets the house and you get the only job you can find.

Working on a salvage boat.

Superior Salvage (SS) is famous for finding the first house that ever sank in Lake Superior. It was an exquisite Victorian being shipped by freighter. It was 1889 and some railroad tycoon wanted the first Queen Anne in Thunder Bay. Somebody thought it was a good idea to load one of the finest homes on Beacon's Pointe onto a cargo barge and then run her up the shore during a rough patch of weather in late October.

The ship made it to Thunder Bay, but the house didn't. She capsized when sudden swells pitched the boat so far to starboard that the house broke her own moorings, snapped them like fiddle strings and crashed overboard, leaving only an orphaned cupola on deck.

When crews went searching for the drowned house, nobody could find it. There was some confusion on the exact coordinates of where she went over, and it was anyone's guess which way the current might have dragged her. After searching in vain and finding only minimal wreckage on the coastline, it was decided the swells must have broken her apart and carried her off in pieces.

That's what people thought happened anyway, until the notoriously unsafe crew of Superior Salvage took their fearsome ship, *Doll Baby*, out for a canyon dive. The area is usually avoided, since it's too deep for salvage, but the crew of SS was combing the very edge of the underwater cliffs, when someone spotted a giant, house-sized box of algae lodged halfway down the drop-off. Of course it was Squid who got his deep-dive gear on first and shot down for a look. When he came back up, he said the algae box had windows, and that's how they found the drowned Queen Anne of Thunder Bay.

Now people call Superior Salvage to retrieve anything under the water that's impossible to find or crazy to try and bring up. Sunken ships, lost cargo, scrap iron, even old timbers coveted by furniture manufacturers and heart pine floor makers. They use high-tech and low-tech equipment on board the *Doll Baby*, which is rigged with everything from side-scan sonar used to digitally read the bottom of the lake to chunks of foam and inflatable inner tubes that float up awkward-sized cargo.

Hickey, the hard-drinking captain of the *Doll Baby* and self-titled "Wreckmaster" of the operation, rattles off a long list of items he's retrieved while watching you do your best to coil ropes neatly and not knit a sweater. "Fuck," he says, "I brought up a thousand whiskey barrels once, with whiskey still fuckin' in 'em! And we found a Model-T Ford and a spiral staircase and once we hauled up a motherfucking *wicked* cigarette boat some douche bag smashed up, it cost like *eight hundred thousand dollars*, and then I was like, *Here ya go, buddy!* and handed him a pile of shit worth nothing. What a *douche bag*. The worst haul was this German freighter that broke into like eight pieces, and the insurance company needed it up before the lake iced over, so we worked day and night in some seriously fucked-up weather. We all nearly died on that one. That's the weirdest shit we've pulled up I can think of. No, wait! There was this huge crate of cheese once! Like all this motherfucking cheese! Some guy said it was from France or something and we also found a cow skeleton."

It doesn't take long to realize Great Lakes divers are a special kind of crazy, because going down to those depths, in that darkness, with those temperatures isn't *natural*. You get to go out with the crew on the dives, but you stay on the boat monitoring the sonar screen as the divers drop down to the murky floor and root around for their treasures.

If they radio up for object location, you're supposed to give them the coordinates for *objects of interest* you see on the screen, which is anything that looks man-made. They might as well let a sack of damp sugar watch the monitor, though, because these guys would rather ask for help changing their loaded Pampers than for help finding a haul. That would be *totally pussy*, to quote Captain Hickey.

In general you get along pretty well with everybody. They're all rough, splintery guys who are too impressed with their own stories to spend much time harassing you about yours. Nobody's even asked you where you came from or where you stay in town, which is at a miserable little hotel that doesn't have cable. So you learn to stay pretty quiet and you pick up as much dive training as you can without anyone really taking the time to show you what to do. It's on an otherwise routine dive when the crew is retrieving a load of coal, which is about as much fun as it sounds like, when you spot a very distinct shape on the sonar screen.

It's a violin case.

There's no mistaking its sharp outline among the blurry marine growth. It's set just off to the side of where the divers are concentrating and you hold your breath wondering if they'll find it. You could radio down and tell them it's there, but something holds you back. An hour drags by and then another, and finally the draining light forces everyone to the surface.

Nobody saw the case.

Only you. It's your secret.

What could be inside a violin case this far away from shore? Your mind reels with possibilities. Maybe it's an innocent-looking transport for wads of stolen cash or a severed human head. Maybe it holds a priceless violin lost at sea when a symphony drowned. God, that's ridiculous, it's probably just empty.

Still, the violin case haunts your dreams, and when you wake up the next morning there's only a brief window of time to decide whether to tell the crew about your mystery musical case. The *Doll Baby* is headed near the same area today, but they're combing farther south with the current, so the divers will be even less likely to make the discovery. If you tell Hickey and Squid you saw a violin case on the monitor yesterday but forgot to tell them, you're pretty sure they're going to be pissed at best and fire you at worst. If you don't say anything, you'll avoid the whole awkward confession altogether, but you'll never know what's inside your violin case lost at sea.

If you keep quiet, go to section 110 (p. 347).

If you tell the guys, go to section 129 (p. 412).

65

From section 32

Furious at your own stupidity, naiveté, and plain bad luck, you furiously pack up Oziyapi and leave immediately, telling your lawyers to let Dirk have whatever he wants. Good riddance. The sooner you get out of here the better.

On the flight home you sit in first class next to a friendly business developer named Steve, who has a big project going on. A real-estate deal in North America, which promises to revolutionize city planning. Steve seems pretty cool and not too pushy at all. He gives you his card and tells you to think about getting involved, but don't take too long to decide, because they're only going to take one more partner on board and there's already a few people interested.

At home it's nice to see your family and friends, even though they all insist they always *knew* Dirk was a jerk. Why is it people think they're doing you a favor by *not* telling you they dislike your boyfriend? Well, because if you end up with him, then you'll be mad at them. But isn't that still a pretty crappy reason that puts your welfare on the back burner and lets your friends avoid potential conflict? Sam is the one person who was always forthright about not liking Dirk. She's headed out for a two-week relaxing vacation and says you should come with.

If you invest in the business venture, go to section 130 (p. 417).
If you take a relaxing vacation, go to section 134 (p. 430).

66

From section 34

·

You take Boy A. Adam, the tall blond who definitely knows massage and really, really passionately enjoys cunnilingus. When he gets done with you, you're afraid he'll have diaper rash on his face. Then he takes you to your gourmet kitchen and whips up a batch of vanilla cupcakes. When things get steamy on the kitchen counter, he takes one of the cupcakes, places it like a creamy target over your vulva, and sinks his cock through it right inside you. You are getting cupcake-fucked.

Soon you're left spread out across the bamboo countertop, smeared head to toe with frosting, legs weak from flexing up in the air and panting like a long-distance runner.

Your session has concluded.

You call up and ask when Adam can come back and the desk says he's in another session, but directly after that. Okay, good. Send Adam.

He comes back and ruts you again and again until you are really feeling a lot better about life. You ask if he can sleep over and he kisses you deeply, saying he'd love to. He even brought a toothbrush just in case. In the morning you order up a big breakfast and a fruit platter and *Good Lord* what this boy can do with a piece of papaya!

You spend the next several days trying out your boy on the special sets. You take him to the executive suite, where he puts on a three-piece suit and you put on a stiff secretary's pencil skirt before he ravages you in the conference room. Then he rows you out on the placid lake in a boat called the *Tru-Luv* and does you doggie-style in front of a pair of elegant, staring swans. Then he lifts you up in the Sex Island ski lift and nearly wobbles the tram off the wire while pressing your face and chest against the steamy Plexiglas windows.

Adam is sweet, but not smart. He's a little glassy-eyed and you're pretty sure he's high, but when you ask, he says, "I'm only high on you, baby." Then, when you're headed over to the fire engine, a small folded-up piece of paper falls out of his uniform pocket (he's dressed as the fire chief) and you secretly look at it. It's an entire list of "Things to say when you don't know what to say," provided to hospitality emissaries while out on dates with clientele. There are lines like:

"I like a woman who eats."

"You're not old. To me you're brand-new, baby."

"I've never felt a connection like the one I have with you."

"Want to buy me a gift at the Companion's Canteen? Leather goods are half off."

"I'm only high on you, baby!"

He has used each and every one of them on you already and you did buy him a leather belt at the Companion's Canteen. You're calling reception to order up a new boy, but you inadvertently press the button that connects you with the automated billing center, which tells you how much your bill is to date.

Holy Jesus, you gotta get off this island.

You've already spent three hundred thousand dollars! You quickly call the front desk and tell them you'll be taking the next helicopter out. You've got to get back to your life. The receptionist says she's sorry you're leaving Sex Island and would you like a good-bye send-off from your favorite companion with complimentary crying and discounted champagne?

No. Thank you.

You leave Sex Island. A week later you're back home and having dinner with your family at the Sizzlin' "T" steak house, when your throat starts to get sore. The next morning you wake up with the flu. Fatigue, sore throat, headache, and a heat rash. You go to your doctor to see if antibiotics or Tamiflu would help, but after you tell him you're glad you got sick now and not when you were on your wild Caribbean vacation, he asks if you've had any unprotected sex recently.

Well, no! On Sex Island everyone wears condoms! (But then your mind sorts through your sexcapades with Adam and there is one, no, two incidents that stand out. Once you woke up and Adam's very sticky, completely nude penis was stuck to your vulva. You practically had to peel it off. Then there was the time you thought the condom broke and you asked him if it did, and he said no but ducked quickly into the bathroom, saying he had to pee.) You tell the doctor no, you haven't had any unprotected sex. He gives you a certain look, just the slightest flaring of the nostrils, and says he wants to do more tests.

He draws some blood and gives you a mouth swab, then tells you to go out into the lobby and read a magazine while you wait for the results. An hour later the nurse calls your name, you go back and sit on the crinkly paper on the examination table, and the doctor comes in with a clipboard.

He tells you that your mouth swab tested positive for the HIV virus. You probably caught it on your "vacation."

Not possible! Doesn't it take years for that virus to show signs? Nope. He says symptoms can start immediately and you're lucky they did, because you have a few more options, but before you go too far down the treatment options path, he says it's prudent to wait for the blood tests to come back, just in case the mouth swab was a false positive. A *false positive?* What the fuck is that? Are these people deliberately fucking with you with these confusing terms? Do you or do you *not* have HIV?

He says he'll know for sure in a week.

So you go home and lock yourself in your bedroom and weep. You pray to any god that might listen. You make deals, swear off all vices, and promise to donate all your money to AIDS research if the universe will just make you healthy. Friends call, they want to go out for coffee, for cocktails, to the movies, but you don't pick up the phone. How can they go merrily along with their stupid lives when yours might be over?

No, think positive. If you believe you don't have HIV and you mean really *believe*, then you won't. The universe will correspond to your thoughts! In fact, your flu starts to lift and your symptoms begin to clear. Hallelujah!

Then the doctor calls. Your HIV blood test was positive.

You have AIDS.

No, you don't have AIDS, the doctor explains. You have the HIV *virus*, and with the right treatment program, you might never get AIDS. HIV only becomes AIDS if your T-cells drop low enough, and you're nowhere near that now. The particular doctor you see recommends you wait to start treatment. Some studies recommend starting treatment right away, but then the side effects of the medications will start right away, too. Diarrhea, nausea, lethargy, chronic fatigue, fevers—it can be debilitating. Many people have to stop working and socializing when they go on meds. All they do is sleep.

This doctor leans toward what other studies say, which is that a newly infected HIV patient should *wait* until symptoms of the disease begin, and that could take up to a decade or more. The idea is to get yourself as healthy as possible before that happens—begin vitamin supplements, exercise regimens, get the body and immune system iron-clad—so when and *if* your viral load jumps, you'll be in the best shape to fight it off. People who go straight onto medication hobble themselves right out of the gate and don't give their body a chance to get ready before the battle begins, if it begins at all.

You decide to take his advice and wait for treatment. You go home and do major research on AIDSMEDS.COM, where you learn about all the things you can do to get your body strong before starting a drug cocktail. You read story after story about people living with HIV, and the one thing you learn is you'll need help. Nobody goes through this alone and no one has to. So you start off by telling your whole family what's happening. You just get it out on the table. *Splat.* The ones who can stay will stay, the ones who have to go will go. So be it.

Then you start exercise programs—jogging, swimming, biking; you take megadoses of vitamins, wagonloads of supplements, and impose strict dietary restrictions on yourself. (No wine! No sugar!) You get tested for any household toxins or food allergies that might compromise your immune system. (Mold! Red meat! White bread!) You fast, you cleanse, you colonic. You eat healthy. You won't allow yourself a single mini marshmallow.

Not one.

Soon you're a regular at the gym. Your body slowly starts to change. Your skin firms, your arms tone, your legs narrow. People say you look *fabulous*! What's your secret?

You just look them in the eye and say, "I have HIV! Isn't it *super*?"

Every night after your cleansing regime, you sit down and power through new studies, recent findings, current reports. There's a new expensive HIV gene-therapy treatment. Scientists discovered that certain people are immune to HIV, because they have mutant CCR5 genes in their white blood cells. Little ugly tough-guy monster genes that inhibit HIV. Everyone else, like you, for example, has normal nice-guy wimpy CCR5 genes that say, "Hi, Mr. HIV Virus! How ya doin'? Come on in and put your feet up! Take cream in your coffee? Of course you do!"

The doctors speculate that by cutting CCR5 genes out of white blood cells, they might make a patient resistant to HIV. It's worked on rats and the procedure is simple. First they do a simple blood draw and remove some of your healthy T-cells (assuming you have any left). They snip out the CCR5 genes, throw them away, and grow approximately ten billion new T-cells in a petri dish. Then those new, improved T-cells go back in you and go to work. Hopefully.

You elect to have the procedure. They say it's new, it's experimental, and it costs about five hundred thousand dollars. *Fine!* I have HIV, you *fuckers! Hook me up!*

So they do. They take an infected blood sample, send you away, and have you come back in two weeks after they've grown CCR5-free T cells in a dish. Then they hook you up to an IV drip and make you sit in a chair reading *Better Homes and Gardens* for three hours while your new T cells march into your veins. You cheer them on. "Hey, new white blood cells! You rock! Get ornery, motherfuckers! Go say, 'Hi, Mr. HIV! How's about I blow your head off with a rocket grenade?'"

The IV drip finishes and now all you can do is go home and wait. On your next checkup three weeks later, the doctors are astonished. They say your

T cells have rocketed and your viral load has plummeted to near zero. Your HIV is "undetectable." That's the word they use. It means there are fewer than twenty-five copies of the virus per *one milliliter* of blood. In your case, there are *no* copies. None.

You are clean.

You fly out of your chair, twirl the doctor around, dancing and screaming. Nurses come running, you kiss them all on the cheek, and you zoom out of that hospital, speed-dialing every person you ever knew and shouting, *"I'm completely clean, bitches! Clean!!!!!!!!!!!!!!!!!"*

This feeling is on fire. You can't afford to keep anyone away from this, you want anyone who ever had the red vine creeping through their system to know what this is like. You start a fund at the hospital for gene therapy, available to those HIV-positive patients who normally couldn't afford it. You take all of your lottery money, every single penny, and put it all in this fund. You have to give up your house and turn in your car but you don't care. You move in with your parents and take the bus. You sing. Burst out laughing. You can't help it, you're going to save people's lives! As many as you can.

The fund is so odd, so unprecedented, with so few, in fact with *no* restrictions, the press takes note. Normally to be eligible for a fund you must qualify. Be of a certain age, income level, be in a specific stage of the disease, and so on . . . but not your fund! Your fund says, "This money is for anyone who needs HIV gene-therapy treatment. Age, gender, income, health condition, treatment compatibility, disease stage, shoe size do not matter."

The local news station does a story on you and it's picked up by the Associated Press. *Nightline* calls you. Senators working on health care reform call you. People start to donate to your fund. Patients, parents, siblings, children, congressmen, Hollywood actors, other countries, and your grandpa. They send what they can, and some of them send quite a lot.

The fund becomes a foundation and elects you CEO. Starting salary of three hundred grand a year. You have friends in Washington, D.C., and in Congress who help pass laws legalizing the federal funding of gene therapy and stem-cell research. Your name is lauded everywhere. Banquets are thrown, hospitals name auditoriums after you, and you receive thousands of packages, presents, and private notes from recovering HIV patients, who tell you their stories and thank you for your work.

In a stunning surprise decision, you're awarded a Nobel Peace Prize. Members of the Norwegian Nobel Committee said their choice was an early vote of confidence in your foundation's ongoing commitment to improving worldwide health. With the HIV therapies you've made available free of cost, the face of this horrific worldwide epidemic is changing.

They see great things in you.

You buy a farm in Vermont and a small condo in Washington, D.C., alternating between the two. In your office there are children's drawings pinned above your desk. For this is the true river running wild over the groundswell in your heart. The drawings you've received from children. They're often of shining suns and families holding hands, and underneath the pictures are large Crayola messages. Block print and determined. Your hand shakes when you read them. They say, *I feel better now. I go in the sun.*

You live a glorious life and don't pass over until you are ninety-nine years, four months, and three days old. They count every single day in heaven.

67

From section 35

You decide to keep the money, for no reason except it's too stupid to give it away and you don't believe in curses or bad luck. What you do believe in now is karma.

It's your fault Sam is gone. It's only because of *you* Sam was on that ship. You are responsible for her death, and now you have to work it off. You have to do something big. Something amazing. A true test of character and courage.

That's when you see an article in a travel magazine about people with disabilities training to climb Mount Everest. *Mount Everest?* Seriously? That's the tallest mountain in the world. One out of every five climbers dies up there! Well, that's sort of the point, isn't it? Absolution comes hard. Forgiveness is found on mountaintops, not in cookie jars. You have to do this. You're *going* to do this.

You can see why mountain climbing is a millionaire's sport. The gear you need is stupid expensive! Climbing helmets, down parkas, pile jackets, climbing boots, wool socks, gaiters, booties, crampons, pitons, ice screws, ascenders, chock nuts, pulleys, snow stakes, carabiners, trekking poles, ski goggles, army knives, water bottles, pee bottles, sleeping bags, stuff sacks, ice axes, and the list goes on.

Gear is one thing, but guides are another, and you find the best. Mr. Brad Kitchell is ranked number one for climbing and guiding on Mount Everest. He runs a training camp in the Himalayas, and he says it's pretty late to start training. His next climb is in four months and usually people train for six. You swear you'll do whatever it takes to catch up, you'll train for as long and as hard as he says and you'll also pay double. That seems to convince him.

One astronomical payment and a stack of signed disclaimers later, you're on your way to the Himalayas. When you finally arrive at the training camp, doctors run a battery of tests: EKG, EGD, VO2 max, pulmonary, blood, urine analysis, and so on. . . . Physical trainers assign you a sadistic schedule, where you exercise for *eight hours* a day, always doing something absurd, possibly for their amusement, like running ten miles while wearing a backpack filled with damp kitty litter, or jogging up and down the aluminum bleachers by the track while carrying big rocks. It's a brutal regimen and your body rebels by vomiting, bleeding, and occasionally just passing out. But those trainers are sadists. No mercy for you. Your freaking heart could pop out your left eye socket and they'd say, "Really? You're giving up *now?*"

So okay, you know it's crucial to push your body past all known limits, but more than once you want to take that seventy-five-pound kettle ball they make you do walking lunges with and lunge it right at their heads. Whenever you're not training, you're playing sports with other members of your expedition. Basketball games, volleyball tournaments, and racing each other in the Olympic-sized swimming pool.

Weeks are spent climbing rock walls, practicing rope techniques, learning crazy-ass knots, walking in crampons, and crossing slippery crevasses on aluminum ladders. (The last two are done in the camp's indoor ice-skating rink.) Your teachers use an effective combination of Zen meditation, careful explanation, patient repetition, and good old-fashioned yelling until you're "one" with your harness, ice axe, and jumar. Until you could teach your mother how to rope-up, tie-in, belay, lead, rappel, aid-climb, lower and climb while attached to fifteen other people and not screw up your rope systems. Knots are apparently not your natural talent. Kitchell says the only way to untie some of your knots is with a hatchet.

At dinner you sit with your fellow trekkers and wonder together what the top of the mountain will be like. You're almost like children gathered around candlelight, sharing bits of knowledge with each other, trying to conjure an imaginary place. You talk for hours and listen endlessly to each other's adventure stories, everyone opening their treasure chest of trips and sharing all the lucky breaks they had, the near disasters, the once-in-a-lifetime sights, the unexpected lessons, the best diarrhea cures.

It's a great group of people, twenty-two in all and from all over the world—Australia, Iceland, Canada, Brazil—and everyone is smart. Maybe world travelers just tend toward intelligence. They see more. Listen more. The group gets along well enough to stumble into heated political debates about environmental policy. You can hardly keep up. It's like a world summit where the dignitaries wear wool socks.

You won't all go up the mountain together, though; the group will be split in half. Mount Everest has two main climbing routes, and in order to keep the treks safe, the groups have to be small. So one group will go up the mountain on the north side and the other group will go up the south, and you'll meet at a prearranged point near the top. Both routes are epic and amazing and safe. Well, as safe as Mount Everest gets.

If you take the north side of the mountain, go to section 140 (p. 449).
If you take the south side of the mountain, go to section 142 (p. 456).

68

From section 98

You push on the smaller door and it creaks open. Dust billows up in your face, making you sneeze and stumble into the room, causing the fragile floor to give way. You tumble head over heels, bumping and cracking along until you land on your back. Painfully.

There's warm, fluttering central pain near your heart, like a dozen red-hot butterflies escaping. When you look up, there's a crude wooden spear sticking out of your sternum. You are impaled on a stick, like a corn dog.

You die slowly, bleeding out in a few hours.

When you're finally dead, your spirit drifts up through the broken floorboards, through the thick slice of earth and the tangled vines and thick trees, through the leafy uppermost branches and into the fresh air and dark sky. Then you bounce back, caught in some sort of spidery net made of chalky ash that hovers over the whole island, preventing escape.

Slowly, you descend back toward the ground.

You are now one of the spirits of the island of San Lucas, doomed to eternally wander these bloody, spoiled grounds. You can see all the other alabaster spirits drifting in and out of the jungle, rough men with torn clothes, all lost, who tell the same stories over and over again. They tell of their hideous crimes, of the prison they endured, of the shackles they wore, of the endless torture, the cruel guards and vicious commandant. They cry. They cry and cry and cry until every frog and bird on the island is drowned out by the constant wailing.

Maurizio doesn't report your disappearance. Instead he poses as you and has the rest of your money wired into his account and business starts to pick up again. Old Santiago goes missing, no one knows where. When your family comes looking for you, Maurizio greets them all warmly and puts them up while they search in vain for you. They never do find you, but they find the old prison remains and play softball in the exercise yard. Maurizio buried the manhole cover in a few feet of dirt—it provided an excellent pitcher's mound.

69

From section 99

You get into the jeep with Gabe and he speeds away, swearing and swerving like a merchant marine. A block later he drives right into the back of a stalled insurgent munitions truck, which explodes on impact. The fireball can be seen from even the farthest balconies in Abu Dhabi. This compels Sheik Nahyan to make the call. Fire the nuclear weapons at will.

In hell you get to explain everything.

70

You pick Boy B. His name is Benoît Beaumont Desrosiers, or "Bo" for short, and the moment he walks through the door you feel something perceptively and uneasily shift inside you. He's stupid gorgeous, as you'd expect any man candy for hire would be, and naturally he's charming and attentive, but there's something else. Not just the heart-starting dimples, or the hypnotic Alsatian green eyes, but a pervasive and authentically feral quality he manages to express in almost every move he makes, even sitting perfectly still and gazing at you. Like a wolf deciding whether to eat you.

His natural comfort around you makes you even more (delightfully) uncomfortable. He sits down on the plush white couch beside you and pours his own wine. You ask how he came to work at the island, then you're embarrassed you said "work," but he shrugs it off and says, "I'm here because I want to be." You end up spending the whole weekend with him, and rather than doing anything unsavory, you spend long hours talking about yourselves. He's originally from a farm in Nice, a quaint coastal town near Monaco. He's working his way through law school because he wants to defend human rights victims. He wants to practice law and own a small farm with lots of children and a wife he adores.

When you tell him about your fears, of growing old alone, of not knowing exactly where you're supposed to be, he listens intently, and then finally sweeps you up in his arms, throwing you on the bed like a rag doll before pummeling all the fears right out of you. Afterward, he holds you naked on the bed as a gentle breeze comes from the sea through the window. He kisses you and it isn't a Sex Island kiss, it's a heaven-on-earth kiss.

You hate that Bo works here. At the end of your stay you make him an offer. If he comes back with you, you'll help him with school. Tuition. Books.

It's nothing permanent, just a place to stay while he takes a few classes. You'll also help him find work that's better suited to a man of his character. Bo looks away at first and you think maybe he's angry, but when he looks at you again, he's smiling and he kisses you long and hard.

Bo settles into your home. He's a tough sell to your family and friends, though, who're sure he's a gold-digging gigolo. But Bo shows them what he's really made of. He applies to Harvard Law School and gets a full scholarship. You buy him a posh penthouse apartment in Boston, where you learn to play tennis while he gets his degree.

While you spend giddy days shopping for lingerie and gourmet dinner ingredients, your darling pores over his law books. He wants to support you and he'll be able to soon. He works so hard! Some nights you have to beg him to come to bed and you shouldn't, you should let him study, but Bo is a god in bed. A six-packed Zeus with ripped arms and hips like pistons. When he opens up inside of you, it's like nothing can come between you. You're one hot, pulsing, electric fire.

Two years later, Bo graduates from Harvard and says he wants to move to Monaco, where he can open his own practice and start helping people, but first he wants to know if you'll marry him. His proposal catches you so completely by surprise it takes you a full minute to find your voice and say *Yes!* You spring into his arms and cry, then he makes love to you in that tender, savage way reserved exclusively for romance novels and the French.

It's Sam who suggests a prenup. You can't believe how unromantic she is, but as your best friend she just wants you to be safe and to know this guy is for real. It's not that you haven't thought of the idea yourself—but you don't want to offend Bo or make him think you're doubtful the marriage will last. Still, if he loves you, a little paperwork shouldn't scare him, should it?

If you don't ask Bo for a prenup, go to section 131 (p. 422).
If you ask Bo for a prenup, go to section 135 (p. 433).

71

From section 35

You give your money away. All of it. Donate it to the Peacefighters, which is an unusual group funded by anonymous titan-of-industry donors who are passionate about extreme social work.

They don't just hand out pamphlets and answer hotline numbers; they get in there and get their hands dirty. Their training programs are extensive. It takes sixteen weeks to become one of the facilitators, which is what they call volunteers trained in a specific field.

After reviewing their work and reading all the many testimonials from elated, enthusiastic volunteers, you even decide to become a facilitator. This way you'll get to see your money at work. You won't be one of those lofty, removed philanthropists up in some ivory tower. No. You're going to get your hands dirty, too.

There are two different facilitator groups accepting new volunteers right now. You can become a "Connector," resolving conflicts and helping people achieve greater awareness through mutual understanding, or you can be a "Liberator," promoting the higher ideals of freedom and change through motivation and education. Both groups get cool Peacefighter tote bags.

If you want to be a Connector, go to section 141 (p. 453).
If you want to be a Liberator, go to section 143 (p. 462).

72

From section 36

You're not having a baby and getting stuck here forever. No way. You call Jim-Junior and tell him that your mother's sick. You have to take care of her. Then you fly to Chicago, check into the Drake Hotel, and get an abortion at the nearby hospital. The nurses, while efficient and friendly, aren't entirely honest about the procedure. It's not quick. It isn't painless. But you *are* relieved when it's over.

Maybe you're feeling uneasy or it's that Jim-Junior keeps calling to see how your mother's doing, but you decide after you've healed you should return to Nutwood and tell him you want a divorce in person. You owe him that. So three weeks later you fly back, drive to the plantation, and let yourself into the house, which is eerily empty. You thought maybe there'd be some sort of "welcome home" for you planned, but no, there's nothing, because you weren't there to plan it. Then the phone rings.

It's the sheriff. His voice is calm but serious. He says they've been trying to get ahold of you all day. Jim-Junior and Miss Meridian Vivcott Rae were both killed this morning in a head-on collision. They were en route to the bank, when the driver of a Birds Eye frozen food truck lost control and crashed through the median, right into their car. It was awful. Blood and broccoli all over the highway. Officers wept, he doesn't mind telling you; Jim-Junior hosted the annual policeman's ball.

The lawyers tell you it must have been fate that took Miss Meridian Vivcott Rae just then, because she was on her way to sign an amended will, one that cut Jim-Junior completely out of her will if he didn't cut you out of his. The papers were all drawn up and ready to go, but they never made it to the bank. The lawyer shakes his head. That woman's going to be mad as a wet hen when she gets to heaven and finds out what happened to the entire family fortune.

The sale of Nutwood is an affair that won't soon be forgotten. So many people wanted to buy the historic property that Sotheby's holds an auction in New York City. The highest bidder turns out to be a Japanese conglomerate that wants to build a large intake facility for all their immigrating employees. It'll be like Ellis Island, but in Louisiana and for Japanese people. Sayonara, Miss Meridian Vivcott Rae!

You move back to LaLaurie and everything is just as you left it, except Mirabelle is gone. She apparently walked in on her husband pile-driving a twenty-six-year-old coat check girl from the country club. She was more than willing to overlook the infidelity, as she had so many times in the past, but her husband claimed to be in love with Cherry-Ann and left her. Poor Mirabelle. *C'est la vie!*

You decide to throw yourself a coming-home party. A big one. Something grand. Something racy and raunchy and where anything can happen. A masked ball. The theme will be Marie Antoinette and you will be the resplendent queen, presiding over your royal court. If any of your loyal subjects don't like it, let them eat cake.

The concept of throwing yourself a coming-home party, or a *Thank God I'm finally free!* party is not new, especially in the realm of the Southern belle. Here women regularly celebrate recent divorces, new widow status, and any newfound ability to move freely in society unencumbered by a male overlord. If that newfound freedom includes a financial windfall, so much the better. You, darling, have a lot to celebrate.

It's a big job to throw the perfect masked ball. So many details and everyone so frequently getting things wrong. Your headaches are endless. The costumers make a gorgeous blue silk gown with matching blue silk slippers, but they forget to sew crystals on the cuffs and hem, which you specifically asked for. Then the decorators put the gold gilt trellises on the east side of the ballroom, not the west, so everything has to be undone and rearranged right at the last minute, which you hate.

The caterers are your biggest challenge. You asked them to make all of

Marie Antoinette's favorites. Sugary pink petit fours surrounding a silver fountain of warm Guittard chocolate, lavender madeleines dipped in lemon glaze, bread pudding with bourbon sauce, mousse au chocolat, profiteroles au chocolat, tarte amandine, soufflé au Grand Marnier, and, in honor of Mirabelle's absence, warm cherry crepes.

To round things out you want a smaller savories table with a selection of soft, medium, and hard imported cheeses alongside silver trays of crawfish profiteroles in citrus butter sauce, miniature beef Wellingtons, shrimp étouffée, brochette Luciana, oysters Rockefeller, and grilled baby lamb chops with dirty rice and maque choux.

Not so difficult, right?

But you'd think you asked for the moon marinated on a platter. Everything they do is wrong. You have to spend half the day of the party sweating in the kitchen showing the chef how to do everything. You hardly have any time to get yourself ready. Impossible. Your head is throbbing, like a ball-peen hammer is trying to pound its way out.

You're still getting ready as your guests arrive, and the kitchen girl comes up to tell you the chef forgot to make the bergamot cupcakes, and you feel this electric arc of white-hot anger flash across your temples, blinding you with fury. You throw the hairbrush you're holding and the girl lets out a scream as she ducks. Ridiculous! The lady of the house is allowed to have a tantrum! It's what you pay for! You stand up, not about to let her escape her scolding, and she runs, terrified, for the balcony. You follow her, shouting. She scrambles to one end of the balcony and, finding herself trapped, makes a mad scramble for the drainpipe, like what does she think you're going to do? Kill her? She does a fine job herself, losing her grip on the slippery ivy, and hurtles headfirst to the ground below, splattering her insides everywhere on the pavement.

You go to jail and the papers call you Madame LaLaurie II. You write your memoirs in prison, but they aren't very interesting.

73.

From section 38

You get permission to work night hours at the Tom-Tom Varietease Club as a "washup" girl. The Tom-Tom is a burlesque show on Bourbon Street that's been running since 1948, when skin artists like Blaze Starr and Evangeline the Oyster Girl dazzled the quarter with unusual and risqué sex acts. Now it's run by a thin, angular woman named Violette who has blunt-cut bangs and smokes her Marlboro Reds in a long black cigarette holder.

Violette gives you the job and says you could even perform onstage, but you say no thanks. This place is a little gritty. The girls are big, one of them is possibly pregnant, and you don't know which dancer the smell is coming from, but there's definitely some questionable hygiene going on.

The girls here are into some weird stuff. Candie-Babie wears short babydoll dresses and sings German ballads while sucking a big bottle of milk. Sheba is covered in tattoos and juggles knives, catching the occasional blade handle with the impressively strong lips of her shaved pudenda. Miss Astrid drips hot wax on audience members while they lick whipped cream off her thigh-high patent leather boot. Honey Bee breathes fire with kitchen matches and aerosol cans of carburetor cleaner, and Betty Cocker packs her vagina with boiled cherries in cream, which she then eats with a spoon.

Bubble, the comedienne, is the only one who tells jokes and the only one who doesn't get naked. She just delivers deadpan monologues while licking a phallus-shaped Popsicle. "This was a popular place once," she says to the darkened room, "but ever since the economy's gone flaccid, we've been hit deep and hard. Recession hitting the sex industry is hard to swallow, but it's normal to expect some shrinkage. If I get laid off, I'll just pull out and spread my . . . wings." Sometimes there's a laugh from the audience, sometimes not. The audience is populated with low-rent pimps, falling-down drunks, and the homeless. At least they look homeless. There's a fight or two every night. Some guy pounds the bar and starts shouting, "HOW THE FUCK DID THIS MAGICIAN BITCH STEAL THE TWENTY IN MY HAND WHILE LOOKING RIGHT AT ME!"

In back is a row of small bedrooms with swinging saloon doors, where ladies take their tricks. Your job is to clean the rooms in between appointments, a job as unseemly as it sounds, and requires you to wear not only arm-length industrial gloves but sometimes a mask. You don't know what the girls do in there, but besides all the standard messes you'd expect to find in a bordello—dirty sheets, condom wrappers, spilled vegetable oil— you also find ingredients you can't imagine in *any* sexual recipe: wads of used aluminum foil, jars of empty salsa, carpet samples, and once, a sloppily stacked pile of telephone books.

The girls each have their own room and every room has a locking red-lacquered Chinese cabinet where they keep their oils and toys and props. *Man*, do you wonder what else they have in there. For the most part you don't talk to them; they're hard at work, and when they're not seducing businessmen in the back rooms, they're pickpocketing customers out front or they're onstage performing.

The best part of work is leaving and walking through the empty streets. By then dawn is breaking and the whole quarter has emptied out. It's quiet and peaceful and you can think for once. The streetcars are mostly empty and you usually ride alone back to Calvary House, stopping occasionally for another night shift worker or a drunk tourist still looking for his hotel. Before you get to Calvary House, though, it's important to shed any evidence of the strip club. There's a strict rule banning residents from working at bars or strip clubs, and you told the Christian ladies the Tom-Tom Club was a music store. Naturally many women break the rule about stripping—like LaFonda, who lives down the hall. She claims to have had parts in *Womb Raider*, *Shaving Aidan's Privates*, and *Star Whores*, so if she can get away with living here, so can you.

Time passes and you stick with your dismal job, but you can't seem to save enough money to move out of the shelter. You're not sure where all your money goes. You eat out a lot, but who wouldn't with the slop the Baptists serve. It's not like you're sitting down at the Café du Monde for beignets; you'll grab a Po'boy on the way to the club sometimes or pick up a slice of pizza on your way home. That's it. Sometimes you have a drink or two after your shift, but that's just so you don't kill yourself. You bought a new jacket and shoes, but you needed those. You've got to find a way to make more money.

Then the curtain falls. You get busted. After work one night, you ring the bell to get in and a staff member comes to the door with all the stuff from your locker in a brown paper bag. Someone saw you coming out of the Tom-Tom Club and ratted you out. *But where will you go? Where will you sleep?* Not their problem. Good day. Door closed. You go back to work because you don't know what else to do. Violette takes pity on you. Mops you up and gives you a drink. She says you can always get up onstage, the money's great. Otherwise she has a cousin who owns the only gun shop in the French Quarter. They've been looking for a girl.

If you work at the gun shop, go to section 42 (p. 137).
If you perform onstage, go to section 89 (p. 277).

74

From section 140

You decide to help the children. When asked how far the statue needs to travel, they just say, "Little ways, little ways." So, with some repurposed carabiners, climbing rope, and harnesses, you hook the wooden platform up to your bikes. Then you start peddling. Unlikely horses with strange cargo. The wagon won't move at first, the wood creaks like a haunted house. But then, just as you're sure this won't work, the wagon heaves and the wheels are off and slowly turning.

You look over your shoulder from time to time and catch sight of the Buddha, bumping and jerking along behind you. Soon enough your muscles are screaming and your calf muscles are ready to give out. How heavy is that statue? Five hundred pounds? You all struggle forward across a barren field of gravel. At one point the guy in the lead stops and asks how much farther and the children just say, "Little ways, little ways," so you trudge on.

By dusk, you arrive at a thatched barn and a very old man comes out. His smile is wide, exposing pink toothless gums, and he motions for you to hurry your treasure into the barn, as though hurrying were an option. It's night and you're exhausted through the bone to the marrow.

By the time you wheel the cart inside you're ready to pass out. Finally the group is led inside a small house and given hot soup with fresh basil. Then you're all shown several mats scattered around the floor, which feel as comfortable and plush as the royal suite at the Ritz. You fall asleep, resting your head on sacks of grain, and it feels like heaven.

Your dreams are short-lived, however, because around dawn the farmer wakes you up, shouting *poh-reece!* The Chinese police are coming.

They're already here, up at the gates and searching for a group of tourists who stole a statue. You stumble up, barely able to grab your pack as you're pushed outside toward a small group of horses, which are already saddled and ready to go.

Madness, surreal flashing. You're on horseback alongside your friends and a lone Chinese guide is just ahead, galloping full-speed down a rocky canyon.

You are fleeing.

Where are you fleeing? You ride for an entire day and through the night and all the next day again. You make camp in another farmer's barn, kept far from the road or where anyone might see you. Apparently, your group is wanted for crimes against the country. You've stolen religious artifacts that belong to the government. The farmer and your guide tell you that if you're caught, the punishment is death.

Death?

Up again riding the next day, it's finally explained you are running for the Yunnan valley, the most southwestern province in China. It's a remote jungle filled with rare orchids and wild elephants. The jungle has been protected for centuries by soaring mountain ranges and steep river gorges. It hosts an ancient section of the old Silk Road, a stone path still traceable through the massive vegetation and towering bamboo forests.

You travel for weeks, first by horse and then by foot, hiking up merciless switchback mountain roads, hacking with machetes through looming, razor-sharp brush, camping on narrow ledges of crumbling rock, zip-lining across raging water. You finally arrive at a forest of banyan trees. Roots thick as elephant trunks grow aboveground in every direction, sloping up toward the canopy, crossing midair to connect with neighboring trees and weave into other root systems.

It's like a cathedral of wooden arms suspended above you, and built into the branches are a collection of small, crooked tree huts, no more than ten or twelve feet square and resting about six or seven feet off the ground. They call it the outlaw forest. It will be your new home for a while, your new village. This is the place to come when running from the Chinese government because they won't allow police to enter the forest. It's too costly. The cost pertains not to the police themselves but to the armaments and equipment they carry. The last time armed guards pursued criminals here, they all came back out stripped of their weapons, ammunition, and uniforms.

Everyone settles in. Your tree hut faces away from the others, the little hand-carved windows looking directly onto the nearby trunk of a neighboring tree. When you sit back you can see nothing through the window but this tree, the dark coffee-colored bark roped with braids of rough, sinewy roots and skirted here and there by small blooms of brilliant green fern. You could stare out the window for hours. Sleep clubs you with your boots still on and you fall into a dreamless slumber, heavy and complete. Paradise.

When you wake the next morning, the air is rain-clean and fresh and everything inside the hut is covered by a fine, pearling dew. There's activity outside; the guides have come back to lead you out of the jungle. After they make coffee, map out the route, and everyone packs up their gear before heading down the path, you announce that you're staying.

They can go on without you, but you live in this jungle now, it's your home.

The truth hits you well and it hits you hard. It's all a crap shoot, every single step a miracle and gamble. That's the beauty of it. That's the unorchestrated gorgeousness, the mad, dizzying light that storms between us. We all have to have fifty-fifty luck every step of the way, without rhythm or plan, and it must be this way just to let all the possibilities in. From now on you'll take your chances here. Luck tends to favor the beautiful.

75

From section 92

You choose the caveman hunt party. They're having it in the woods behind Bennigan's and the stage crew built these lifelike papier-mâché caves with a stone fire pit at the center for roasting a pig. They even put up extra green privacy fencing to block out the automatic motion-sensor security lights in back of Bennigan's, which flood the loading dock with bright light every time an employee takes garbage out to the Dumpsters.

Your role will be "Mogra," cave-wife to one of the important clan leaders. You will skin animal hides while your bushy-haired husband threatens to kill inappropriate suitors who have come from neighboring clans to capture your young virgin tribeswomen. You asked to tend the fire, which is a much more interesting thing to do for six hours straight, but someone else already had dibs on fire tending, so you were stuck with animal skinning or flea picking.

You chose animal skinning.

The party gets festive right away. Many of the participants went to Bennigan's while dressed in their caveman outfits for several rounds of green rum Shillelagh Shakes before showing up here and are guzzling even more cave brew from bowls shaped like plastic skulls. People are really into the prehistoric theme. They grunt and drag their clubs and have sex in the cave dirt without breaking character, probably because sex goes well with caveman language. It's got to be hard for the French Civil War reenactors to stay in character while they're humping. If they want to cry out during sex, they still have to conjugate verbs. These guys just go *Uh-uh-gah-uh* and it sounds perfect.

The night wears on and the cave brew flows, causing several people to pass out right on the ground next to the caves, which are filled with drunk captors and their conquered virgin tribe girls. You have to move your animal skins twice to keep out of the . . . *Klunk!*

Some jackass clonks you in the head with his fucking wooden club.

Everyone *knows* their weapons and implements of war must all be made from plastic, foam, or rubber for this exact fucking reason. It's written right on the information sheet everyone gets with party rules and driving directions.

Ow! The jerk doesn't even know he hit you.

He's gyrating in some elaborate mating dance with a fake-frightened cave girl. They don't even see you're bleeding. You feel a sharp pain in the back of your head, then you keel over and hit your head on one of the real rocks around the fire. You now have multiple head injuries and are surrounded by drunk, dancing cavemen.

When they find you in the morning, the last of the cavemen will be heading for their cars in the parking lot as a pearling lavender light breaks over the roof of Bennigan's. Someone shouts, "I don't think this one's sleeping!" Everyone's clubs will be confiscated so the coroner can determine which caveman hit you.

76

From section 36

When you return to Nutwood you sit down in an easy chair and put your feet up. Miss Meridian Vivcott Rae comes hobbling in demanding her tea, you tell her to get her own damn tea. *You are with child.* She pauses for a moment, studies your knowing smile, and her eyelids flutter briefly before she clutches her chest and rolls her eyes upward, as though an attack was upon her. "Don't bother," you warn. "If you pretend to faint, I promise you I am not getting up from this chair."

So begins the short-lived yet lovely era of carrying the Wadley heir. You no longer have to lift a finger. Everything is taken care of, nurses are brought in, nutritionists, massage therapists. Jim-Junior even hires an estate manager to run Nutwood, so you won't have to. He treats you like a goddess now, a sacred deity to be obeyed. Now you call the shots. You tell him that if he expects a healthy heir to his fortune, then the two of you should stop having sex, for the baby's sake, and you should sleep in your own master suite, and to keep your spirits high, you'll need at least ten new pieces of jewelry.

The coup de grace is when he moves Miss Meridian Vivcott Rae and her full-time nurse out to the guest cottage behind the house. You told him she was fraying your nerves and it might affect the baby. Lord, they could probably hear her tantrum in Shreveport! Yelling, throwing things, cursing people, threatening to change her will, threatening to take her own life . . . and when Jim-Junior allows her to hobble into your room to "say good-bye," she points a crooked finger at you and keeps her voice low so no one can hear her. "I got a girl on you," she hisses. "She's working right now and she'll put a curse on you!"

You just ripple your fingers merrily in the air and say, "Toodle-oo!"

The hag gets her wish, though. The delivery was brutal. Primal. Like pulling a piglet out of a pickle jar. Afterward the doctors are quiet, and in your epidural haze you can't tell what the matter is. Whispers. You get glimpses of the baby as she's passed from arm to arm; she's crying loudly and a healthy pink, but she's covered with strange brown streaks. Smudgy baby.

Then you sleep.

When you wake up, you are alone. No Jim-Junior, no flowers, no nobody. Then a nurse comes and introduces you to Dr. Baumeister, who specializes in genetic disorders. He tells you that your baby has Ambras syndrome, or *hypertrichosis universalis.*

Translated from the Latin as "very hairy all over."

He blathers on about statistics and studies, but ultimately says that due to the disorder's rarity, they don't know much about it, only that it causes "universal hair growth" at an accelerated rate. What he's telling you is you just gave birth to a girl version of Jo-Jo the Dog-faced Boy.

Your return to Nutwood is dismal. Jim-Junior stays locked in his study and Miss Meridian Vivcott Rae has moved back into the house. You've had no visitors, no calls, not even a card from your family. The staff won't make eye contact with you; it's like you're unclean now. Not to be touched. It is perhaps for this very reason that you and Tallulah, your baby girl, become so close. She loves touching you and you love touching her. Tiny little follicles crown the tips of her fingers and the top of her toes, fanning back into long silky swirls of caramel-colored hair that shifts and waves around her body like ripples in the sand made by water.

Tallulah is beautiful, perfect with bright eyes and strong hands, but no one else will touch her. Jim-Junior won't look at her and Grandma only comes to stare hatefully. When Miss Meridian Vivcott Rae tells Tallulah she's cursed, you're done. You tell Jim-Junior you're leaving and he can send divorce papers if he wants to. You couldn't care less. They can call themselves blue bloods if they want to, but all you see is white trash.

Then you pack your baby girl up and move back to LaLaurie. You research her disorder, even though it's an unfair word, "disorder"—who's to say she isn't the perfect specimen of this particular happening? What if there's a whole planet of people just like her not too far away? Your research shows congenital hypertrichosis, or Ambras syndrome, are extremely rare. Fewer than fifty cases have been documented worldwide. It's not terminal, has no known side effects or complications, and simply seems to be a case of good old Mother Nature having some fucked-up fun. It isn't fun for Tallulah, however, as she gets older.

She's afraid to go outside. She hates meeting people, doesn't want anyone to see her, and how can you blame her? Once she came into the kitchen to ask for a glass of water and the new maid screamed before running out of the room. When Tallulah watches TV shows and movies, she looks endlessly for someone like her, but there is no one except werewolves.

She wants to know why she's different and how to make the hair go away. She steals your razors and shaves off big patches of hair, which grow back more thickly each time. She burns her arms with scalding hot water, scrubs them with Brillo pads and sandpaper until she starts bleeding. You tell her she's beautiful, you tell her it's all right, but she says she's ugly and nothing will ever be all right in her life.

Then one day you see a strange woman outside the front door, staring.

You open the door. "Yes?"

"The girl Madame hex is here?"

"Excuse me?"

"The girl who was born like a dog, the one who hexed."

You tell her to get off your property and slam the door shut, your heart racing. Could it be possible? Did Miss Meridian Vivcott Rae put some spell on your daughter?

Tallulah will only leave the house at night. You get a limo with tinted windows and take her to Miss Edelle, who lives now in a wooden house by the river. The priestess is happy to see you and gives you her Masonic handshake before studying Tallulah with large eyes.

She lights the olibanum and takes out the asson. Then she tells you to leave, she must work on the child alone. Tallulah says she's okay, so reluctantly you wait in the car for two hours until you're summoned back inside. Tallulah's playing with marbles on the floor. "I cannot move de curse," Miss Edelle says, "because there is none. This girl's as she's meant to be."

Tallulah looks up from her game.

"What me say?" Miss Edelle asks her.

She grins. "I'm as I was meant to be!"

After that Tallulah is a different person. The curse is lifted. Tallulah starts to venture out more. Walking through the French Quarter you realize that if you're different, New Orleans is the place to be. The French Quarter is filled with characters, people who look strange and act delightfully even stranger. Tallulah loves it. She makes friends with the shopkeepers and everyone knows her name. She adopts a stray dog and names him Handsome Tom.

Months after visiting Miss Edelle, you're both out at the park when your cell phone rings. It's the sheriff calling from Nutwood. He tells you Jim-Junior and Miss Meridian Vivcott Rae were in a serious automobile accident this morning.

They both died at the scene.

You take your daughter shopping to celebrate.

The Wadley fortune goes to the only remaining heir—Tallulah. You ask what she wants to do with all that money and she says start a modeling agency.

For freaks.

Cirkus is the name of her agency, and she has models with every imaginable oddity: Siamese twins, lobster boys, albino dwarfs, women with scars, burns, and surgical implants, models who are blind, some missing arms or legs, "Trunk Girl," who's missing both. It's a great, strange success, this agency. Not only does Hollywood use Tallulah's clients regularly, so does the fashion industry and world-renowned photographers. The agency's motto, "Ugly is the new pretty," becomes so well known that the following year, the *Oxford English Dictionary* enters it as an official English idiom.

You don't sell Nutwood, that would be sacrilegious. It will stay in the family. Instead it becomes Sosyete of La Belle Deesse—Miss Edelle's school of Vodoo. You start as a *serviteur*, a newcomer, but after a while you study up to become a mambo.

Priestess.

The world is very fine after that. Very fine indeed.

77

From section 38

Working in a lab sounds much more promising than working in a bar, even if the hours are ungodly. You're told to show up at the office on Canal Street by five a.m. When you arrive, still sleepy and wishing you'd stopped at the Winn-Dixie for a free cup of coffee, you find yourself standing in front of the New Orleans Insectarium.

The building isn't open yet, but a security guard buzzes you in and tells you to go through the lobby, down the main corridor, and to keep going until you see the offices in back. You thank him and hurry down the shadowy corridor, passing glass display cases and dark entryways to exhibit halls. Butterfly Atrium, Insects of New Orleans, Beauty Queens, Creepy Crawlies, Base Camp, Swampland, and the Tiny Termite Café.

It's a bug museum.

The back offices seem empty, but then a small man with a friendly smile and a trim white mustache comes out. He introduces himself as Mr. Nicholas, the entomologist you'll be working for, and thanks you for being early. He leads you back to his small cluttered office, where he puts on a white lab coat and an old tweed fedora.

"Very exciting day!" he says and rushes back out of the office. He doesn't tell you to come with, so you sit there for a second before you get up and bolt after him. He walks briskly down the hall, whistling and flicking on light switches. "Morning, Louise!" he calls out, you have no idea to whom. "Morning, Quelle Belle! Astrid! Ichabod!"

Hurrying behind him, you catch fleeting glimpses of the now-illuminated exhibit halls, some of which are built like big Hollywood sets. There's a Louisiana swamp, a subterranean cave, a Japanese garden, and then a room walled with giant glass cases that hold thousands of live insects. You stop short at the Beauty Queens hall. Mr. Nicholas keeps walking, but you're transfixed by the back wall, which is completely covered with glorious, iridescent butterflies. Then you hear Mr. Nicholas whistling far down the corridor and you run to catch up.

Mr. Nicholas shows you the lab downstairs, otherwise known as the Bone Room, a low-ceilinged clinic with white counters and cabinets filled with live specimen containers and preservation chemicals. There's a refrigerator by the door and a deep freezer, which he says to never open or samples will be lost. The room smells faintly of nail polish remover, which he says is from the acetone they use to denature protein.

Chip manages the Bone Room, Hilda and Rick are technicians. Being at the bottom of the lab ladder means your jobs are mundane, like mounting unit trays, refilling naphthalene in insect drawers, labeling specimens, and so on. . . . There are delicate insects, dried dragonflies and butterflies with torn wings in small specimen boxes, which show how even damaged insects survive. One satyr moth had its wings nearly eaten off by a bird, but had just enough surface area available to still fly. So said the notes of the entomologist who sent him. There's also the occasional bizarre bug, like the wandering violin mantis, *Gongylus gongylodes*, with legs that look like elongated miniature violins.

You also get to have sex with Chip in the supply closet. After a few innocent flirtations and suggestive metaphors tossed around over the Bone Room tabletops, he asks you to help him get something from the other room and wham, hello, Chip! His penis is delightfully misshapen, like three partially interfused kielbasas. You start in the supply closet, but gradually screw all over the museum, your favorite place being the butterfly atrium. You like how the little live wings flutter on your face while lying supine by the koi pond.

On two sides of this domed room, past a row of high arched windows, is the busy street outside. Only a pane of glass separates the two worlds—on this side of the glass it's stone quiet, only the splash of the fountain can be heard, as iridescent green, gaslight blue, and royal red butterflies flash through the tranquil air, exploring the world with fragile, spider-lash-thin antennas. On the other side of the glass is a churning world of grit and grime, where all manner of muggers, thugs, and ne'er-do-wells roam the streets with heated hearts and sharpened knives. It makes you feel safe to be in here; you wish you could stay forever. If you were an Indonesian swallowtail, you could live in this climate-controlled sanctuary permanently and never have to brave the world outside.

Chip says he's going to Indonesia in three weeks to collect rare insects. He asks if you want to come with him. Mr. Nicholas says if you stay, he'll promote you to lab technician. A bit more money and a lot more work.

If you keep working in the Bone Room, go to section 22 (p. 60).
If you go to Indonesia, go to section 133 (p. 428).

78

From section 40

You get back to the ranch early. Ralston's already home. You don't know what crazy cover-up scheme Ida Mae has planned or how far she'll go to protect her little brother, but you suspect it's pretty far. So be it. You don't want in on it. All you want are facts. So you park, go inside, and call Ralston's name.

"I'm here!" he shouts back.

"Where, Ralston? It's a big house!"

"Office!"

Queer dread. Cold feet. Thick tongue. You grip the office door frame for support. Then you ask Ralston to tell you straight out what's going on with the Cutter family and all this Pecum River business. "Say what?" He smiles. "Who you been talkin' to?"

"Just tell me, Ralston. Tell me everything. Tell me about the river and the pastures drying up and tell me your . . . connection with the Cutter family."

He walks up to you and touches your cheek. "See now, I hate it when you talk like you're back in the city," he says. "It makes me feel stupid. You think I'm stupid? Or is it you think you can run a ranch now? Is that it? You think playing around with them ranch hands in the horse pens makes you an expert? Honey, you ain't even come close to knowing what goes on around here. You best stick with what you're good at. Whatever that is."

He grins and goes back to his desk, where he sits and takes out a stack of papers.

You don't budge from the door. "I saw the red folder. I know you want their land."

His head snaps up and you step back. You don't like the look in his eyes.

They're blank, like he's not even there anymore. "I'm sure sorry to hear you say that, darlin', because now I gotta fix your lying mouth for good." He smiles and then lunges at you, springing catlike over the desk and getting his hands around your throat. He starts choking you and forcing you to your knees. Your hands feel around blindly as your eyes roll up in your head. You can't breathe and start jerking in hacking, convulsing spasms.

This is how you die.

Then you hear a powerful crack and the pressure releases, letting harsh, sharp-edged air rush back into your lungs. You sputter and cough, eyes watering as you heave and try to catch your breath. Ralston is slumped over on the floor, his neck twisted and bent at a sickening angle. Above him stands Ida Mae holding a ball-peen hammer. She looks annoyed. "I said be back at six. You better hope there's no blood on the carpet."

You help her drag Ralston by the boots out back—to the slaughterhouse. "Where is everybody?" you ask.

"The hands are in town. Gave 'em tomorrow off. Here, pull him like this."

You get him into the slaughterhouse and Ida Mae hoists him over her shoulder, gunnysack-style. "What are we doing, Ida Mae?"

"No harder than a sow," she says and heads to the rendering stall. There she tosses on a mask and grabs a chainsaw. You turn around just in time.

The chainsaw whines for a half hour.

When Ida Mae comes into the kitchen her cheeks are flushed, her hair is damp, and she glows as though freshly released from a sweaty lover. She washes her hands in the sink twice over with a bar of soap and boiling hot water. Pours bleach on her arms without flinching. She says she could use some help with the feed grinder, so you follow her to the feed barn, where you help her lift an industrial-sized plastic garbage can.

"What's in here?"

"It ain't chicken!"

You gag. It's chopped-up Ralston parts. A pulpy dark red slurry, which you pour into the feed grinder. When he's all in, she follows with a few bags of grain, sluicing everything together and pumping it out into long, soft, sausagelike tubes that run down conveyor belts to the cattle troughs where the cows feed. Ida Mae is cheerful when it's over. "The dogs will eat good today!"

"Ida Mae, are you sure you're okay?"

"Why wouldn't I be? It's a good thing to put an animal down when it's time. Ralston was turning for a while now. I thought maybe the wedding would sweeten him up, or maybe a baby would give him new energy. But no," she says and sighs. "It was just his time."

You can't believe the tenacity of her buoyant attitude, especially as the night wears on and you spend hours hosing everything down. "If any of those *CSI* shows are right," you shout at her over your pressure-washer, "and they have those fancy lights that detect blood even after you clean it up, then this won't do any good!"

She laughs and says, "Still, nice to keep things clean!"

Two days later, while Ida Mae is in the barn and you're up at the house alone, the sheriff pulls up. He comes up, knocks on the door, and you step outside, where the wind is blowing and the sun is bright. "Looking for Ralston," the sheriff says. "He was supposed to pick up a straight-loader in town today. Seen him?" You tell him you haven't. He puts one boot up on the split railing and looks over the wide rolling fields.

"You expect to see him?"

"Um, no, sir, I don't."

Sheriff spits. "Well, I expect he's gone then."

"I expect he is."

"I miss ranching," he says. "Got your own world out here." He takes his boot off the railing. "You staying on here?" he asks as Ida Mae appears from out of the barn and starts walking up to the house.

"Yes, sir, I expect I will."

"Well, I imagine two ladies out here running a ranch might work real well."

You smile and shade your eyes against the setting sun.

Ida Mae waves.

"Could be, Sheriff. You can't know nothing for sure."

79

From section 23

You decide to go home. It's time. You miss your family and you've learned your lesson about money, which is you need some, but not as much as you think. Ida Mae cries up a storm when she hears you're going and begs you to stay. Ralston gets real quiet. He clams up and says, "Well, all right then," and won't look at you.

Some men just can't afford feelings.

You call your mom and she's so happy to hear from you she starts crying. Everybody's been so worried and nobody knew how to find you. You tell her everything's okay and you're coming home.

At the bus station, there's a lot more people than usual. A tan cowboy in a patriotic country-western shirt tells you everyone's here for the Renegade Rodeo. *The Renegade Rodeo!* You'd completely forgotten. The prize money for bronc riding is a hundred thousand dollars. Not bad for seeing who can hang on the longest. If you were to win that money, you'd have a much better start on a new life. If you didn't win, then you haven't lost anything, but then again, you could get your head smashed in or your intestines torn out, which would put a decided crimp in your plans. *Hi, Mom, hi, Dad, can I stay with you for a while? I'm a paraplegic!*

The overhead speakers crackle and a lady says your bus is ready for boarding. It's time to make a decision. Do you enter the rodeo, or get on the bus and head home?

If you get on the bus, go to section 52 (p. 176).
If you enter the rodeo, go to section 88 (p. 275).

80

From section 41

This has gone too far. You're out. You tell them you're not comfortable installing a dock for the commercial drug trade and you're selling the island. Maybe the next owners will let them use the island as a pirate playground. The drug runners don't like this, and before you know it, they grab both you and Aidan, clonk you on the heads, and drag you to their boat.

You wake up in the arid region of Port-de-Paix, Haiti. Sexy Star and Dumas have kidnapped you and brought you to their coffee farm near the small town of Bonbadopolis and you are now their slaves. They do give you a choice, though: Do you want to work outside on the coffee farm here or travel to Port-au-Prince, where you'll work in their warehouse?

If you stay in Port-de-Paix, go to section 82 (p. 255).
If you go to Port-au-Prince, go to section 146 (p. 475).

From section 107

You bid on the Key West cargo and what turns up is remarkable by anyone's standards. The salvage company drags up seven dark wood trunks from the Mediterranean Sea, which smell rankly of algae and are blistering with microscopic barnacles.

The crates are thought to be of Egyptian or Phoenician origin, and inside are seven hundred alabaster vials of *stakte*, *susinum*, *cyprinum*, and *mendesian*.

Ancient bottles of perfume.

The opaque cloudy blue oblong vials, circa 650–550 BC, are scientifically analyzed and declared to contain elements of blue lotus, cedarwood, myrrh, frankincense, cinnamon, and cassia. Among the perfume are unbroken vessels containing Tyrian purple, the legendary imperial dye used to create "royal purple," inspiring the lasting Roman ideology *Eserre a la Viola*. "To be of the purple." To be of a superior breed. To be what others are not.

Eternally royal.

The concept had to do with the intensity and permanence of the dye. Once something was cast in Tyrian purple, it was to last a lifetime and beyond. Created from the mucus of a predatory sea snail in the eastern Mediterranean, Phoenician indigo was used on Roman ceremonial robes and royal ornaments. Only the wealthiest, most revered wore this color. Now you own three hundred bottles of this antediluvian dye, along with seven hundred bottles of the oldest perfume known to exist.

Even though you're splitting the profits with the salvage company, you make a killing at the auction. Two lifelong enemies start bidding against each other and can't stop until one's hemorrhaging enough cash to call your antiquarian maritime treasure "one of the most lucrative Egyptian antiquities sales of all time" . . . and that's saying something. (Think King Tut's tomb, or the temple of Taposiris Magna, Cleopatra's final resting place.) Your load of rare perfumes and dye is on par with these discoveries, and you're paid handsomely for them.

You end up staying in Key West and buying Hemingway's old house. A grand old Mediterranean gem, formerly a museum in honor of the writer, but then someone finally realized the old goat would rather rise from his grave and blast everyone's head off than let hundreds of tourists file into his bedroom every day and take pictures of his bed linens and beloved six-toed cats.

You like living where Hemingway used to live. There's a certain elegance and responsibility to it. You adopt his army of cantankerous pugilist cats, cultivate his garden of exotic plants, host many dinner parties, and let various dignitaries and diehard fans (mostly other wan, ne'er-do-well writers) stay over for holidays or weekends. You even adopt his personal routine, rising early every day and working until noon, having a big lunch, and then heading for the coast to go fishing for the rest of the day.

You marry a local art dealer and live together in boisterous, cantankerous harmony for decades. He likes to yell and you like to throw things, smashing up your valuables so that there's room to buy more. Life is a crashing thunderstorm of endless, unpredictable passion.

When you die, it's due to a simple tumble down the steep front stairs. Then it's lights out.

Upon waking, you find yourself in Hemingway's heaven at the Paris Ritz. It's a fine summer night and you're knocking back martinis, Cambon side. After a wonderful dinner in Le Petit Jardin, under a flowering chestnut tree, you wander up to your room and get into the big brass bed loaded with goose feather pillows. Two for you and two for your heavenly companion. (In your case it's not your husband but a nicely tanned waiter named Maurizio who doesn't speak much English and has a cock that's too big to fit into a Mason jar.)

Afterward you fall asleep, dreaming of the treasure under the ocean, fragile glass vials of perfume waiting down there, smelling sweetly in the dark.

8 2

From section 80

Port-de-Paix is a small, dry, dusty town on the northeastern edge of Haiti. It's a trading post for smuggled goods from Miami, but you don't get to see any smuggled goods, because you and Aidan are put right to work in the bean fields. At least Dumas and Sexy Star kept you together. You couldn't make it through this alone. Aidan says eventually your families will find you. Someone back home has to be smart enough to figure out what happened, right? Or at least smart enough to hire someone who's smart enough?

You spend long, backbreaking days in the fields, sweat stinging your eyes, and cuts and scratches crosshatching your arms and legs. You dream of feather pillows and food. Sizzling steaks and whole coconut cakes. Ice seems like a faraway fantasy, a myth. Everything around you is hot on hot on hot. No relief, even in the shade.

Then one night you get the shivers. Aidan heaps blankets on you and rubs your forehead until you finally fall asleep. Then you're on fire with fever and Aidan wipes your arms and legs down with a washcloth soaked in tap water. By dawn your fever breaks and you descend once again into violent shivering. What the hell is wrong with you?

Plasmodium falciparum takes seven days to develop after you're first infected. In your case it was a mosquito that bit you while you were working in the field. You even killed the little bastard, squashed him dead, smearing your own blood on your exposed ankle, but the damage was already done, as it so often is.

You have malaria.

The sweating/sleeping/shivering cycle goes on for three more days.

You have nightmares and delirium. They roll over you all night long. A little stuffed bear like the one you had when you were little says *you're too late* and tells you to look closely at your family's faces, which loom up covered with oozing larvae and sticky sap. Something's chasing you! You're trapped and they won't let you out until you solve Haiti's economic crisis. *What's the answer?* the little bear asks. You don't know. You don't know! He leans close and whispers: *The answer is trees.* Then he explodes into raw meat.

You wake up to Aidan blotting your forehead with a washcloth. Dumas and Sexy Star let him stay with you and don't make him go work the fields. That's nice. You should tell them about the trees, but you feel too weak to talk. That's because the parasites are attacking your red blood cells and changing their structure.The cells become sticky and start clumping together, restricting blood flow to your kidney and spleen. You drift into a coma, which is just like waking up refreshed, after rain has come.

You see a bright white light, which you're drawn up into. It's a glorious, renewing light, completely revitalizing. There's a stern-faced nurse waiting for you at the other end. She's tapping her pen against her metal clipboard.

"Name?" she asks.

You give her your name.

"Date of birth?"

You stare at her.

"Oh, brother." She rolls her eyes. "Harry! Got another one still fuzzy! I don't know what you're putting in the tunnel but you're putting in too much! See if you can get this one to wake up, would ya!" A nice-looking gentleman in a male nurse's uniform comes over and leads you off to the side as a new person pops into place behind you.

"Now then," Harry says, flipping your chart. "I'm going to look in your eyes and give you a little shot of angel dust if you don't recall anything."

Two little blue pixies, bright as LED flashlights, come buzzing out and over just next to your corneas as the angel peers into your eyes. "Fine, just fine," he says. "Any thoughts?"

"Well, I'd like to know what the heck those two flying things are."

"All right then, here we go!" He gives your arm a little tap with a metal wand thingamajig and all of a sudden a great silver wave crashes down over you, thundering in your head so loudly you hold your ears.

"Oooh, sorry, kiddo." He touches your head, which feels like heaven. "Too much? Man, maybe I am putting too much stuff in the tunnel. I am off my game. You okay? All better now?" You look around, light now thrown in. "I was here before. I . . . I'm from here."

"Yes!" The angel nods and the little blue pixies fly in behind him, sorting through the files and collecting up your paperwork. "Very good. And the Earth Experience?"

"The Earth Experience is . . . for developing the soul."

"Yes. And the soul develops in direct relationship to?"

"The soul develops in direct relationship to the difficulty of the life. It's why all lives on Earth are difficult, without exception. Difficulty expands soul capability. We can't deepen or strengthen the soul here because . . ."

The angel tilts his head. Small feathery dusts of silver twirl lightly around his head. "Because here, everything is perfect."

"Yes." You nod. "And perfection brings beauty, but not peace. I went to Earth this time to gain . . . equanimity. Balance at all times."

"Yes."

"How'd I do?"

"You know, you can go over it with your intake counselor. It's a tough one to learn. I had to go back to Earth three, no, four times before I got equanimity. Disorganized down there. Always something to tip you over."

"Right."

"You okay to walk? Need an escort? Bathsheva here can go with you." One of the little pixies zooms up and pulses brightly with light.

"No, I'm going for a swim in the Luminary Pool before intake counseling."

The little light flickering in midair dies down and flies away.

"Too bad," the angel says and sighs. "They love getting out of the office."

83

From section 41

You tell Sexy Star they can use your dock, but you have conditions. They can only use it at night, and if they come up the dock, they can't go farther than the lighthouse. You never want to see them anywhere else on the island except the old docks. Also, they can't boat past your house again. They have to go around the other way. You can't be explaining all this to your staff, let alone your friends and family. *Okay?* You stick out your hand and Sexy Star grins, shaking it vigorously. Each boy shakes your hand before heading out into the night.

You're very happy with the deal you've struck, but Aidan acts like you've invited the devil into bed. "You wait," he says. "This will not end well." But life goes on after that, and you begin to forget about the boys. You don't even know if they come anymore. You never see them or hear them, but then, you wouldn't. That was the deal. You focus your energies on planting a new botanical garden and greenhouse as well as entertaining family and friends.

Aidan fishes, you cook. You learn how to make seared conch with mango chutney, blackened citrus scallops, banana fritters, corn fritters, dirty rice, sweet potato bread, squash soup. Aidan masters the art of making cocktails, achieving the perfect kefir lime mojito and a sublime Cuba libre. He's a real snob now when it comes to rum. He only drinks Barbancourt, and if someone serves him the cheap stuff, he acts like they tried to poison him.

It's sort of adorable.

Aidan's out fishing one afternoon when Sexy Star shows up. *Bang!* Out of nowhere, the skinny Haitian ringleader appears like a wolf out of the woods with his gold teeth and a T-shirt that says FEMA SUCKS! He smiles before pulling out a sweaty brick of cash from his bag and handing it over. There's a hundred grand here *at least*. You take the money and ask what *exactly* are they transporting anyway? But Sexy Star just winks. "Don't worry your pretty head," he says. "Women shouldn't think so much." Then he takes off, stopping midway and shouting, "Next payment in two weeks! We put a bigger dock in soon!"—cheerfully adding—"Much bigger!" Then he disappears into the trees.

You debate telling Aidan about this little conversation. He wouldn't appreciate it. He'd be livid. He'd say, *I told you so! Why don't you ever listen?* Then he'd drink a pitcher of Long Island iced tea and go shoot at coconuts. Maybe there's nothing to worry about. These kids have been straight with you so far, and *a lot* more honest than other workmen on the island, like the pool contractors from Miami! They were the *real* criminals, with what they charged. You'll just leave Sexy Star a note and remind him *no boats in front of the house* and ask him please to build an *eco-friendly* dock without churning up the dunes.

A week later, you and Aidan are drinking mimosas on the deck when a huge industrial-looking barge chugs past. Aidan sets down his glass and says, "You realize that your lack of hysteria implies your guilt, right?"

On the south shore you find the barge. Two dozen workmen are installing industrial-sized storm-proof pilings made of reinforced concrete for a dock big enough to host a small cruise ship. You're livid. The workers are loud and have completely flattened the dunes.

Aidan says he's going to get his gun and put a stop to this. You convince him to come back to the house. No confrontation. He seems fine. Well, at least okay. He definitely seemed okay. Around midnight, though, you can't find him. He's gone off on one of his rum-soaked walkabouts. You look everywhere until you think to look in the one place he shouldn't go. The dock.

He's down there all right, not just *at* the dock, but *on it*. You can see him standing on the dock shouting at the workmen as you hurry down the serpentine path from the lighthouse. As you get closer you can pick up parts of his tirade through the wind. "Not your property!" he yells. "Absolutely over! Serious . . . call the authorities right now!" Great. Here you thought you'd brought him around to accepting the idea of an international drug dock on the property.

A burst of rapid-fire gunshots makes you drop to the ground, your heart splintering in fear. *Oh God, oh God, oh God, oh God, oh God.* You peek out from the tall grass where you luckily dropped down and see Sexy Star wiping off his gun. Two other men are dragging Aidan's body off the dock, while the rest scan the perimeter of the hill where you're crouched, slowly fanning out and looking for any witnesses.

You scramble-crawl back to the house as fast as you can, flying into survival mode and heading not for the phone or the gun or even your own boat moored mere yards away. No. You run for the shower, ripping off your clothes and throwing them on the floor as you go. You blast the hot water, letting it burn your skin as the glass steams up around you. Seconds later you hear whatever spy they sent tiptoe into your bathroom. He's not even subtle. Knocks into something, but it's conceivably hidden under the sound of running water and your shaky but gregarious humming. *She'll be comin' round the mountain when she comes....* At the last moment, just as your animal instincts are sizing up the distance between the shower and the window by the toilet so you can pole-vault through it, you hear the little monster leave. He even shuts the door.

You can't run. If you run, they'll know you saw Aidan's murder. There's nowhere to hide and you can't beat them to the mainland. With your night vision, you'll slam the boat into a breaker wall before they even get you. You force yourself to shampoo and rinse twice before stepping out onto the plush bath mat. The one you ordered from Restoration Hardware in beignet, but it arrived in bisque and you spent an afternoon on the phone berating some poor customer service person over a bath mat, and now . . . Aidan is dead.

Footsteps creep up the stairs. You towel your hair. Should the universe decide to let you live, you'll build Aidan's underwater hotel. Your mind works quickly. You move through the bedroom, carefully opening closet doors and looking inside. It could be a really nice but eco-friendly hotel, too. Showcasing not only the sea's beauty but its need for protection and stewardship. You could hire that architect who built the underwater sea voyage ride at Disneyland. You *love* that ride. Aidan loved that ride. You could call the hotel Chimera, after the mythical monster. Your mind is *so sharp* suddenly. You stand on tiptoe with your back to the door, arms reaching overhead as the bedroom doorknob turns. *The Chimera was feared wherever she went.* Sexy Star enters the room. He points his gun at the back of your head.

She caused trouble in the lands she traveled.

He closes his eyes, about to pull the cold, hard trigger.

. . . and for all the men around her.

You spin around to face him. Shots fire. Three consecutive.

Sexy Star drops. You're left alone in the room, holding Aidan's smoking gun. On the ground the skinny boy sleeps. Blood blooms across his Doral cigarettes T-shirt, which bears the once- popular slogan TASTE ME! TASTE ME! COME ON AND TASTE ME!

Ten years later, on this very same spot, Chimera, a sea-sleep hotel, is open for business. It opens to rave reviews and the underwater suites are sold out for three years in advance. When the secretary-general of the United Nations decides to host the world's first underwater UN meeting at Chimera to highlight global warming, his security detail uncovers the Haitian drug smugglers working off the south end of the island. There's a stakeout, a complete sweep, and the runners are now behind bars. The chief security officer says this outfit was once led by the notorious heroin trafficker Jen-Baptist le Fleur (a.k.a. Sexy Star), but ever since he went missing ten years ago, his younger brother Dumas le Fleur ran the show.

You feign surprise and later on lock yourself in your penthouse pod (deepest one, furthest out) and cry. Yes, you own an amazing luxury underwater hotel, but at what cost? Would you have been happier in a modest home in the suburbs raising a family with the man you loved?

You consider this as you sip champagne and press the button that retracts the shark-viewing window. Then you press the button that releases chum and watch the amusing frenzy ensue. Aidan was a good man, but the sharks are pretty good too.

84

From section 92

Okay, you tell your boss you'll work the Puritan war on Christmas. Sounds like fun. He gives you a preperformance briefing sheet, which says in seventeenth-century England, Oliver Cromwell enforced an Act of Parliament banning Christmas celebrations. Puritans thought the holiday was a wasteful decadence that threatened their core Christian beliefs. All the drinking, merrymaking, and unnecessary gifts were an affront to God.

Wow, fun theme for a party.

You arrive at the museum early so you can suit up in your garb. The linen sackcloth dress, thin lavender shawl, demure bonnet, bloomers, and scuffed leather boots make you look quite the waif. You don't know. Is this really supposed to be a sex party? Something about wool underpants and anal lube just isn't right. Tonight, you'll be a bar wench and in charge of delivering clay mugs of ale to men who order them. (The ale is so pungent it makes your eyes water when you sip it.) If a woman orders ale, you are to request permission from her "Governing Lord" and ask "May the lady partake of spirits?"

The party is just getting started at the south end of the compound, in the Ye Olde England area, with Tudor houses and a small town scene. The caterers set up in the town tavern, serving coarse wheat bread, crumbly Stilton cheese, and fried chicken. You ask one of the waiters if they had deep fryers in 1644 England, but he just shrugs and sticks to his preapproved Ye Olde English Speake and says, "I dunno if they was fried, but methinks they had chicken."

You don't really get the point of the party, but it seems that it's supposed to be Christmas Day and the villagers cower in their homes and scurry down the street as Oliver Cromwell prowls around the village with his Puritan henchmen looking for anyone who dares to celebrate the sinful Catholic holiday of Christmas. When he finds someone unwrapping a Yuletide gift or sitting beside a hidden Christmas tree, the henchmen pounce and women are dragged off to the fornication rooms while the men are forced to impregnate Irish barmaids.

Punishment/fornication rooms are located in the little thatched cottages behind the tavern. The dark rooms have wattle and daub walls and dirt floors. People lie on sackcloth mattresses grunting and writhing in the dim, flickering candlelight. The Irish wenches, oh my, they get it good, but the room is briefly interrupted when someone shouts, "Hell yeah, bitch! Bring a ruckus to that ass!" causing everyone to briefly cease grunting and groaning. There's fierce whispering, probably about appropriate phrases to shout during climax, and then the party carries on as before.

You wander in and out of the various little village scenarios, men and women getting off on acting in a very strange way, all grasping at this collectively created pretend world. Man. They are really, really into it. You're struck with the peculiar nature of fantasy. Are we the only species that makes-believe? Do whales copulate while imagining their mate is a Japanese goldfish? And why do fetishes evolve? It seems like whatever fetish people have, when acted on, it's never quite enough. It's an itch that intensifies the more it's scratched.

Where do fantasies even come from? What's the exact genesis? You begin researching and reading up on the psychology of desire. Primitive human sexuality, cognitive controls, and behavior urge modification. Freud's theory that we walk around all day looking for penis substitutions. Skyscrapers, cigarettes, hot dogs, pickles, lipstick tubes. . . . Apparently, our entire civilization is fashioned after the cock.

You engage several of the more educated reenactors in this psychology of fantasy discussion. So by the time you finally save enough money to quit working at the Living Museum, you've got investors and seed money for your own tandem venture. Something that gets at the quick of the whole reenactment world. You open a personal-fantasy-fulfillment center in Las Vegas called Aphrodisiac.

Aphrodisiac is an adult entertainment center catering to fantasy fulfillment. (It's also a Quonset hut far off the Vegas Strip on Clark County 215.) So yes, you start small but think big and expand quickly. You build a series of closed-circuit-monitored, soundproofed rooms inside the air-conditioned Quonset hut in which men and women can partake of any manner of "alternative services." Leather dungeons, stuffed animal pits, adult diapers, asphyxiation, kidnapper/rape role play, smearing poop on walls . . . the whole fetish works. If someone wants a straight-up stripper or a prostitute, you send them back. This is for people with *unique* needs. Not all requests are granted, but they're all considered.

Business booms, in large part because you've hired the only albino pygmy in town and the center provides an unusual free service, fantasy divination. Some people know what they want, but others haven't quite found the right key for their little locked box.

By using a patented "Desire Divination Method," your team of Desire Divinationists can uncover hidden fantasies quite easily. Customers are surprised to discover what's motivating their fetishes and even more shocked when hidden desires they didn't even know they had are found. You warn everyone beforehand that the desire divination process is quick, but it's not always pleasant. Some enjoy it more than others. People familiar with therapy do well, but others don't like answering unpleasant questions about their pasts, though this is the quickest way to find out what they really want.

Therapists only have to locate a person's deepest hurts in order to find their wildest desires. Childhood traumas, bad memories, lasting negative impressions, they're all the mysterious dulled-down brass keys that open those treasure chests of brilliant want. The chain of command is simple. A wound creates a deficiency. The deficiency creates a desire. The desire negates the hurt by wrapping tightly around it like pearl forms around an irritant. Absentee fathers create daughters who often like to be dominated. Icy mothers create sons who like to spank. Walking in on your parents having sex can promote an interest in public sex.

Basically your people get in there and root around until they find out what really fucked you up, then they know what turns you on. Sounds a bit barbaric and it is, but you have a higher, less-publicized goal, which is to ultimately help cure people of their more destructive and obsessive desires. The ones that are getting out of control. If you can hunt a fantasy down to its initial "parent" hurt, you can often identify a person's unmet needs, and when those are met, the fantasy, particularly the really odd ones, dies down or disappears altogether.

Clients who come here to act out fantasies of molesting little girls or raping women think they're getting what they paid for. They think they're doing those things even though they're not. (How do you trick them? Easily. By using imagination, smoke, mirrors, and Hollywood magic, as well as offering talented, top-tier sex-industry professionals, and hiring every midget in the quad-state area.)

The center expands its service menu to include faux medical suites accommodating acrotomophilia for people who fantasize about watching an amputation, catheterophilia for those sexually aroused by the insertion of a catheter, and necrophilia for those who like to do it with the dead. It's your introduction of a "Kiddy Menu" for pedophiles, however, that gets Aphrodisiac shut down. You wish you could advertise the fact none of it is real, but that would kill business. The whole fantasy is the whole fantasy. They have to believe it's real.

You move operations from Las Vegas to Amsterdam, where people are more tolerant of sexual deviants, but even there people get uncomfortable with what *they think* is going on. You'd love to reassure the public that you're actually trying to help people, but can't very well publicize the fact you're helping to cure pedophiles of their urges or the motherfuckers wouldn't come in the first place.

Eventually you move Aphrodisiac to Indonesia, where there are no extradition laws, laws in general being nonexistent, not upheld, or largely irrelevant, and officials can be bought. The other bonus to being in Indonesia is that you can handle the really crazy motherfuckers. The ones who are too damaged to be fixed. In this way, the center's notoriety and negative reputation work in its favor. Coming here is usually a secret. Not the kind of trip people announce to their spouses or colleagues. Like a Thai sex-slave trip.

In fact, that's exactly the kind of trip you're trying to reduce in the world. If you can get horny businessmen to come here and "abuse" your Thai girls (who are all actually youthful-looking Thai boys with extraordinary kick-boxing skills), you can hopefully cure them of their deviant behavior.

As time goes by you run into some real sickos. People who don't have "wounds" so much as they have "serial psychopathic tendencies." You learn these people can't be cured. And if you can't cure them, you feel you have a moral obligation to kill them. Indonesia's awesome that way. Lots of forest.

85

You head for the shelter to regroup, trudging down the street, ashamed and humiliated and lower than low. It's raining and cold out. While passing an alley, you see a dog lying on a dirty piece of cardboard. He's a little guy, some kind of terrier mix, and he's as down as you are. He whimpers and ducks his head shyly when you approach him, as though he wants to lick your hand but thinks you might kick him. His hair is so tangled and dirty that when he gets up he can't even wag his tail, because it's matted to his leg.

How can you leave this little guy outside alone?

You scoop him up in your jacket and carry him to the shelter, where a sign says NO PETS. The nice woman at the desk says you could take him to the pound; they have vets there. So you carry him across the city to the pound, but they won't help him unless you surrender him, and if you surrender him they'll euthanize him in two days if no one claims him.

You know damn well no one is going to claim him. This is not the kind of dog that gets taken home. This is the kind they put down.

Nope, he's all you've got. So you name him Lucky.

You need some luck right about now, plus it's your favorite hobo name, and that's what you two are now. Hobos. And the one thing any good hobo knows is you can't get a handout in the city. Too much competition. So you carry Lucky farther out of town, following alongside a highway, resting every mile or so, until the sun starts to set and you make it all the way to the big mall out by the cineplex.

You know about this place from a summer job your sophomore year in high school, when you and your zitty teen friends worked at Fatlinks, the jumbo hot dog place with pretzel-bread buns, and you used to take smoke breaks out back. There's a little covered loading dock nobody uses with a big metal air duct that blows warm air all winter.

Using some old dusty loading blankets, you make yourself as comfortable as you can wedged in the far corner of the loading dock. You dig around in the Dumpsters until you come up with some uneaten hamburgers, which you feed Lucky. You also find a hose thrown down on the ground trickling water; probably someone was hosing down teenager puke and left it running. You're able to give Lucky a trucker bath and even loosen that crusty tail from his leg. His skin sure looks sore, though. You wish you had money for a vet.

You spend the next few nights like that, you and Lucky camping out together behind the mall foraging for food. What you don't know is the night-shift security guard at the mall has been watching you on his grainy black-and-white monitor. His name is Ed and he's a by-the-book kind of security guard. He's turned in plenty of vagrants and runaways to the police, because that's his job and he takes it seriously.

You, though—you're different.

Something about you makes him hang the phone back up after reaching for it. He sees you sleeping, the dog's head on your shoe. He watches you every night, all night, neglecting the other camera screens behind him. He had a dog once, when he was a little boy. Chex. Chex was hit and killed by a car one day and Ed saw the whole thing happen. The dog's dashing legs, the screeching brakes, the sickening *thud*.

Teddy had locked himself in his room and sat there for two days. He didn't cry, he didn't eat, he just sat while his parents banged and yelled at the door, finally calling a locksmith to break in. After that his parents forbade any more pets, believing Teddy was overly sensitive and couldn't survive another loss. Teddy would stop at pet stores on the way home from school sometimes and stare through the windows. He only did that a few times and then something wild and unmanageable kicked in his heart and he couldn't look anymore.

Years passed.

Even after Ed grew up, moved out, got a decent job, married a nice girl, and moved into his own house, he never had another pet. To this day the security guard has never allowed himself to have another dog, not even when his own boy begs for one. Especially when his own boy begs for one. Maybe if his boy never has a dog in the first place, he'll never know what it's like to lose one.

Now, as Ed watches you on his grainy monitor, he can feel that wild, unmanageable kicking again. It's painful and it makes him shift in his seat. He picks up his coffee cup and sets it down again without taking a sip. He's late punching out, and he's never late punching out. His manager asks if he's feeling all right and Ed says *yes*. The manager asks if he's still taking his vacation time next month and Ed says *yes*.

For six days Ed watches you, and on the seventh he leaves work early. When you wake up the next morning, Lucky is whining and sniffing at a white paper bag on the loading dock. There's thick black Magic Marker on the bag, deliberate printing that says:

Get yourself safe.

Inside are two ham sandwiches and three thousand dollars in cash. You look around, call out and ask if anybody is there. But there's no one. Just the distant sound of the delivery trucks backing up and the cars driving by.

You rent a small basement in a house on Delaware Street. It's a good neighborhood and the owner is a sturdy little Jewish lady named Mrs. Roseburg, who loves dogs and feeding anything small or scrawny. She immediately takes you under her substantial wing and in no time Lucky is looking ready to win a blue ribbon and you're eating potato knish at her table. Her cousin gives you a job at the register in his deli. She says you're going back to school, and as long as you're making something of yourself, you and Lucky will always have a place to stay. She says the world is full of miracles. More than we know.

You wonder who left you that money, what angel came to your rescue. You'll never know it was the security guard who helped you. You never cross paths again.

The day after you found your miracle money, Ed went home and told his wife and son there'd be no family vacation this year. Just as the boy started to cry and his wife crossed her arms in her "this better be good" stance, Ed opened the door leading out to the garage and in bounded a mangy yellow dog named Max. Max leapt across the living room and onto the couch, knocking over a vase of fake geraniums and slobbering all over Ed's son, who fell apart in piles of giggling and twisted with laughter.

His wife raised an eyebrow, unable to fully suppress her smile.

"It's about time," she says.

You've graduated from veterinary school and open the city's first no-kill shelter, which accepts any injured, lost, or unwanted creature and will never put any animal down. It's a lot of backbreaking work, and you never knew how many people buy iguanas only to surrender them about three months later, but it's worth it because, as you learn eventually, a truly happy life is not parented by money or success. In the end, it's only nearly killing yourself over something that really matters that can turn your miserable life into a masterpiece.

86

From section 43

You decide to meet with Niobe, flying on Dolly's dime to London and leaving Captain Marquardt and crew to sail the *Bête Noire* behind you. It'll take awhile for them to catch up with you in England, and you want to meet Niobe *now*. If the psychic has information about your future happiness, you'd like it sooner rather than later.

Ironically, she's asked to meet you on another ship. The *Hispaniola* is docked along the River Thames and has a small restaurant on board. You wander up the gangway jet-lagged and spacey and the maître d' brings you to a small corner table, where a positively ancient woman with milk-blue eyes sits facing the water. You introduce yourself. She nods, but doesn't say anything, and so you sit as a waiter sets down a teacup for you.

You're nervous but don't know why. You find it absolutely impossible to look directly at Niobe's face, which seems like a series of thunderclouds congregating under a snowy plume of ash-white hair. She pours your tea, carefully lifting the pot with her long weathered fingers. You try unsuccessfully not to stare at her dirty yellow fingernails. She sips her tea and finally speaks. "Look to create your own sanctuary here on Earth. Yes? Don't search for someone else's idea of the way. Sometimes people are afraid of cultivating their own power, especially women. People tell you to *keep sweet and play nice* and warn you not to cause a mess. But the Furies are here to tell you: Make a mess. They *need* you to make a mess. Build shit. The stronger you become, the more you protect. The taller your shadow, the more who are shaded. Do you understand?"

You take a sip of water.

"The Fury watching you says maybe you're scared or nervous or want to read self-help books first, but there isn't time for nonsense. Grab hold of yourself. There's a hell of a lot of shitheads out there. People who are broken and cruel and abuse animals and hurt little kids. They smear their evil on the walls like sticky tar, trying to black out the light. So, while it would be really awesome to get all *organized* and ready before you start on that thing *you know you should be doing*, there's no time. Jump. *Now.* We need more strong, good people. Be one."

Niobe opens her eyes.

"There are two paths for you," she says. "Choose one or the other, but not both. If you want to be lucky in love, go to Ireland. You'll lose all your money, though. All of it. If you want to secure your fortune, then stay here in London—but whatever you do, sell that godforsaken red boat. It's going to sink and take all souls on board with her."

If you want to be lucky in wealth, go to section 21 (p. 54).
If you want to be lucky in love, go to section 39 (p. 121).

87

From section 18

You can't marry Mr. John Harris Wadley Jr.! It's not right. He's too old, your cultures too different. It would be an unending negotiation for footing on a slowly leaking yacht.

You stand up, smile frozen. Lacking any eloquent comments or even the ability to utter a sound, you simply grab your purse and dash out of the room, hot tears starting down your flushed cheeks.

You run out onto the street, frantically hailing a cab, only to be struck down by a horse-drawn carriage. You ran right out in front of the wheels without looking, spooking the Clydesdale, who reared up and brought his massive hoofs down quite completely on your head.

It happens.

Now you're dead. You're on EZ Pass this time around and so are immediately reincarnated and reborn in the village of Lona in the foothills of Taiwan. This time you become the respected leader of a Bunun tribe, but to counterbalance all the money you spent in your previous life, you will be poor for this one.

Poor but not unhappy.

You go on to have a good marriage, five children, and become a popular full-time DJ on the country's only all-aboriginal radio station, Ho-Hi-Yan.

88

From section 79

You're riding in the rodeo! Normally it's forbidden to sign up so late, but Mrs. Undershaw, who sings in the choir at Bible Baptist Church with Ida Mae, is running the sign-up table at the Llano County outdoor arena, so she writes your name down anyway and gives you number 338, which you pin to your shirt.

You jog past all the concession stands selling ice cold beer, blooming onions, boiled peanuts, and something called a Tornado Potato. Then you climb a flight of stairs on the red metal bleachers and make your way down to the Cowboy Pen, where you wait with all the other riders. It's packed. Thousands of cowboy hats bob around in the stands and the crowd suddenly roars as someone gets thrown from a bull. The barrel men help him up and another man with a huge silver belt buckle walks out and ropes the bull. Three guys help lead him off.

Now the last bull is up and a horn sounds. The metal chute opens, releasing the snarling, kicking black bull, who kicks and foams as the cowboy on him jerks around and the barrel men scatter. The rider is crap, goes flying off before the bull even gets to the center of the ring. He gets up and dusts himself off while the crowd boos.

Someone shouts, "Go back to Idaho!"

Then the ring is cleared and a marching band comes out. They're wearing blue and white uniforms with silver pom-poms on their hats and they play "Hoe Down Rodeo" while their mascot, a large pecan, chucks candy at the crowd. Pecans are as Southern as peach pie, but they don't really make for a good costume. If you squint, it looks more like a dog turd.

Finally, it's time for the bronc competition and you watch with increasing anxiety as cowboy after cowboy gets thrown off. When it's your turn, you take a deep breath, think of Ralston, and let the barrel men lower you down into the chute onto the horse's tawny-colored back. *What are you doing here? Going for the hundred grand!* This is not a good idea. The horn sounds as the chute breaks and the horse takes off full gallop across the ring. You can hear shouting in the stands, the arena lights whip by, and then your grip loosens and you fly off. The barrel men rush over for you, but they can't always get there in time. The tawny horse gallops back around, and either in a vengeful plan or a freak accident he plants his iron-hard hoof full force down on your skull.

You're in critical condition. The doctors can't stabilize you. Your mother makes them wait until she can get there and touch you one last time before they unplug you. The worst part is you can see everyone as you drift out of your body. Your mom crying, your dad shaking his head. They'll never know you only tried the rodeo to make some money before you came home. You feel like crying, too, if only your damned tear ducts still worked.

Then you see a river of spirits whistling along outside the window. You can't give your parents another thought, you just have to jump in! It's like a white-water river with rapids and waterfalls and deep pools of churning, bubbling life. You ride that wave to the outskirts of the city, where everyone seems to break off and shoot like stars in their own direction.

89

From section 73

You only have to dance onstage for a little while. A few months. You'll save up enough money, then you'll get out. You're not going to become one of those old beef-jerky-titted strippers who have to compete with nubile sixteen-year-olds for sweaty dollar bills. Chick-a-Dick is your stage name and you make a chicken costume out of a white leotard and feathers ripped from a down pillow. In your act you peel your feathers off slowly, revealing pointed yellow pasties that look like little beaks. It's kind of weird.

Violette likes it, though, and signs off on your first night performing. You get the jitters real bad and stall, letting Candie-Babie and Honey Bee go on before you. Finally it's time to get up there and you feel nauseated. Violette gives you a push onstage, digging her long purple nails into your back, and there you are, a chicken caught in headlights. The entire room is staring. Heart thumping. Music playing at a bizarrely soft level. You can barely hear it. You start to dance, but you're so rattled you don't remember the steps and you end up doing this little bounce-bounce thing that probably looks like the actions of an actual chicken.

For the finale you're supposed to lay a golden egg, but the one you made is just papier-mâché spray-painted gold and actually quite brittle, so when it drops from the hidden black box onstage it breaks, revealing its interior newspaper walls, made from an abandoned *Times-Picayune*. The audience boos and someone throws ice from their cocktail at you. People yell and cat-call as you waddle offstage, your costume bunched up around your ankles.

Total humiliation.

The girls are nice about it, they say everybody bombs their first time, you just have to get it over with. But you can hear them tittering in their dressing rooms and someone calls you Quackers. Violette says to cheer up and you better glue your egg back together, you're on again in a half hour. No fucking way! You are not going out there again. It doesn't matter if you end up homeless, you'd rather die alone in a gutter than go back up there! You quickly gather your stuff and run out the stage door, dropping the damn papier-mâché egg again. Why did you even take it? You chuck it in the Dumpster.

Then someone says, "I'm sorry, that was the funniest thing I've ever seen in my life." Great. Parking lot hecklers. You give him the finger, and march off, but the prick follows you. "No, wait," he says, "I meant that in a good way." He runs in front of you and blocks your way. He's actually a pretty clean-cut guy and he's wearing an unstained, recently dry-cleaned sport coat, which is unusual for Tom-Tom clientele. You stop and put a hand on your hip. "What?"

He says his name is Michael Ross and he's a television producer from L.A. He's been scouring venues for a comedy show he's trying to launch, a live Lucille Ball–type variety show, and until tonight he hasn't found anyone who's got the right stuff. You, though, you're amazing. You tell him that's about the worst come-on line you ever heard. He asks if he can buy you a coffee and you say no, but he can buy you a steak.

So a porterhouse, loaded baked potato, and three beers later, you admit his ridiculous story has an odd ring of truth to it. The details are consistent and he isn't drunk. He offers to fly you to L.A. and put you up in an apartment while you shoot one single episode. The pilot. He'll give you a per diem, and after they're done shooting you can leave. Go anywhere you want. You can think about it if you want to, but really, what do you have to lose? Where could you end up that would be worse than that stage?

He does have a point.

So off to L.A. you go. You get a small sunshiny apartment in Venice and a car picks you up every morning and brings you to Sony Studios for rehearsal. The director and other actors want to practice till everything's perfect, because when the show airs, it'll be live. Easy to make mistakes. Michael says whatever you do, no matter what happens, don't swear and the show must go on. If you remember those two things, you're golden.

The show is called *Sunday Night Live* and features a series of funny skits on prebuilt sets, just like *Saturday Night Live*, but instead of an ensemble cast you're the star. There's lots of physical comedy that involves falling down, slipping, or spilling things on yourself and you're starting to figure out why Michael thought you'd be good for the part.

Finally, after two weeks of rehearsals, the big night comes and everyone is humming with anticipation as the band strikes up. The first actors dash out onto the kitchen set for the "My Baby's an Alcoholic" sketch. Everything goes perfectly and the audience is laughing loudly until the "Amish Stripper" sketch, where you have to get up on a little stage much like the one back at the Tom-Tom Club and dance a jig.

Just as you jump onstage wearing your frumpy dress and bonnet, you accidentally trip over the butter churn and fall flat on your back. The audience laughs. Then you try to get up and knock over the wooden cutout cow, which cracks a fellow actor in the head, and they roar. The frantic assistant director, a normally even-tempered woman, wildly spins her fingers, saying, *Keep going! Keep going!* So you finish the rest of the sketch and go on with the show. After that the calamities are constant, though your shattered nerves cause you to drop things, miss cues, forget lines, bump into people, and accidentally burp. Your fellow actors are shaken and the crew look like zookeepers with a four-hundred-pound gorilla that's out of control.

After the show you lock yourself in your dressing room and refuse to come out. Michael pounds on the door until you let him in. You fall into his arms weeping, mascara running down your face. You sob and hiccup as you tell him you didn't mean to let him down, especially after he's been so good to you and pulled you out of that crap hole in New Orleans. As you go on and on, your voice gets higher and higher until only dolphins can hear it, and Michael finally shakes you hard by the shoulders. "Stop!" he shouts. "I don't want to hear it!"

You sniffle and wipe snot off your upper lip. Classy.

"I don't know what you were thinking," he says, "but I brought you here to be the funniest woman on air since the *Carol Burnett Show* went off the air in 1978!"

"I know," you whimper miserably.

"And you did it!"

He grabs you and squeezes you, covering your face with kisses. *"I love you, I love you, I love you!"* he shouts and spins you around the dressing room.

"But, I ruined everything!"

"Yes! And I knew you would! After that fiasco with the paper egg, I knew I've found my girl. The klutziest, most reliably dangerous stage performer the world has ever known." This time he takes you in his arms and kisses you for real.

Your show rockets to the top and the studio picks up another nine seasons. Your career in television makes you famous around the world. Little old men playing dominoes in bamboo-thatched bars in Fiji know who you are. You never quite make the transition to movies, but who cares. You love what you do and the people love you. You become America's favorite funny lady, a Hollywood goddess revered for her brains as well as her beauty.

You don't lose your footing, though. Fame doesn't change you. In fact, it allows for more of you. You get active in charity work, become a spokesperson for women's rights, and donate money to rehabilitation centers around the world. Your crowning achievement is building a nondenominational women's shelter named Open House in New Orleans's ninth ward, where women can stay as long as they like and get free child care, health care, job training, and clothing. They can watch TV and they can even take untimed hot showers. You build it right across from Calvary House. You send them a sweet note on monogrammed stationery that says *Suck it!* The Baptists are praying for you. Hard.

You marry Michael and buy a palace in Malibu. Your family relocates to Southern California, all except Grandpa Joe, who says California is for derelicts and the Army Reserve. He does let you fly him out for holidays, though, and he even puts one toe in the ocean before declaring it too cold. Michael produces several more hit shows, but he takes a break when you get pregnant. It turns out to be a beautiful, robust, wacky little girl who enjoys knocking things over and chatters like a jaybird. You name her Camilla.

90

From section 142

You decide to climb up. It's about forty feet. That's not so much, right? Godzilla was forty feet tall. Why you remember that is a mystery, but you could climb Godzilla if you had to, right? It's not like belaying the Empire State Building. Of course, you have no ropes, no ice screws, no harness. There's just you and one Latin saying to remember.

Semper ad alta—Always to the summit.

Okay then.

This will be your first free-climb on ice. This will be *anybody's* first free-climb on ice. Then again, there's probably some insane free-climbing ice club in Fairbanks. (Fairbanks is where the *truly* insane run free.) Besides, free-climb purists would probably say your ice axe and crampons prevent this from being a *true* free-climb. They believe nothing outside a climber's body should be used for assistance—to which you say, self-important adrenaline junkies who hyper-focus on fine print are no better than bratty, obese children who pitch fits when served the wrong pie.

Just do what you gotta do. Get yourself home. Just do what you gotta do. Get yourself home. Just do what you gotta do. Get yourself home. Just do what you gotta do. Get yourself home. Just do what you gotta do. Get yourself home. Just do what you gotta do. Get yourself home. Just do what you gotta do. Get yourself home. Just do what you gotta do. Get yourself home. Get yourself home.

Up you go. Lots of things to think about now, but only one thing matters and that's *swing the hammer, hoist and hold. Swing the hammer, hoist and hold.* The pain in your leg gets bad, but you decide it can go fuck itself. You are going home.

You move quickly, using animal instinct over actual ideas. It's easy when you're terrified. In twenty minutes you've made amazing progress, already covering a quarter of the distance. Amazing. In the next twenty minutes you don't move at all. Can't find the handholds, uncertain of the grip. It's a slow, tedious process and you're getting colder every second. Your hands are so frozen you can hardly make them bend. You think it's because you stopped and patted yourself on the back.

No more of that.

Just embrace these lovely stupid decisions. Each one. All the way from here to the top, because they're going to get you home. Climbing without a helmet, or harness, or movie crew to film your death. Not to mention what you did bring. A head injury, a broken kneecap, and an ice axe that splinters off more ice than it grabs. Forget that. You like the sound. Remember, you got yourself here and you can get yourself out. Like Grandpa said, stupid works both ways.

Thank God.

You keep moving. You embrace any and every thought that comes into your mind and you don't focus on what's actually happening around you, sort of like reverse meditation. Color and chaos and clutter are welcome. You recite recipes, remember past relationships, unfortunate haircuts, disaster vacations, dead pets, funny stories, kindergarten songs. A farm you once visited. Chickens.

When you slow to hoist yourself over a jagged ridge of ice crusted on the wall, you discover that you're singing, but you don't recognize the tune. You also notice your hands are bleeding. Never mind. Inch by inch you pull yourself up. Your knee is really throbbing now; it's definitely broken but it's getting lighter as you climb higher, and you allow your mind to entertain the brief thought you might live. *Is anyone looking for you? Will there be a helicopter buzzing the mountain or will you have to drag yourself back to base camp?* You lose your footing over and over again, but you refuse fear. Only anger and annoyance are welcome on this journey.

Semper ad alta.

Fuck! Why did you even do this stupid thing? Isn't life sort of difficult enough without you flinging yourself up the side of a mountain and then needing to be rescued? Wait, that's Grandpa talking. Well, he does have a motherfucking point. Isn't life sort of hard enough, with just its preset run-of-the-mill obstacles? Is it really necessary to go creating Mount Everest–sized motherfucking drama? (The swearing escalates as the ice gets harder and you have to smash the axe into it like friggin' Paul Bunyon. Your arm is about to give out and that just makes you angrier. Why . . . are . . . you . . . so . . . stupid!?)

You reach the top of the sheer ice wall, hair wild, eyes in maniacal slits, hands and arms covered in pulpy blood, and you hit a ceiling of iron-hard snowmelt.

Oh, *come on!* You've got to get home, for fuck's sake!

You're stuck underneath a wide shelf of hard-packed snow, which means you're going to have to crawl across upside down. If you jet, speed-axe through, you know you can make it, but then you have to haul your ass over the lip. You need an anchor to throw over the ledge! So fuck! Make an anchor! There must be some motherfucking kind of rope around here somewhere! (Even this blatant, utterly irrational declaration doesn't snap you from your angry certainty.) Don't think about it, just do something stupid. Stupid will save you.

Done and done.

You remove every stitch of clothing you have on, tightly tying them all together and weighting the line with—what else—your ice axe. There's no time to think about the fact you're buck naked at the top of a ten-story crevasse with all your clothes bundled up and pinched in your teeth, as you scamper quickly and monkeylike along the ledge. Snow starts giving way underneath your hands and you push harder, causing more to give way, and in one final act of complete stupidity you launch yourself headlong into the wide-open space of nothingness and hurl your ice-axe anchor overhead just as gravity does its work and pulls your body back down into the black mouth of the crevasse.

The axe catches.

You hoist yourself up, nether parts awkwardly exposed like a sashimi plate. You finally arise from the crevasse naked, covered in blood, and just in time for the last yellow rescue chopper to see you. They were about to call off the search, as everyone else is dead.

You are the sole survivor.

See that? When you are right, you are motherfucking *right*. And when you are wrong—shit *really* gets figured out. *Semper ad alta.* Always to the summit. By hook or by crook, by ice axe or by insanity. Do what it takes to get to the top. Climb Godzilla and use your own pigheaded, stubborn anger to do it if you have it. Use whatever axe you get.

Newscasters, local officials, professional climbers, field experts— nobody believes you scaled that sheer wall of ice unassisted, except there's video footage. They replay it on the news over and over with your nude torso digitized out, the details missing, but not the color. Many people initially speculate on your actual race, as it was impossible to tell through the amount of dark red blood caked everywhere. Funny. You remember feeling just fine at the time.

When you get home, you're like a foreigner in a new and hard-to-grasp land. Everything and everyone seems equal parts ridiculous and miraculous. Everything in this world seems bizarre. Dinner reservations, lawn ornaments, strip malls, it's like you never saw any of it before. You're prone to long bouts of sudden laughter and sudden, unplanned moves. You don't like being inside. Can't stand it, actually. You're always aware of the walls.

You ask your grandpa to move with you to Bali. You're going to build a tree house. He says it sounds damned bizarre, so yes, he's going so someone keeps an eye on you.

You build a magnificent four-story tree house on the Ayung River in Bali with open-air pagodas and teak floors built among the jati trees. Hand-carved furniture and running water. Large airy rooms, all wide open to the elements, letting the wind and leaves blow in along with songbirds. Three religious ladies from the nearby village work tirelessly to keep nature from taking hold in your home. They brush away forest debris and insects, pluck out the tiny ferns that sprout right on the ceiling joists. At night large canvas sails are hoisted up along the outer walls to protect you from sudden thunderstorms and strong winds.

Most of the island is Hindu and rituals are regularly practiced. For instance, every day before the ladies go to work in your kitchen, they leave woven baskets filled with sugar cane, bananas, rice, and flowers by the statue of Ganesha beside the black lily pond. These colorful baskets are called canang offerings and they're meant to show thankfulness and attention to detail to the gods. The Hindus in Indonesia believe the universe is carefully structured, not random. Balance must be kept between the dark (adharma) and light (dharma) forces of the world to maintain this equilibrium, and these offerings help that. They believe in reincarnation and the idea that the fortunes or misfortunes of the next life will be dependent on their actions in this one.

The women who work for you dote on your grandpa, even though he mocks their religion (and all religions) pretty much every day. They won't let him lift a finger, though, and scold you if they find you together and his teacup is empty. Grandpa enjoys this treatment, and let's face it, he's earned it. Within a few years he's slid right off his rocker and has four wives along with eight goats. *Why not?* he says. He likes goats and he likes women. If he met a goat or a woman who could hit a grand slam . . . he'd die a happy man.

But you're meant to die before him this time around. Grandpa's still alive and well when a fever steals you away and you close your eyes for the last time.

The ladies gather all their friends and family for your funeral, as is the custom in Bali, and repeat *Om Swastiastu* until the holy man gets there. Dogs sniff along the ground and dark-eyed men smoke clove cigarettes as the women prepare you on a grass mat lying on a bamboo bed. Grandpa won't come to the funeral. Nothing will sway him. "Save yer chanting for a ball game!" he shouts. Then he demands a plate of fresh papaya and wants to know where his goat is. Meanwhile, the holy man pours water on your hair, places flowers on your eyes, in your ears, and in your mouth, preparing you for your departure. They wrap you in white silk and tie it with yellow silk sashes. You look like a strangely shaped gift.

Heaven is a breezy dome with two distinct sides. Light and dark. Sam is there to greet you and she socks you right in the jaw. "That was for the cruise!" she says and then tells you this place has amazing cupcakes.

She shows you around the city. God lives on one half and his sister Lucy lives on the other. Like all siblings, they're similar, but different. The devil is a very charming woman who wears a lot of perfume. God is a cinnamon-colored antelope-like creature with white robes who is endlessly trailed by singing doves, which actually seem to annoy him at times. He takes time to speak with you whenever you meet and answers all your questions one by one.

You ask him, "Where did the Mayans go?"

He rolls his eyes. "Built a spaceship when we weren't looking."

"What causes cancer?"

"Complaining."

"If the devil is your sister, why don't you stop her from doing her work?"

God looks toward Lucy's workshop, which is always chugging with colorful steam, even late at night. Peals of laughter emanate from the windows and little hobgoblins fly this way and that, collecting ingredients for her complicated and delicious-smelling recipes. "The truth is I'm a fan of her work," he says and sighs. "We're both classically trained—just different aesthetics." You're glad to hear that. You tell God if you ever see Lucy coming, you'll be sure to introduce yourself, but his eyes go wide and he puts a warm, cloven hoof on your hand. "If you ever see the devil coming, you do what I do," he says. "Just run. Run like hell."

91

From section 140

It's too risky to help the kids, not to mention inconvenient and labor-intensive. Enough with the roadside camping, you need a freaking shower already.

You finally arrive in Kathmandu around dawn and check into Dwarika's Hotel, a private mansion turned luxury auberge. Besides the thick feather-top mattresses and lemon balm–scented rooms, this lavish building is constructed from so many ancient sculptures, salvaged carvings, and fifteenth-century architectural artifacts, it's actually listed as a world heritage site. Plus, the restaurant serves a twenty-two-course meal, which is pretty nice after a week of noodles.

After a good night's sleep, a big meal, a steaming hot shower, and an achingly good crap, you and the group head out to explore the city, stopping first at Asan tole, the largest market in the old quarter. This ancient bazaar is packed with people buying fragrant spices, sticky incense, steamed dumplings, stone idols, dime-bright aluminum pots. You're pressed into the crush of people, swept past shops and wooden tables piled high with baskets of lentils, peanuts, colorful saris, candies, dried sardines, incense, clay pots, and henna.

You stumble across the bright lights of an American camera crew filming at one of the food stalls. Not a big crew, just five or six guys with a camera pointed at one big bald guy, Andrew Zimmern, the star of the show, who's dangling a steamed yak eyeball by its tendon right over his open mouth. He pauses and says into the lens, "If it's crunchy, I'll like it!"

The guys on the crew offer you a ride back to your hotel, just hang tight till they're finished shooting. Thank God for not-so-small favors. You stand aside and watch the shoot, but just then you feel something sharp and painful in your side and you sink to your knees beside a table piled high with yak pelts. Two Chinese youths on a top-secret assignment hurry to roll you over onto a large pallet. You have no idea what's happening. What is it? Appendicitis? Where is your appendix? At first you think maybe these guys are trying to help you, but when you reach up one smacks your arm down with a big animal pelt. You try to yell but they quickly wrap your head in animal skins and keep piling these heavy, oily, musky hides across you until you can't move or breathe. The smell is unbearable. Pain spreads from your back to your abdomen.

They stabbed you!

The boys, members of the Young Communist League (YCL), are now whispering fiercely to each other. You try to scream but you can't. Thick tufts of yak hair fill your mouth, making you cough and choke as they hoist the pallet up and load you into the back of a waiting canvas-covered military truck.

As the truck jerks forward and rumbles down the gravel road, you work your head back and forth furiously to make more space and air underneath the heavy pelts. You can hear Chinese rap music on the radio and the boys are talking to each other. It's muffled and you don't speak Chinese, but they seem pretty cheerful, laughing even. Sure, why not? They just got away with bagging a tourist in a public market; now they're probably talking about zit cream or banging their girlfriends after tonight's celebration rally. It's like some perverse sitcom. *It's just two crazy communist kids and a wacky hostage! What'll they get into next?*

Suddenly an animal skin is lifted off your face and the kid in the passenger seat offers you a slice of orange. He takes the small translucent wedge of mandarin and taps it lightly on your lower lip until you take a bite, the small burst of juice brightening your mouth and washing away the vile sandy yak hair. The kid smiles and says, "Good! Good!" Then the truck turns sharply and you go up a steep incline.

What the hell are these kids doing?

They actually talk about what they're doing in exacting detail as they speed across the landscape. (Only they converse in Chinese, so they might as well be reciting dumpling recipes.) They're driving you to a remote area of the Terai region, along the southern border of India, where they've been instructed to dump your body in rival territory. Nepali Congress activists have organized protests against Maoist lawmakers recently and are even garnering support from key political figures, which must end. The Nepali Congress are terrorists, violent thugs determined to undermine the fabric of the country, and are practiced in their abilities to masquerade as loyalists. That will all change quickly and for good after authorities find a dead, dismembered tourist in their headquarters. Then they'll see. Meanwhile, back at the market, the camera crew who was going to give you a ride is packing up. Andrew Zimmern eats another eyeball and wonders where you went.

Once dead, you pass up through the celestial bodies and cross over through a milky white river of light to a vast place of healing energy. It looks like an endless sea of warm sparkling water and feels like you're swimming in an ocean of fizzy pink, Bengay-scented, unconditional liquid love.

Here you splash and play until you reach a white sand beach, where you're given a plush terry-cloth towel and a fizzy cocktail. A little motorized gadget-gizmo thing with wings whirs by, asking if you require anything else. You just want to know how long this place lasts. The whirring gizmo checks his little silver BlackBerry and says:

In saecula saeculorum! (For always and forever.)

You can stay as long as you like. That's the best part of enduring a sucky life. The one that's waiting when you cross over and join the sweet hereafter will be amazing to a commensurate degree.

92

You take a job at the Living Museum, which is located way out on Highway 494 between Home Depot and Bennigan's. The museum director, a wiry, spectacled man named Mr. Bickles, welcomes you. He says they strive to keep history alive by not only displaying pertinent historical artifacts, like genuine reproduction suits of armor and a gruesome medieval iron maiden, but also through reenacting history, so people can see what really happened. They've built several different structures on their property, a jousting ring, a sawmill, a castle with partial moat, and a penal colony work camp.

The Living Museum also does reenactments of Civil War battles, Roman gladiator fights, medieval jousting; most recently, they portrayed the First Battle of Saigon in the Vietnam War, which did not go over nearly as well as they thought it would. Even though the staging crew tried to meticulously re-create the jungles of Indochina in the woods behind Bennigan's, a bunch of real-life Vietnam vets showed up and booed everybody and shouted things like, "This is horse shit!" and "I saw good men die!" and tried to ruin it for everybody.

You're hired as a "Composite Character," which is a reenactor who plays anything and everything. A person who romps around in old-timey clothes and does old-timey things while museumgoers watch and take pictures, and whichever particular old-timey time you're reenacting varies from week to week. Sometimes it's World War II and you reenact battles dressed as a military nurse or a Nazi sympathizer. If it's Old Colonial Life, you sit in one-room wooden farmhouses and knit or churn butter and say things like, *"'Tis the year of our Lord 1771. Prithee, allow me to describe ye my adventures in the colony of Virginia...."*

Some reenactors specialize in certain time periods, like the Black Powder Enthusiasts, who are mostly fat guys who like to shoot muskets, or old Mr. Henry, who always plays President Lincoln. He never plays anything else. He brings all his own costumes from home, the black suit, the top hat, even the wiry black beard, which he keeps in a special wooden box. Becky, his fifteen-year-old granddaughter, plays the president's wife, Mary Todd. This is as creepy as it sounds, especially when President Lincoln is finished delivering a speech and takes his wife's hand while leading her offstage.

In general these specialty guys are a pain in the ass. They shout at anyone who's not being "authentic," which is the almighty point of everything around here, according to them. If anyone does something, says something, or even wears something historically incorrect, they'll catch an earful. "FARB!" someone will yell. That stands for "Far be it from me to tell you that was not around during the Civil War!" You'll be doing your thing and some idiot will yell, "FARB! Civil War soldiers wore their canteens on the left side! The *left* side! Fix it! Christ, next you'll be chewing gum!"

Besides the occasional FARBing, you like your job okay, but it's hard to make money since you're working for minimum wage and nobody thinks to tip the reenactors. In fact you're thinking about getting a second job waitressing at Bennigan's, when Mr. Bickles approaches you and asks if you'd be interested in picking up any side work. "As you know," he says, "we occasionally throw private parties here and we have a few coming up for the holidays. I'm looking for another Composite Character and the pay is double."

You say yes right away. Double pay means you can put off slinging buffalo chicken drummies at Bennigan's for another month. Mr. Bickles stresses you don't have to participate in any "extracurricular events" if you don't want to, but many employees do, since it gets bigger tips. This month the Society of Prehistoric Enthusiasts are hosting a caveman hunt. A week after that there's an "adult-themed" reenactment of Oliver Cromwell's seventeenth-century ban on Christmas. You can choose whichever sounds like more fun.

One of your fellow reenactors shrugs and says these after-hours events are just lame sex party boink fests for perverted old men who like to watch Puritans having sex in period clothing. You decide it's definitely creepy, but you definitely need the money.

If you work the caveman hunt, go to section 75 (p. 238).
If you work the Puritan war on Christmas, go to section 84 (p. 263).

93

From section 46

You sell the house. Jeremy's probably right. A museum would be crazy and weird, so you let him bring in a Dumpster and a crew, watching anxiously and with growing despair as he lays all of Miss Dottie's valuables outside on big blue tarps across the lawn, then slaps price tags on everything. Your anxiety coagulates into a thick, viscous disgust that makes it hard to breathe. When the house is finally emptied out, the Dumpsters full, and Miss Dottie's things gone, all you can do is stand in the middle of the living room and cry. Jeremy wants to know what's wrong.

You tell him *what's wrong* is you never want to see him again in your entire life. You leave and vow never to let anyone talk you out of a gut instinct again. That is, if you ever *have* a gut instinct again. All you can feel now is a blunt, gooey sadness and a widening tar pit of depression. You've got to do something before you sink too low.

At home your mother asks what's wrong but you have no idea what to say. Everything's pretty okay really, your rental properties are starting to chug along and they're producing a modest monthly income, just like Jeremy said they would. You're not rich-rich, you can't buy a yacht, but you don't have to work, so you have no idea why you're so unhappy. Worse, you have no idea which direction happiness is.

"Well," your mother suggests, "follow a honeybee. It's the only way to find the honey. Just stand perfectly still in one sunny spot and wait until you see a honeybee. Then follow him as far as you can, until you lose his trail. Wait right there until you see another bee. Then follow him. Keep going, bee by bee, until you get all the way to the hive. Where the honey is. Just follow any one little thing that pleases you as far as you can. Then wait there and slowly, pleasure by pleasure, you'll find your happiness, just like the honeybees!" Okay. You're a honeybee. You think about what makes you happy, but you just keep coming back to Miss Dottie's house. It was something about how she saved everything, protected her fragile belongings and preserved her history.

On a frustrated, blind whim, you do a Google search for: *Save everything, protect belongings, preserve history.* Lo and behold! Up pop thirty pages about historical preservation classes, architectural conservation seminars, museum collections care, and the conservation of cultural objects. There are several local universities and colleges that teach everything there is to know.

God love the honeybees.

You enroll in classes and dive headlong into the strange, cultish, somewhat closed society of historical conservationists, museum curators, and artifact conservators. This last group interests you the most. The *conservation of cultural objects* is basically just the science of saving things. Everything from rare artifacts to everyday objects has a life span, just like humans do, and that life can be greatly lengthened with proper care. It is the conservator's job to extend an object's life to the greatest degree possible.

What if everything in your life was handled with such care? To a future archaeologist, every single item in your life would have meaning. A sapphire ring, a prescription bottle of painkillers, a cookie tin filled with sand dollars collected on the beach. Who's to say what's valuable in the end? And if your life was the source material for a museum a thousand years from now, what artifacts would be on display? What documents would be archived in stacks, what events catalogued, what memories inventoried? Love letters? Photographs? Certainly your treasures from childhood. Soft scuffed-up jump ropes, dolls with dubious haircuts, broken dog collars, bracelets of braided yarn, all artfully presented and bearing index-card corsages of information nearby.

This pink plastic comb was most likely used on a daily basis—and not just for combing hair. The missing teeth and splayed ends of the uppermost tines are consistent with bite marks taken from Citizen X's dental trays (Exhibit A3) and would indicate it was chewed on frequently. This would also co-

incide with diary entries from the same time period (Exhibit C4), which reveal an ongoing nervous condition all through third grade, struggles with the early morning ritual of "getting ready."

The Museum of You would showcase a night garden of dried flowers. Paper-thin petals pressed and dried in sheets of feather-light white tissue, delicate specimens from a variety of significant moments. There'd be an entire wing for paper. Birth certificates, birthday cards, grocery lists, phone bills. It would all be of great interest to the careful team reconstructing your life. Every bit.

This makes you think—and it makes you get organized. You move into a small apartment on one of your properties and the first thing you do is paint everything arctic white. Wall-to-wall shelving units are installed, also white, and then you sort out all your worldly belongings, just as that archeological team might.

You store items in appropriate containers: photographs in airtight boxes, documents inside Mylar sleeves, breakables in undyed cotton muslin, organic matter (such as toenail clippings and stray eyelashes) pressed inside acid-free buffered tissue paper. You keep logbooks documenting the history of each item. Information and anecdotes that would be lost over time if not written down. The clothing has some of the more detailed entries.

ENTRY #3072 Gray cashmere sweater. Purchased at about fifteen years of age. Kissed for the first time while wearing this item. Spilled grape juice on it same night. Wore casually for years after. Stopped wearing it after Debbie Magers said it looked "spinsterish." Kept for sentimental value.

ENTRY #1027 Black combat boots. Purchased at unknown time from army/navy surplus store. Bought to achieve a "tough" look, but they hurt my feet. Kept because I liked how they looked in my closet. Like I was a person who would own combat boots.

It gives you a weird voyeuristic thrill to collect and comment on your own life, a life that seems more and more like a moving work of art, a living sculpture with removable, adaptable pieces. When you take something out from "the collection" to actually use it—say, if you want to wear a sweater out shopping or thrifting—you unwrap it from its heavy-duty plastic bag, go out, come back, and return the item to its proper place. Then you take out the logbook and enter anything interesting or historically significant that happened while wearing it.

ENTRY #3072 Gray cashmere sweater. Purchased at about fifteen years of age. Kissed for the first time while wearing this item. Spilled grape juice on it same night. Wore casually for years after. Stopped wearing it after Debbie Magers said it looked "spinsterish." Kept for sentimental value.

+Added 04/15 Wore gray sweater to movies. No negative comments.

+Added 06/03. Wore gray sweater to yogurt cart. Got ogled by man with large head. He might have been mad, but Debbie Magers can suck it.

There's a great and unsuspected therapy in this process. It makes you think about what you do and buy and say out loud. It creates a portrait, delineates a form in the smoky mist of uncertainty. This is who you are. This is what you wear, this is what happened. Instead of being a haphazard jumble of unrelated events, you have a picture now, you are a story.

Plus, you seem to acquire far less crap. Before you buy a disposable razor or a plastic box of paper clips, you ask yourself, "Will I want to catalogue this? Will this make a good addition to the Museum of Me?" Pondering this idea winnows out 99 percent of new purchases. You save your money and buy better things of higher value, like a whalebone-handled straight razor from an antique shop. It doesn't shave your legs well, it's for men and cuts quite a bit, but it's lovely and the shopkeeper said it was recovered from a sunken ship during World War II. Possibly a lie, but a good lie, so accepted.

After a while, though, you get so good at cataloguing your life, it gets a little routine, a bit boring. You need a bigger challenge, so you take over the apartment next to the one you're already in (perks of being the landlord) and you give it the museum makeover. White walls, floor-to-ceiling white shelving. Now you just need something new to collect.

You use your modest income to find bargains in thrift stores and second-hand shops. You go to estate sales, garage sales, and study the obituaries in search of the next great cache of treasures. You slowly build a collection of strange art and certain artifacts and keep going to preservation classes at the university. About three years later, you've taken them all.

You've studied artifact appraisals, preserving furniture coatings, conservation of specialty papers, the chemistry of pigment, proper framing techniques for papier-mâché, the safe handling of ivory, the unpredictable world of varnishes, housing options for ancient textiles, caring for Chinese woodblock prints, and how to kill mildew on over forty-five different surfaces.

You're offered a rare opportunity. An anonymous collector named Mr. X offers you a mysterious job. He wants to expand his art collections. Fine art, modern art, ancient artifacts, architectural antiquities, you name it—he wants to make sure he owns the very best of it. You'll act as conservator for the artifacts he's already acquired and you'll help him expand his collection by buying whatever you think is best. You'll travel quite a bit, have a generous salary, and can work from anywhere you want.

You accept the position with Mr. X but you never meet him. He doesn't want to reveal his identity. Your paychecks are direct-deposited, as is the generous "starting bonus" of two hundred thousand dollars. Mr. X's secretary, Miss White, recommends that you use this bonus to buy a wardrobe "worthy of the White House," and adds, "Our clients usually don't feel comfortable around people who wear camouflage-print sweatpants or scuffed-up flip-flops."

Okay, how did she know that's been your daily ensemble for the past two weeks? Has Mr. X been spying on you? Is there some van parked outside your house? A guy in a trench coat obtaining long-lens images of you leaving the lab late at night while eating microwaved hoagies from the vending machines? If you'd known you were being watched, you would have at least worn a bra.

Your first official assignment from Mr. X is to buy "something Russian." What kind of work Mr. X wants, what genre, what influence, what artist, what time period, is not specified, so you go to Sotheby's on Bond Street in London and bid on a work you'd like in your own home. It's an oil painting by Boris Grigoriev titled *Faces of Russia*, and many critics have called it the most important Russian work since the Communist revolution. The piece comes from the collection of the late Mstislav Rostropovich, one of the greatest cellists in Russia. You figure Mr. X will like added intrigue. He does. Very much. Miss White relays his approval of your purchase and gives you your next assignment. He wants something "big, cool, and conceptual."

Big and cool and conceptual? Can do! You manage to secure a work by the hot American artist Cameron Gainer. It's an eerily realistic sea serpent that stands over twelve feet tall and is hieroglyphically titled _/. It's meant to be floated out on a large body of water where it lurks like a real-life Loch Ness Monster. Mr. X loves it. He even builds a pond for it. Miss White tells you now Mr. wants some "old stuff," so you fly to Greece and buy him a marble statue of Adonis, which once stood at the Acropolis.

So it goes, you wandering the world, attending auctions, browsing museum collections, being extravagantly received by art dealers and prestigious galleries. It isn't until you're in Hong Kong buying a Simon Birch painting that someone pulls you aside and says, "What's it like working for a dictator?" You think they mean "a tough boss," and so you happily explain Mr. X is actually very accommodating, but they mean an *actual* dictator. It turns out you are expanding the art empire of Kim Jong-il.

Furious, you send a final purchase to Mr. X: Anselm Kiefer's *Buch mit Flügeln* ("Book with Wings"), which is a beautiful sculpture made of a large book affixed with wide wings and then dipped in metal. You include directions with the piece, as you usually do, and tell Mr. X the artist intends for the viewer to *lick* the sculpture every day. It's how he intended this piece to be "experienced." The visceral sensation of running one's tongue along the metal pages is the only way to truly understand its meaning. What you *do not* tell Mr. X is that the entire work is dipped in lead.

Six months later, when Miss White mentions Mr. X hasn't been feeling well, you don't say anything. You're dead a few days later. A soft-shoed man with a silencer takes you out from behind. Kim Jong-il, who's listened in on your every conversation with Miss White, thought your silence was suspicious. It was worth it, though, because Kiefer's lead sculpture, which the North Korean tyrant licked for good luck every morning and every night, takes its toll. He's dead inside a year.

94

You go to work at the Pancake Ranch. It is the quickest way to make some money and get out of the house. Your parents' depressing, sad glances were making you go crazy. You're not going back there. You'll go to a homeless shelter before you move back in with them. Besides, you make enough money at the Pancake Ranch to pay your rent *and* you get to eat unlimited pancakes, so it's sort of a sweet gig.

You pick up waitressing right away. By just pretending you're a kindergarten teacher for a bunch of legless retarded kids who ask stupid questions and can't get anything for themselves. You have the menu memorized by your third day at work. There are forty different kinds of pancakes at the Pancake Ranch.

Buttermilk, Buckwheat, Dollar-size, Sourdough, Flapjacks, Pigs in Blankets, Belgian Style, Cherry, Strawberry, Blueberry, Raspberry, Raisin, Lingonberry, Lemon Curd, Apple Cinnamon, Almond, Banana Bran Nut, Honey Oat, Bacon Bit, Cornbread Crumble, Cinnamon Spice, Smoked Sausage, Peanut Butter and Jelly, Hazelnut, Chocolate Chip, Coffee Chip, Cookie Dough, Butterscotch Chip, Pineapple Chunk, Pistachio Mint, Caramel Crisp, Georgia Pecan, Tahitian Lemon Coconut, Caramel Orange Whip, Pralines and Cream, Rocky Road, Rice Krispy Bar, M&M, Chocolate Bacon, and Wheat Germ.

You have never once had anyone order Wheat Germ. They order everything else, though, and they eat it, too, which is disgusting considering the pancakes are as big as the plates and the plates are as big as steering wheels.

Everything is supersized at the Pancake Ranch, *especially* the people. The overcrowded dining room is packed with ravenous, walrus-sized customers wedged into red vinyl booths, and their similarity with chunky marine animals does not end in size. They waddle around, knock things over, bleat for syrup, belch out loud, and roll their big bellies heavenward after eating enough not just for a person but for a whole pod.

They're mathematical idiots, often leaving 2 percent tips or nothing at all, but everyone's a self-starter when it comes to complaining. When the slightest thing upsets them—perhaps their flapjacks weren't properly slathered in butter or their coffee wasn't instantly refilled like Harry Potter's magical goblet—they fluently and vociferously recite their civil rights and your legal obligations to the customer. The customer is always right! They demand satisfaction! They're not paying for wagon-wheel-sized pancakes that weren't hot as the sun!

The manager, Gross Gordon, which is what everyone calls him, always sides with customers no matter how ridiculous their complaints are, because he's *king* of the pig-tusked walruses, a greedy little reptile-eyed man with thick, stubby Vienna-sausage fingers who sits on a cracked vinyl stool at the register all day making creepy comments about female customers walking in, like, "Damn! Like to get that one in my van!"

He's always rubbing up against you and saying he'd give you better sections and more overtime if only you'd be "nice" to him on the drums of canola oil in the janitor's closet. Besides the instant heave the idea of touching Gordon gives you, those drums are also disgusting and old. All the food is cheap at Pancake Ranch, but the ingredients are even cheaper. The cheapest. Like army-surplus cheap. Gordon buys "irregulars" from discount warehouses, whole pallets of expired canned fruit, big plastic buckets of sugar from China, which taste like sweet drywall powder. Real butter is too expensive, so he buys only large drums of dehydrated canary-yellow granules, which get mixed with water to make a chemical version of whipped "butter topping." By cutting costs Gordon can skim off the top. You've seen him stack oily wads of cash in a padlocked cabinet in his office.

Creep.

Sometimes you dream about shoving Gordon into the walk-in freezer and suffocating him in an industrial-sized tub of pancake lard, but he's just one cast member in this theater of the oily and the damned. There are so many others. Backstabbing waitresses, mean-as-hell fry cooks covered in murky prison tattoos, thieving busboys who steal tips off your tables, cheap customers, bad tippers, messy eaters, furniture rearrangers, separate-checkers, people who scream, *Hey, waitress! Hey! Yoooooo-hooooooooo!* Persnickety penny-pinching senior citizens, boorish husbands, impatient wives, snotty toddlers, screaming babies, and your personal favorite, the loud, obnoxious, rage-inducing teenagers who create sugar art on the table and spend a dollar on a donut while hogging a table for an hour.

There's the physical hell, too. The headaches, muscle aches, sore back, and bunions from hours on your feet, gaining considerable weight from all the employee-discount pancakes, and of course the nasty burn you got on your ass from accidentally sitting on a plastic drum of chemical grill cleaner left out back. You're a wreck.

Then you find out Aidan is dating a girl *half his age* and he apparently started dating her *while* you were still together. Her name, and this is the best part, is Shitaye, which sounds like French for "shitty." Worse still, your friends knew, but didn't want to upset you. All this presses like a vise grip on your brain. You feel like if one more thing happens, you're going to kill yourself or someone else. Then one more thing happens.

At the end of an already long day, just as you're about to clock out, Gordon gives you a table of fifteen that walks in with no reservation. They're irritable and cranky from the start, asking why you don't have regular food instead of just pancakes. "Well," you say, unable to keep the sarcasm from your voice, "I guess because it's called the *Pancake Ranch*, not the *Regular Food* Ranch. You know?"

Well, this just about unnerves some guy at the head of the table, who stands up and puts his finger right in your face and starts shouting that you shouldn't talk to a man that way, you're *just a waitress*. He says, "Just because you didn't do anything respectable with your life doesn't mean you shouldn't show respect to people who have!"

You look at him with his hands on his hips, his impertinent face stuck deliberately too close to yours . . . and you slap him. Just haul off and give him a big ol' slap right across the face. The entire room comes to a screeching, silent halt and everyone stares at you, speechless.

Then you slap him again.

Everyone in the room starts shouting, Gordon waddles over in a flubber flash and apologizes profusely, pushing you away and telling the man his whole meal is free. Then Gordon fires you and says to get out right now. You're hysterical.

Fired? What a freaking joke! *Fired?* How could he fire you?

You go home and lie down. Over the next few months, you look for work, but there's nothing. Your money runs out. You can't make rent and you're not going home. What are you going to do? There is actually a shelter run by a women's group who offer job training and career services. If you go there, they might help you get back on your feet. You could also break into the restaurant and steal Gordon's money out of that goddamned cabinet. He's probably got big money in there right now. It's stolen money anyway, and he owes you. You've suffered enough for a big oily cash settlement.

If you go to the homeless shelter, go to section 85 (p. 268).
If you rob the Pancake Ranch, go to section 118 (p. 371).

95

From section 46

You tell Jeremy that despite what he thinks, you're still going to turn Miss Dottie's house into a museum. You know it doesn't make a ton of sense, it's not exactly an investment, but still, your gut is telling you to protect this woman's collection.

Well, he thinks it's crazy. He doesn't want to own a weird museum. You put your foot down and tell him you've made your final decision and you're doing it whether he likes it or not. He doesn't like that *one bit* and tries harder to reason with you, which makes you try harder to reason back. Pretty soon you're arguing and he loses his temper and starts yelling. "Why are you so controlling?" he shouts. "Who made you Queen of Sheba?" You inform him you made *yourself* Queen of Sheba, and if he doesn't feel like bowing down, maybe he should go find a concubine to date.

That's it. He *knew* you were unstable, but this is ridiculous. He can't have a partner who comes up with half-cocked ideas and ignores plans that were already made and agreed on because of some "gut feeling." He's not staying here and running some freaky side-show exhibit of crap. He's leaving. He grabs his stuff, says good luck, and bids you good day.

Good day?

After he leaves, you stand there alone in Miss Dottie's mint green kitchen holding a ceramic chicken, telling yourself everything will be fine, even though you're sure it won't be. A fuse blows and all the lights in Dottie's house wink out, leaving you alone in the dark, holding a ceramic chicken. *Fabulous.* You venture down into the basement, feeling your way gingerly over the cobwebby, crumbling walls until you find the fuse box, which looks part tractor engine, part evil robot. You throw the switch and the lights blink back on, revealing a small door you hadn't noticed before.

Behind the boiler is a little hidden room, which must have been used to store coal, judging by the smudgy black nuggets strewn around the floor. But as you turn to go, your eye catches something farther back in the room behind the low wall of neatly stacked firewood. There, lying on the basement floor just next to the drain, is an old black coffin. You take a step closer. On the coffin lid sits a small white card, turning yellow from age and bearing small words handwritten in a tiny, spidery scrawl.

DO NOT OPEN.

If you do not open the coffin, go to section 107 (p. 340).

If you open the coffin, go to section 119 (p. 373).

96

From section 49

You're not crazy or stupid and you're *not* staying in that pit. You go back to the lodge and tell Maurizio everything. He laughs and tells you not to worry, there was never a prison here, it was more like a boot camp for soldiers and to his knowledge there was never even one death. Then he fires Santiago. In fact, he fires the entire staff and rehires Hondurans who hardly speak English. He says it's because the lodge is losing money and needs cheaper labor, but you don't like this new crew. They don't talk much and they're secretive. The chef cooks things that look dumped out of a can, and the busboy is always sharpening his knife.

Maurizio starts selling inventory to make ends meet. The hotel's motorboat, the spare generator, all the china used for weddings and special occasions. Your paradise is taken apart piece by piece as chaise longues and microwaves walk out the door. *Not to worry!* Maurizio has a plan. Tonight he's having the chef prepare a celebration dinner. Something to cheer you up. You appreciate his attempts to boost morale, but the meal leaves a lot to be desired, soggy garlic bread and some red-sauce pasta resembling a creation *du Chef Boyardee*. The wine, however, a French Côtes du Rhone unearthed from Maurizio's private stash, more than makes up for the tinned noodles.

As does the second bottle and the third.

When you wake up the next morning, you don't know where you are. *Why is it so cold? Ice cold!* You're sitting in a tub of ice water. Your arms won't move. *What the . . . ?* You're in fact sitting in a long cardboard box filled with ice. The ice comes up to your waist. *How long have you been here? What the hell?* "Maurizio!" you whimper, the pain stabbing you hard in the side. A wave of nausea knots your stomach as you look around the cold, blue-tiled room. You're in the . . . *refrigerated storage shed?* It's where the kitchen keeps surplus meats. Frozen foods. Extra ice.

That's when you see the little note taped to the side of your box. Damp ink running into the slushy ice water.

> *Don't move. Your kidney has been taken.*
> *Help will come tomorrow or the day after.*
> *Whatever you do, keep still.*

The lightbulb swings overhead. You realize no one is coming. Suddenly, the seams of the wet cardboard box give way, spilling soupy blood-water and diamond-bright ice all over the floor. You'd been there awhile.

97

From section 63

You stay on the island. It's got to be safer than venturing out onto the violent, stormy waves. All your guests herd themselves into the main lobby and huddle together on the floor away from the windows, which shudder and bang in the growing wind. The building groans as palm trees thrash outside and beat the clapboards with spiny wind-whipped hands. You expect people to cry or pray, but everyone stays quiet, grasping at one another, holding on to one another, looking up toward the walls and ceiling and waiting for what's next.

There's the sound of tearing fabric. Glass shattering. The windows blast open and a torrent of wild air comes charging into the room, slashing and ripping at everything with frantic claws of lacerating debris. Your hands and face are instantly cut, forcing you to fall back onto the floor just as the first wave hits.

You could hear it first. Like a deep engine troubling its way across the island. You look up just as water explodes through the room from every direction—through the windows, through the doors, through the floorboards. It's up to your chest before you can even stand, then it pulls you away hard in its vortex. You're under way. The lobby becomes a churning cauldron of seawater, catching up women, children, sofa cushions, grandfather clocks, and loveseats without preference.

The salt stings your eyes blind. You paddle furiously, trying in vain to head for an open window as they merry-go-round by, hoping to get out before you drown inside the room. The water surges up, carrying you toward the ceiling, and soon you're clinging with a few others to the chandelier. Then you're choking. Sputtering. Animal instincts kick in and you grab for anything, kicking and thrashing.

Then it's over. You're a paper doll drifting through a room of water. Arms raised up as though ready to play a piano. The picture mechanism in your head sputters out, trailing out the last vestiges of memory and thought. All is dark. Then a warm light reappears. Calming. Steady. You hear no voice and see no face and yet a woman is calling you forward. You swim to her.

It's your eighth grandmother on your mother's side. You'd never even heard of her, but she's your spirit guide come to help you cross over. She drowned, too, when she was only six years old. She takes you sky aspiring into an ocean of spectral light. There you feel a comfort and peace you've never known. You're reconnected with all your family, and not just immediate members, but *everyone*. There are over five thousand generations to meet, all the way back to the dawn of man. It's incredible getting to know them, because everything you are is actually from them. Not just how you look (and everyone does look related, even Caveman Grandpa), but everything else about you, too. Your likes, dislikes, psychological temperament, physical strengths, medical weaknesses, sexual tendencies, even the music you like and the foods you hate—it can all be traced back to genealogical roots.

You spend most of your time with your clan up in heaven, always meeting new family members, since people are always coming and going. Often you're called to assist on Earth; it's your duty to guide any family members who drown and need help crossing over. You have an Irish cousin (sixteen times removed) who drowns in the Atlantic Ocean while jet skiing off the coast of Mumbles, Wales. Another distant uncle chokes on his own vomit after a seizure. And twin girls have a tragic accident in an inflatable backyard swimming pool. You're always extra gentle with the little ones, who are often confused and want to go home, not caring or understanding that the rest of their family, the larger part of their family, is actually right here, waiting.

98

From section 49

You decide to stay in the pit. So finally, on the chosen night, you and Santiago steal away, creeping along the old oxen trail that winds its serpentine path toward the prison, trying your best not to think of the hidden creatures under the thick ipecac vines that bramble along the forest floor.

When you arrive at the yawning oubliette, Santiago gives you a canvas bag containing a bottle of water, a chocolate bar, a box of wooden matches, a flashlight, a green fluorescent glow stick, and a spidery, hand-drawn map with a red X on it. Then he lowers an aluminum ladder down into the hole until you hear it touch the ground. He pushes it around to make sure it won't slip and he hangs on to the top while you begin to climb down.

"Stay till dawn," he says, "then you come back up. One night, it's all over."

Okay, just focus on your hands, see them reaching right in front of you. Breathe slowly. One rung, two, three, watch your foot. Steady on, you can do this. You force yourself to breathe slowly but your heart is fluttering like a hummingbird caught in your throat. Your mouth is dry and your legs feel rubbery, as though you're spelunking down a perilous cliff instead of just climbing down a ladder. "Okay?" Santiago whispers from up top. "You holding on?"

"Yes! Almost there!"

You descend deeper into the heavy, humid, rotting-butcher-shop air; it's hard to breathe, and you've no sooner gotten to the bottom and taken a tentative step onto the soft mossy ground than Santiago yanks up the ladder. *Ffft-ffft-ffft-fff-ffftt!* The ladder disappears over your head. You start shouting at Santiago to *stop!* But he hushes you. "No!" he says. "You don't want to wake them up!" Then with great effort he drags something big and heavy over the mouth of the hole, blocking you out from the world completely.

This was not part of the plan. Fear rushes in and smothers you. It's pitch-black, you can't see your hand in front of your face. You turn on your flashlight and immediately stumble over the crushed body of Mr. David Sunderland. Given his proximity to the opening, it looks as though he fell through the hole, or was thrown. He's covered with insects and maggots; you have to turn away so you won't vomit.

The pit is shaped like a wine bottle, the narrow entrance expanding down into a large vaulted room, part of which has crumbled away, exposing a hallway that traverses its circumference. You investigate carefully, moving slowly through the dusty corridor, and that's when you remember the map Santiago gave you. It shows the main holding cell where you first descended and the narrow hallway that you're in now. Maybe Santiago was trying to kill you, but maybe not. You locate the red X on the map and set out to find it.

The dark hallways snake along in an underground labyrinth and you have to retrace your steps a few times through the airless, dead-silent darkness until you come to where you think the red X should be. It's at the end of a hallway that leads to two wooden doors. One door is big, and one is small. They both have cast-iron handles and rusty iron hinges. The X you're looking for must be behind one of these doors, but which one?

If you open the bigger door, go to section 44 (p. 152).
If you open the smaller door, go to section 68 (p. 223).

99

From section 63

You evacuate the guests quickly, using every available boat on the island. The cruiser, the ferry, even the skiffs. Everyone's wearing life jackets and clutching their thrown-together luggage as the boats storm across the choppy water. Dear God, please don't let one fall overboard. No way will your insurance cover it. When you land in Jumeirah, however, you realize something else is happening. At first you think it's typhoon evacuation, but military men are running down the street in full riot gear. Camera crews in satellite vans barrel past and explosions are going off somewhere in the city.

You herd your guests across the street, all of whom have gone from brave to irritating the minute they got on dry land. *What's happening? What's going on? What are we doing? Where are we going?* How should you know? Nobody told you to have a natural disaster/civil unrest plan ready for these people! You spot people rushing into the Hyatt and say, "Okay, everybody, let's go to a real hotel!" You're hurrying them inside when a jeep speeding by slams to a stop. It's Gabe Stone. He says Iranian insurgents have planted bombs all over the city and thirty-six people were blown to hell at the mall. Sheik Nahyan, president of the UAE, has declared war on Iran.

"Do you hear me?" Gabe shouts. "Motherfucking Dubai has gone to war with motherfucking Iran! This ain't no British tea party! These fuckers are nuclear! This whole place will get blown to hell! Get in!" You tell him your hotel guests are inside the Hyatt, and he says, "They're not your guests anymore, they're motherfucking refugees! Let's go!"

If you get in the jeep with Gabe, go to section 69 (p. 225).
If you stay with the guests, go to section 53 (p. 177).

From section 54

You invite Auguste and Philippe to stay with you. Initially they refuse, but eventually they cheerfully and with much gratitude relent. You like having these two in the house. Auguste makes magical beignets with a bit of flour and sugar she finds in the pantry. Next you're savoring lavender-scented crème brûlée with chilled gooseberry tea and seared lamb chops with rhubarb-mint chutney. Everything she makes is unique and divine. She should open a restaurant; she'd have a Michelin star in no time.

And while Auguste is an excellent cook, Philippe is a genius botanist. He procures seeds, shoots, herbs, and saplings from all over the island, which he diligently plants in the garden. (You suspect he steals many of them from the resorts with sprawling manicured lawns with lax security.) He's actually started an entire section of the yard that attracts the most unusual and exotic-looking butterflies. Sometimes you'll drag a lawn chair out there at dusk and watch them flutter and go.

Finally you're not alone. Well, sometimes you feel alone, especially when you hear the two of them having unabashed, boisterous sex—and they have a lot of sex. Morning, noon, tea time, dusk, twilight, evening, night, witching hour, you name it, they've had sex at all hours of the day. The house seems to pause and listen when they do, the birds temporarily silenced, the china rattling faintly.

They stay for two weeks and then two weeks more. Their passports are delivered but nobody seems to want to go home. Why would they? You buy all the liquor and food, and what else is there to want? The house is lovely, the view superb, and the easy lifestyle tranquil enough to drink. Philippe eventually says he has to go back to work. He has to pay off student loans. He tells you how much he owes and you're surprised how much botany school costs. Seems like you could wander around in the woods and learn it all yourself.

You're sad to see them go, especially because this time of year it's cooling off just a bit and everyone's going home. The island's population dwindles down to the size (and to some degree the mentality) of a suburban high school. Half the little shops close down and the lively restaurants aren't so lively anymore, not only because they cut their hours, but oftentimes the liquor supplies dry up. The islanders all ease up on working and retreat back into their neglected lives, which were put on hold for the lucrative but exhausting tourist season.

It's this time of year that's the loneliest.

As you load Auguste and Philippe into your new Range Rover (shipped direct from Tanzania), your heart is heavy and you feel sluggish, depressed, like gravity is turned up too high. You drive them to the port and see the vast ship waiting to ferry them back to the mainland. Philippe starts to say you'll see each other again soon, but you know you won't. As he pulls his bag from the car you're hit with a wave of misery like nothing you've known. If you have to go back to an empty house you may go crazy, too crazy to even figure out how to get back home.

They are boarding their ship, just stepping onto the gangplank, when a cold feeling of isolation looms up and you hear yourself shout, "Stop!"

They turn and look at you.

"How much are your student loans? I'll pay them!"

You tell them you're a millionaire, a multimillionaire, something you haven't told anyone. Not exactly. Surely they knew you had money with this gorgeous house and no job, but you tell them you can afford just about anything . . . and that changes everything.

They come back with you to the house and you're grateful, even though you don't know why. You just don't want to be alone, or maybe you don't want them to go or maybe you just wanted them to stay. You open one of your best bottles of wine to celebrate and they seem happy and you seem happy, but somehow they aren't and you aren't. Strange things happen when people look at you differently.

They do. Look at you differently, that is. Philippe still busies himself in the garden and Auguste cooks up her creations like never before, but there's something in their eyes, a pause before they speak, and you can't quite tell what's in that pause. Are they shy now that they know about you? Incredulous? Angry? Jealous? You can't tell. Things are the same except they're different.

You insist on happiness. If you're in paradise, then happiness is required. You pay off Philippe's student loans with one wire transfer to the bank. Then you buy them each expensive gifts to cheer them up. They seem cagey, though, restless, and you're always thinking of new ways to make them happy, but it feels very much like Siegfried and Roy with their trained white tigers performing in Las Vegas. Everyone has diamonds and gold, they have everything they could possibly want, but they can't go anywhere else. They're stuck in their particular gilded cage in a particular freak show that isn't running anywhere else. It's draining them all to death because a cage is a cage, even if it's gold.

One night, after a beautiful dinner, Auguste makes you a warm pudding. Chocolate thyme with crème anglaise. It's rich, decadent, absolutely heavenly. You eat two bowls and tell her this dish should go on her menu. "But the chocolate," she says, "it was from Switzerland. You only had one block of it left."

"So we'll buy more! We'll import whole crates of it!" And then your lips start tingling. "Was there pepper in the pudding?" you ask. "Cayenne?"

Auguste shakes her head no and walks out the back door, leaving it open so you can see the balmy night. Wow. Your head feels strange and there's a bitter taste on your tongue. You go and lie down. Philippe checks in on you in a few minutes. Your heart is hammering in your chest and you're sweating, but your arms and legs feel like they're made of cement. It aches to move them.

Philippe sits beside your bed and takes your hand. Then he ties a green rubber band around your wrist, winding it twice, painfully tight so your skin turns white underneath it. After a moment he says, "We poisoned you. It was in the pudding." He pauses to see if you're listening and goes on.

"Water hyssop," he says. "It's a plant. A creeping vine, really. People use it to cure lots of things. Epilepsy. Asthma. They even rub it on the skin for rheumatism."

He hears something, checks his watch, and returns his steady gaze. The paralysis is spreading up your fingertips now, through your arms and toward your heart. It's as though someone is laying sheets soaked in ice water on top of you, one after the other, each layer bringing a new depth of cold to your blood. "In larger doses, though," he says, "it's quite deadly. Nerve damage, central nervous system collapse. Very complete."

You try to say something but you're frozen, unable to speak or move. It seems darker, too, like someone is pushing you very slowly under black water.

"There is an antidote," Philippe says, "and we'll give you some, if you sign some papers." Then Auguste appears, and without looking at you she hands Philippe some official-looking documents. "This is power of attorney," he says. "Sign it and we'll give you medicine." Auguste then brings him a small silver tray carrying a small brown glass bottle with a black eyedropper. "A few drops of this and you can move again," he says and makes an abrupt move toward you. He shoves his hands underneath your armpits and pulls you up to a sitting position. Then he picks up your hand and holds it above the signature line.

"The rubber band kept most of the poison from getting to your fingers," he says. "It'll be stiff, though." You look at him and feel wetness on your collarbone. You realize you're drooling. With great concentrated effort you scratch out your signature. Your hand feels like a lightbulb at the end of a string; it and it alone responds to the nerve signals firing down your arm. It looks freakish, like Frankenstein's hand. When you're done he removes the green rubber band from your wrist and the toxin in your body floods through your fingers, making them as inoperable as the rest of you.

He gets up, and there's Auguste at the door with their bags all packed and ready to go. She silently hands him the keys to your car. "It isn't personal, you know," he says as he hoists a duffle bag onto his shoulder. "We like you very much. Don't think we didn't like you, because we did." Auguste remains quiet, looking at her feet. She clears her throat.

"Oh, right," Philippe says and takes the brown bottle off the tray. He administers twenty drops of liquid, which you cannot taste because your tongue has gone into premature rigor mortis, too. "This should work in about two hours," he says, "and when you can get up, you want to call the clinic immediately. I already checked and Mrs. Soro is there till dawn. The good thing is you cooperated and we got the medicine in fast, before the poison stopped your heart." He smiles and kisses you on the forehead. "Philippe!" Auguste snaps, looking at her watch. "All right then, au revoir, cheri!" He stands and they go out together, leaving all the doors to the house wide open. You close your eyes and let the darkness come for you.

101

From section 50

You tell the ranch foreman, Buddy "Smokin' Gun" Stewart, that you're turning the BS6Q into a dude ranch. He'll continue running the daily operations, while his younger brother, Billy "Big Boy" Stewart, organizes all the guest activities—the riding lessons, horse clinics, overnight campouts, cattle drives, fishing trips, skeet shoots, trap shoots, and river rafting. Billy's wife, Lilly, can take care of the guest accommodations, cleaning crew, and kitchen staff. That means all you have to do is be the consummate hospitable hostess, something you had hoped to do part-time, possibly while traveling, but the one thing that becomes immediately clear is that even though they told you this was going to be easy, no work at all, it isn't true. You have to live on a ranch in order to run it. If you're going in, you're going *all* in.

You give notice at work and move out to Montana, where you oversee the construction of a thirty-five-room log cabin guesthouse. A pool, spa, and state-of-the-art shooting range is added. You join the Montana Association of Dude Ranchers and advertise in several travel and leisure magazines— but a year later, despite the first-class accommodations and spectacular scenery, the BS6Q Dude Ranch is mostly empty. It turns out dude ranching is a very competitive industry, and there are bigger, more established ranches nearby, which all have great reputations.

After months without any guests, Lilly says she has a friend who needs a room to rent. Tessa-Mae works from home and has lots of gentleman callers. About five a night, in fact. It doesn't take you long to figure out she's turning tricks. At first you want to kick her out, but Buddy talks you out of it. He says this may be the one thing that separates the Big Sky Ranch from all the others. Plus, Tessa-Mae has lots of other girlfriends who want to rent rooms. Why not give it a try? You can always stop the cowgirl rodeo later, if you want to.

So the girls move in one by one and make themselves at home. Their clients are perfect gentlemen. You never have a problem. Some drink a little too much, but in general the men seem downright grateful and humbled by this palace of sex they've been allowed into. They treat your place like a sanctuary, a mecca. The only incident is when a fat guy named "Big Larry" has a heart attack while on top of one of the girls and you have to call the sheriff. He doesn't care about the girls turning tricks; he's one of your best customers. Plus, you routinely make donations to the police precinct ball. That's one of the tricks to staying in business. That and keeping your neighbors happy. You roll them cash from time to time, ensuring your little secret world here stays protected.

Running a whorehouse isn't all fun and games. There's lots of scheduling issues, advertising headaches, and hooker drama. Jealous interactions, possessive boyfriends, violent ex-husbands, and constant day-care issues. It feels a lot like being a full-time therapist and part-time mother to a group of women who consistently, without fail, make the most asinine decisions possible. The girls like working on the ranch, though, and your reputation spreads until you pretty much can pick the cream of the whorehouse crop. Your prices go up and your clientele gets more and more well-heeled. Pretty soon you're providing services for mayors and governors, who come out and stay for whole weeks at a time. You have to build adjoining accommodations just for the many men who come on sex holidays. They love the ranch, because not only do they have their sexual fantasies fulfilled any time of the day or night, but they can play eighteen holes on the golf course and shoot AK-47s afterward. It's a perfect world for men, which could only be built by women.

There's another world women can build perfectly and that's one for themselves. You get the idea to expand services one day when a group of women pull up to the ranch. They got off the highway and got lost, meandering down country lanes until Billy found them. When they asked him where the nearest hotel was, he shrugged and told them to follow him. Naturally you offered them a place to stay for the night and when they found out about the extra amenities available on the property, they wanted to know if you had any gentlemen available for consort.

Why didn't you think of that before?

So starts the next chapter of life on the ranch, which people now call the Biscuit Ranch. You build an adjacent guest house, paint it all up like a cute New England cottage, landscape the hell out of the lawn, create a Zen garden, a walking path, and a tranquility fountain. You construct a full-service spa, a yoga studio, and a bakery. The guest rooms all have Jacuzzis and complimentary mineral bath bars. The service rooms are decorated in a variety of tasteful themes: the newlywed apartment, the high school sweetheart room, the jungle room, the Queen of Sheba room (more of a chamber), the executive office suite, and so on. Finally you populate your new Casanova Cottage with half a dozen sexy little boy toys and offer full-service companion packages to women.

Soon you have to hire a dozen more.

Once word gets out that there's a five-star vacation destination with botanical gardens, in-room chocolate fountains, and on-demand oral services, your reservations list books out a year in advance. It soon seems obvious you ought to expand—especially after you find a loophole that allows your bordello to be legal. All you have to do is make the Biscuit Ranch a church. Then, not only can you charge for sexual services, you're also tax-exempt. Your guests must become "members" of the church when they arrive by signing a ledger and receiving a Biscuit Ranch ID card. They don't get billed for rooms or services; they simply receive a tab at the end of their stay suggesting a specific donation to the church. This amount reflects their activities while at the ranch. Their electronic ID card is swiped for every meal, massage, and blow job. Then when they check out, the computer politely asks for a contribution. Often it's quite a substantial contribution; it's not unusual for a weekend at the ranch to run ten thousand dollars.

Of course, it takes some work at first to become a church. In order to meet the IRS guidelines for a nonprofit religion, you must adhere to strict rules.

You already have a place of worship, hold regular services (tent parties), send out monthly newsletters—and boy, do you have devoted congregations. Your board of directors is comprised of your ten best, richest customers (board meetings are held on their yachts), and your official statement of belief says: OUR MINISTRY BELIEVES IN LOVE, LAUGHTER, AND THE PURSUIT OF HAPPINESS. Naturally your application for church status meets immediate and fierce opposition, but no one who stands against you is quite as convincing or connected as the state senator, two lieutenant governors, and retired justice of the Supreme Court who are all regular Biscuit Ranch clients and who would just hate to have surveillance footage end up in the wrong hands.

So the "Biscuit Ministry" is born.

As the ordained pastor of the church, you regularly visit the satellite Biscuit Ranches all over the country. They're not all ranches, though; there's a Biscuit Ranch penthouse in New York and a Biscuit Ranch steamboat anchored on the Mississippi in New Orleans. The Las Vegas ranch even has a drive-thru, where cars pull into a large illuminated building and proceed onto automated conveyor belts so drivers have their hands free for "counseling sessions," as they're now called.

To say your business venture is successful would be like saying Bill Gates has some pretty good pocket money. Your empire builds and expands across seventeen states and overseas to Paris and Stuttgart. (You never enjoy the Stuttgart visits. Those people are into some weird shit. You drew the line when customers asked for horses to be brought in.) Your fortune amasses into the vicinity of sultans and teen pop stars. You buy islands, sports teams, hotel chains, and the San Francisco Zoo.

The media vilifies you, the religious right endorses crucifying you, and some oil titan in Texas offers a bounty on your head. Anyone who successfully assassinates "the Queen of Sleaze" will be put in his will and inherit a fortune. This of course invites rebuttal. You tell Barbara Walters on *The View* that only a natural-born idiot would put an assassin in his will. "The bad news is he might actually convince someone to blow you to hell," Whoopi Goldberg says, "but the good news, he'll probably be joining you shortly after!"

They like to make fun. Everyone likes to make fun—especially of your failed romances. Like any titan of industry, you have a great social life—you even get invited to the Princess of Denmark's birthday ball—but your love life is poisoned with a seemingly unending stream of pricks, dicks, gold diggers, buttheads, jackasses, and one transsexual. Seriously. You had a brief relationship with a lovely man, who finally confesses he was once a Balinese cocktail waitress. So be it. You can have anything in this world you want. Diamonds, yachts, cars, estates, a small genetically engineered parrot that changes colors every two months, but the one thing you never have again is love. Not the romantic variety anyway.

You finally take to traveling incognito, wearing disguises and using fake passports, just so you can find people who like you for your personality, of whom there are few. All these years of being a whorehouse madam and running a Fortune 500 company have turned you into a bit of a shrieky shrew. Things just annoy you now. How slow waitresses are, how rude hotel managers can be, how no matter how many times you stand in line to see the *Mona Lisa,* you can't even get within fifteen feet of her due to the crowds. Finally you just make an astronomical contribution to the Louvre and the fine arts curator takes you there himself after hours, where the two of you enjoy chilled champagne and he lets you touch the edge of the canvas.

That's the problem. Try as you might, you can't stick to a humble budget. When the lines back up at the airport, you get frustrated and charter a jet. When you discover there's not one room left in all of Madrid, you buy a villa. Once you've tasted the luxuries of life, it's impossible to settle for the little things. The little things suck. On the other hand, the more you buy and purchase and obtain, the less thrilling it is. You have the world. Everything and anything you could ever want is at your immediate and easy disposal. If you asked any of your stealthy and eternally poised staff members to bring you the world's largest black pearl so you could crack it in half, they'd move quickly and without question. If you wanted an ampoule of Egyptian perfume raided from Cleopatra's tomb or twenty kittens brought before you because you felt like strangling something adorable, these items would be brought to you forthwith.

But no one can bring back your father, who was kidnapped from his bed and bludgeoned to death in an abandoned gas station, despite the fact that you paid every penny of ransom that was asked for. No one can retrieve your mother from her catatonic depression. You're like King Midas. Everything he touched turned to gold, but when he touched people, he lost them forever. Your entire family has become irretrievable. They all hate you either because you made your fortune from a despicable trade or because you made your fortune but didn't share it—not enough of it, never enough of it.

No matter what you buy them, they want something else. Always something else. Dangerous things. Deadly things. Everything you buy ends up hurting them. Fast cars that crash into trees, big boats that collide into bridge towers, exotic trips that give them malaria. They move into big houses and lose each other somewhere in the vaulted, drywall rooms. The parents travel, the kids smoke pot, the new Pomeranian drowns in the pool because no one remembered to keep track of him. Nobody remembers to keep track of anything anymore. Ever since you won the money, there's too much to keep track of. It's only after you have the world that you realize— the world is not enough.

Finally comes a perfect evening. The kind of evening that reminds you just how beautiful the world can be. You're in Paris and there's an extraordinary sunset beginning and a warm, fragrant breeze all around you as you stand on your rooftop terrace overlooking the city. It's early in the season and unseasonably warm. Not so many tourists yet. Parisians stroll along the wide boulevards and pink clouds sail overhead. You pick up the phone and tell your house man you'd like some stationery and that bottle of 1907 Heidsieck. The one you just bought at auction.

Moments later you're seated in your patio chair sipping champagne and writing a letter. It's good wine. They found this particular bottle with about two hundred others on the ocean floor off the coast of Finland. The bottles were en route to the Russian Imperial family when the ship went down. A hundred years later the champagne was retrieved from the wreck and finally put up at auction. If you remember right, this bottle cost a little over two hundred and fifty thousand dollars. You study the citrine-yellow champagne. It's actually a bit disappointing. Vinegary. Not right away but there, behind the muted fruits, bitterness lurks. Perfect for the evening.

After finishing your note, you polish off the bottle (on principle) and stand at the terrace ledge, looking down at the people below. In the distance a small silver airplane is cutting across the clean lavender sky. The patio chair allows you to step carefully onto the ledge while gripping the cool stone wall beside you. You take a deep breath. What marvelous air.

Then you step off.

You plunge downward, your clumsy body a lost bird in broken flight. The speed at which you're falling is so tremendous it's surprising. You'd hoped for a few moments to reflect. As it stands your last thought before joining the concrete below is of the silver airplane. You wonder about the passengers on board and where they're going and if they're as happy as you are, to find themselves in the sky.

102

From section 51

You decide to stay on Skellig Michael; you've gotten a bit used to this peculiar world. Plus, now that the population of the island has doubled, why not enjoy the excitement? You dive right in and invite the new lighthouse keeper, Ian, over for supper.

He accepts.

You show him your little beehive home and he shows you the lighthouse he's come to watch, a comely plaster structure with Spartan comforts but a breathtaking view of the bay below. He says every time he climbs the tower the same feeling comes over him. He knows he's following in the steps of countless others who went before him. Every time he polishes the brass handrails, or cleans the lens, he thinks of those who did these same things for hundreds of years.

He teaches you chess, cribbage, poker, and dominoes. He starts a vegetable garden for you on the small patch of land by the lighthouse. He teaches you the names of all the birds on "the rock," as he calls it, chief among them the elegant black and white gannets, which turn the steep sides of the island white each summer as so many come to nest here. Soon you can easily identify the pretty little gray kittiwakes from the penguin-like auks and striped razorbills and tiny charcoal pipits. Ian's like an ornithologist, only from time to time he'll climb down the sheer face of the rock and steal eggs for his exotic seabird omelets.

All talk of your ruined reputation is gone. Evaporated on the howling wind. You can be anybody here. You can just watch dolphins. They swim around the island as they hunt for fish. You love how they jump and play. One morning you spot the distinctive fin of a minke whale slapping the water. Ian says they're migrating south to lower latitudes for winter. He knows so much about nature and how things work, you love listening to his stories. When the boat captain comes two weeks later, he doesn't ask if you're staying. The only thing he takes back is the stack of handwritten *I'm still alive* letters to your family and a sternly worded letter to Mr. Bossrock, telling him he's fired.

Time passes and seasons roll through. You never tell Ian you're a multi-millionaire, you just say there's a modest trust fund, which provides a small monthly income. Who cares if you're a millionaire, anyway? The seagulls? The stones? Your television set is a three-hundred-and-sixty-degree view of the rolling sea. You knit your own sweaters and grow your own herbs and vegetables. You start keeping bees and make your own lavender honey. Out here it isn't money that makes you rich.

You're married on the mainland in a little stone church. The twins come a year later, Madeline and Violet, with tiny fingers, rosebud mouths, and riveting glacier-blue eyes just like their father's. It's not easy raising two girls on a remote rocky outcrop, especially when they're afraid of nothing and climb like monkeys.

As they grow older, they become fierce and wild as the wind, fearlessly walking on the stone walls, shooting skeet with their father's rifle, rock climbing the craggy cliffs, and talking to the dolphins, which eerily seem to talk back. The girls take a boat to school on the mainland every day, and when bad weather prevents them coming home, they stay with Ian's mother, who lives in town in a little thatched cottage. Madeline will become a prominent marine biologist and Violet will win seven gold medals in four consecutive airgun championships at the Olympics.

It's a storybook life, a fairy tale with occasional illness, injury, and in-clement weather, but even when the radio man says the storm of the century is coming, you don't worry—you just batten down the hatches and hang on. Skellig Michael has taught you there's strength in staying put and that all weather passes—in time.

103

From section 51

You decide to leave the island. You've had all this time to think and stare at the ocean; what you're really craving now is lights, action, and people—so you take the ferry to Dublin, where you check into room 526 on the fifth floor of the posh Cromwell Hotel on St. Stephen's Green. It's a very nice hotel, but you wake that night to a pale little girl standing at the end of your bed. She asks you where Sophie is. Then she disappears.

You tell the reception desk about a little girl who's looking for Sophie and the manager grins wide, exposing a gold incisor. "That'd be Mary Masters!" she says. "The little girl who got run over by a train round turn of the century. Her and her little sister, poor lambs. Harmless, though. Nothing to worry about! In fact, you should consider yourself lucky! Lots of people stay in your room hoping to spot Miss Mary and never do. She only shows herself to some." Lucky it may be, but Mary returns that night—her face smeared with blood—and you check out in a hurry the next day.

You check into the Four Seasons. A fine American hotel, where ghosts are not appreciated or acknowledged. You're just settling into your posh bed, prepared for a lovely night of spectral-free sleep, when Mary appears. This time she's holding the hand of an old man. They just stare at you. Then the old man says there's a baby buried down in the rocks. You lunge out of bed and stumble downstairs, where the manager hails you a taxi.

You're freaked out. Are you even safe? What can ghosts do? Can they hurt you? You buy a little silver pistol from a pock-faced teen in the parking lot of a grocery store. When you ask him if he knows anyone who can get rid of ghosts, he shrugs and says there's an old lady in his neighborhood named Fiona, and people say she can remove curses. She can cast them, too, though, so whatever you do, don't steal from her.

You find Fiona in her tenement apartment on the north side of Bally-mun. She looks old enough to have built Stonehenge, and curls her gnarled, purple-spotted hand around your wrist as she leads you inside to her living room, which is packed with worn, overstuffed floral-print furniture and yellowing porcelain figurines.

Fiona says you've picked up *Taibhsean*. Ghosts. Powerful ones. Very alive. "Yes," Fiona whispers with her eyes closed, "a little girl, her grand-father, and the grandmother now is getting closer. They've been traveling with you since . . . yes, the hotel. You picked up a curse on the island . . . Skellig Michael, and now bad luck will follow you."

What? Get rid of them! You don't care what it costs! Fiona leads you through her cramped little house to a tiny backyard that's surprisingly tidy. At the middle of the garden is a craggy white granite rock, with a large hole cut from its center. She calls this a sword stone and says it'll remove any ghost, curse, or negative energy that's attached to you. She lights the candles hanging in iron lanterns on either side of the sword stone and then pours table salt in a large circle around it. Then she starts to chant and blesses herself three times before instructing you to crawl through the hole at the center of the stone. "As you pass through the heart of this stone," she says, "it will pull everything bad out of you."

You take a deep breath and awkwardly crawl through the hole, which is just big enough for you. (Huskier citizens must not be able to use sword stones. Not this one anyway.) You wonder if Fiona is filming this so she can laugh at it with all her other fake-witch friends later. As you crawl through the hole, though, you notice the temperature inside the ring is different. It's colder. Also there's a faint humming sound, like a distant vibration. Prob-ably all explainable, but suddenly your headache lifts and you feel better, lighter, easier, and like maybe something good just happened. Then she tells you the sword stone cleansing costs five hundred dollars. It's not usually so expensive, but you had a lot of negative energy to suck out. Now the stone will be tired. *Fine*. You give her the money and apologize for "tiring out" her stone. Now it's time to get the hell out of this witchy place.

You fly to London and check into the grand St. Regis Hotel. After two days of soaking in a hot tub and finally getting some decent, entity-free sleep, you decide the medium was worth the money. Whether it was actual magic or the power of suggestion, you feel normal again, and to celebrate, you decide to take a bottle of champagne on board one of those big red double-decker tour buses. Time to see the city.

You're sitting on the top deck, just cruising past Big Ben, when a nicely dressed gentleman carrying a black umbrella and a leather briefcase boards the bus and sits down next to you. He's British and says his name is Harold. When he inquires about the paper bag you're holding, you confess it's champagne and he promptly snaps open his briefcase, removing two small clear plastic cups.

"I insist you allow me to join you," he says. "As a gentleman I must spare you from the indignity of drinking alone." At first you wonder if this guy is some kind of con artist. What kind of British gentleman carries plastic cups in his briefcase or rides touristy double-decker buses? Well, Harold does. You come to learn he's a man who's prepared for sudden situations. His briefcase is primarily used for work, but it's also stocked with a penlight, a Swiss Army knife (with tweezers and corkscrew), a small first aid kit, a package of wet wipes.

Harold is fascinating. In fact, you start to pay more attention to him than to the tour. When you ask what he does for a living, he shifts uncomfortably and says he always wanted to become a barrister, but managing his family's estate is a full-time job now that his father passed away. Upon further pressing he admits he's the son of a duke and the head of a rather powerful family. Still, he remains down-to-earth and friendly, and after the tour you can't help but admit how much you enjoyed meeting him, and since you'll be at the St. Regis for another week, maybe the two of you could have tea sometime? Adorably, this causes him to redden and look down at his polished wingtips, before saying that would be quite nice.

The very next afternoon he takes you to tea at the St. James, and then the following evening he takes you to dinner at Belvedere and then for a sherry at the Mayfair Hotel. He regales you with funny stories and intelligent insights on art, music, opera, the world market, and politics. You end up spending the whole week with Harold, who shepherds you around to museums and the opera and even procures tickets to the coveted and spectacular final night of the Royal Proms at Prince Albert Hall, where the BBC Symphony Orchestra performs with Andrea Bocelli, Placido Domingo, and Anne Sofie von Otter, just to name a few. During the finale, when the magnificent choir sings "Rule Britannia," thousands in the audience join in, whipping themselves into a frenzy and wildly waving Union Jacks. Many start crying. It's a night you'll always remember.

Every night with Harold is one to remember. He has this marvelous way of making you feel at home, which is remarkable considering how different your backgrounds are. You know nothing of the upper-crust society he lives in; you're constantly asking who people are or why they're important and what's appropriate to wear when you go out. In fact, you worry that you're too high-maintenance, you ask too many questions, but Harold laughs and says he doesn't mind at all. He's tired of dating English women, whom he finds not only haughty and judgmental but cold and unemotional. Your eyes go wide with surprise and you ask him if you are in fact *dating*. He laughs and says, "If we're not, then consider this a formal request, my dear."

That's when you decide to extend your trip by another week or two.

Maybe ten.

Since his family comes from old money, he never talks about it, so you don't, either. He always pays for everything, and the few times you beat him to the check it was because you spoke with the maître d' beforehand, but it put Harold in an awkward place and you could tell he didn't like it. His home is a simple three-story building in Notting Hill, sparsely furnished but pleasantly located right on the busy markets. He invites you to stay with him and your love affair grows.

Then one night Harold puts on a particularly smart suit and a peacock blue ascot. He takes you to dinner at a lovely little French restaurant by the river and just as you've finished the last course, before the waiter has even cleared the dishes, he suddenly proposes. He doesn't have a ring with him and he doesn't get down on one knee. He seems terribly sheepish and embarrassed as he takes your hand and says, "I'm bloody awful at this, forgive my stumbling. Damn. Sorry, darling. Would you marry me?"

He left the ring at home. He was so nervous he convinced himself he'd drop the damn thing in the Thames. You do wish he'd kneeled down when he proposed. That would have been romantic, but then again, you have to remember Harold's not only British, he's *aristocracy*, and if he had a heart attack during dinner, he'd rather excuse himself from the table and go die quietly in the other room than cause a fuss. You know that about him. You know lots of things, but do you know everything? How well can you know another person after only six months? At least you're sure you love him and you're sure you love how he makes you feel. So, do you want to marry him?

If you accept Harold's marriage proposal, go to section 112 (p. 355).
If you decline Harold's marriage proposal, go to section 117 (p. 369).

104

You tell Mr. Cook it's *your money* and you demand access to it. You want a bigger house! This does not go over well. Mr. Cook is flustered and angry, he stumbles over himself explaining how it's not the right time, you'll incur penalties, and so on. . . .

Why is he angry?

Finally, after much persistence, he says he'll pull some strings, get the money together, and call you later. He doesn't call you later. Instead, a lawyer representing a class-action suit calls you. Turns out all your money was lost in a Ponzi scheme, a scam where the promise of high returns entices scores of new investors, who turn over their money in the hopes of high dividends. They are paid off over time not with returns from investments but from the principal cash contributed by other investors. It basically means everyone throws their money in a pot and one crook in the middle just keeps shuffling it around until it collapses or he's caught.

Silverlock Trust was just a guy in New Jersey, a single guy who created a fake fund and made millions, possibly billions of dollars off the backs of his clients. Wealthy families, working mothers, retirees, trust funds, volunteer organizations, hospitals, other scam artists, everyone. Nobody suspected him. The SEC gave him a clean bill of health. Nobody knew the extent of his empire or his reach. He had clients in Dubai, Tokyo, London, San Francisco . . . nowhere was safe. Was Mr. Cook a willing or an unwitting assistant in your demise? Did he know about the Ponzi scheme? Did he lose any money?

You'll never know, because one very windy day, after he told his secretary he was going to hang the silver wind chimes his wife had given him as a birthday present, Mr. Cook "fell" off his office balcony. He'd been wiped out by the Ponzi scheme too and even though he'd hoped his family could live on his life insurance policy after his sudden and unforeseen death, the insurance company declared his demise a suicide, nullifying the policy and leaving the Cook family out in the cold.

What an utterly ridiculous thing to do. Kill yourself? There's always a way out. Or that's what you think, until things in your world get bad. Really bad. The cars are repossessed, the bank demands mortgage payments, the electricity is cut off. You can't sleep and hardly afford to eat. You lie awake at night unable to calm your mind. Why is this happening? You followed the lottery board's advice, you weren't irresponsible with your winnings, you were just unlucky. Trusted the wrong people.

It gets you thinking about Mr. Cook's suicide. What if you pulled off a phony suicide? One that no one could catch? It's extreme, but your family is going to pieces. They're all suffering and no one knows where they'll go next.

Most of the cousins go get jobs and Aidan becomes the manager at an auto parts store. The same store where he used to buy parts for his motorcycle (which is now sold). The kids offer to sell their toys. Michael must go without swimming lessons. This makes you want to weep.

You take a look at your life insurance policy one insomnia-fueled evening. Mr. Cook wasn't good for much, but he did get both you and Aidan five-million-dollar life insurance policies. It would take care of your family and children for life. Of course there's a suicide clause, so you'd have to make it look like you and Aidan died accidentally. If you pull it off, all your financial problems are solved. If you don't, you'll both go to jail.

If you don't fake your own death, go to section 113 (p. 359).
If you fake your own death, go to section 116 (p. 366).

105

From section 59

You decide to buy a big house and settle in until this feeling of imminent peril leaves you. Coming up against people who want to kill you is a very eye-opening experience. You don't know who to trust. Aidan shows up at the new house with a big bouquet of roses. He just heard about the attack and you fall into his arms, weeping.

He promises to never leave. He never wants you to feel vulnerable like that again. He helps you update your state-of-the-art mansion with every high-tech security system available. High-definition cameras, infrared lights, electric fences, hydraulic gates, voice-recognition locks, body-heat motion detectors, and a twenty-four-hour guard who sits in a little hut at the end of the drive. Still, there are gaps in security everywhere. What's to stop the pizza delivery kid from whipping out a gun and shooting you right in the face, or a passing car from tossing a hand grenade over the fence?

Every day the papers are filled with kidnappings, murders, shootings, stabbings, and worse. Last week in broad daylight two kids walked into someone's backyard during a family barbecue and robbed everyone. Took all their wallets and cell phones. When some guy put up a fuss, they just shot him in the sternum and ran down the street. Nobody knows who they were or has seen them since. They're still out there somewhere planning their next insane crime spree. People may think you're crazy for being cautious, but at least you're alive, and you plan to stay that way *despite* the fact absolutely everyone in this town knows who you are and where you live. *You're that big lottery winner; you're the one they saw on TV!*

Some woman even recognized you at the dentist's office and asked you what you did with all that money. What a rude question. Would you ask her what she does with her money? Everyone thinks lottery winners waste their money on something stupid, so you told her you used up every penny buying a whole fleet of brand-new Mercedes-Benz convertibles, and then you hired clowns to drive them around and smash them up in a big spectacular demolition derby. That woman didn't ask you anything else.

You hire a burly security specialist to assess your property for potential risks, and after a careful inspection he recommends bulletproof glass on all the first-floor windows, but better yet, on all the windows in the house. He was a big guy, that specialist; his arms looked like pregnant pythons. He could have strangled you with one hand and you let him right in the house! You have a judo instructor come out twice a week to teach you self-defense, and you hire a security guard to keep on the judo instructor whenever he's there. It goes on like this for a while, every security feature needing another security feature to watch over it. You become nervous and withdrawn, unable to sleep. You'd take the sleeping pills the doctor gave you, but then if there was a fire you might not wake up and you'd burn alive.

You don't even like your family to come around anymore; they're always monkeying around with the windows and doors, leaving something open or unlocked. Your stupid nephews left the gate by the pool wide open, not just unlocked but standing *wide open* so any burglar in the world could waltz right in and slit your throat. You just can't stand this growing panic in your gut, this feeling, this *certainty* something's coming for you. You have to find somewhere safer.

You spend a full year in Greece in an unusual dwelling near Mount Olympus called a *meteora*, which is Greek for "suspended in air." It's a fitting name for these tall sandstone towers built by eleventh-century monks on top of cliffs jutting abruptly from the flat Thessaly plains. They were originally used as monasteries and provided total safety, absolute seclusion, and literally brought the monks closer to God. A helicopter has to drop you off on a stone helipad just to get there, leaving you to behold the breathtaking three-hundred-and-sixty-degree views all around you.

The tower has three floors. The main floor has a formal little entryway, a vaulted living room with a large stone fireplace where the altar used to be, and a small but excellently appointed kitchen with appliances that connect to large underground propane tanks. The second floor is primarily a reading room or study, with a small library of floor-to-ceiling shelves carved right into the stone. The third floor is the master bedroom and bath, providing spectacular views from both the modern egg-shaped bathtub and the dreamy, mosquito-netting-strewn bed. You can't believe your luck. What an idyllic retreat. No people, no worries, no unexpected surprises, no unwanted visitors.

After a year of soaring sights, however, you and Aidan are bored. Your sex life has dwindled down to a very unelaborate series of pump-'n'-grunts. He has a hard time getting it up, says he must be getting old, but you know it's because he's getting bored. So you want to change things up while still feeling secure. Living in a tower isn't even all that safe. Helicopters, planes, hang gliders, and birds can zoom past any time they like, and you for one have had it.

You find these underground tunnels for sale in London, enormous steel caverns built during the war to serve as public fallout shelters. They're fifteen feet underground, sixty feet tall, and big enough to house five football fields. The owners decorated this underground castle as a dreamy netherworld with airy white furnishings and a true-to-life celestial skyscape that with the flick of a switch illuminates the entire ceiling of the main tunnel.

The designers thought of everything. They installed sectional climate control, atmospheric ionizers, humidifying atomizers, and a high-tech detoxifying water filtration system that can turn wastewater into Evian. The place is like a bunker, with enough food and supplies to last a year. (The delivery boy, Jamil, brings fresh groceries once a week.) Several fun elements were installed as well, like a secret tunnel that opens when the candelabra above the den bookcase is pulled. It leads to a small terrazzo-tiled room with faux grass and a private hot tub. Then one day as you're perusing the spice rack in the chrome pantry, you see an old bottle of paprika on the uppermost shelf. You have to get a stepladder to reach it, and once you take it from its little segmented slot, a small door to your left *whooshes* open. It's a child-size opening that you need to crouch to get through. It leads down a dimly lit tunnel, the LED lights flickering lazily on as the motion detectors sense your presence. The hall leads to a wood-paneled room with a black chair and black table at its center. On the table is a large metal box with a translucent plastic yellow lid. Inside is a fat red button. The button is labeled DIRE STRAITS ONLY.

If you don't push the red button, go to section 139 (p. 448).
If you push the red button, go to section 145 (p. 473).

106

As a bon vivant, you're in perpetual motion. Whether dashing over in a taxi, pulling up in a limo, or boarding your own private jet, you're always en route to something spectacular. Celebrity-studded parties in L.A., fundraisers in New York, political receptions in D.C., wine tastings in Paris, theater galas in London, nightclub openings in Ibiza, winter solstice parties in Reykjavik.

You buy a penthouse on Park Avenue in Manhattan, a mansion on the coast in Malibu, then a villa in the south of France and a palazzo on the Grand Canal in Venice. All your homes are staffed with private chefs, limo drivers, and round-the-clock security details, as well as twin Rolls-Royces and a yacht in the nearest port.

Naturally your new lifestyle comes with a lot of new friends, mainly other bon vivants who jet-set around going to big events, throwing big parties, and, of course, spending big money. You learn to shop where all the other bon vivants do, which is mostly on Rodeo Drive in Beverly Hills and in the Harajuku district of Tokyo, where Asian teens loiter outside the elegant shop windows dressed up in colorful crazy costumes fit for cartoon porn characters.

You learn that bon vivants don't spend every hour of their lives shopping or partying, though. Many like to "invest" in projects, like art galleries, theater companies, record labels, even vineyards, as a means of looking marginally productive if not fractionally lucrative. Your bon vivant gal-pal, Jordan, who inherited her fortune, has been producing movies lately, which she says is a riot. Write a little check and you get to meet celebrities, attend exclusive parties, and see your name on the big screen with a producer credit.

You also get to sleep with handsome directors, solicitous producers, and if you're feeling extra-gritty, there's easy access to the more feral crew members, like the grips. Jordan needs another producer for a movie she just got on board with. She asks you to be her coproducer on an "adorable little indie film" shooting in a few months.

Sterling, your bon vivant guy-pal, has a different investment idea for you. He's involved in a space tourism program named Starlink, which has loose connections with NASA and aims to be the first official tour operator in outer space. They'll cater to everyday citizens, offering John Q. Public pricey rides on space shuttles and hopefully accommodations on the moon. That's right, Sterling's business partners want to open the first luxury lodging available in space. He says if you invest in his project, you'll not only get a VIP tour of NASA, you'll get your own personalized spacesuit and passage on the first-ever all-civilian flight to the moon.

If you invest in Starlink, go to section 137 (p. 441).
If you produce a movie, go to section 144 (p. 468).

107

From section 95

You don't open the coffin. It's too scary and falls directly under the category of "What good could come from it?" This isn't really your house, after all, it's someone else's, and it's always going to be someone else's. You're glad you kept the house but you don't have to live here. The important part is done. You saved it. When you turn around to go back up to the kitchen, you trip over a wrought iron grate embedded in the floor; it's like a little hatch, and when you open it you find several coffee tins filled with gold coins. They turn out to be priceless pieces, mostly traceable to known pirate booty, probably a piece of Miss Dottie's mysterious Caribbean past. They're also estimated at over ten million dollars.

You transfer responsibility of Miss Dottie's Museum to the Germantown Ladies Auxiliary Club. You agree to pay for the museum's upkeep and they can use whatever profits come in for whatever they like. Planting community tulip beds, installing NO UNNECESSARY LOITERING signs by the public fountain, regilding the testicles of Washington's horse outside the courthouse, et cetera. . . .

Dottie would be proud.

Now it's time to create your *own* collection of oddities, rarities, and hand-selected treasures.

After a thorough investigation of every antiquities auction and estate sale coming up, your eye catches on an estate collection at Christie's. One anonymous lot is simply described as belonging to a "deceased collector" and possibly containing "rare artifacts." Auction houses do this sometimes when they have large estates to sell off, randomly grouping properties together so neither the sellers nor the buyers know what they're bidding on.

You could bid on lot 408 and wind up owning a vintage merry-go-round or a rare collection of taxidermied tarantulas.

There's another tempting item for sale. A deep-sea salvage company based in Key West is auctioning off anonymous marine salvage. Using infrared cameras, unidentified parcels are located on the ocean floor across the globe and assigned random numbers. You pick a number, divers retrieve the parcel, and you get to keep half of the profits, if there are any. These "parcels" could be anything from swamped Igloo coolers to sunken shipping containers to lost atom bombs. They've found all of the above and make no guarantees. You may drag up pirates' treasure or just big buckets of sand.

If you bid on the deceased collector's property, go to section 20 (p. 51).
If you bid on the salvaged ocean cargo, go to section 81 (p. 253).

108

You give the couple some money for a hotel and send them on their way. Thank goodness, too, because shortly after they depart there's a rash of unexplainable murders on the island. Tourists are robbed and killed for no reason. If you hadn't made sure your friends were safe and off the streets, it might have been them. What nice people.

The experience reminds you that not everyone has won the lottery and has a big chunk of money to lounge around with. In fact, a lot of people who would love it here will never even see it because they can't afford to get here, let alone stay in one of the high-priced hotels.

You decide to start Simple Exchange of Art, or SEA, a foundation that imports writers, musicians, and artists overseas. At first it's like a student exchange program—you send a local artist or student over to a country and they send one to you. The artists stay in each other's houses, which eliminates housing costs and turns out to be far more inspirational for the participants than if they stayed in hotels. All artists, whether they create with paint, musical notes, or words, seem to surround themselves with the same ingredients, solitude and light.

The program is free; all that's required is that both artists donate three pieces of work to the foundation. George Clooney, who eventually dropped all charges against you, even donates some money to the cause, maybe because he's a really good guy or maybe for the press, but either way it allows you to put together the first traveling show of your international art program, which opens to great critical acclaim.

The program grows and starts sending artists to different countries all over the world. Albanian modernists are painting in the Alps, Icelandic musicians are dancing next to the Nile, Greek sculptors are digging out red clay from the banks of the Mississippi. The program is honored by UNESCO and the World Bank. Donations and grant money start to pour in and you have to expand your tropical home to include a world headquarters, where a staff of ten is constantly organizing travel arrangements between strange destinations.

You live a serene life surrounded by artists and their creations, by people who are grateful to you for your vision and generosity. You hardly remember your old life, this one seems so complete. You meet one of your artists, Mada, an oil expressionist, who paints nude portraits and makes love to you on sweaty, paint-smeared drop cloths. Together you roll around in gymnastic back-arching positions until you're washed and streaked with glitter—an unusual and exotic-looking butterfly.

You use your money to start a starfish sanctuary. Many starfish are wounded by jet skis and boat propellers. They lose arms, get diseases, and become more and more pale until they die. At your starfish sanctuary, you have starfish of almost every imaginable color—red, yellow, green, lavender—and all of them as intelligent as a house cat. They work together to build bridges and frequently escape the tanks.

It's a tranquil, exotic, peaceful yet thrilling life. Your future lives will be good, but none as perfect as this one.

109

Onward O Pioneer!, the Wild West town, opens to excited crowds who wander around the lifelike streets and establishments. The Swamptick Saloon serves whiskey shooters and sarsaparilla milk shakes in miniature wooden barrels; Chompy Joe's Steakhouse features five-buck pork chops; Fixin's! is an all-you-can-eat family-style buffet; Chuckleheads Comedy Club has cowpoke clowns telling jokes; the Rusty Blade is a barbershop offering two-dollar haircuts; the Soiled Dove is a faux brothel offering shiatsu massage and mini-facials; Darn Them Barkin' Dogs! sells replica pioneer footwear and beaded moccasins; the Tomahawk Shop sells Civil War weapons and flintstone scalping implements; Applejack Blacksmiths shoes a horse every hour; Lil Digger Creek is where kids can pan for gold nuggets; and the Guttersnipe Dropoff is where kids under five can enjoy supervised activities while their parents drink. Whippersnapper Amusement Park and Petting Zoo is quite popular. It has a log ride that drops down through a series of big fake chopping blades in an old-timey sawmill.

The only attraction more popular is the Rickety-Splits Coal Mine. Guests sit in wooden coal cars and wear hardhats with headlights as they ride along the rails through the coal mine, the diamond mine, and the gold mine. A small sign on the ride says SOME EXHIBITS MAY BE GEOGRAPHICALLY INACCURATE. It's a huge hit. People come from all over to stay at Onward O Pioneer! The hotel is booked through next summer. There are pony rides and outdoor pig roasts followed by fireworks. People love the safe family-fun atmosphere, and much to your surprise, Onward O Pioneer! makes Rush Limbaugh's "Top Ten Best Places for Conservatives to Vacation" list.

The money just pours in. The more you have, the more you want and the more stuff you buy. You also enter the delightfully seedy world of cake sitting. It's a fetish, but also an art. The main premise of this particular group is the erotic sensation felt when watching someone sit on a cake. A big, round white-frosted or densely delicious chocolate cake. Well, you never know if the cakes are delicious, tasting them isn't part of the deal. It's better when someone wearing fishnet stockings or who is clean and well-shaven presents and hovers. Then sits, slowly, slowly, slowly. The more slowly the better, but after the point of no return is reached, then speed is desirable. Cake sitters like to smear the frosting up, up, all over and around.

You've tried sitting on a few cakes yourself and, while you prefer to watch, you cannot deny the startling "oh no!" sensation that thrills your body when you do something so perfectly wrong. You even start taking the cakes into public. Hostess cupcakes actually. You have special underwear made that can hold three Hostess cupcakes in place. Then, when you reach the desired location for the "big squelch," you just sit right down and work yourself into it. Some people think God will send cake sitters to hell, but God made the cake sitters and those particular parts that like big-squelch feelings, and he made the damn cakes too, in a way, so shame on you, Mr. Man.

Shame on you.

You love eating. You become obsessed with the edible nest of the swiftlet, found only in Java. You ate your first swiftlet nest in China. Delicate as spun glass and collapsing into a gelatinous heap when added to soup, this small engineering marvel is made only from the bird's saliva, and of course purported to possess extraordinary medicinal qualities. These tiny nests, which sell for thousands, are said to improve skin tone and cure respiratory disorders, blood disorders, nervous conditions; and of course, the Chinese don't eat a damn thing if it doesn't enhance sexual skill, stamina, or performance. Swiftlet nests are said to do all three.

Swiftlet nests are tasty. Gummy, a bit gamey, but good. You begin collecting the nests and storing them in a special temperature-controlled room you have built specially. Several of your friends are curious about your odd hobby and they want to taste these nests themselves, which stirs an odd and fiercely protective feeling in you. You even kicked some people out of the house last week when they made too much about seeing the swiftlet nest humidor.

Next you find yourself choosing to stay inside for weeks at a time. You don't like to go out. Too uncontrollable, unpredictable, and windy. Plus, you've started to get a skin rash and it creeps up your neck sometimes, making you look half sea creature in need of being returned to its brine.

When they eventually find your body, it's weeks after you actually died. The servants were terrified of you and would never dare knock on a door for fear of losing their employment.

Toxic epidermal necrolysis is the official cause of your death. A rare disorder causing rashes, lesions, and blistering before the skin starts to separate from itself. Severe reactions to medication is the usual cause for this disorder, but in your case it takes the medical examiner weeks before he stumbles across the swiftlet nests. After running extensive tests on the chemical compounds, cell structures, fungal presence, and bacterial components found in the swiftlet nests and saliva, he finally concludes that long-term exposure to this unique and complicated blend of elements can prove toxic.

To some.

Your funeral is oddly empty, except for the protestors.

In heaven you're assigned a new life. You will become a swiftlet so you can see just how much fun it is to be constantly building a nest for your children on the sheer face of a windswept cliff, just so some jackass can come and turn it into soup. Also, God assures you he did not make cake sitters, he made cakes, which he intended to be eaten, not sat on and filmed. Some people just have too much time on their hands and can get pervy with just about anything.

110

From section 64

You keep quiet. You had a chance to say something and it was yesterday while the divers were right there. Everyone goes on about their business and you sit silently boiling with regret. It's always this way. People want whatever they can't have. If you're within reach of a mystery violin case, you're too scared to take it. Then, only when the mystery violin case is *long gone* do you set about getting it. Just freaking typical.

You know right where it is, the coordinates are seared in your brain. All you have to do is find divers who will take you there. If you told the guys on your boat, you'd have to share whatever's inside with them, but if you hire divers, then the case is yours. There's another salvage outfit on the opposite side of the bay, who you'll have to swear to secrecy or your crew will keelhaul you (a grotesque medieval punishment Hickey explained, where traitors were tied to a rope that circled the belly of a boat and were then dragged around and around from the keel to the hull, until they either choked to death and drowned or the barnacles below ripped the skin clean from their body).

The guys at the other salvage yard know who you are and it takes some convincing that this isn't a joke and you aren't a spy. They finally believe you when you lie and say you were dating Squid for a while, but then you broke up with him and he got so mad he threw your beloved violin overboard, and if he knows you're going to try and retrieve it, he'll intercept the boat and there'll be a nasty scene at sea. That they believe completely.

Then there's the uncomfortable topic of money, of which you have little. The new crew is not terribly sympathetic to the idea of buzzing you out there for free, but hating Squid as they do and wanting to help piss him off any way they can, they offer you a job. They just hauled in a big load of ornamental railings off some supply freighter and the customer is paying extra to get them back clean. So if you want the job, they'll go get the violin.

You say you'll take it.

So for two long weeks you scrub sharp, cold barnacles off ornamental wrought iron. Your back aches, your legs throb, your hands get cut right through your gloves and bleed, which at least makes them a little warmer. You go to bed each night drained and exhausted, with only the image of the violin case on the sonar screen to soothe you. Some nights it doesn't seem like nearly enough. Still, you keep on.

Finally, mercifully, the day comes when you stack the last piece of clean iron and tell the guys you're done. They stay true to their word, and in short order you're on board Salvage Marine's wrecker speeding home with your mystery violin case safely wrapped in plastic on your lap. It's cold and damp, a soggy baby heavy in your arms.

When you finally sneak the heavy bag into your room, you pull down the shades and set the plastic package on the table. You unwrap it carefully, slowly and with bated breath, as an archaeologist might undress a brittle mummy. You tell yourself it doesn't matter *what's* inside this violin case. Not anymore.

Because you realized something sitting on the deck of the speeding Salvage Marine wrecker. You realized that for the first time in a long time you saw something you wanted and you worked really hard to get it. You didn't lean on luck or hope someone would help you, you just worked bloody bone-saw hard until you got it.

The feeling is glorious. Comforting, like how your face feels warm when you come in from the cold. It wasn't anything like winning something suddenly, which felt more like hysteria, or getting a sudden adrenaline shot that your body didn't quite know how to handle. That feeling caused your heart to race and your palms to sweat, and in the end, those really aren't very pleasant sensations. They leave you disoriented and confused, not really happy.

This time, though, when you didn't get what you wanted right away, you had to sit with your frustration and anxiety and unhappiness. You had to make plans that then got rearranged against your will and led you to uncomfortable roads, which you traveled painfully and at a glacial pace. It's easy to see why this, the long way, wouldn't be the preferred way to get what you want, why winning the lottery seems easier, but you bear with the journey one step longer.

When you take the long way to a dream and you finally arrive at the small green pasture where what you wanted is standing in front of you, having appeared like a mirage after miles of endless travel, it isn't with panic or hysteria you'll greet each other.

No. This was a long time coming and you're ready. There are no sweaty palms, because now you know exactly what this is. This is how it feels to come in from the cold. This is home. If you're willing to take the long way, there's nothing in the whole world you can't have. This violin case is proof. So, when you open it, as you're about to do, you know that the treasure is not *inside* the case, the treasure *is* the case.

Close your eyes, take a deep breath, and open the lid. Water, slugs of algae, and the pungent smell of rot seep out. You look more closely. Under the lumps of viscous seaweed are twenty-five black velvet bags, all soaking wet and cinched by thin black cords that are hard to untie. You have to tug hard at the stupid little knots to get them loose, but finally out spills the other thing you're getting today. Eighty-five million dollars' worth of mother-fucking diamonds, which roll out like a sudden celestial constellation on the black plastic covering the dingy kitchen table.

Oh yes. This is how it works.

Exactly.

You strike out on a spending spree unlike anything the world has ever known. Well, unlike anything you have ever known. You buy your entire family mansions, Bentleys, jewelry, yachts, and luxury cruise trips. Then you buy yourself a ticket to New Zealand and take only a hundred dollars with you. It's a new game you've decided to play, called "Get Yourself Home." The rules go like this: Based on the premise that all things are possible, hard work renders the sweetest rewards, and most people are actually good, you believe that you can get yourself home from anywhere in the world without money, power, influence, or status.

All you need are friends, and you make them along the way.

It's a fun game. You make it back home starting with no money from New Zealand, Iceland, South America, Taiwan, Madagascar, and Easter Island. You work odd jobs along the way, volunteer, get help from strangers in the shape of rides, meals, shelter, and stories. Oh, the stories you hear. Secrets, scandals, gossip, confessions, lost loves, new passions, amazing recipes. People tell you things you never would have heard if you'd been a tourist. Tourists take the paved roads and you like the dirt. Dirt is better than all the damn diamonds in the world.

111

From section 55

You're not going to get pressured into an unwise decision, even if it drives away the man you love. *Especially* if it drives off the man you love. You tell him that if there's no prenup, there's no wedding. Much to your astonished shock, he actually finishes packing and leaves. You're stunned. Horrified. After a long cry, you're oddly relieved to have found out the man you thought you loved was a gold-digging son of a bitch who clearly couldn't have loved you. Then you indulge your post-breakup hunger by gorging yourself on leftovers in the dining room, you lie alone on top of the dining room table in the dark. It's so uncomfortable here; you're so unhappy and still bizarrely wide awake.

In the morning you set about your new life in the empty building. The management company tells you it won't be long now till the tenants arrive, which is a blessing, because the building gives you the creeps from the start, even though it's almost finished. All the condos are finished, all the hallways are carpeted, all the gym equipment has arrived, and the super-smooth chrome elevators already play calypso Muzak as they whisk you down to the main level, where the white marble floors have been polished to such a high shine the lobby looks like an ice-skating rink flanked by a reception desk.

It's eerie. It looks like people should be here, like maybe they were here and then a silent plague or a serial killer picked them off one by one. There's no valet or concierge yet. The glass doors in the lobby *whoosh* open automatically when you leave but stay locked from the outside, so to get into the building you must swipe a wallet-sized keycard in front of a little black magnetic reader. Sometimes it doesn't work right and you have to stand there waving your keycard back and forth like you're fanning a fire.

Life in the condo is weird. The worst part are the mystery sounds. Sometimes the noise is traceable. A janitor drags a garbage pail across a hallway or an electrician sets up an aluminum ladder to work on a panel or a landscaper comes knocking around watering the big palm trees in the lobby. These sounds, if you know what they are and who's making them, are fine. Good, even. It's nice to see the occasional face, and the faster the building gets done, the sooner your world stops looking like the opening scene in a horror movie and you can stop buying discount jumbo cans of Mace online.

The overly friendly rep at the management company tells you until the garage is built the building can't open. Well, *it can*, but no one would come because there'd be nowhere safe to park their cars. No way are your tenants parking on the street; they'd rather leave their grandkids on the street, because the only thing these people love more than their overpriced luxury condos is their overpriced luxury cars. You tell her you're glad she's so fucking cheerful; however, you're not cheerful because you are stuck like a prisoner in this damn tower after the sun goes down because you are too scared to leave your apartment!

Then you hang up on her.

Something is definitely going on. One night you order Chinese food, and two hours later, when the nice deliveryman who always gives you extra fortune cookies still hasn't called your cell phone announcing his arrival outside the lobby doors, you call the restaurant and they say the deliveryman *was* there and when he walked up to your building, the lobby doors automatically opened, so he came inside and left your food on the reception desk. You run downstairs and check, but there's no food waiting for you. You don't know if the lobby doors are locked or not—the technical maneuvers required to test them from outside without actually getting locked out are way beyond your current state of mind. Either the Chinese restaurant is lying to you—and you don't think they are—or someone is in the building.

That's it. You've had it. You decide to leave that night. You run upstairs, throw your crap into garbage bags, and march downstairs. Just as you're getting off the elevator, a big bottle of shampoo perched on top of your bag opens up and glops down the front of your sweatshirt.

You storm into the service hall to throw the sweatshirt away. You don't want anything anymore! You fling the Dumpster lid open and a huge man stands up, inexplicably, who's inside. He's staring at you like you're food, like you're something he's going to tear into pieces. He raises his arms, hand thrusting out, and you run. You run away, flying across the lobby, sprinting wildly, screaming, not looking, you're outside, your heart hammering, and then you trip.

You're falling.

Tomorrow, they'll have a hell of a time trying to figure out what happened, as there are so many clues and none of them make any sense. Ripped garbage bags of clothes are strewn everywhere, your sweatshirt is covered in what they assumed was semen but turned out to be Vidal Sassoon shampoo, there's a bizarre shantytown set up in the service hall, and worst of all, there's you. Dead in the pool with a fractured skull splayed facedown on top of a tangled lounge chair with the words "EAT DICK" spray-painted on the pool walls around you.

Tomorrow, they confirm you weren't attacked and your injuries were all self-inflicted. You died when your head hit the edge of the pool, and while they briefly considered you might have slipped, it's later concluded this was no accident. This was an elaborate suicide carried out by a very unwell girl. The police piece everything together and gently explain it all to your mother. After Aidan left, you became distraught. You refused to leave your apartment and became more and more paranoid of human contact until you actually abandoned your apartment and moved into the downstairs service hall, which was tactically the safest place in the building. No windows and easy access to multiple escape routes. You even set up a little bunk in one of the unused Dumpsters, providing an extra level of protection, which might seem odd to us, but is a very normal, very comforting habit for someone who's clinically paranoid. Then in a fit of agonized fury you put on Aidan's sweatshirt (crap! it was his) and before you threw all the lounge chairs in the pool you spray-painted the words "EAT DICK" all over the walls, then you took a flying leap. The forensics guys say you must have started running from the other side of the patio and threw yourself into the pool, accomplishing what you'd set out to do, *end the pain*. Everyone in your family is devastated, wracked with grief. Everyone thinks you killed yourself except your grandfather.

He's not interested in some cockamamie cop's idea of what happened, he wants proof, so he gets an old recruit who works down at the station to send him a copy of the crime scene photos. "It's right there!" he barks at your parents, tapping on a grainy picture of the service hall. "That's a military man's camp!" he says. "Look how the blanket is folded, look at the tin can!" and when no one knows what he's talking about, it takes ten minutes to bring him back from his torrential outburst of swearing. Finally, after the family leaves, Grandpa sits next to his old pal in the TV lounge so they can watch *Matlock*.

112

You say *Yes*. Harold's overjoyed, happier than you've ever seen him. He arranges for you to meet all of his extended family. You never knew there were so many of them! Aunts, uncles, cousins, even his Grandmother Isabelle receive you with exceptional warmth, considering they're British.

Harold wanted the wedding to be at Westminster Abbey, which would be an extraordinary feat considering only members of the royal family are allowed to marry there, but he was firmly turned down. Your nuptials are held at the beautiful Parish of St. John the Baptist in Burford, Oxfordshire instead. Everything is *perfect* as you walk down the aisle. Your whole family is there, and Harold looks perfect in his top hat and tailcoat. Even the rare, pale green orchids you wanted for your bouquet were found. You clutch them against your heavy ivory brocade dress, which has hundreds of thousands of Swarovski crystals sewn into the bodice. (The wedding costs you a fortune, but you've never felt better about spending money.)

The honeymoon in Scotland is idyllic, but the best part is when it's over. Once you've returned to Harold's bachelor pad, you begin turning it into a real home. Harold's a huge help, showing you where to buy the best furnishings, driving you as far as Bath and Cotswold to find the perfect pieces.

Harold's also very good with finances, and when he suggests you don't need Mr. Bossrock anymore, who after all got you into such an embarrassing predicament in Hollywood, it's a point well taken. Besides, now you've got Harold, and look how well you're doing! Life is near perfect. So you fire Mr. Bossrock, who says you'll be sorry.

Life in the UK carries on and you're consumed with running a household. You want your husband to be happy, you love it when he smiles. Sometimes that seems to be not so often anymore, and you can't figure out why. Everything is going smoothly, you never fight, you attend all the best events and parties in London, his friends all like you, his family even likes you, so you can't imagine why he's starting to fall into these funks. He takes long walks in the city, and then after he convinces you to buy a cottage in the countryside, he refuses to leave it, preferring to go on longer and longer solo journeys through the fields.

You stop having dinner together, you stop making love, you almost stop talking completely. You try and talk to him about it, but that makes it worse. He snaps at you and tells you to leave him alone. It's in your third year of marriage that the Bank of England calls to see if you still want your separate monthly checks sent to the same post office box in London. You're confused. What separate checks? Upon investigation it turns out your beloved husband, the true gentleman and English blue blood, has been siphoning funds from your account.

Three million pounds is missing.

At first you refuse to believe it. There must be a mistake or some reason Harold had for transferring money without telling you. You confront him out at the stables, where he spends so much time with his beloved horse, Persephone. "What's the meaning of this?" you ask, shoving a bank statement at him.

He's very quiet at first and reads the statement as though it was for the first time. A fleeting part of your panicking heart holds fast to the hope that it is. Then he folds the statement up, puts it in his coat pocket, and continues saddling Persephone.

"Time you knew," he says, and proceeds to explain in a chillingly calm voice that he only married you for your money. Why else would a member of the extended royal family marry a commoner? As is the case with so many lords and ladies on the fringes of the royal family, he has a title, but no wealth. It was all spent by relatives before him, idle, pampered gits who never knew a hard day's work in their lives.

The only way for a gentleman who's fallen on hard times to acquire a fortune these days is to marry into one. He was involved in some scandal years ago, an affair with a married woman, and no British socialite would have him. He's a black sheep. A scoundrel. He needed a wealthy, unassuming foreigner. Preferably an idiot.

That's where you came in.

This is the curse at work, you can feel it. Fiona didn't get rid of it, she just took your money. You look at Harold tearfully and ask, "Don't you love me, even a little?"

He cinches Persephone's saddle. "Of course I love you," he says. You saved us. The whole family. Grandmother was about to lose her house, and it's been in my family for centuries. You're the reason she still lives there."

He looks so convincing as he says this, it takes a moment to shake off a desperate feeling of tenderness. *No!* Why didn't he just ask for the money? Why did he sneak around behind your back? Well, there's an easy answer for that, too. He assumed that now that you were married, committed to each other for life, what's his was yours and what's yours was naturally his as well. He assumed you'd want him to take care of his family and you wouldn't want him to suffer the humiliation of asking for help.

It all hits you at once. It all makes sense. Why Harold wanted you to fire Bossrock and transfer your funds into a joint account in the UK. It wasn't because he was protecting you, it was because he was *stealing* from you. You run into the house knowing full well Harold won't follow. Sure enough, he doesn't.

Love is an untrustworthy thing. It won't always lead you to happiness and health; it will sometimes lead you into dark places. Maybe it isn't love you feel for Harold, maybe it's an addiction. They say you're addicted to something if you keep returning to it even though you don't want to, and that's exactly how you feel about him. You want to leave him, you know you should leave him, he's confessed to a terrible, unforgivable thing.

But has he?

He hasn't been unfaithful and he does love you. Maybe not in the traditional romantic sense, as you love him, but he does love you in a way and might that be enough? Must all love be matched ounce for ounce, depth for depth? How high are the statistical probabilities of that even happening? One in a hundred? In a million? The inconvenient truth is you still love him, even with solid evidence he doesn't love you.

So you stay and give birth to four girls, each a year apart, who bring your heart to a tender capacity you never knew before. They, with tiny hands, teach you patience. The long hours treading the floorboards, the constant gymnastics of diaper changing, the endless spoonfuls of mashed vegetables that end up on the floor, or in the nostrils, but never, hardly ever, in the mouth. The reluctant bundling every dawn, the uncertainty of it all, the accidents that could happen, the worrying, the waiting, it all acts as a meat tenderizer on your already lenient heart, and before you know it you're someone you were sure you could never be. You are a mother.

Even Harold finds them impossible to ignore. His reclusive activities wane after the first baby arrives and by the third he seems to come around to a different place regarding you. He takes your hand one evening as you both read by the fireplace and says, "I love you," and he means it differently now. Then the unexpected night comes when he climbs in your bed and makes love to you in an achingly tender way that's totally unlike before. He weeps afterward and says he never thought he could do it. He never thought he could break through the wall of anxiety and fear placed on his shoulders by his forefathers at birth. He never thought he could love someone.

But he does, he does love you, and it didn't come about in a traditional or even romantic way, but who cares what road brought you? We're told true love has to do with luck, chemistry, and kindness, that those are the building bricks of love, but then so must be patience, forgiveness, and dedication. Simply deciding to stay with someone and riding it out, even on days you have every reason to leave. Maybe especially on those days.

In this manner, through odd, unadvised persistence, you dodge the Irish curse. You simply had more stamina than it did, which is all anyone needs to outrun bad luck. You become quite happy in your estate in the English countryside, your family comes to stay during the summer, the children grow up and start families of their own. You start trust funds for the grandchildren. It won't be the giant sum you received so suddenly, but it's enough to get them going and not enough to get them in trouble.

No one is allowed on Skellig Michael.

Freaking Irish curses.

113

From section 104

You can't fake your own death. The ramifications are too severe. Where would you live? What would you do? You rid yourself of all thoughts of death, real or faked. It just isn't the way to go. You're thinking all this as you're crossing the street. You step out into traffic and the wind is terrific. Refreshing. Then black. The force throws you and all pictures light out. Blackness.

You wake in a vast storehouse. A warehouse packed with tall, cluttered racks of odd objects and miscellaneous items. There's a little old man in a gray cashmere sweater, and at first you think it's Grandpa Joe, but it isn't. You ask him where you are and he says *heaven*.

Heaven is mostly a lost-and-found depot with some waiting rooms thrown in. It's where everything anyone ever forgot goes to stay. If a person forgets something, the memory flutters *up, up, up*, through the clouds, past the magnetic fields, into the inky black, and up to the grand wire shelves where God keeps watch.

Occasionally as you walk slowly through these dim halls, something will jump up and fly away. A little rag doll, a chipped baseball bat, a hand-painted porcelain vase filled with brightly blooming pink roses, they zip up and vanish, taking flight through the window.

You watch as they disappear. "Where are they going?"

"Back home," the old man says. "Someone just remembered them."

Just then a small dog on the bottom shelf sneezes. He's old, with bald spots on his coat and cloudy eyes, but he gets up from his worn blue pillow wagging his tail.

"That you, Biscuit?" The man peers over his glasses.

The dog barks suddenly and then whisks up into the air. Then he's gone.

"Good for you, Biscuit!" the old man shouts and then registers the look of confusion on your face. "Well, someone just remembered Biscuit," he explains. "Someone down there. Probably looking at old family photos or something. So now good old Biscuit gets to see his family. That's how it works."

You nod, looking around at all these forgotten things.

He hands you a clipboard. "We take inventory. This is just the pets and childhood memories section. Wait till you see the souls section. Whole place is one big coffee shop where people hang out reading until someone down there thinks about them. Some folks never leave. Others go all the time."

"What's that place over there?" you ask, pointing out the window to a dark building in the distance made of green glass and surrounded by some kind of electrical storm. The old man shakes his head. "Don't go that way," he says. "That's the nightmare warehouse. You *do not* want to see what they have waiting over there. Shoot. There goes one now. Look!" An electrical arc flashes as a horrific gorilla shoots up into the sky and flies away. "Gorillas again?" he says, shaking his head. "I tell you what: someone down there's got gorillas on the brain."

114

From section 60

As an empire builder, you quickly learn there's no way to get filthy rich without getting filthy. The financial whiz kid you hire is named Mica Baum and his consulting fee is fifty thousand dollars an hour. He advises such other financial gorillas as Ovitz, Winfrey, Trump, and Woods (before the affairs). He single-handedly got both President Bush Sr. and President Bush Jr. elected. People say he can do anything, but his first piece of advice to you is if you want to get rich quick, you have to do exactly as he says.

Mica has a short, compact, sparkplug-shaped body and bright blue, slightly wild eyes, as though he was hooked to some invisible low-grade electrical current or perhaps fueled by some form of moderately legal speed. He walks and talks in quick bursts and has a jerky, overanimated way of using his hands. He says the best way to make big money *fast* is to get dirty. Be willing to do what others won't. All societies, whether you like it or not, whether you dress it up or boil it down, are built on two principal things: drugs and weapons. If you want to build an empire, you have to lay a pipeline. So which is it?

If you manufacture drugs, go to section 138 (p. 444).
If you manufacture weapons, go to section 148 (p. 481).

115

From section 26

Mr. Cook has gotten you this far, so maybe continuing to trust him is the best thing to do. You'll just have to make some cutbacks—maybe you could get rid of a few luxury items, like the solar tanning bed or Grumbles the hermit crab, who refuses to die and has cost more in care and maintenance expenses than all the other animals combined.

You tell the family they have to cut back. Now is the time for low-flow shower heads and automatic dimmers on the lights. The thermostat is to stay at sixty-five degrees, which causes your uncle Sydney to constantly complain about how cold the house is and run around plugging in space heaters everywhere. He finally gets so fed up with your "Gestapo regime," he goes and buys a big old Airstream trailer and parks it on the lawn.

Aidan says maybe it's lucky, at least he's living outside the house now and in charge of cleaning out his own Porta Potti. Then Uncle Sydney's new pal, Irv, pulls up in his more modern, more massive RV and parks it right next to the Airstream. You'd be annoyed but the guy is really nice and actually offers to pay you some money for the parking space. Then more RV buddies show up, each asking to park on the lawn, and before you know it you're running a mini trailer park.

The phone wakes you up early one morning. Who could be calling at this hour? It's Mr. Cook's assistant. She very slowly, very painfully explains that Mr. Cook has killed himself. He took his own life earlier in the day after it was revealed that Silverlock was a Ponzi scheme. A scam. His weepy assistant tells you that your accounts have been drained. You're broke.

In the morning you gather all the adults in the house and tell them you're broke. You have to sell the house, everyone will have to find a new home and . . . just as you're about to break apart crying, Grandpa Joe stands from his wheelchair. An act that silences the room. He tells everyone to quit worrying and start thinking. "Got a lot of land here," he says, "got a lot of people that seem to want to park on it."

"Grandpa, are you saying we should turn this place into a trailer park?"

"Got a lot of *crap* here, too," he says. "These damn kids don't need it all. Sell the crap! It's cooking their brains from the inside out!"

At this point several of the children who had gathered around the perimeter of the group to listen in start crying and the group dissolves from there, but Grandpa's speech has an impact. It is unanimously decided that you will open the first-ever trailer park in Airedale Downs.

Since no one ever tried, or even *considered* trying to open a trailer park in this neighborhood, there are actually no laws against it. Nevertheless, the neighbors fight like hell to get you thrown out, there's even a big town hall meeting about it and the local paper crusades to end your plans, but eventually even Airedale Downs' lawyers give up on changing the many, many old ordinances that uphold a person's "God-given right to prosper."

Your neighbors are livid. Terrified. Fears of wild teenagers and knife fights run rampant. They expect your property to look like a postapocalyptic landfill crossed with a nude beach within a week. All hell will break loose. Incidents of social disorder will rise, teen pregnancy and graphic vandalism will rocket and it is *all your fault*.

You don't know what other trailer parks are like and you don't care, you just want to make a nice little community that's safe and aesthetically pleasing, so you create Ritzy Acres, *the little mobile home park that could*. Pretty soon word gets out that there's a nice new trailer park in the middle of a safe residential community, and before you know it every one of your trailer slots is filled. There are people from every walk of life. Retired snowbirds, long-haul truck drivers, divorced dads, single moms, and a whole lot of kids.

There are two boys from Juarez, Jorge and Diego. Brothers. Teenagers. Hardworking. Not only do they attend high school full-time, they both work night shifts seven days a week at the gas station on Highway 169. Their parents are back in Mexico, they have no other family, so you look out for them. So does Maggie, the young, one-armed war veteran who lives in the trailer next door. She has two kids of her own but no husband. He never came back from Iraq. When she sees Jorge or Diego sitting outside late at night, she sticks her head out the door and asks them what time it is. Then, no matter what they answer, she says, "Know what time I think it is? Time for bed." Then she stands there and watches them until they ease up from their lawn chairs and put out the fire.

Miss Doll, the old lady who lives across the way from Maggie, says the Lord never intended for a single mother with only one arm to raise children all alone. She drops off chicken casseroles and apple pies on Maggie's doorstep almost every day and if Maggie protests, Miss Doll gets quite snappish and says, "It's nothing! Just scraps! I was going to put it out for the raccoons anyway!"

Bob, the grumpy old man living next to Miss Doll, is retired and doesn't say much, but he's always fixing things. He used to be a water engineer for the city and even though his pension came up and he was free to roam the world and never work again, it's like his hands couldn't stop fixing things. Maggie's crooked steps, Miss Doll's Cadillac antenna, even Too Tall Tom's guitar bridge.

Too Tall is part Cree and he plays acoustic guitar on his stoop almost every night. He was a shepherd in Montana and still has his border collie, Samson. Whenever he tells stories of living alone on the mountain, a crowd gathers to listen. Among them is always Beth, the bone-thin seamstress, who brings her mending with her. She gets a strange look on her face when Too Tall speaks, as though she's listening to something far, far away.

JoAnne is the park's den mother. She loves making big meals and organizes Sunday supper for everyone each week. People listen for her Sunday dinner bell, a bullhorn that usually sounds at around five o'clock. The kids all race around on bicycles and the teenagers sulk on the fringes. The women fuss over details and the men swap stories. What an odd, happy little world you've created.

Time passes and you develop an odd condition called synesthesia. It's a condition where your nervous system mixes up signals. Confuses sounds with colors and colors with numbers. Beer tastes like cool terra-cotta and a car horn sounds like lemon-yellow walls. Space and taste become one. Sound and color blend so as to be inextricable from one another. Cats meowing is silver spray. The taste of butterscotch raises a vibrating plaid pattern in front of your eyes. You can remember almost anything by assigning it a color. People's phone numbers become variant rainbow ribbons, your own phone number being canary-orange-caraway-bisque-blue-oatmeal-gray. Some colors have no names.

First you thought it was just fuzzy thinking from all the headaches you've been having, but then you're diagnosed with the condition and the doctors order all kinds of weird treatments and mind-altering medicines. Well, you're not about to put that crap in your system. Besides, one of your favorite things is sitting on the porch at twilight silently and with great stealth, watching your neighbors take care of one another. You sip tea and taste mountain ranges. Too Tall comes out with Samson, who barks, and you see the most beautiful color blue.

116

From section 104

Faking your own death has been done by many people. Since the beginning of time and until the end, certain people will want to disappear. They all have their reasons. Personal crisis, financial disaster, legal despair. Sadly, there's little news about successful phony deaths, because those people got away with it. Only the stories of failed absconders can be found, but they provide useful information anyway.

Murder is out, as you don't want to implicate anyone or come up with a body. Sadly, gone are the days when you could dig up a fresh corpse, put it in your car, douse it with gasoline, light it on fire, and run away. Damn forensics. Suicide is out because it voids your life insurance policy. The bean counters don't like planned exits.

That leaves an accident. A mystery.

You make a simple plan. You and Aidan announce your decision to finally take a honeymoon. You're going camping in the Blue Ridge Mountains.

One week into your camping trip Cousin Beth calls the police and reports you missing. She tells them you were supposed to return yesterday and didn't. The police call the rangers, the rangers sound the alarms, a massive search launches, but no one ever finds you.

You never return home.

That's because your brother took a trip out to these same mountains a week earlier, slunk in on foot, and never registered his name at the rangers' guard window. He hid fake IDs, cash, and disguises for you in the parking lot, just put them in a knotted garbage bag and tucked it behind the retaining wall near the Dumpsters. Then he shadowed his way back out.

When you and Aidan show up and check in at the guard window, you make sure you're conspicuous as you sign in. You ask questions, get maps, ask for directions, and tell them you'll be hiking for six days. You park the car and haul all your camping gear up to your first campsite, about a half mile into the woods.

That night, after the tent is up, the steak dinner cooked and cleared, the sleeping bags unrolled, and the lanterns extinguished, you and Aidan creep out of the campsite, both of you wearing only black long underwear and flip-flops. You make your way back to the parking lot, where you quickly retrieve the hidden disguises, don them with as much care as possible in the dark, and then, using your brother's hand-drawn map, take a shortcut through the woods back to the main road. Then it's a short walk to the nearest motel, where your brother's marine buddy's Dodge Dart is waiting for you.

A week later your cousin Beth calls the police and reports you missing. Then she calls back with increasing measures of panic when it's been twelve hours, then twenty-four, and once again after forty-eight hours, when legally they can file a missing persons report. A massive search is launched. Dogs, helicopters, Baptists. Everyone looks for you and Aidan . . . but by now you and Aidan are safely in Mexico.

When enough time passes, the police declare you and Aidan dead. An obituary is placed in the paper, a large funeral is held, and the insurance company is contacted. There's a lot of paperwork but not much trouble. They pepper your family with questions: *Were they unhappy? Suicidal? In debt?* But no matter what they ask, the family just shrugs and says they don't know. Clever liars give details, but the cleverest don't.

You and Aidan make your way down to central Uruguay, where you live on a small ranch about an hour outside Trinidad. Your family arrives six months later and with the policy money you buy a little ranch with wide-open acreage and a tiny, fast-flowing creek running through its middle.

Eventually Aunt Phyllis and Uncle Sydney come, along with cousins Beth and John and their girls and, yes, all their dogs. One by one everyone makes their way down to the ranch, Rancho Paradiso. A simple name for a very simple life.

The kids all grow up riding horses, little gauchos who ride barefoot and bareback. Your cousins plant fruit and vegetables, which they sell every Sunday at the open market. You and Aidan become fairly successful ranchers—your hands worn and calloused from the unceasing rhythms and hard but satisfying work all around you. Nobody ever discovers your identity—no one ever finds out about your crime. Here they probably wouldn't ever consider faking your own death a crime, if it meant providing for your family.

Twenty years later your car collides with another while you're on a short trip to Buenos Aires, where you go once a year for certain supplies, like antibiotics and double-ply toilet paper. This time you were on the prowl for dog vitamins. Then you take a wrong turn onto a one-way street and slam into a taxicab. You die instantly on impact. No pain, just light, a freshness, and then gone.

In heaven you learn identity theft is a beloved pastime. After all, what is the body but a flash of electricity in a fleshy Motel 6? Souls are the passengers, bodies are the ride. People get in and get out. Anytime a person is unconscious, even for the briefest of moments, a soul can transfer. One soul can leave the body and let another soul enter.

That's why so many people seem different after accidents. They are different. Literally. When you experience déjà vu or something that ought to be foreign but isn't, you're only seeing something someone using your body before you left behind. A memory, a fear, a forgotten thought. It's like finding someone else's umbrella in your room at Motel 6. A memento from the passenger before you. Returning the memory to its rightful owner isn't necessary. All we are is a series of stolen identities and the whole of heaven is just one big celebrity in disguise.

117

From section 103

You tell Harold that you love him dearly and *treasure* time with him, but you just don't know him well enough yet to marry him. After all, you only met six months ago. Maybe in a year or two the idea of marriage would make more sense? You smile warmly, but as your words register, his eyes grow hard. He drains his cocktail and barks rudely at a passing waiter to bring him another.

He's upset, naturally.

It's understandable anyone who's just had their marriage proposal rejected would be a bit disappointed, but Harold's reaction seems . . . odd. The waiter brings his drink and Harold slams it back before demanding the whole bottle. The waiter hurries toward the bar. Harold crosses his arms and says, "What a colossal waste of time. Grandmother warned me, of course, but naturally I didn't listen."

"Harold, are you not feeling well?"

"I say people are teachable. Grandmother, however, thinks people are born where they belong and they ought to stay put. The subtle nuances of high society are too complex to learn, really. How one crosses a room or shakes your hand—they have etiquette books for that. It's all the unwritten rules that trip a person up. I suppose it's how old money can spot new money a mile away. It isn't any one mistake, just a hundred little ones."

The waiter sets down a tray with a small silver ice bucket and crystal decanter of scotch. Harold pours himself a drink.

"Are you insulting me, Harold? I can't tell."

He rolls his eyes and says, "Not yet," then downs another drink. "I'll cut to the chase. I've been trying to work up to it and I'm failing splendidly. Just bear with me. All of this is to say I am a complete and resounding failure."

"Harold, you're not! You're lovely!"

"Well, in Grandmother's opinion I'm a prime example of our family's decline, which she says is producing fewer titans of industry, and instead populating her Christmas brunches with thick-headed, overweight leeches. She's even begun to suspect infidelity somewhere in the family tree, because she doesn't think it's possible for a family with our heritage to give birth to *so many idiots*."

"Harold, that's awful! You shouldn't let her say those things. It isn't right."

"Well, it's *nothing* compared to what she says about you."

"Beg your pardon?"

"The first time my grandmother ever saw you, she took me aside and said, 'Harold, that girl doesn't have greatness in her. She'll never fit in.' Of course she was right." He tosses his napkin on the table. "You're terminally stupid. You could've at least offered me compensation for the long, agonizing months of being your escort. You really are dull."

You almost can't breathe. "Is . . . this a joke?"

"Not a bit. Did you really think I wanted to marry you? I wanted your money! God, you're daft. Utterly, completely, an entire waste of—"

Sha-boom! A huge explosion ricochets through the place and people scatter, knocking over tables and dinnerware. In your trembling hand is the little silver pistol purchased in the grocery store parking lot from a pock-faced teen.

You just shot Harold. He's dead. Splayed back and limp, blood draining from his shirt.

It was worth it.

118

From section 94

You decide to rob the Pancake Ranch. Let it be known! The world will pay! You don't even plan it out, you just sort of start moving, like you've been a stone-cold criminal from day one. Around midnight you grab half a can of compressed air and a wrench from your parents' garage. Then you walk to the diner, giving yourself plenty of time to get good and cold and plenty fucking mad. Mad enough to start whistling.

You walk up to the large plate-glass window of the Pancake Ranch and raise your wrench, smashing the glass with one blow. Stepping through the shards, you keep whistling and stride through the dining room, kicking open Gordon's office door. There you hold the can of compressed air upside down and spray the padlock until it smokes over a frosty white. You saw this handy maneuver on a TV show once; you have no idea if it actually works. A second later you bludgeon the lock with your wrench and it clatters to the ground like a tin toy.

What do you know? It works!

You grab the cash and stuff it inside your sweatshirt before smashing the back window and whistling off into the night fifteen thousand dollars richer. You walk home, get in your car, and drive over to Aidan's house, where the Lexus SUV you bought him, the one he cherishes, sits in the driveway behind Shitaye's red Camaro. You park on the lawn, hop out with your wrench, and smash out the headlights on his truck. You're working on the windshield when the lights come on and he comes running out of the house in his boxers.

"What are you doing?"

Smash! Smash! "I'm working out some issues, Aidan!" *Smash!*

"Stop!" he shouts, trying to grab your wrench. "Why are you doing this?"

You make a move like you're going to hit him and he flinches. You throw the wrench down at his feet, laughing, and say, "I would never hit you with a wrench, babe!" Then you punch him with your fist. Crack him right across the jaw, bare knuckles splitting against the stubble on his chin. He stumbles back and sinks to his knees. Shitaye appears in the doorway, terrified and clutching her pink robe.

You grin at her. "You look scared, honey. Wanna hug?"

Her eyes go wide and you lick the blood off your hand as you scoop up your wrench, pausing to smash out the driver's-side window on the Camaro. Then you hop back in your car and peel out, after shouting at Aidan, who's still lying on the grass.

"Like you said, babe! Good people go bad if you push them hard enough!"

Then you hit the road with the radio on full volume and a hot stack of cash. You're heading to a new city, another place. It doesn't matter which way you go, you're going to start over now and it's going to be fucking beautiful.

119

From section 95

You hold your breath and heave open the coffin. The lights flicker and you almost drop the lid, but it's empty inside. There's nothing there. Very odd. You give the coffin a good look before closing it, even daring to let one hand dip down and skim along the bottom of the cool interior. Nope. Nothing there. You close it and go back upstairs feeling a little silly. Miss Dottie is full of surprises.

You dive into a cache of Miss Dottie's private journals from 1925, which you found on the lower shelf of the living room bookcase. The more you find out about Miss Dottie, the stranger and more exotic she seems. The youngest and only girl of seven children, Miss Dottie's name was Dominique Anastasie Lully, born in 1898 on Martinique to parents of circus lineage. She traveled through the north of France with her family and at the ripe old age of six became a bareback rider. She rode in circus rings all over Europe until she was seventeen and met a French painter named Modigliani. He begged her to come be his model in Montparnasse, that infamous area on the Left Bank of Paris known for *les années folles,* the crazy years, when the square mile was lousy with geniuses: Picasso, Cocteau, Rivera, and Brancusi. You couldn't swing a dead cat without hitting one.

In her journals Dottie scolds herself for not knowing what exactly "being a model" in Paris meant. After she joined Modigliani in Montparnasse, she became his lover and he became fiercely jealous. No one even knew if she spoke French, because he never allowed anyone to speak to his new favorite model. Dottie eventually left Modigliani and traded her services around the quarter, becoming one of the most popular models at the time. Cocktails at Café du Dôme, discussions with Diego at La Coupole, dancing at Café de la

Rotonde. She even went on to perform at some theaters, singing and dancing for appreciative audiences. When she met an American soldier named Stanley Daniel, however, she was at last smitten. *Stanley Daniel?* You have to double-check her handwriting to be sure, as it's not quite as sexy a name as Modigliani. Then you hear a crash in the basement.

You tiptoe downstairs and find the coffin facedown on the floor. You back away slowly, whispering *Everything's okay, everything's okay, everything's okay* and then you dash/scramble up the stairs to the kitchen, slamming the basement door shut. You're breathing hard, heart hammering loudly enough for the ceramic chicken to hear. This is ridiculous! Just relax. The coffin just fell over. No big deal!

You force yourself to settle back down and continue reading Miss Dottie's journal and learn that Stanley Daniel's real name was Stanislav Daniel and he was born in Slovakia to a hard family who she calls "brutal and dangerous." Gizella, Stanley's mother, is referred to as "the witch," and Dottie seems to use this term in the literal sense. One entry recounts her first introduction to them, when Stanley announced their engagement. *Gizella looked at me with hate in her eye and started mumbling something. Stani told her to stop—but she would not. Later when he was out of the room, she told me that she'd put a curse on me. Any children I had with her son would die before I did. I said I wasn't afraid of her and she started cursing me again. Such rubbish. Oh, how I cry for Montparnasse!*

The young lovers moved to New York City, where Stanley, or "Stani," as his Slovakian friends called him, got work as a bartender while Dottie studied to become a nurse. They kept planning to get married, booked dates at City Hall, but some catastrophe always befell them on the day they were to wed. The first time was in spring when Stani fell on the steps outside City Hall and landed on his elbow, fracturing it. The second time was in high summer and it was Dottie who fell this time, on the church steps. She twisted her ankle and went tumbling down the whole flight of stone steps, winding up with a concussion and cracking one corner of her top left tooth off. Their third attempt at marriage was in the fall, and as they hailed a taxi in front of their apartment, the little neighbor boy came running to give

Dottie a bunch of dandelions he'd picked for her, and he fell down the steep tenement steps, fracturing his skull. After that they decided not to get married. Stanislav's mother could work curses even in America.

All of a sudden you hear pounding in the basement, like a hammer on a garbage can. You freeze. Cold creeps across your neck. Your heart begins to beat faster. Your hands go cold. You can sense something breathing just behind you. You suddenly spring up and dash to the front door—but it's too late. She's standing there in front of you. Her lips are full and pink, exquisitely curved like a cupid's bow. Her nose is strong, nostrils flared. Her eyes are wide and almond-shaped, liquid black but lucent. High cheekbones, skin the color of smoked cinnamon. Her forehead is wrapped tightly with a parrot green turban. "Dottie?" She nods.

"Merci, cherie," she says, "for releasing me."

You step back. "But there was nothing in the coffin!"

She smiles. "But there was."

"What are you?"

"Gizella made me *lamia.*" Her smile widens until her black teeth envelop her head and she turns inside out, a slimy, slithering creature.

Great. Here we go.

"Choose the coffin or the night," she hisses. "You can go into the ground or forever walk the earth, as one of the damned and undead."

If you choose to die a natural death, go to section 152 (p. 490).
If you choose to become undead, go to section 153 (p. 491).

120

On the way back to Rome, the bus breaks down, and while the driver is going for help, a group of Gypsies walk by and offer to perform for the stranded tourists. You tell them, "No Grazie," but the tourists whine and say, "Why not? Why can't we hear music! We want to hear music!" until the fillings in your teeth ache and your eyeballs go dry and your brain feels like a hot plate. *Fine! You want Gypsies? Have Gypsies!*

The Gypsies produce violins and a tambourine. The moon rises high above and little Gypsy children dance on the side of the road as their mothers clap and sing. It's one of those strange, marvelous moments that happen too rarely in life, when everything comes together in one harmonic moment, a moment you never could have predicted or orchestrated. When it's over, the tourists clap and cheer and wave good-bye to the Gypsies as they disappear into the night. Then they realize all the luggage is gone.

While everyone was on the roadside clapping and singing, the bus was stealthily being emptied out. It's also discovered that the adorable little children who danced with the tourists pickpocketed everyone. You! You let this happen! The tourists are enraged, furious. When they return home they launch full-scale legal suits and smear your name into a pulp.

The lawsuits, thirty-four in total, bankrupt you. You're completely finished. Aidan leaves you for a Sam's Club cashier who buys him bulk spices and discount kitchen appliances. You move home with your parents and land a job at Olive Garden, where you start mopping floors, but with the right attitude and hard work, you hope to work your way up to salad bar replenisher. Sometimes you look at the row of glass-and-chrome crushed red pepper shakers and you cry.

121

From section 147

You decide to go for it. You bet all four hundred thousand on the last race. The bell sounds and the entire stadium roars. Cameras are trained on you and the words BIG WINNER? flash underneath your face on all the monitors. It's the question you've been asking yourself all along. Are you a big winner? Has everything that's happened to you up until now been good luck or bad? Winning the lottery, paying for all your family's bills, losing Aidan— you could play it either way, as bad luck or good luck. Just depends on how you look at things. Maybe if you decide it's all been good luck, that will make it true. The big question now is . . . will your luck hold?

Sirens blare and the crowd goes wild as you snap out of your reverie. Quite a time to get lost in your thoughts. Your heart leaps to your throat. Only one thing could make a crowd cheer like that! You must have won! Frantically you scan the boards . . . and there it is.

You lost?

Rick's got his hands over his face. He's moaning. "I don't get it," you whisper. "Why are they cheering if I lost?"

" 'Cause the only thing that makes people happier than a big winner is a big loser. Take a look around. You're broke, kid, but you're the most popular person here."

Homeless, jobless, depressed, and unfit for public viewing, you move into your parents' basement and spend the rest of your life addicted to online poker, rarely leaving the house except to go buy wet wipes and nachos.

122

You sell the vineyard to Mondavi. Why fight Goliath when you don't even have a rock to throw? The vineyard is too much for you.

After returning home, you feel a little deflated. You miss the vineyard and move to St. Helena, California, the hub of Napa Valley winegrowers. It's a gorgeous town where Robert Redford can be spotted shopping for organic strawberries at the farmers market and Joe Montana checks books out for his daughter at the public library. The life here is not cheap, and despite the money from Mondavi, your previous winemaking enterprise has set you back considerably. You'll need half a million just to buy a small one-bedroom house in town with a tiny backyard. The nicer houses start at two million and you just can't part with that kind of cash right now. You've got to find a way to turn the money you have left into a livelihood!

In the end you take some random emergency housing on Mobile Home Way by Slurry Pond so you can use the last of your savings and open an Italian bistro named Bella Ovunque, which loosely translated means "Beautiful Everywhere." (You think that's what it means. Your Italian is not the greatest. It's close.)

You renovate a tiny yellow cottage just on the edge of town and turn it into a small rustic dining room. You pay for Vincenzo to relocate to Napa Valley and be the head chef at your restaurant and you host free wine tastings every Sunday night. Soon your small establishment becomes a lively hotspot for intellectual oenophiles everywhere and quite a few locals. People love Vincenzo's Tuscan bruscetta and the cheese he imports (illegally) from his cousins in Florence.

When you learn you can allow dogs into your restaurant by putting a simple sign on the door that says THESE PREMISES HAVE LIVE ANIMALS ON THEM—

PERSONS ON THE PROPERTY WITH ALLERGIES OR OBJECTIONS ARE FOREWARNED AND ABSOLVE MANAGEMENT OF ANY RESPONSIBILITY FROM SAID FACT, you become the first eatery that allows dogs inside the restaurant and the seating reservations go off the chart. The only thing vineyard owners like better than fine wine and good food is fine wine and good food with their canine companions. Let's just say a lot of them get along better with animals than with people. Bella Ovunque is a runaway hit. You're soon turning a profit and able to buy a small tract of land, which you flip without trying to an aggressive vineyard on the south side that was never told the land was going up for sale. (The rivalries in this community could fill a three-hour documentary and already have. *Mondo Vino* gives a peek into the rarefied world of the wine industry and its ugly underbelly.) You're able to buy an even bigger tract of land and lease that out to a winegrower.

Slowly, over the next decade you save enough money to start a modest vineyard of your own. Of course, being a vineyard owner is far more expensive than being a restaurant owner, and not just because of operating costs. Besides the initial four million it costs to build the winery, you have to go to the Napa Valley wine auctions, which cost seven grand a ticket; you need to throw routine fancy-pants dinners so you can keep up on valley gossip; and you have to join the Meadowood Country Club, which has a thirty-thousand-dollar initiation fee. If you're not a member, you might as well leave. It's where most business gets done.

On the upside, you have your own vineyard and produce a nice Cabernet table wine called Bella Ovunque. You start to do yoga in the vineyard, lining your mat up with the horizon at sunset and stretching until your lungs fill with sweet, deep breath. You invite others to join you, friends and then friends of friends, until you're actually teaching yoga classes and serving wine and organic meals afterward. It becomes an enterprise almost as lucrative as the winery and restaurant.

Aidan and you like to walk through the vineyard at twilight, look at the grapes, and see how the vines are growing. The sound of crickets all around you.

Bella Ovunque.

123

From section 62

You decide to become a roaming philanthropist. A Guerrilla Miracle Machine. You travel the world and give the money away. There's a Chinese proverb that says: *an invisible red thread connects those who are destined to meet, regardless of the time, place, or circumstance. The thread may stretch or tangle, but it will never break.* Now it's time for you to set out and start walking the red line. The red thread that will connect you to all the people whom you're meant to help and destined to meet. You and Aidan decide to take a round-the-world trip in which you will hand all twenty-two million dollars away.

You boil down your worldly possessions to fit inside two Eagle Creek Grand Voyage backpacks. In your pack:

- Two North Face antimicrobial T-shirts in frost and inkwell.
- Two Columbia Omni-Dry long-sleeve shirts with underarm venting and convertible sleeves in black ibis and fresh lox.
- One Amana Tunic with built-in UV protection, lightweight nylon, and four-way supporting stretch fabric in hamachi.
- One pair of paratrooper porter pants with abrasion-resistant nylon fabric and zip-off legs in pumice.
- One pair of Zambian Insect Shield Ambush Pants with built-in UV protection and high-strength canvas impregnated with insect repellent, good for seventy washings, in night moth.
- One set of 100 percent New Zealand pure merino wool long underwear in glacier blue.
- One women's Khumbu TKA 200 midweight fleece jacket in bitter chocolate.

- Three pairs of travel panties in smoke, smudge, and smirch.
- One Nimbus Sombrero Hat with plastic-reinforced edging channels and adjustable chinstrap in tom-tom macoute.
- One ugly horrible bathing suit you'll never wear.
- Two chamois towels.
- Nike running shoes.
- Merrell lightweight hiking boots.
- Teva Women's Hurricane 3 Sandals in mud.
- Small goose-down sleeping bag.
- Battery-operated pedometer/pen.
- Self-filtering water bio-bottle.
- Passport.

In Aidan's pack:

- Two Columbia Men's Titanium Omni-Dry Mountain Tech short-sleeve T-shirts in night train and moon dust.
- Two men's Air Strip Lite Fine-Line Plaid long-sleeve shirts with built-in UV protection and climate-control ventilation in pebble plaid and lettuce.
- One pair Men's Scrumbling Pants in condor grey.
- One North Face Men's Khumbu TKA 300 midweight fleece jacket in anemone green.
- One set of 100 percent New Zealand pure merino wool long underwear in riverstone.
- One O'Neill Grinder Boardshort swim trunks in Oakland.
- Three pairs of Capilene underwear in smoke, smudge, and smirch.
- Hurley Men's Puerto Rico Flexfit baseball hat in cholo plaid.
- North Face Men's Ultra 104 GTX XCR trail running shoes with Northotic ergonomically designed footbed and Poron heel inserts plus TPU toe cap and gusseted tongue in loden green.
- Teva Men's Hurricane 3 Sandals in rubble grey.
- Small Hypnalis goose-down sleeping bag.

- Big Swiss Army knife.
- Two LED mini flashlights with extra batteries and headlamps.
- Guidebooks/maps.
- Xeroxed copies of passports.
- Extra passport photos (ten).
- Solar-powered alarm clock/radio/compass.
- Digital camera.
- Flash cards.
- Panasonic Toughbook H1.
- ATM card.
- Traveler's checks.
- International driver's license.
- Passport.

You start in London. Your first miracle is to buy a homeless man a sandwich. He was sitting on the sidewalk in a tatty trench coat with his scabbed hands covering his face, like maybe he'd just stopped crying, or was just about to start. You handed him a roast beef on rye. You didn't mean it to be your first miracle and certainly not your last, but it was both. He took the sandwich, flashed you a confused look, and then ran off with it. You and Aidan just shrugged at each other and then headed to your hotel, but you got lost. The map was kooky or your directions were wrong, and before you know what happened, you're pulled into a dark alleyway and mugged. Clubbed on the head with a tire iron. The men were strong.

Smart, too.

"By three methods we learn wisdom," one of the thugs says cheerfully as he rips your backpack off. Someone else pushes you down on the cracked asphalt.

"First, by reflection," he says, "which is noblest."

You can hear your backpack being unzipped as Aidan groans.

"Second, by imitation, which is easiest."

Someone hits you in the spinal cord with a cold blunt object and everything goes black, but you can still hear the thug's voice. "The third method of learning wisdom is *experience*. Much like the one you're having now, and naturally, the bitterest." Poet thug seems quite pleased with himself but the rest of the pack seems uninterested.

"Hey!" one says. "Look at this. Wick-away underwear!"

You and Aidan both die due to injuries.

Your career as a guerrilla philanthropist lasted one day. In heaven you enter the Hall of Truth, a grand room cut from white marble, with vaulting ecclesiastical arches and a chandelier of living, breathing, crystal-clear songbirds with liquid sapphire eyes perched on the branches of an illuminated tree. They chirp and chatter. A lovely woman stands behind a marble podium in a long cerulean green dress; she's alabaster white and seems to be made of stone herself. Then her pale purple eyes flutter open. Her face is smooth white and small illuminated firefly creatures begin to dart around her spun-silver hair. She picks up a plumed pen and holds it with her extraordinarily long alabaster fingers.

"The life you just completed?" she asks.

You're nervous. "Yes?"

She blinks her large lavender eyes. "Did you mean it?"

"Pardon?"

She stands, waiting with her pen poised. You stammer out a half answer. "Yes. Sure. I don't know. I didn't do very well—but I meant to. I *tried*."

"She meant to!" the woman says, but not to you. She says it to the birds above her, which rustle and rearrange themselves, singing out loudly in unison: *True true true!*

"Very well," the woman says. "The lovelies say it's true."

She carefully marks something down on the tablet in front of her before smiling and directing you down the hallway to her right. "This way, please." The entrance of the hall is blooming with opulent, extraordinary flowers. A quick look over your shoulder reveals the hallway opposite yours, a sinister-looking entrance tangled with thorny dead branches.

"So, I'm going to heaven?" you ask hopefully.

"Yes," she says. "God's quite a mistake maker himself. He prefers the company of imperfect dreamers and those who are hopelessly romantic and/or wildly impractical. Hell is reserved for perfectionists." The lovelies above her sing: *True true true!*

In heaven you learn you're not a complete fuckup after all. The unseen second act of your unfinished miracle is shown. Ivan, the homeless man to whom you gave a sandwich, was going to kill himself that day. He hadn't been able to find work in so long and his family was starving. After he ate that roast beef on rye, though—it was delicious—he went to the shelter where his family had been given a room and he made quick but passionate love to his wife, Yuliya. Yuliya gave birth to baby Nikolas nine months and two days later and he, this little one—will become a legend.

After enduring many hardships, Nikolas will be placed in foster care with a kind couple who are overjoyed at finally having a child. The wife is a ceramics instructor and the husband is a research assistant at the Royal Marsden Hospital, which specializes in treating cancer. Nikolas will grow up to become a world-renowned geneticist and he'll discover the world's first noninvasive treatment for both brain and pancreatic cancers.

The boy cures cancer.

The angels explain most miracles aren't grand gestures. They're strange kindnesses flitting around out there like lost fireflies with interminable spirits. These are not miracles in the historically or hysterically *ecclesiastical* sense of the word, they're not crying statues or incorruptible corpses or the Virgin Mary appearing on toast. No. Your miracle was better than all those put together. People don't need stigmatic nuns or shrouds in Turin. They don't need million-dollar all-terrain ponchos or cholo-plaid microfiber wick-away underwear.

They need roast beef sandwiches.

Roast beef sandwiches are the kind of miracle people can use.

124

From section 61

You decide to keep the vineyard. You've worked too hard for too long to give up now. Unfortunately, the crops get black rot and suffer for the next two years. No bottles of wine are made in that time. The winemaking aspect of your enterprise is a disaster. You're stewing over your problem in the field one day when an idea hits you. Why not open a restaurant? Isn't that how it all started—with fantastic food? So you open Maison, a family-style bistro, in your converted hay barn, which has a gourmet kitchen and lofty, vaulted dining room. You serve French countryside favorites, pan-fried steak, duck liver, beef bourguignonne, bouillabaisse, crêpe frontenac, as well as a wide variety of delectable pastries created by a local chef from the village.

You love the electric energy in the kitchen; the chef sings when he debones chickens and the waiters flock through the kitchen during the dinner rush like startled white doves. The vineyard recovers from black rot, and while you fall far from winning any awards, you do produce a nice table wine, which your own chef won't drink, but he *will* cook with.

Aidan proposes and you have a lovely spring wedding right there in the vineyard, your whole family flying over for the ceremony. That's when you let them know you're pregnant, with twins. Alison and Isabel. It's hard to believe you are now raising a family in France. You love living here. It feels like home. The neighboring vineyards, the quaint village, the rolling fields of lavender and sunflowers banked by the rich-smelling olive groves. You can even speak a decent amount of French now, after years of effort. Naturally Alison and Isabel are fluent before they're two and run wild through the vineyard like French monkeys. You're not rich, but you have enough.

It's a beautiful life.

125

From section 48

You meet with Dr. Silvern, a very expensive and sought-after fertility specialist. His clinic is in Denver and looks like a penthouse apartment with carpet and soft lights so as not to rattle the wealthy, highly rattleable, pre-pregnant/still-pregnant/post-pregnant women who collect in his posh waiting room.

After several visits and prescreening tests, Dr. Silvern decides you are a great candidate for in vitro fertilization, a procedure where eggs and sperm are united in a petri dish under the fluorescent lights of a lab instead of joining in a uterus. After carefully reviewing all the information, consulting with your family doctor, and discussing it with your family, you decide to do it.

You go to the clinic for twelve consecutive days of gonadotropin, a medication that encourages the growth of multiple egg sacs. Then you check into Methodist Hospital, where Dr. Silvern carefully suctions your eggs out. (It only takes about twenty minutes and you're sedated but it hurts like almighty hell.) Your eggs are then inseminated and allowed to develop until they're ready to be put back in your uterus. Dr. Silvern implants eight embryos and says he can almost guarantee success.

Success indeed. Thirteen days later you find out you're pregnant. Thirty days later you find out you're pregnant with *octuplets*. All eight embryos took—which means you have eight small people riding around in your stomach. The idea makes you go into a state of suspended shock and you can't quite focus on Dr. Silvern's words as he explains your options regarding the disposition of the remaining embryos. You just sit there nodding, panic spreading like a slow fever. He sends you home with an armload of pamphlets about embryo donation, disposal techniques, and the cryogenic freezing process. When you know what you want to do, just give him a call. You go home and sit in the bathtub for two days. Then you tell Aidan. Then you cry for a week. Then you eat your weight in fudge-chunk ice cream. Another two weeks pass and you can't quite account for them. Then your phone starts ringing and Dr. Silvern's nurse leaves messages. First they're friendly reminders: "Please let us know your excess-embryo choices as soon as possible!" Then they're curt requests: "Please contact the office as soon as possible." Then outright scoldings: "We've attempted to contact you for three months. This is your final notice. The procedure contract you signed absolves the clinic of all repercussions should you miss your embryo disposal window, which is quickly closing. Call us today."

You nod at the answering machine. You agree. You should call. Instead you lie down and you sleep. Aidan wants to know what's wrong, he begs you to get up. Your family comes around, your friends, but you don't want to talk to anyone.

You go over it again and again, but none of the options seem right. Keeping them all is insane but disposing of them seems impossible. How do you pick which zygote comes home to a sweet bubble-gum-colored nursery and which one gets chucked into a medical waste bin? Donating an embryo is the same as giving it up for adoption. How could you let your biological children grow up in someone else's house? And freezing them for later? You picture little fetuses with frosty eyelids sleeping in a silver canister. Plus, what are you supposed to tell some future child of yours who was frozen? "Sorry about that freezer burn on your arm. We hated making you wait, but we really wanted to meet little Billy here first."

All the options and choices and possibilities and precautions whirl around your head until you fall into an exhausted, unconscious heap. You usually sleep sixteen to eighteen hours a day with the door locked, the phone off, the shutters drawn. Aidan leaves your meals outside in the hallway but you rarely touch them. You're not yourself. Time seems to collapse in on itself, and before you know it, it's finally too late to dispose of the embryos.

People want answers. Your doctor, your family, Aidan—they want explanations, but you don't have any. Aidan tries to look on the bright side.

What if they haunted you? Little demon fetus-ghosts whipping around and stinging you with tiny safety-pin pitchforks?

No, thank you.

Once it's clear you're having eight babies and there's no stopping the juicy octo-bus now, people come around. They tell you that your "decision" was brave, that you're a hero, that life is precious, and so on . . . even though the truth is it wasn't a decision. It was paralysis.

Your belly gets big, skin distending and stretching like an alien cage match is happening inside you. Your body swells and bloats until it resembles the head of a big bulbous man-eating octopus twenty thousand leagues under the sea. You feel sick. Nauseous. Like you ate an oil tanker of chum. Your stomach is brimming with roiling eels. Symptoms akin to biblical plagues set upon you. Sleeplessness. Nausea. Heartburn, headaches, hemorrhoids. Explosive diarrhea. Incontinency. Excessive saliva, food cravings, food abhorrence. The sensation of being seasick twenty-four hours a day, even when you're lying perfectly still.

There is no escape from the torment, the disgusting, vile sensations. You get to the point where you beg the doctor to take these demonic creatures out of you. Give them to a surrogate, throw them in a wooden barrel of brine, do anything!

Dr. Silvern assures you everything is fine. You assure him he has no idea what it's like to have eight creatures from the black lagoon trying to claw their way out of you.

Then the tabloids arrive. Some janitorial assistant called in a hot tip to Fox News and got a cool five thousand just for telling them there's an octomom at the hospital. He gets another ten thousand for the blurry image he of your manatee-like body beached on the hospital bed. Bastard. Who knows when he took it. You're sleeping in the photo, all the sheets are off, and your exposed, misshapen belly looks ready to Jiffy Pop babies all over the walls any second. The press calls you *Big-Tum Octomum* and says you're obsessed with starting your own race of superhumans. Talk shows, chat rooms, radio jocks, the airways fill with people vigorously debating just how irresponsible, horrible, stupid, backward, careless, and inhumane you are. Your face is plastered across so many news stations and magazines that Aidan has to ban all media from your room just to stem the flow of hourly weep sessions. Aidan does his best to console you. He says when the babies are born, everyone will focus on how wonderful and perfect they are.

The day the babies are born, however, there's confusion. You went to sleep with an auditorium of medical staff crowded into the viewing room overhead, but when you wake up—everyone's gone. You're in the room alone. When the nurses wheel the babies in one by one, your first thought isn't how much you love them or how amazing they are but—*Whose kids are these?*

Each child is a different color. One has light brown skin and ice blue eyes. One is cinnamon. Another has fine cornsilk-white hair and peach-pink skin. One is clearly African American, and yet another is definitely Asian. What the hell happened?

It all comes out. There was a mix-up. None of these kids are biologically yours. *None of them.* The doctor put the wrong eggs in you. The hows and whys are still unclear, but the eggs are traced back to a batch left over from a health-care study for undocumented aliens that paid quick cash for non-Anglo eggs, which are in high demand for stem-cell research. Due to a simple printer malfunction the eggs were labeled incorrectly and accidentally vetted into the egg bank.

The upshot is you have eight children from eight different countries. Mexico, Canada, Haiti, Cuba, Puerto Rico, Korea, Africa, and Cambodia. Your anger is only outweighed by your confusion. What does it mean? Whose kids are these? Are they yours or do you have to give them back? The hospital administrator says the children are 100 percent yours. It was a blind study and the eggs were legally purchased from the donors. Besides, since the donors were anonymous, you couldn't even find them if you tried.

You name the babies after their parents' "place of origin." It's the only personal information available on their anonymous egg donor sheets. Juárez, Alberta, Jérémie, Havana, Isabela, Suwon, Nairobi, and Battambang (a.k.a. Baby Bang) come home with you, and the press uncovers everything. The "racial inconsistencies" of your children, the "baffling stupidity" of your doctor, and further evidence that winning the lottery can't buy you an easy life. Those horrid paparazzi flash-monkeys even manage to get several shots of your children as they are whisked into the waiting van ferrying them home.

You're finally home, although it's not a home now, really, so much as an industrial way station to manage an endless pipeline of urine, poop, spit-up, snot, and tears. Man, are babies messy. They *hate* each other, too. It starts right away, a blaze of shrieking, angry punching, kicking, biting, and smacking. The kids attack one another from the get-go. You don't care what scientists say about nature versus nurture or learned behavior versus blood memory—if you let the Cuban baby and the Haitian baby anywhere near each other . . . there will be blood.

Getting all eight of them up and out the door takes one adult for every child, plus two extra helpers to get the doors and run back for various items forgotten, dropped, launched out of the car, and on and on. . . . You come to hate going outside. Not just because the kids are so much work, but because people are so asinine. The stupid questions and comments never stop. "Why are they all different? Did your husband pee inside you during sex? Are any retarded?" You hate taking them out in public, afraid they'll pick up on all the bigotry and stupidity that flows like a muck river around them.

Staying at home is no picnic, either. It's clear who's in control now, and it's not you. Despite the fact the kids are all the size of variegated potatoes (except for Alberta, who's a full pound heavier than the rest), they take over. They set the schedule. They decide when they cry (constantly), when you sleep (never), and when they need something (unceasingly). They're aggressive, demanding, and mind-numbingly loud. Aidan does his best to help, as does your mother and his mother and any other relative you can rope into helping, but it's no use. *There're more of them.* You end up hiring a full-time staff of nurses, just to keep up with diapers.

As they get older, they get worse. Alberta's the most difficult, the biggest, and the loudest. She's the first to speak, walk, and read, and she's the de facto leader, if not by silent secret unanimous vote then by outright size. Anyone who disagrees with her gets a black eye. You secretly ply her with sweets and candy (big girl, loves to eat) because the only way to control the kids is if *she* keeps them in line. That's one thing you have to be grateful for. Alberta coerces the children into an uneasy truce. They all look to her for instruction. For what to do next. They all look at Alberta. If ever there was the perfect training for a violent dictator, this is it. Kim Jong-il couldn't have done it better.

Your Ghastlycrumb Tinies start their own language, their own code, holding entire conversations at the dinner table without you or Aidan having any idea what they're talking about. Alberta forbids anyone to teach "outsiders" the language. It's infuriating. Teachers at school berate them. Classmates tease them, but they couldn't care less. They don't need anyone's approval or acceptance. They have one another. You can't ostracize eight people because eight people are a tribe. They stick together, forming a perfectly enclosed, unbreakable society that has no need or desire for other citizens. They're full up already.

This makes you an outsider in your own home. A barely tolerated staff member who's constantly in the way. The children have no need for you. It's bizarre. They never cry for Mommy when they're hurt or ask Daddy to read them a bedtime story. They get everything they need from each other—affection, advice, camaraderie, companionship—they've got it all in-house.

It's incredibly lonely. Therapists tell you to accept them for who they are and one even suggests studying simian pack habits. Monkeys. She wants you to learn about monkeys to better understand your children. (In the end you do buy a few books on proper ape handling.)

Try as you might to understand these kids, the damned truth is they're not yours. Not really. They know it and you know it. It's there every day. Legally they're yours, the state can lock you up if you refuse to feed them, and you're socially obligated to clothe them . . . but you can't make them love you. Aidan feels it, too. You both struggle to battle back an ever-increasing sense of resentment. It's looking more and more like you gave up your entire life to raise eight people who will never want you.

The children develop odd skills. Alberta can lie with the pathological ease of a serial killer. Juárez is a master builder: ham radios that pick up the neighbors' cell phone conversations, long-distance rockets that can light buildings on fire, concealed weapons so cleverly crafted he can get them through airport security. Jérémie is fluent in multiple languages and has a photographic memory. Havana can contort her body into any shape, hiding in suitcases and dresser drawers just to scare you. Isabela can hear electrical frequencies and see clear as day even in the dead of night. Both Suwon and Nairobi have unusually advanced mathematical skills. Baby Bang lived up to his namesake by loving anything loud. Homemade bombs especially. He and Juárez built a catapult capable of launching a dishwasher over the house. (Poor Mrs. Bennet. She loved that dishwasher.)

The children combine their skills to mastermind complicated schemes, such as how to steal a train car, how to free reindeer at the zoo, and how to break into the waterpark after hours.

These schemes take planning. They cover the walls of their rooms with intricate carefully coded maps and diagrams. Fill journals with cryptic notes and sketches—all pieces of their big, secret puzzling ideas, of which they have many. You stare at those walls for up to an hour at a time, trying to decode their messages, but it's impossible. All the symbols are foreign and the notes are in that damned language. From a purely visual standpoint, however, Aidan agrees it looks like they're planning a war. How did you give birth to this gang of criminals?

And criminals they are. Chores, as it were, do not exist in your house. Not for the child-pirates anyway. Instead of making their beds or studying (to think you actually made them a *chore wheel* from a pattern in *Woman's Day*!), they spend long days and nights running wild in the back woods, or roaming into the neighbors' yards, where they steal and vandalize. If anything gets stolen, goes missing, or is torn to pieces in your neighborhood, people call you. It is always your kids who did it. They come back at all hours, sometimes late for dinner, covered in brambles and scuff marks and looking like they were in a tactical skirmish. It doesn't matter what locks, bars, or security techniques you use—the kids get through them. When a nice man from the electric fence company comes out to better enforce your property, Alberta turns a hose on him and Nairobi steals his car.

The counselor at school tells you to try disciplining them more. Fat chance. You can't punish what you can't catch. They're like flying squirrels. They're quick, strong, and can climb straight up bare walls unaided. Plus, if one is caught, the rest immediately engage in troop-retrieval tactics. They create diversions and run interference (sounding carbon monoxide alarms, ringing front and back doorbells repeatedly, calling grandparents, starting a car and rolling it down the driveway, sticking an oven mitt on an open stovetop flame . . .). If you do manage to separate one from the group (rare), the remaining uncaught will orchestrate heroic prisoner rescues, going so far as to use ball-peen hammers and spatulas to unlock doors or kitchen knives and toenail clippers to slash and/or remove window screens. Punishing them just isn't worth the energy or the home owner's insurance. They're too good at ganging up on you.

Take on one, take on them all.

So it's with some relief, years later, that one of them calls you finally needing help. It's Havana. Calling at three o'clock in the morning. Turns out they all got caught while robbing a convenience mart, or almost caught, and Juárez suffered a gunshot wound when the clerk surprised him with a shotgun pulled from under the counter. Now he needs medical attention but he can't go to the hospital. Can you help? Will you help? Should you aid and abet known criminals, even if they are your own children?

Of course you shouldn't, but you do.

They are your children, and crappy circumstances aside, you'll do whatever it takes to help them. So you find one of Aidan's friends who's a golf buddy, an EMT, and an ambulance driver. He knows basic stitch-up protocol and operates on Juárez in his basement rec room. No questions asked, no explanation needed. He knows all about your kids.

After that the children ask for help more often. Usually when something goes wrong, or someone gets hurt or an emergency pickup is required. You're so relieved to finally be part of this clandestine group, finally needed and wanted and, yes, maybe even loved, that when Alberta asks you if you want to participate in a heist, actually join them while they're doing something illegal, you say yes. It's only driving the car, and despite knowing better, the pull to be loved and included by them is far greater than any fear you have of the law.

So it goes. You (and even Aidan) start to participate in the petty and eventually not-so-petty crimes your children commit. Some families go to Disneyland, others have dinner every Sunday night. Your family is a gang. You do lay down ground rules. No violence. No victims. No collateral damage. That's your rule and it's absolute. Also, everyone has to eat a good meal before a job. Low blood sugar is a killer.

As your heists increase in scale and success, the rule about no victims gets harder to keep, especially when people keep pissing you off. Like the mean old man down the street who leaves his dog tied to a tree even in the worst weather. (Fido was mysteriously stolen and relocated to an alfalfa farm.) Or the restaurant owner who sniffs and mumbles something derogatory about your son's appearance while seating you one night. (His place burned down the next day.)

126

From section 62

You build a sanctuary on a big piece of land. There are several different sections, like the one for tired mothers who just need a freaking nap. Lovely airy cottages decorated in pastel hues are filled with comfortable furniture, fluffy, oversized beds, and the soothing sounds of prerecorded ocean waves. There's also the creative sanctuary, where writers and artists can get away from editors, curators, deadlines, distractions, and their worried families so they can actually do some work.

There's a dog sanctuary for dogs who don't like their owners. For German shepherds who have owners who listen to Jimmy Buffet. For cocker spaniels who can't stand all the cats in their house. And for quite a few Chihuahuas who are damned sick of being dressed up in prissy little outfits and made to look like Tinkerbell or a bumblebee, when in actuality they are quite fearsome creatures who'd gladly rip out the throat of those who would dress them thusly, if only they were a little bigger.

There's a sanctuary for children who want to run away from home. They're all welcome here, because children often need sanctuary from their situations more than anybody—and while the authorities and parents dislike you harboring minors, they have to admit it's better to have them running to your place (which is safe, well lit, and provides counseling as well as an all-night taco bar) instead of the streets of some metropolis, where perverts, thugs, and creeps abound.

You live a long, wonderful life and die peacefully, in your sleep.

Heaven is a cabin in the woods beside a still lake. Inside is a place to rest, relax, and read up on everything you did wrong in your last life. It plays out like a thriller. The tabulations. The number of good deeds you did in your life, subtracted by the number of times you hurt people, multiplied by your "moments of selflessness," then rounded up by the number of times you called your mother. The only bad thing about heaven is the bears.

They're like bill collectors who make you pay off your debts. If you were really bad in life, one might eat you a few times, or maybe a few hundred times if you were really, really bad. In your case, the bears just bring you snacks and cocktails with plastic toys on the lip. In the cabin next to you, though, is someone who must've been bad and whose punishment includes being chased.

"All right," a bear outside the window says. "Time to play scared camper."

They always tell him to go away. "I don't want to play scared camper!"

"Them's the rules," the bear says, and easily smashes a big paw through the window.

127

From section 48

You and Aidan decide to adopt because, when you think about it, there isn't exactly a shortage of people in the world. In fact, what with the millions and millions of orphans looking (desperately) for homes, one could argue there is a bit of a surplus.

You want a kid? *Great!* Go get one! Any color, any size, any age, they're out there by the *millions*. It could be soundly argued that having biological children in this day and age, when so much of the world is in crisis, is a profoundly ugly, selfish thing to do. Try bringing that up in a moms' fertility chat room or a Catholic church.

Plus, you don't have to look far to find a heartbreaking story. So many children without parents or medical care or even enough food.

You adopt a little boy. A beautiful blond-haired, blue-eyed boy named Nikolai, from the Nizhegorodskaya region of Russia. You and Aidan fly over and spend three weeks in cold, drafty government offices filling out paperwork, handing out bribes, and waiting endlessly for your little one to be in your arms. (Still, three weeks in Nizhegorodskaya is slightly better than nine months of pregnancy, and you get to skip the labor pains altogether.)

Finally they hand Nikolai over. You've never seen such terrifically electric blue eyes in your life. You love him immediately. Instantly. Deeply. Awfully. You love him so much it hurts.

Even as a baby he already has such a tremendous personality. He loves when you sing, and when he's tired or fussy or frightened you sing lullabies to him, which you must learn from listening online or memorizing from books. Your childhood somehow didn't have singing in it. Your *life* somehow didn't have singing in it. There was a brief stretch when you were a teen and would sing in front of the mirror to pop beats as they pulled and tweaked your hormones, but then you grew older and singing felt silly.

He seems healthy at first, the doctors all gave him a clean bill of health, but then one day you're carrying him and you cough. He's startled, grabbing you around the neck hard, and you hear his arm crack. It's broken. At the hospital they run tests and want to send him to a specialist. The specialist says he has *Osteogenesis imperfecta*, otherwise known as brittle bone syndrome. His bones are as brittle as honeycombs.

The slightest bump can break his bones in half, any sudden movement or abrupt pressure. He is the world's most breakable boy. You're plunged into a world of special needs children—the doctors' visits, the research, the studying, the worrying, the wonder. Aidan is a champion of finding new alternative treatments, flying as far as Australia and Oslo to meet with doctors who think they're close to a cure.

But no one is close to a cure and you become keeper of the crystal collection called Nikolai. He walks in a padded jumpsuit, lives in a room of soft things. No sharp corners, no hard furniture, even his forks and knives are made of bendable plastic. Nothing hard must touch him and it is your unceasing job to protect him. A lifetime of careful planning and tedious inertia stretches ahead of you like a steaming hot tarmac of black asphalt, no shade, no shelter, nothing between you and the brutal elements. It is all on you now.

Why is it this way?

You don't know why; no one knows why.

You cry, Aidan cries, you all fall down. The initial adrenaline blooms into a manic, unmaintainable schedule that wears you out. Then the exhaustion and anxiety bleed out into a muddy swamp of grim acceptance. Grueling submission to your particular sorry lot in life. So this is it. This is how it will be for you. Your life, as it were, is over. You will live in servitude to another for all the rest of your days.

Time passes. Seven years.

Your money buys doctors, time, experiments, trials, excellent advice, excellent care. It buys you everything but bones that don't break. Nikolai is what the nurses call "a trouper." He has a sunshiny disposition and is always air-kissing people and telling you not to worry. He likes to color and sing and look out the window. When a bone snaps, which it still sometimes does, Nikolai says it's okay, it doesn't hurt if he doesn't move. He will lie perfectly still while you nap. He says you look tired—he, the orphaned angel thrown on a scrap heap with all his little broken bones. He says *you* look tired. You kiss him, long and soft, on the forehead. Then you sing him to sleep. When you put him to bed, he dreamily murmurs that he wants to go swimming. He's always wanted to go swimming. Like a sea creature, like a seal.

You lay him down.

Then a diamond bullet drives itself deep into your cortex.

Swimming! Think of all the creatures in the sea that exist in robust vibrancy underwater, but bring them onto land and they shatter. Coral, starfish, seahorses, sand dollars, shipwrecks, they're all strong but only in water!

You get permission to bring Nikolai to the hospital therapy pool. They reserve the whole thing for him and he is lowered down gently in a hammock of white cloth. You stand in the pool beside your son, freezing cold in your bathing suit despite the warm water. *Please, God, let it work.* The physical therapist helps Nikolai stand on the soft mats placed over the tiles. The boy is hesitant at first, his narrow chest breathing heavily as he takes his first cautious steps out into the water. He clings to a kickboard and stands stock-still, as though he expected the liquid around him to seize up and drown him even though he's not moving.

The therapist shows him how to hold his nose and blow bubbles underwater. Then how to cling to the padded side of the pool and kick gently. Every stroke panics you, because no one knows if the force of Nikolai kicking his legs underwater is enough to break them. It doesn't seem to be hurting him. In fact, after his initial hesitation, the therapist says he's moving along quickly, faster than most in his swimming lessons. He takes to the water like a fish. Aidan says he's never seen Nikolai smile like that. To move freely through space, unhampered by protective clothing and cumbersome gear. The boy looks so serene, like he's become part angel.

You and Aidan sell the big house and build a long single-story house on a piece of rolling green property in southern Tennessee. Temperate weather and one story allow you to build a house of interconnected swimming pools. Giant tubs are installed in every room of the house and connected by wide padded canals that Nikolai can drift down easily without the fear of falling.

You hear your name being called. "Mahmmy? Mahhhhhmy!" Nikolai wants you. He will always want you. It is all on you now. Why is it this way? You don't know why; no one knows why—but here is why. The honor of watching over that boy goes to you.

A groundswell of joy hits you, knocking you over with liquid white light. Pure drops of stupid, grateful tears roll down your face. Sobbing, rocking, hugging your knees because now you understand. You see, your life, as it were, is over. You have the overwhelming good luck to live in servitude to another for all the rest of your days. His injuries are your roots to this earth. The call and response in the temple of here.

The only reason to sing.

128

From section 55

You decide you don't need a prenup. You're not going to let negative think-ing and fear drive away the man you love. You rush into his arms and he kisses you in a way you'll never forget. Strong yet tender, knee-buckling yet somehow soothing. A kiss that goes deep, yet keeps you completely buoyant, bubbling over with happiness in this, the most perfect of moments.

The kissing gets more aggressive, clothing starts to come off, and you tumble down on the designer sofa in the living room and perform acts so strenuous that when you're finished no one's going to need a UV light to know something unseemly happened.

After indulging postcoital hunger with leftovers in the dining room, you lie naked together on top of the dining room table. It's so comfortable here; you're so happy and sleepy. The marble cools your heated skin and you start to drift off, watching the fire overhead blaze in its glass case. It's disquieting, as common sense would say the flames would heat the glass and burst out, catching the whole room on fire, but this will not happen.

No, it will not.

Because the fire is in a magic box and today your life is a storybook. The flames above you can't get out, but they still breathe brightly, safe inside that lovely glass coffin. In the morning you call your family and tell them the great news and you sound pretty happy despite your killer hangover. They're not happy about your decision to have a wedding on the beach with only a witness attending. "Doesn't Aidan want a big wedding?" your mother asks. "He was always such a nice boy." You try to explain, which is always a mistake.

"It's not him," you tell her, "it's me. I don't want a big wedding; I don't want this to be about money." Well, now your mother has heard enough.

Before hanging up she says that's the worst thing she's ever heard come out of your mouth and that's saying something.

You set about your new life in the empty building. The management company tells you it won't be long now till the tenants arrive, which is a blessing. It's not so bad living in a building that resembles an empty airport at first, but after a couple of weeks it starts to get weird. The building is almost finished, it looks finished. All the condos are finished, all the hallways are carpeted, all the gym equipment has arrived, and the super-smooth chrome elevators already play calypso Muzak as they whisk you down to the main level, where the white marble floors have been polished to such a high shine that the lobby looks like an ice-skating rink flanked by a reception desk.

Maybe that's why it's weird. It looks like people should be here, like maybe they were here and then a silent plague or a tidy serial killer picked them off one by one. They haven't even hired a valet or a concierge yet. The glass doors in the lobby *whoosh* open politely when you leave but stay locked from the outside for obvious security reasons, so upon returning you must swipe a wallet-sized keycard in front of a little black magnetic reader. Sometimes it doesn't work right and you have to stand there waving your keycard back and forth like you're fanning a wall fire.

The overly friendly rep at the management company tells you until the garage is built the building can't open. Well, *it can*, but no one would come because there'd be nowhere safe to park their cars. No way are your tenants parking on the street; they'd rather leave their grandkids on the street, because the only thing these people love more than their overpriced luxury condos is their overpriced luxury cars. At least you get celebrity parking every day, right next to the dry fountain out front. The fountain features two big bronze trumpeter swans, which are supposed to be in love or necking or something, but they're identical, neither one more masculine or feminine, and their eyes seem locked in a steely stalemate, not a loving gaze, and their wings are thrown back a little too wildly, like they're possibly about to attack each other and resolve some territorial dispute in a bloody trumpeter swan smackdown. Maybe it'll look better with water.

Life is pretty good inside the condo, it's actually pretty close to perfect;

and you like tooling around Palm Beach. It's filled with manicured gardens, excellent shopping, and the best-looking waiters in the entire country. Even the guy who replenishes the salad bar at Red Lobster looks like he belongs on the cover of *GQ*. The problem lies in the expanse of space between your apartment and the outside world. It's weird walking through the lobby alone. When you come home the big glass doors *swoosh* closed behind you and the sound of the birds and the wind and the street traffic die away.

Your steps echo as you walk to the elevator, where the piped-in sound of the calypso Muzak seems overtly phony and completely desperate, like some overeager cruise director trying to convince bored passengers a really fun, really big party is happening soon. You *really* start to hate that Muzak, covering your ears and trying to hum more loudly than it, but nothing helps. You even go to the trouble of tracking down a maintenance man, braving the eerie service hallways, calling out in the darkness like some lost tourist in the bowels of a haunted coal mine. The janitors say they're not allowed to touch the elevator panels, so you call the management company and they say they'll get someone out in the next few weeks. You end up dragging a kitchen chair onto the elevator and covering the speakers with duct tape, which does nothing, the music is just as loud, but now it sounds like there's a mattress over the speaker. You want to kill yourself.

The worst part of the building is the mystery sounds. Mystery sounds have all sorts of origins. Sometimes they're traceable—a janitor dragging a garbage pail across a hallway or an electrician setting up an aluminum ladder to monkey with an electrical panel or a landscaper knocking around watering the big palm trees in the lobby. These sounds, if you know what they are and who's making them, are fine. Good, even. It's nice to see the occasional friendly face, and the faster the building gets done, the sooner your world stops looking like the opening scene in a horror movie.

It's the sounds without a justifiable cause that scratch at your nerves. Loud thuds in the middle of the night, repetitive banging after all the workers have gone home, a scraping sound, like something heavy is being dragged. Sometimes when you're alone walking through the empty halls you swear you hear whispering. You think other people might be living in

the building, kids or squatters or worse. Aidan says it's probably just workers on other floors, their voices coming through the ventilation ducts. *Right.*
If that's true, then your voice would carry just as well as theirs. If you hear
voices and shout back at them, *Hello, who is there, please?* then based on the
laws of sound or physics or ventilation ductwork, shouldn't they be able to
hear you?

Something is definitely going on. One night you order Chinese food,
and two hours later, when the nice deliveryman who always gives you extra
fortune cookies still hasn't called your cell phone announcing his arrival
outside the lobby doors, you call the restaurant and they say the deliveryman *was* there and when he walked up to your building, the lobby doors
automatically opened, so he came inside and left your food on the reception
desk. You run downstairs and check, but there's no food waiting for you.
You don't know if the lobby doors are locked or not—the technical maneuvers required to test them from outside without actually getting locked out
are way beyond your current state of mind. Either the Chinese restaurant
is lying to you—and you don't think they are—or someone is in the building. You race back upstairs and lock yourself in the master bedroom walk-in
closet. You feel safest there; it's the only room in the whole freaking place
that locks and doesn't have any windows.

The next morning you wake up to find someone has thrown all the lounge
chairs into the empty pool and spray-painted the words "EAT DICK" all over
its dry walls. The scariest event takes place a couple weeks later around
four in the morning. You're both in bed sound asleep when someone rides
the elevator up to your floor and pounds on the door. Aidan calls the police
but they're no help. By the time they show up anyone could escape down
any number of stairwells or elevators; the complex is huge and the security
cameras still aren't hooked up.

You burst into tears. You're at wit's end living in a third world country
twenty stories in the air! This is not how you wanted to live! You wanted
luxury! A clubhouse and a private marina! Aidan tries to console you but
you push him away. He's useless. He just waltzes around free of charge, not
paying a penny for anything, content to freeload off your ever-dwindling

bank account. Without tenants the building is forcing you to hemorrhage cash; you still have to pay the management company and mammoth utility bills. This building is taking you down like a Coral *Anchor*, that's what it's doing!

Four months after moving into the Coral Arms, you call Miss Sumpter and tell her you want out of the building. You're not happy, the building is scary, the elevator plays hateful music, and lying by a bone-dry Olympic-sized pool with "EAT DICK" spray-painted all over isn't relaxing at all. You called the management company to report all this but they're useless. It's like they aren't taking your calls anymore. Miss Sumpter listens patiently as you rant, she doesn't interrupt, and when you're finally done, she quietly says she's been waiting to call you. She wanted to gather more information before she said anything, but since you called, she should just let you know there's been a development.

She takes a deep breath and begins. Apparently the sellers of Coral Arms were far from honest about the building. They suppressed important information regarding the extent of Eli Esteban's tax problems and pulled strings with friends in local government to keep certain documents sealed. She keeps talking, but you feel light-headed. You fade in and out, catching words like *tax fraud . . . misappropriation of development funds . . . tax lien . . . bankruptcy . . . probate court . . . halting construction.*

What?

She says there's a tax lien on the Coral Arms because the IRS, which launched an exhaustive hunt for Esteban's assets in order to recoup unpaid back taxes, had already arrested him and frozen his accounts a full month before you signed paperwork on the property. The government was too busy tracking down Esteban's major holdings, his hidden funds, and off-shore accounts to run around repossessing dead assets like the Coral Arms. They'd get to that later, which they have—right about now. In the mean-time, however, it looks like the few remaining Coral Arms investors who were left decided to sell the property to someone, knowing it had already been seized.

What all of this means is the IRS owns your building. You didn't buy it from Esteban, because it was never his to sell. It's called an affinity scam, a conceit constructed around a tight-knit group of people or parties who consider themselves friends. Miss Sumpter's voice catches and she lets out a small, pained sound. It was her old friend, the county tax assessor who owed her a favor, who turns out to be one of those few remaining developers. When his feet were held to the fire, he had to find a buyer for it, so he called all the people who trusted him most.

The upshot is you've basically been squatting illegally at the Coral Arms this entire time. Not only that, you've been using your personal funds to keep an empty condo tower running and now it looks like there will be no tenants and no building and no income or profits of any kind, leaving you basically broke. Miss Sumpter tells you not to worry, the IRS is aware of your situation and knows you were the victim of a scam. You should just stay there and sit tight while she sorts everything out.

She'll call you in the morning.

But you don't talk to her the next morning, because you can't sleep that night. You pace the apartment like a Las Vegas show leopard and walk around that bloody balcony in circles until you feel like a gerbil on a wheel. Aidan is asleep, no one back home answers their phone, and the pressure in your head is ready to make it explode off your shoulders, so you decide to take a drive and go anywhere, just to get out of the building. You write a note saying you'll be back in an hour and set out for the long trek to the lobby. You never make it to the car, though; you're intercepted as you get off the elevators.

The vagrant who's been living behind the unused Dumpsters in the back service hall has a variety of mental illnesses: schizophrenia, anxiety disorder, PTSD, and violent, unpredictable flashbacks of his memories from Vietnam. Most of them are progressive diseases that have gone undetected, undiagnosed, and/or untreated. He likes the back service hall because it's quiet and dark and there are no people, which is good, because he doesn't like himself around people anymore; the feel of it is uneasy; he's losing hold of the thread that separates the pictures in his head from the pictures in his eyes. Sometimes on the street he'll look up and everyone is dead. Blackened eyes, dried lips, blood coming from their ears and pooling around their feet. Then the picture clicks over and everyone's alive again, walking down the street. He knows something's wrong, but he doesn't qualify for any programs anymore and he has no money, so he hides.

He's been hiding in the Coral Arms and keeps himself on a strict schedule. He only comes out at night, when it's safe. You startle him when you get off the elevator; he's never heard anyone in the halls this late. He feels a rush of panic, a cold, clawing sensation that tears through him, and then you're hanging limp in his arms. He doesn't know what he's done, it was over so fast. Maybe he did it again. Maybe it was an army hold; they taught him lots of army holds and made his hands so quick they think faster than his head now. He thinks he killed you, he doesn't know you're just unconscious, so he lays you gently down on the polished lobby floor and leaves.

You wake up in the hospital, a ring of ugly bruises around your throat. Your whole family is clustered nervously around your narrow bed. Why is everyone here? *Because we thought you were dead and we wanted to see who'd get the money!* Big laughs all around; people are relieved to see you awake and smiling. It was a little dicey there in the ambulance after Aidan discovered you collapsed in the lobby. You tell him about the strange "military man" who came out of nowhere and had such a *look* on his face—you will never forget that look. Then he moved with a swiftness that was robotic, automated, not attached to thought. It was like he was sleepwalking or daydreaming or both. You want to find out who that man is and you want to help him. *Help him? There are professionals for that! People! Programs!*

You ask everyone to come back with you to the Coral Arms. The whole family's invited, including everyone back home, all your cousins, aunts, uncles, second cousins, anyone who wants to should come down to Palm Beach, and this time everyone gets their own keycard and their own goddamned luxury condo. You want to make sure Grandpa's coming. Who can go get Grandpa from his old folks' home?

Your family's nervous. *You want to go back? Aren't you scared? Are you ready? Do you really want to go back to that building?* Oh, yes, you do, and this time you're not fucking around. You get on the phone and order Mr. Cook to round up a bloodthirsty pack of his meanest lawyers. They're coming down here and getting free albeit mandatory housing at the Coral Arms. So is Miss Sumpter and the rest of her entire office. They're all coming, or else.

Affinity scam? IRS seizure? Tax lien? Bullshit!

The next time you walk through the sliding glass doors of that building your shoulders are square and your jaw is set. The whole family is behind you now; there's twenty-five other people here who'll occupy twenty units plus. They all pick out their own condos and you assure them once again the Coral Arms is absolutely secure now; they did a thorough security sweep of the building and everything's clear. All the keycards have been swapped out, all the locks changed, and they should feel perfectly safe. You also apologize about the condos being unfurnished, but you have an idea. If they're willing to do a little leg work, there's tons of furniture all over the building, it just has to be "reallocated."

An all-night scavenger hunt starts up, people laughing and running around all over the building, dragging up couches from the party room, tables and desks from the business center, overstuffed chairs and standing lamps from the lobby, game tables from the community room, massage tables from the spa. If it isn't bolted down, it's gone. The one thing nobody has is a mattress. There's a lively debate about the cheapest place to buy beds and whether Wal-Mart sells a decent air mattress, and then it hits you. *The pool house.* Locked inside the service building behind the trellised cabana are two hundred unused lounge chairs and two hundred matching full-length lounge pillows. They're long and thick, and when you lay three on the floor side by side, instant mattress.

Everyone bundles their bedding into the elevators. (For the first time you didn't even notice the Muzak; unfortunately you noticed not noticing.) They all get situated in their new apartments and you encourage everyone to spread out and take up as much space as they can. They should make noise, have parties, invite folks over, and leave their doors open. You want life in this place. Life! By the end of the first night, everyone falls asleep exhausted, worn out from moving furniture and laughing and having so much fun.

They might be having a good time, but you've already implemented a serious plan. All you have to do now is wait for Grandpa. The next day Cook's lawyers arrive and good-naturedly check into their bizarrely decorated condos. (Poor Mr. Cook got stuck with the apartment outfitted primarily with patio furniture.) They spend five solid days in the empty restaurant pacing the floors and arguing as they hatch an intricate legal plan. Meanwhile, Sumpter's flock show up and get their condos. You have preassigned tasks for everyone, which you hand out as professionally as you can, considering they're all handwritten notes on yellow legal pads. They get busy making calls, checking local maps, buzzing in and out of the building. One of them dashes out to her rental car and the glass doors open, letting a rush of warm air in that rustles the big potted palm trees in the lobby. Those palm trees have been motionless for five months and right then you realize, *this might actually work*.

Finally Grandpa turns up in his wheelchair. He's escorted by one of your cousins and he looks a little pale when you show him to his special apartment, the manager's suite on the main floor, which you've outfitted with all the best furniture and stocked with all his favorite foods. He asks you *What the hell is this all about!?* and you ask to speak to him privately. Four hours later you emerge from Grandpa's suite more certain of your plan than ever.

As the weeks go by some of your guests leave, but a surprising number return with their kids, who band together and form a tribe of miniature lunatics racing up and down the halls screaming their heads off, playing games, building forts, and shrieking like monkeys. They fill the pool with a garden hose, which takes five days and contains no germ-killing agents, but it's still nice to have the pool full of water again, even if it does turn green and sludgy in a few weeks.

Those lawyers! Beautiful bastards who can confuse a straight line. They ask question after question until they mentally wear down or physically wear out their opponents. Pretty soon they have your case so crossed-up with loopholes and antiquated zoning laws nobody knows who legally owns *what* anymore. They muddle things up even more. A judge finally issues a temporary order that says the tenants of the Coral Arms may remain in their residences until a final verdict is reached.

Step one, complete.

The ladies have been working hard, too. It started slowly at first; a lone man shows up one night, he has one eye and a dirty green backpack. He picks an apartment in the rear, one with the fewest windows and closest to the ground exits. A good tactical choice. He stays quiet, keeps to himself, like you thought he would. You're not even sure if he's still in the building when the next two show up. Brothers built like grizzly bears with bushy beards and dirty necks. They pick the unit next to the man with one eye.

Then more come. Some look so young you have to politely ask what war they served in. They come alone or in pairs and occasionally in small bands, but they all have one thing in common, their eyes. Whether they're friendly or quiet their eyes never stop moving; they tread back and forth, back and forth, as though reading something invisible written in the air. Grandpa says it's from combat and being caught off guard once too often. After the war you might stop fighting, but you always stay ready. You're always scanning the crowd, looking for sudden movements, potential risk factors, points of attack, closest exits, any way to get out in a hurry. You pause before opening doors or starting the car because of booby traps. After a while you don't even notice it, but it never stops.

Miss Sumpter finds therapists willing to move into the building and trade free therapy sessions for the vets in exchange for luxury condos. More soldiers come until the building is nearly full. Every single unit has someone in it and many are occupied by two or more. A local television station shows up at your door one night and asks if the rumors are true. The Coral Arms is supposedly the most luxurious veterans' home in the nation. How did it happen?

You just tell them your story with no bells or whistles, just the truth: the lottery, the investment, the IRS, the empty building, the attack, and now this. "So you were inspired to build this place for veterans because a vet attacked you?" But you correct them and explain the soldier didn't attack you, he was just startled and reacted before thinking. Military training comes back quick, especially when a soldier is startled. You just want to help the guy.

The TV station hotline lights up with charities wanting to help, veteran advocates offering resources, and, brother hallelujah, the attorney general calls and tells you the Coral Arms is a sanctuary giving peace to our nation's most troubled and he'll fight for you all the way to the Supreme Court.

Step two, complete.

Finally Thanksgiving comes and it's wonderful, but you don't get your holiday miracle until two days later when your grandfather rolls up to your door. "Got him," he says, "in the boiler room. His name's Archie. Vietnam, so we talked a little."

"I *knew* he was still here."

"Hasn't eaten much since you two tangoed. Told him you were a tough kid and you'd be just fine. Then I got him to eat a cookie."

"You told him he can stay as long as he likes?"

Grandpa nods.

"And he doesn't have to come up or talk to anybody, we can send food down, and there are people here if he ever wants help?" Grandpa rolls his eyes. "We're men!" he says. "We don't blab on like you idiot kids. It's all in here." He taps his temple. "We talk up here. I told him I'd come down and check on him sometimes. He's gonna be okay."

You exhale. Archie's gonna be okay. Step three, complete.

Now when you and Aidan, now your husband, sit on the balcony, you look out over the sea and feel the warmth from the city streets below. The Coral Arms gleams like the fireplace over your dining room table. A structure made of metal and glass, filled with strange, dangerous, beautiful, improbable men. Here's where you live the rest of your days.

A big box of beautiful fire.

129

From section 64

You decide to tell the crew about the violin case and it goes over as well as the *Lusitania*. You say, "Guys? Um, guys? I think I might have seen something on the monitor yesterday, I'm not sure, but it could have been something. At first I thought yes, but then I wasn't sure, and then I was thinking about it later and I thought maybe it *was* something, but maybe not."

Squid just looks at you, blinking, as though you might be speaking Farsi. Hickey punches the console and flicks his lit cigarette overboard. "Okay, then," he shouts, "let's go find the motherfucker."

Luckily, the violin is right where you remembered it being and Squid goes down alone to pull it up. While he's under, the suspense is awful. Maybe he'll just find a violin-shaped rock and they'll toss you overboard right there. Maybe it'll be filled with vials of toxic poison that will kill you all dead the moment the case is opened and you'll be forced to drift around for eternity on board a ship of the undead.

When Squid surfaces, the case looks small in his arms. Slimy. Like nothing much at all.

When you finally open it, you're back in the warehouse and the whole crew stands around the table. Hickey undoes the latch. Eighty-five million dollars' worth of diamonds roll out like a sudden constellation across the table. Right then and there Squid pulls out a fucking gun and points it at your heart. He tells you to get out of Thunder Bay tonight, and if he sees you again, he'll shoot first and ask questions later. Great. Another gun pointed at you. You storm out swearing and cursing, which actually makes you look pretty badass.

Still. You've had it with action and adventure for the time being. You want a placid, nonterrorizing line of work for a while, so you hop the next bus to Duluth and decide to take whatever the unemployment office has got.

The only job is working at a musical instrument shop.

Undersea Instruments is run by two brothers, identical twins in their eighties, who've been making musical instruments out of wood salvaged from the bottom of Lake Superior for over forty years. The twins, Mr. Hansen and Mr. Hansen, are hard at work on a violin made from five-hundred-year-old red birch when you show up for your first day of work. Mr. Hansen says this wood is particularly rare, as red birch never regenerated after being cut from the forests, and the only way to find a red birch tree now is under the water.

You're put to work cleaning a wall of ancient instruments thick with fine wood dust, because apparently the city inspector has informed the Hansens that their shop has become so coated with decades of dust the whole place is a fire hazard. "But we don't have time to clean the shelves," Mr. Hansen tells you almost apologetically. "We have orders to fill, instruments to make, symphonies that are waiting on us." So that's why they hired you, to meticulously hand-clean each and every surface in their shop. Judging by the crammed room filled with shelves, drawers, cabinets, and hundreds of tools hanging on every available wall, you have job security for the next five years.

You set about cleaning the shop and over time you work yourself into a slow, methodical rhythm that reaches an almost Zen-like quality. You mostly keep quiet, not wanting to disturb their work, but your occasional curiosity is always rewarded by Mr. Hansen the younger (by five minutes, you're told), who explains that waterlogged timber has unusual qualities that make excellent musical instruments. The cold temperatures, low oxygen content, and microscopic marine life in the lake compress the wood over time into a finer, denser grain less prone to flaws. Stradivarius used water-soaked wood for his violins, and scientific studies have shown these instruments made today with ancient Lake Superior lumber equal or surpass the tonal quality of those violins made over four hundred years ago.

When you ask how so much timber got to the bottom of Lake Superior, he tells you around the turn of the century loggers cut down trees and herded them across the water toward the mills. Invariably during the journey many trees sank, which the loggers called "sinkers," but more trees survived the journey than didn't, so the sinkers were left to drift down into the darkness of the waters and rest on the muddy lake bed for decades until a salvager brought them back up.

The Hansen brothers must know more about logging than the loggers back then. Mr. Hansen can peer over his bifocals and tell just by the axe marks on a log which woodsman cut it down and what mill he was taking it to. Every timber is branded with the logger's personal mark. That way when the logs were collected, the mills knew which logger to pay for what timber. In a weird way you become a little envious of these ancient trees. People go to such great lengths retrieving them, take their time studying them, and then fight over who gets them. You wonder if anyone will ever track your life with such care and concern. You have a sinking feeling you're not even worth as much as this dead wood.

Still, it's a cozy place to work, filled with the rich smell of burnt coffee and ancient wood. The sounds of chisels tap away while National Public Radio plays on Mr. Hansen's antique RCA Victor Console. They're kind men, reserved, but good-hearted, and you wonder why they both remained bachelors their entire lives. They would have made good fathers, being so naturally patient and consistent. They show you certain elements of their trade, tricks and techniques they've learned over time, but the one thing they'll never share is their drying process. Everyone who works with waterlogged wood keeps his drying methods secret, and the Hansen brothers are no exception. Their drying barn is in a separate building behind the shop. You've never been inside it and the doors are kept padlocked. The timber must have to stay in there a long time and go through several different stages. Mr. Hansen stops his work every day at twelve and two and goes out to the drying barn, but there's no telling what he does.

The natural-born enemy of Undersea Instruments is the flooring industry. The only time Mr. Hansen or Mr. Hansen gets upset is when a particular piece of timber they bid on winds up going to one of the mills that specializes in luxury hardwood floors. Mr. Hansen says it's a travesty, a crime against wood to turn it into a bathroom floor rather than a violin. You can tell when he's mad because his ears turn red, while his brother vents his outrage by furiously polishing his glasses.

Your favorite moments are when Mr. Hansen allows himself to play the violins, which happens once in every violin's life at the shop, just before it's ready to be shipped out to the customer. Mr. Hansen strings it and tunes it, then allows himself one mad twirl, his bow dances, and his eyes close as if he is remembering something wonderful from long ago.

You surprise them one day by booking the small park on the steep cliff that cantilevers over Lake Superior. It's available for rental, mostly weddings and the occasional poetry reading or small musical concert. You tell them it's time they play their music out in the world.

They take quite a bit of convincing, but finally both brothers grudgingly concede a concert outdoors might be all right. Might be suitable. Might even be good for business.

The day of the concert every chair is filled and people crowd around the sidewalk behind the audience. Just at sunset the elder Hansen bows deeply and looks over. "Mr. Hansen?" he says. His brother bows back. "Mr. Hansen." Then the men turn their dusty tuxedoed backs to the audience, face the water, and begin to play.

Everyone in the park looks around at each other in polite confusion. Since when do musicians turn away from the audience? The brothers play the most delicate, delightful sonata you don't know the name of, but your glance goes past their swooping bows, out onto the surface of the wide-open water, where barges chug past and sailboats tack and turn. When they finish, the polite Minnesotans clap and the brothers bow deeply, still facing the lake and exposing their threadbare rumps to everyone sitting behind them. They begin to play again. This time a grand waltz.

As you sit there, the waves crash more loudly on the rocks below and foam spits up higher than you've ever seen before. You suddenly understand. The brothers have not turned their backs to the audience; they are indeed facing the grand orchestra hall in which they intend to perform. Lake Superior. After all, their violins are made from an underwater forest and the brothers do not play for people. They play only for the sea.

You live the rest of your life here, working for Undersea. You learn to play the violin and join the Duluth Symphony. Fifteenth chair, but hell, that's not so bad. Plus you get to travel around the region performing in small theaters and concert halls. Playing the violin up north is like walking through the dark holding a candle. It gives you just enough to go on. That's all you need. That and to remember three things: Don't get in your own way. Keep playing after they tell you to stop.

Expect miracles.

130

From section 65

You decide to invest in the real estate opportunity. It's called Operation Redo **Detroit**. Steve, along with a bunch of his buddies, is buying up all the run-down properties in downtown Detroit, Michigan, which is pretty much everything.

"I mean, let's face it," Steve says. "Detroit as we know it is finished. The destitution, the declining population, the crime? The American auto industry as we know it is finished. It may rebuild, but not here."

They want to start the city over again. Raze all the buildings and then turn it into farmland. Start back at the beginning. No more skyscrapers and auto factories and ghettos and violent crime. Just farmland and little towns with main streets and mom-and-pop stores. Kids will ride their bicycles to school. It'll be Detroit, with a do-over.

You move to operation headquarters in Detroit, where the investors occupy one of the last fully functioning apartment buildings downtown. Steve and his assistant, a local kid named Lil Michigan, take you on a tour of the city in a rusted-out van. You tell Steve he needs a new car, and Lil Michigan says, "Shit, you can't drive nothin' nice! They shoot you!"

"It's safer to keep a low profile," Steve says.

"Yeah," Lil Michigan says, "*low profile*. 'Cause some motherfuckers don't like other motherfuckers doing better than them."

You drive through the sprawling ruined neighborhoods and it's like you're on another planet. It's a ghost town. Hundreds of once-pristine blocks are now filled with abandoned, dilapidated houses, lawns littered with debris.

Now it looks like an atom bomb went off. There are no people, no cars, no bicycles. It's silent except for the sound of birds. The playgrounds are empty, the stoplights have been turned off, garbage pickup was canceled a long time ago. Every house has been looted, windows broken, walls gutted, plumbing and wiring ripped out, unidentifiable debris dragged out and heaped up on the lawns. In the driveways are abandoned cars, burned-out boats, and empty mobile homes tipped on their sides.

The few neighborhoods that still have residents are heavily guarded and if you want to drive down a block, you better have permission. "'Cause if you don't," Lil Michigan says, "you gonna get shot."

It's not just the wealthy neighborhoods that are ruined. Detroit's homeless shelters are mostly closed due to lack of funds, bedbug infestations, scabies outbreaks, and scarlet fever.

"We want to mow all the ruined buildings down," Steve says. "Turn all these lots back into what they started as. Farmland. It's already changing back on its own. See that?" He points to a low-flying bird circling overhead. "That's a hawk. Right here in downtown Detroit. Mice and rats take over the abandoned buildings and then their predators come. Next you'll see deer walking through the empty houses."

"You ain't gonna see no deer," Lil Michigan says. "Those motherfuckers gonna shoot Bambi and have a motherfucking barbecue."

Okay, you're all for things changing, so when do we start?

"Next week," Steve says. "We blow it all to hell."

Sure enough, next week they start demolition on Brush Park, a section of town that's been totally destroyed, houses bulldozed or lost to arson. Shrubs and grass grow shoulder-high, vines carpet the sidewalks, alleys look like overgrown nature trails, lawns have practically reverted to prairie.

But demolishing a neighborhood isn't that easy. Careful planning is involved, the city shutting off electricity and gas lines, hazmat crews identifying potential toxicity leaks, the police double-checking vacant houses. Then the demolition team sets the dynamite and runs the explosives, which takes weeks. An emergency shelter has to be set up in case there are injuries. The fire marshal has to establish an emergency evacuation route, and finally all residents of surrounding areas for three miles in every direction have to be notified.

Finally the day comes for the "Big Brush Blast." News crews have assembled, as have protestors and supporters and throngs of people just there to watch what happens. You stand on a podium in hard hats with a REDO DETROIT! banner overhead. After a series of speeches by the mayor, lieutenant governor, and Parks and Recreation commissioner, the cameras pan to Eminem, who declines to comment.

Steve gets the honor of holding down the FIRE button on the detonator, which starts a violent domino of blasting caps.

The explosions begin.

One by one every building, house, and standing object in the neighborhood is blown sky-high, sending up cloud after cloud of dust and raining debris. It's a spectacle caught by the Channel 5 Skycam as news helicopters buzz over the necklace of explosions.

Over time, neighborhood by neighborhood, the demolition crews blow everything up. Highland Park, Greektown, Osborne, 8 Mile, Brightmoor. It all falls down. The cleanup crews come with wrecking balls, wide-mouthed bulldozers, hydraulic cranes, brooms, chippers, and backhoes, chucking all the debris into a man-made pit the size of a football stadium. Once the pit is filled, the earth movers come. Giant rumbling machines that steamroll everything flat. When they're done, half of Detroit is gone.

Engineers take over. New roads are built, sewer lines are laid, property lines are marked out, and fields established. A five-foot layer of rich black earth gets spread over each plot. Then, rather than build new housing, the Redo Detroit planners, as previously decided, take historic homes cherry-picked from the demolished neighborhoods and drop them on each new farm. Extraordinary houses, gabled Victorians, stately Tudors, Arts and Crafts ranch houses, they're all delivered like unwrapped presents to each farmstead, where they're assaulted by armies of engineers, construction workers, utility crews, stonemasons, carpenters, plasterers, and painters until they each pass inspection and are deemed ready for habitation. Landscape crews come in and dot the lawns with large shade trees and rows of hedges. A tasteful, proportionate number of apartment buildings are built near commercial zones, meant for the field hands and other trade workers not living in the single-family homes. The commercial zones themselves, only eight in total, resemble old-time mom-and-pop main streets, each with small grocery stores, hardware stores, Laundromats, and diners. It's like you're playing with a Tinker Toy city, only everything is life-sized.

It isn't until the families arrive that the project comes to life. Applicants were chosen by lottery and assigned lots in New Detroit (pronounced New *DEE-twah*) at random. They move in one by one and the little stores open for business, the restored homes light up, and the new streets (named after more current dignitaries—Obama Boulevard, Clinton Way, and so on) host a sparse flow of traffic.

New Detroit is beautiful. A falling-down metropolis of poverty and crime has been transformed into bucolic farmland. Of course, there was the unfortunate business of the relocations, all those citizens who neither wanted to live in your new town nor leave their old homes. They're shipped to Chicago. The mayor of Chicago went all the way to the Supreme Court in protest, but in the end, how can he stop busses driving south and unloading passengers?

Of course your piece of paradise isn't perfect. The project is a success, but as an investment, it's a complete disaster. You'd hoped to sell large tracts of land to wealthy parties interested in developing the new farmland you created, but nobody's buying. The project is too avant-garde, too utopian for big business to be comfortable with. Yes, you tore down an urban blight, and this new pastoral community is lovely, but where's the Starbucks?

Your money swirls down the drain. You end up living on a small tract of land with Steve, who also lost most of his money. You're sort of a couple now, thrown together by fate but grateful to have each other. It's not his fault the project wasn't profitable. He really believed in it and gave it everything he had. Together you decide to grow soybeans, and your modest fields yield just enough for you to live on. You never have kids or decide to adopt, but Lil Michigan does move in with you, as well as some of his friends who didn't win the lottery and didn't like Chicago.

"It's too motherfucking crowded down there," he says. "I need some motherfucking space."

So you all live together in a tiny little farmhouse. You're poor, it's true, and some months it's hard to make ends meet, but Steve has schemes and you have dreams and you just know that one day one of them will catch. For now you cut coupons. Some might say you got caught up in the wheels of your own monstrous machine, you had no right to interfere with the city, and you've got your comeuppance. You'd have to agree. Sometimes, though, on still nights, after everyone's had their supper and the dishes are done and you're all sitting around the fire telling stories and laughing, Steve will reach out for your hand and start massaging it. They get so sore from all the hard work you do. Right then, as the fire crackles and Lil Michigan is telling a ridiculous story and Steve is tenderly tending to your fingertips, right then you feel like the richest person in the world.

131

From section 70

Prenups are for people who don't believe in love—and you do, so you marry Benoît Beaumont Desrosiers and become Madame Desrosiers. Beautiful! You and Bo move into a posh apartment in Monaco, which overlooks the ocean. The luxe rooms on Boulevard Princesse Charlotte are filled with baroque furniture, grand chandeliers, and ornate gilded mirrors.

You're surprised by how popular Bo is. Everywhere you go, it's "Bonjour, Bo-Bo!" He throws lavish parties, with celebrity chefs, string quartets, belly dancers, even a juggler with flaming swords on the balcony. You're wondering when exactly he's going to start his law practice.

Soon, cherie!

Six months pass, then a year. It costs a fortune to rent this place and still Bo isn't working. When you ask him when he's going to start making money, he says, "Why? Haven't you got any?" And you tell him you probably have eight million left. To which he says, "Well, then we stay here for eight million more dollars."

What is that supposed to mean?

Things aren't working. Besides being a leech, he spends your money like Princess Grace. You've never known anyone who could power through cash so fast. Every week there's a shiny new toy. Bo is possibly gay. You caught him kissing a young man in the back room of the club one night, but he laughed it off, saying they were just old friends and Europeans kiss.

You fight, you shout, he shouts, you cry, he cries. Then you kiss and make love until all is forgotten and all you know is that you love him.

Bo decides to take up car racing after making some friends on the Renault team. It's madness, completely dangerous, and you forbid him from doing it, but you might as well forbid a storm from coming in off the ocean. Bo starts training for the Formula One Monaco Grand Prix, one of the world's most difficult races. It takes place on the city streets of Monaco; they close off boulevards, reroute traffic, and create a loop that changes every year but always runs past the Grand Hotel, which creates one of the slowest turns in professional racing, at just thirty-one miles per hour. The race also has one of the fastest turns, a deathly jog inside a tunnel, which drivers hit at one hundred and sixty miles per hour. Every year idiots (like Bo) take a shot at that loop and die. You beg him not to do the race, but your protests only fuel his determination.

Luckily Bo doesn't qualify for the team or even come close. The city fills up, the megayachts sail in and set anchor, all the celebrities fly in on private planes; Stallone, Britney, Jack Nicholson, Bruce Willis, J. Lo, and P. Diddy are spotted at the track. Everyone's watching the Monaco Grand Prix, but not poor little Bo. He stays at home and refuses to go out, even when you get invitations to Vijay Mallya's *Indian Empress* yacht. That's when Bo's drug use starts, or maybe that's just when he stops hiding it. Cocaine, heroin, just about anything he can get his hands on.

You threaten Bo and start withholding money. You say you'll take it all away if he doesn't go to treatment, and he throws all the coats from the front hall closet off the balcony in protest. He's impossible. Childish. Churlish. You pack your bags to leave and he begs you to stay. He says he'll kill himself if you leave, so you unpack. This goes on and on, back and forth, and your family starts to get worried. Your parents fly in and beg you to go home with them, but you just can't abandon your husband.

Bo decides it's Monaco that's the problem. This party lifestyle is making him act crazy, so you buy a big house in Tuscany and move him out there, where it's quiet and peaceful. Well, that's a problem, too; he hates quiet and peaceful, so you go to Paris, but he starts using again and you spend night after night looking for him or dragging him back from some girl's apartment. So you take him to his grandmother's place in Gijon and leave him there. Damn it all to hell. *Men!*

You go back to Paris and stew on Bo's complete lack of emotional maturity. Why are some men so broken? You go to the gym and start tai chi lessons to get out some of your anger. Talking to him doesn't help, reasoning with him doesn't help, the only thing men like Bo understand is brute force. Primal responses. You meet several other women with the exact same problem. Men who cheat on them, treat them badly, who can't learn or don't want to.

It gives you an idea. Why not open a reeducation center for men?

L'ÉCOLE D'HOMME
The Man School
A Training Academy for Men

The school's motto is: THEY COME IN KICKING—BUT THEY'LL LEAVE SWEET. It's a huge hit. Frustrated women from all over the city deliver a steady stream of inconsiderate, boorish, selfish, self-absorbed, addicted, weak men whom you retrain and make better. The men don't come willingly —if they did, they wouldn't need treatment. Besides, the "willing" part comes in time. You employ a talented cadre of Korean girls trained by the kkangpae (Korean mob), who are truly excellent at low-profile abductions, not to mention the art of persuasion and Gestalt therapies. The gang provides free transportation to incoming clients after they're drugged sleeping in bed or while leaving their offices.

Once in your care they go through a series of response-technique therapies; they're strapped down and electrodes are clipped to their private parts. Then they're shown pictures of strippers, and if the sensors detect even the slightest indication of arousal, they're given a short, hard electric shock. It continues with pictures depicting infidelity, teenage girls, and raucous nights out with the boys. Tougher cases get water-immersion therapy and food privileges withheld. (The Korean girls in particular are very precocious at inventing successful behavior modification techniques.) By the time your subjects are blindfolded, shoved in a black van, and dumped back in front of their houses, they're new men. Supplicant, grateful, and wary. Younger women make them uneasy now. They keep sensible work hours, eschew out-of-town business trips, and dislike taking colleagues or clients out for drinks, preferring to be home in time to eat dinner with their families. The wives and girlfriends write you tearful letters and e-mails of thanks.

It becomes a very popular service.

Your riches increase tenfold as L'École d'Homme expands. You buy a magnificent apartment overlooking the Seine and travel all over the world with a cadre of rotating partners, including Bo, who was brought in and rehabilitated nicely. You're never quite so in love with him again, however. Something's missing.

132

From section 40

You race down the highway to the Cutter house, wondering how to alert them without causing undue suspicion or harm. What are you supposed to say? "My husband might have murdered your girl, but I'm not sure. Probably you should keep your boy inside just in case"?

No.

Maybe you could leave a note? Something like: *Dear neighbors, Ralston might have gone crazy and stabbed people up, so please keep an eye on your loved ones.* Or you could just have a cup of coffee with Mrs. Cutter and explain that whatever the situation is, she can depend on your help no matter what. You will help protect her family. Yes. That's it. That's what you'll do. That's got to be the way.

The Cutter house is dark. Nobody answers the bell. You walk around back, through their little yard. Toys are scattered around in the gravel, laundry flaps on the line in the wind.

You knock on the back door. "Hello? Anybody here?" Your voice sounds weak. Tiny. The wind kicks up and the screen door rattles. You hear whispering inside. You open the door and step in.

"Hello?"

"Now!" someone shouts and Mr. Clutter's face rises up from the darkness. His pitchfork barrels down, piercing your sternum and lung.

You fall forward into the house, landing sideways on the linoleum floor. The pain in your chest is searing and blood bubbles from your mouth. The lights flicker on and the Cutter family comes out of hiding. They're talking. They know it was Ralston who killed their daughter. The sheriff knows it, too. He told them to wait awhile, then take care of the situation themselves. Easier that way. Now they got you, they'll get him next.

You fall forward into the house, landing sideways on the linoleum floor. The pain in your chest is searing and blood bubbles from your mouth. The lights flicker on and the Cutter family comes out of hiding. They're talking. They knew it was Ralston who killed their daughter. The sheriff knows it, too. He told them to wait awhile, then take care of the situation themselves. Easier that way. Now they got you, they'll get him next.

You lie on the floor gasping.

They make sure you're dead before they call anybody.

Heaven has a complaint window, and the line is long. People demand to know why they were taken from their families, ripped away from their loved ones, snatched up before they got to retire. A woman in front of you says she just needed *two more minutes* to tell her daughter something. Something *important*. The teller stares unsympathetically behind her little caged window as the woman goes on and on. "My daughter needs to know she's ruining her life!" she shouts. "That man she picked is the worst!"

When it's your turn at the window, the teller asks what the nature of your complaint is, and you haven't a clue what to say. Couldn't the powers that be have helped you more? Taught you better lessons? Let you ride wild horses more often? The whole thing seemed like one long hurricane. The storm drains in your heart are full.

"Better luck next time," the teller says, and hands you a ticket for your next life.

Now the whole ride starts up again, and this time you don't care who they say you are or where they set you down. This time around, you know what you're doing. You're busting out early and heading right to the hills. You're gonna catch you some horses.

133

From section 77

This epic insect quest will take you to the rural jungles of Sulawesi in the northern province of Indonesia, which is made up of over seventeen thousand islands tossed across three and a half thousand miles of ocean. All the islands sit on the "Ring of Fire," an arc of volcanoes and fault lines that circle the Pacific Basin. It's hot, buggy, and filled with dangers ranging from earthquakes to insect-borne diseases, so you have to be prepared.

You spend a sizeable chunk of your savings on gear. Water sandals, hiking boots, pocketknife, polypropylene underwear, a headlamp, a rain jacket, and a big waterproof backpack made just for rain-forest trekking that has breathable mesh sides and a "low-profile" configuration, so you're not whacking yourself on trees and getting caught up in vines.

You fly from New Orleans to L.A., where you sprint through the airport to catch your connecting fourteen-hour flight to Taipei. Then you get on another five-hour flight to Jakarta. When you finally get off the plane at Soekarno-Hatta International Airport in Jakarta, you're hungry, exhausted, and unsure what day it is.

You wind up sitting at a McDonald's eating a "McRice Burger" (two rice patties on a bun), while Chip writes a postcard back to the lab that pictures an incredible ice blue ocean and a sunset that's stupidly perfect. He says you're both having a great time.

By the time you arrive in Palu, you're nauseated from bouncing up and down on the bus and you decide to relax on a nearby beach before the eight-hour bus ride on to Sulawesi. The idea of another eight hours in motion makes you want to cry. A cab drops you off at a glorious white-sand hamlet filled with fishing boats and villagers, where you spend three glorious hours sleeping. Then it's time to go. You didn't even have time to swim in the water.

On the crowded bus, you can't set your backpacks down because of the coffee-can-sized holes in the floor. The ceiling leaks, too, so when it starts raining, water drips through the roof, and wet rusty splinters shower down on you.

An eternity later, the bus drops you off in a village called Doda, where a taxi driver named Budi offers to takes you into the surrounding hills of the Besoa Valley. He charges you a fortune, but it's worth it because he hooks you up with a family living deep in the jungle in a rickety wooden house on stilts. They don't speak English and you can stay there for three dollars a day.

Every morning you and Chip trek through the jungle loaded with collection jars and specimen boxes. You wield machetes, hacking your way through the undergrowth. You collect hundreds of butterflies. Iridescent bluebottles, absinthe-green birdwings, Caribbean-blue *Papilio ulysses*. The highlight is the magnificent swallowtails. Operatic creatures. Like small colorful kimonos lighting through the banyan trees. They have large, velvety black wings with broad brushstrokes of marzipan, cherry, and lollipop blue. You and Chip stop to make love in the most remarkable place, on an ancient stone statue, a ruin deep in the jungle, which Chip says is probably thousands of years old. Afterward, you sit under a banyan tree and stare out across the valley. That's when a gorgeous *tambusisiana* alights, flexing its beautiful black velvet on iridescent blue wings.

You wake up.

You were dreaming. There was no bus, no Budi, no swallowtails. You're still sleeping on the beach in Palu. You didn't hear the sirens or the people shouting as they ran for higher ground. You only wake up as the water thunders down on you, enclosing you in a cold airless space. You're dragged up into the streets, somersaulting with the tidal wave, churned with debris and buried in mud within minutes. It takes aid workers two weeks to find you, scraping back the red mud from your face.

134

You decide to go on the retreat with Sam. Why not take a break and relax a little? Your lodge on Lake Superior didn't turn out to be the oasis you'd hoped for; maybe Sam's retreat will be less of a soul-torturing suckfest. The brochure looks nice.

You'll be going to a holistic healing center in Sedona named the Celestial Center, which focuses on helping you find your own Inner Oracle. Ted and Arabelle Markowitz are the owners and they welcome you to their "co-creative program." Ted says that by using the earth's energies, your guardian angels will help you discover your "Oracle Within," which will forevermore guide you and help you to stop constantly screwing up.

The schedule at the center is flexible. You can pick and choose from various events and workshops, so you decide to attend a class called "Conscious Cash: Healing Your Relationships with Money." Ha.

The leader of the workshop, an airy nymph named Kym, opens with ten minutes of deep breathing, then asks the group to write down their most precious belongings on narrow strips of paper, which she passes out along with Bic ballpoint pens. Everybody sets about listing the things they love most and then Kym collects the strips of paper and puts them in a box.

She leads the group outside, where a bonfire is already going in the sacred spirit pit, and she tosses the box on top of the flames.

"Let go of what you love," she says. "Material possessions are temporary, fleeting. As impermanent as everything you wrote down."

"But I wrote down my daughter," one woman says. "Weren't we supposed to write down things we loved?"

"I meant objects," Kym says. "Like cars or television sets."

"Well, I wrote down my new diabetes monitoring device," another man says, holding up his arm. "Wear it right here on my wrist. I'd be dead without it."

"Okay," Kym says. "Let's just do our primal scream." She tells everyone to release their negative soul-sucking money gods by screaming as loudly as they can for as long as they can.

The sound is maniacal.

Then class is over.

Next you get an energy massage, which is kind of peaceful, but the masseuse doesn't actually touch you. She waves crystals over your body and sings. At one point you think she starts crying. Later that evening there's a bonfire after dinner and you're given the choice of going to bed early or participating in a sweat lodge. Sam chooses to go to bed, but feeling as though you haven't gotten quite enough out of the day, you choose the sweat lodge, which you expected to be a teepee or some other sacred-looking structure, but it turns out to be just a big eight-by-twelve-foot plywood box.

Ted reads a long ancient Druid prayer before anointing everyone with palm leaves and instructing them to disrobe as they enter single-file into the box. Inside, benches line the walls, and the only light comes from an oil drum at the far end of the room. It's heaped with glowing red rocks. You sit down bare-assed on a wooden bench without even a towel between you and the slick cedar boards. (Ted says towels prevent the oracles from speaking, but maybe you should tell him they also prevent bacterial infections.)

It's hot. Sweltering. More people come in and crowd around you. There must be enough oxygen in here, they do this kind of thing all the time. You just have to keep calm as you acclimate. Ted says another prayer and pours water onto the rocks, making them sizzle and hiss into the air.

It's really hot now. Like being inside someone's mouth.

Ted says to let your impurities sweat out your pores and let your negative thoughts come out. If you feel like crying, then cry. If you feel like groaning, then groan. Do anything you have to and let the darkness come out. He says after two hours you'll feel fresh and new. *Two hours?* You fan yourself with the back of your hand and ask if there's any water. No. There's no water. Ted says prayer and meditation are the only things that should be consumed in the sweat lodge.

So you pray. But after a while you feel faint. Others around you are making strange sighing sounds and resting their heads on their naked knees. Some lie down on the floor. You ask if you can leave and Ted strongly encourages you to stay because it's only once you push past your comfort zone that your oracles will start talking to you.

You sit down. You start to feel light-headed and weak. The air is thick, as though you're trying to breathe through a wet blanket. You see visions. Is this what he meant? Is this your oracle? Then you lie down on the floor. It feels so cool down here. There must be a draft from the floorboards. Then you drift to sleep. Tomorrow, the headlines will read: TWO DIE, OTHERS OVERCOME AT SEDONA SWEAT LODGE.

The county sheriff declares the tragedy an accident. No one else there the night you died presses charges, and the hazardous materials team tests for carbon monoxide, carbon dioxide, and other contaminants, but they find nothing unusual.

135

From section 70

When you request a prenup, Bo throws an ugly fit, screams his head off, starts throwing things, smashing framed photos of the two of you. He even takes your mother's picture and hurls it into the trash. The ranting and name calling continue, until you manage to physically push him out the door and lock him out of the apartment.

You're devastated. Destroyed. Heartbroken. Heavy. Unable to breathe, think, eat, sleep, or get up. Finally Sam arrives to save the day (again, again, and always again) and spends a week with you, washing your hair and force-feeding you home-cooked meals, like you were a little baby. You are a little baby now. You're starting over. Now is the time to restart your entire world, and you decide the best way to Etch A Sketch your brain is to do something so epic that it takes over all your thoughts and makes all the painful thoughts and bad memories blur in the distance.

Safari! That's what you need! An exotic trip to a completely foreign locale. Bring on the big-ass safari. It's every millionaire's wild card, to be played at any time, without much notice. There's no time to mewl about Bo, you're too busy buying eight-hundred-dollar binoculars and digging out your passport, because you and Sam are going to Africa! Two weeks later, you're embarking on "Tanzania Trek," a luxury safari catering to "intrepid travelers and adventurous singles."

The journey starts at the Intercontinental Hotel in Nairobi, where the tour group spends a few days in the city acclimating and waiting for strays to arrive.

You meet lovely Sinethemba, the six-foot-tall Zulu tour director, who walks and speaks with the grace of a Zulu queen. Everyone's a little scared of her. She introduces you to your guides, elderly and sweet Mr. Morompi and his handsome son, Kotikash, or Koti for short. They're both Masai. They speak English to the group but prefer to use their native Masai language, Maa, when speaking to each other. You like it because you sometimes learn the Masai names for things. "Fruit stand" is *m-bosoré* and "singing" is *ranyaré*, which is what Mr. Morompi keeps telling Koti to stop doing while he's driving so we don't get killed.

Finally your tour loads up onto the "White Elephant," which is what they call the big ivory-colored tour bus. It's a great time to get to know everybody and to figure out there are two people, no, really just one person, on the bus you can't stand. Steve Burmeister, or "Hateful Steve" as you come to call him, is a short butterball-shaped man from Fresno. He knows everything, he corrects everyone, he's been there, done that, if you think something's cool he saw something cooler once, and so on and so forth until you want to kill him. His wife, Shelley, rolls her eyes a lot when her husband talks, and at one point says, "Just ignore him. Better yet, listen to your iPod. That's what I do."

Finally, after a long, bumpy ride across the border at Namanga, where the paperwork required to get into the country exceeds a college loan application, you enter Tanzania and drive to the Masai Mara National Reserve, where the Masai live. You spend the first night at the Naárri Lodge, which is built on stone stilts so all the elephants and giraffes can walk right underneath your rooms. Koti says the name of the lodge means "Long Ago Place" and it feels that way. Like you're seeing the land exactly as it was a thousand years ago. It's a wondrous, heavenly place where you feel deeply at peace.

That night, however, you hardly sleep. Despite the posh room and yards of mosquito netting over your bed, Steve and Shelley, occupying the room next to yours, launch into some argument that goes on forever, and then some damn little insect, some creature of a hateful disposition and evil nature, bites you unmercifully until you're covered with tiny red welts that itch like hellfire. When you finally get up around four in the morning to find ice for your bites, there's Steve standing in the hallway in his striped pajamas looking quite red-faced while pointing his little white uncooked sausage finger at Shelley, who's also in her nightgown.

"Hemingway *was* a great writer!" Steve says.

"He might've been a great *writer*," Shelley says, raising a fist to her hip, "but he was no great *man*, Steve. His only way to commune with a lion was to blow its *head* off."

"He was a hunter!" Steve argues. "He wrote 'Snows of Kilimanjaro'! He won a frickin' Nobel Prize!"

That's when they finally notice you're standing there. Shelley gives you a saccharine smile. "Did Steve tell you he's working on a novel?" she asks. "We came to Africa so he could find *his voice*."

Steve glares.

"Um, I just need to get some ice," you say, eking past them and heading for the stairs.

"Why can't you be more supportive?" Steve demands.

"You're never going to finish that goddamned book and everybody knows it. You don't have the discipline. You're not a novelist, Steve, you're a page-ist!"

When dawn finally breaks, you've only gotten about an hour of sleep, which puts you in a very bad mood. Today you're touring the reserve, and then the tour is meant to stay overnight in the Enkang, or traditional Masai village. There's a big dinner and dance ritual planned and you don't want to be tired, so you pop a few caffeine pills you brought along for just such an emergency.

The reserve is incredible. Magnificent. Koti drives the unwieldy behemoth of a vehicle down the rutted roads while Mr. Morompi points out water buffalo, elephant, giraffe, dik-dik antelope just over a foot high, herds of Thompson's gazelles, and even a lion, although it was a brief sighting, a female retreating from a freshly killed wildebeest. You could only get pictures of her powerful haunches as she trotted into the brush, and you can hear Steve from the back of the bus whining, "Great! All I got was her ass! Lion ass! Perfect!" Sinethemba shushes him and you love her even more. She's really like the armed guard of the outfit.

The Masai people seem lit from within. Resounding with vitality. They wear loads of beaded jewelry on top of red and purple cloth and do tribal dances where they jump straight up and down to see who can go the highest. Their village is surrounded by a tall circle of stacked thorn branches, which helps keep wild animals out. Since the seminomadic tribe lives off their cattle and moves the village at different times during the year, their huts are semipermanent as well. They're built with tree branches and sticks, then covered with cow dung and mud.

After the cattle are brought into the safety of the thorn circle for the evening, a dinner of roasted meat is served (which wasn't of completely identifiable origin), then there's some more singing around the fire and general revelry until everyone turns in for the night at their various Masai host families' huts. (Part of a high-end "luxury" safari is getting to rough it. If you weren't so rich, you couldn't afford to stay in a shithouse.)

Late that night you wake up and have to pee bad. You were afraid of this. The "toilet ditch" is on the other side of camp and requires you to squat in a most unseemly position to use it. You decide to just pee behind the hut. It's late, no one will know, and goddamn it, you're paying too much money to have to use a toilet ditch. You should be able to pee anywhere you want. You finally get up and tiptoe around back, to the edge of the thorn circle, where you squat down in the shadows just in time to hear voices coming your way. Not Masai voices, either, and they get closer until you recognize their owners.

Shit. It's Steve and Shelley, who are for their own reasons taking a three a.m. stroll, and once again they're in midfight. Perfect. You lean in, hoping they won't see you—and they don't, stopping mere inches away from where you're crouched as they try to scream at each other without raising their voices. "You can't make me stay!" Shelley hisses, her angry face illuminated by the thin sliver of the moon high overhead.

"I never told you to come!" Steve whispers. "I wish you hadn't! I knew you'd ruin it! You ruin everything—the only fucking talent you actually have!"

"I'm leaving!" she says. "I'm going back to the lodge and your fat old liposuctioned weeble-wobble ass can't stop me!" She starts marching toward the gate. *Good Lord.* You really don't feel like witnessing this. What is she going to do, cross the reserve on her own, at night? And . . . ouch! *Thorn in your ass! Thorn in your ass!* You bite your lip as stinging nettles burn like poker-hot pinpricks on your butt.

This is the worst safari ever.

"Shelley!" Steve shouts. It's loud enough to start a dog barking somewhere. She reels around, her travel bag gripped tightly in her hand. "What?"

"You know what you need?" There's a strange metallic clicking sound. You can't see what he's doing. There's a series of loud pops and a scream as something hits you in the eye. It's you screaming as you stumble up and catch your foot on something in the dark, forcing you to fall backward full weight into the thorn wall as you black out in pain.

You die and go live on your star. Obsidian-Absalom-Elysian-Eight. Even though it's never been recorded by any scientific database, it was seen once by a small Masai boy who was walking alone at night.

Due to a rare astronomical configuration and a particularly clear magnetosphere, when the boy looked up as he walked away from the village, he saw a star up in the sky that had never been there before. There was no name for it. Later he tried to describe it to his friends, pointing up to *énk-áí,* the sky. He said it was a star so far away it was in a sky beyond the sky, but they did not understand what he meant. The boy was searching for the word "universe," but there is no Maa word for this.

136

From section 59

You take over the restaurant on Orcas Island in the little town of Eastsound. It's a crab shack called the Blue Plate and it's on the harbor in an old white wooden building, originally a cannery with clapboard walls and a stained pine floor. It's not fancy—the tables have red-checked paper tablecloths and the fish tacos and crab cakes are served in red plastic baskets—but it's a popular place, popular with the locals and with tourists, with families and the grizzled longshoremen.

You like the chaos and noise of the place. It's impossible to feel down when there's so much going on around you. Running a busy kitchen is like waging a small ongoing war. There's an endless need for supplies, recruits, marching orders, and strategy. You handle the pressure remarkably well; it's nice to get lost in something bigger than you are. Scouring the pots and cracking the pink crab legs, a curtain of steam and sweat always engulfing you, has a Zen-like repetition to it, like those monks who spend days and weeks creating ornate pictures of sand, only to let the wind blow it away as soon as they are done.

Then one night you meet an astronomer named John, a quiet man with eyes that remind you of a night sky, dark with small diamond lights. He comes in for a bowl of hot chowder and says he's studying the magnetosphere, the invisible shield that envelops the earth and protects us from all the dangerous, poisonous rays and particles we're bombarded with every day. You peer out beyond the red-checkered curtains into the darkness. Who knew we were under such threat?

He takes you out to his cabin, where all his computers and communication links are hooked up with the ESA, the European Space Agency. He worked at NASA for a while, but they were too rigid, too orderly for him.

"The universe is one chaotic mess," he says, "a gorgeous mess, and sometimes studying it has to be messy, too." He says NASA wouldn't let him work out of remote locations as he wanted to, insisting instead he stay in the lab, because they had perfectly good billion-dollar telescopes right there. "The director didn't believe in running amok," John says. "He was British and that's what he told me. *I don't need you out there with your toy telescopes running amok.*"

His specific area of study is the "balance points" of the magnetosphere. He says every two entities strike a balance at five gravitational points. At least two of the points are so stable they can capture asteroids, space particles, dust and debris. Solar flares create magnetic storms, which we can sometimes see in the aurora borealis. When you ask him *why* he's studying the balance points of the magnetosphere, he explains there've been rapid, almost sudden changes taking place in Earth's magnetic field recently, while changes are simultaneously occurring in the liquid metal nineteen hundred miles below the surface of the earth. The changes may suggest the possibility of an upcoming reversal of the geomagnetic field. In other words, Earth is getting ready to reverse.

You're confused. "You mean, like, start spinning the other way?"

Yes. Exactly.

Apparently the magnetic field has reversed hundreds of times over the past billion years and the process takes thousands of years to complete. No one knows where we are in this cycle—we could be smack in the middle, or we could be toward the end—as these recent signs would indicate. He says geomagnetic storms affect brain waves and hormone levels and all kinds of other things scientists don't even fully understand yet. All they know for sure is that any time there's a solar flare, heart attack rates spike.

You had no idea.

John shows you all the constellations out in the fields. His arm brushes against yours as he leans in to adjust the telescope for you and he smells heavenly. Through his lens you see Cassiopeia and Orion and the Big Dipper, which you already knew but you let him show you anyway. Then you kiss him. You can't help it; you've wanted to for so long that it becomes an irrepressible urge. He looks utterly shocked and then kisses you back with a forceful tenderness you had not heretofore experienced. It turns out humans have five balance points, too. Sound, sight, smell, taste, and touch. When two bodies lock orbit, these points pull. They must look right to each other, sound right, smell right, feel right, and taste right.

You tell John about your millions after the wedding. He seems to take it for a joke, until you confess to buying one of the grandest homes on the harbor for him as a wedding present. You live there together for the rest of your life, running the restaurant and spying on the heavens. You live relatively simply and credit the restaurant with your sanity, as strange as it sounds. The steady work, the hard work, the scouring and rescouring of the same pots burn off some slippery layer on you, some unpredictability and uncertainty you never thought you could lose.

Years later, many years, when you are old and John is even older, you stand together in your backyard at twilight, watching your grandbabies run and tumble as they catch fireflies. The moon is rising red as a blood orange and you're struck dumb with a kind of happiness that usually only visits small children. A strange giddiness, because there is no reason for it. Any of it. The magnetic field warding off asteroids, solar flares licking waves of plasma at us, the earth spinning, molten lava running underground, rainstorms, bumblebees, kissing on a dock, whales migrating, the wild unpredictability and uncertainty of the world, it's all a statistical impossibility, yet here it is—spread out before you on this beautiful evening, with fireflies.

137

From section 106

You decide to invest in the space tourism program. Starlink is a great talking tidbit at parties for fellow bon vivants and for would-be sexual conquests. Men perk right up when they hear you've "invested in the space program." It's not standard party banter and triggers their deep-rooted childhood desires of growing up and becoming cowboys, firefighters, or intergalactic outlaws, otherwise known as astronauts.

You can hardly blame them. Astronauts hold appeal for you as well. In fact, you usually imagine it's an astronaut in bed with you instead of these guys you pick up at parties. It's not meant as an insult, it's just that nothing tops astronaut. Money, looks, personality, popularity, and fame bleach up and blow away in the face of space travel. Simple fact. The only terrestrial-based male who can hold a candle to an astronaut is a firefighter. Sexy as they are, however, they're still government workers. With astronauts, you get it all. Money, power, prestige, and fame. (Looks are officially unimportant if you've docked in a space station.)

When you finally fly to Cape Canaveral for a big fancy Starlink dinner that Sterling's hosting at NASA, you're almost too excited to go. You'll be mingling with dozens of sexy, square-jawed astronauts interested in becoming pilots for your company. Apparently the idea of civilian space travel has already "taken off" (Sterling's pun) and the first flight is sold out to the tune of twenty million a ticket.

It's a beautiful evening, hosted at the Kennedy Space Center in a massive white tent that's set up on an actual launch pad. One thing you learn that night is that astronauts can party. Some of them anyway. You're seated between two of them, Mikhail Demidov, an aerospace engineer originally from Odessa, and Eric Sorensen, a mission specialist from Ohio. Both men are charming and funny, and after dinner they both offer to dance with you. Then they offer to take you on a private tour of the Starlink shuttle, which is in the final stages of construction over in hangar 42. One hour, two orgasms, and a lost shoe later, you all emerge sweaty and rumpled, having officially completed a very important mission. Your first aeronautical three-way.

After that you put every effort into launching the Starlink program. You hold fund-raisers, court politicians—you even sell off some of your personal assets for the final funds required. You love fraternizing with astronauts, they're freaks. Set above and off to the side of normal society, these celestial cowboys are aware of their appeal and they use it. You've been to astronaut parties where every moment, every event, could or actually does become a viral video on YouTube. Your personal favorites are the nude river dancing and monkey knife fights. Besides, the idea of pioneering a new frontier, really the *last* frontier, is thrilling. You will actually be on board the first civilian flight to the moon!

The day of the launch is amazing. All the weeks of preparation, training, and drills you and your fellow passengers, mostly Asian businessmen and one Texan, went through are worth it. When you're all strapped in, heart hammering away like a piston, and the shuttle thrusters fire, an immense pull hits. There's intense pressure on your eyeballs and your internal organs feel like they're changing position. Then there's a flash of white, the sensation of speed, and then nothing. The shuttle has exploded.

The flight deck on the ground goes utterly silent for one almost imperceptible split second before flying full speed into their disaster recovery procedures. It will all be in vain. The plume of smoke, which is taller than both the Twin Towers standing end to end, says it all. There are no survivors.

The ambulances waiting on the tarmac turn off their lights, TV stations interrupt their regularly scheduled programming. One reporter recalls the words of the rocket scientist Wernher Von Braun: "Don't tell me that man doesn't belong out there. Man belongs wherever he wants to go."

In heaven you ask God why he allowed your spaceship to explode. He rolls his eyes and says he didn't *allow* it, he *caused* it. It annoys him when people traipse across his sky lawn. He's mad at you and says in your next life you'll have to choose between becoming a writer or being a carpet salesman. He raises a warning eyebrow and says, "If I were you, I'd go with carpet."

138

From section 114

You decide to manufacture drugs. At least some drugs heal people, so you can mass-produce them with the full intention that people will choose to use them for good instead of, say . . . um, self-destructive purposes.

Mica is pleased. He says he was hoping you'd go with this industry because he already has a complete business plan ready to go for the hottest category of prescription drugs. He not only has the business plan ready to go, he's already picked out a cherry management team, located the perfect factory, secured a distribution center, and picked the company's name.

Meddie-Dins
(Din-Din and a Dose!)

It's a cute name for a company that makes a wide variety of special food just for children. Snacks, beverages, and frozen entrées, which are special because they're loaded with prescription drugs. All the medicines kids hate taking. Moms are always trying to trick their children into taking their medicine, and now they have the ultimate stealth weapon. No more sticky spoons of cough syrup, no more grinding up pills and hiding the gritty bits in peanut butter. Kids don't fall for that stuff anyway. Now they can get every remedy they need and never know it.

There's *Copsicles* (cough syrup popsicles), *Ty-Ty Nums* (Children's Tylenol chocolate-chip cookies), *Adderbutter* (Adderall-infused peanut butter), *BioticPops* (antibiotic lollipops), *Pro-Chickies* (Prozac chicken drumsticks), *Insadillas* (insulin quesadillas), *Paxi-Mac* (Paxil mac-and-cheese), *Rafforli* (Effexor ravioli), and other such products that turn the headache of administering medicine to already ill wee ones into the relief of giving them a treat.

Mica says the amount of drugs being prescribed to children has more than doubled over the past decade and trend research indicates that within another ten years this number will double again. It's a pint-sized pill gold mine.

Meddie-Dins launches its debut line despite ongoing debates about the ethical implications of surreptitiously drugging children. The mood-stabilizing products sell the best, with *Rell-O Pudding Cups* (Ritalin pudding cups) and *Stratta-kix!* (Strattera-laced cornflakes) in the lead, followed closely by *Lexy-Bears* (Lexapro gummi bears).

As a side venture, you open a children's "Emotions Management Center" called Bashville, where kids can deal with problems in a tangible, proactive manner. After donning protective gear and watching a short safety video (where Sunny, the slightly cracked cartoon egg, gives them tips on avoiding injuries while "letting all the uglies out"), they're taken to "therapy rooms," where they can safely express their emotions by chucking rocks at windows, smashing living room lamps, throwing whole pies onto pristine white couches, and hurling clods of dirt at photos of their parents. There's always "venting specialists" on hand to make therapeutic suggestions. *Try smearing peanut butter on the walls! How about pouring soy sauce onto the carpet?* Short of hurting themselves, kids can do whatever they want to.

The centers were initially just meant to be a Meddie-Dins delivery vehicle. Every kid that comes through the door goes home with a goodie bag of sample snacks and convenient Meddie-Dins coupons redeemable at markets nationwide. But then the demand outgrows the supply. Parents who bring their kids to Bashville don't question the center's venting techniques, or worry too much about safety, as they stand in the observation room watching their children smashing up furniture and going wild with rage—they just want to know if they can use the therapy rooms themselves.

Mica immediately draws up plans for a chain of centers called Big Bashville, where adults can enjoy the same therapeutic sessions as their children. Soon Big Bashvilles and Little Bashvilles spring up in every major city in the United States, then around the globe. It turns out the one thing that connects us all is the universal desire to smash things.

So too the Meddie-Dins product line gains popularity in other countries, the name changing according to locale. In France it's d'Entrée de Jeu, "Right from the Start"; in Germany it's Drogenbrot, which is quite literally "Drugged Dinner." Mica hires sharp marketing teams to adjust the company's image as needed and the result of all these international industries and services is financially phenomenal.

You become a mega-billionaire. A true empire builder at last. Now you can use your money philanthropically. You fund cancer research centers and Russian ballet troupes and civil rights causes. You send aid to foreign countries, building schools, hospitals, and water treatment plants in every abandoned, disenfranchised, forlorn place you can find. You help children, starting arts programs, pediatric clinics, literacy outreach organizations, and college scholarship grants, and you donate so many gymnasiums, auditoriums, and libraries that half the elementary schools and high schools around the world bear your name.

You buy a few things for yourself, too. Like an entire village in England. The village of Blackshire in Gloucester includes a Baroque castle, two thousand acres of land, five hundred acres of forest, a manor home, twenty-odd Tudor houses, a cricket club, a blacksmith shop, and a greengrocer. The only building not included in the sale is St. Christopher's Church, which holds services on the third Sunday of each month.

You're able to turn your acreage into a wildlife preserve, securing protected land for indigenous animals, endangered species, and migrating birds. You take it a step further by hiring a team of conservationists, botanists, and landscape architects to cultivate habitats for such endangered species as the Scottish wildcat, the long-eared owl, and the water vole. You find a brilliant apiarist, Mr. Simon White, who says with proper funding he can augment the return of the bumblebee, which is not only the UK's most critically endangered species but the world's. So fund him you do.

The Tudor houses on your property are turned into a foster-care facility for children in crisis. A large parcel of land is donated for the construction of a new children's hospital with a state-of-the-art cancer treatment wing and physical rehabilitation center. The architects are instructed to incorporate as much of the surrounding natural beauty as they can, building indoor waterfalls and connecting walking paths that allow patients to take short walks through the woods as they're able. You like to think it's one of the few hospitals in the world where people can get well.

You build an extraordinary life for yourself. Sure, the products you push create a generation of mentally unstable, malnourished freaks, but they don't really affect society for another two decades and you have lots of fun till then. Money can buy you anything, and "anything" gets weird fast. Like the purchase of a robot squad, automated servants who power up and down at the flick of a switch. Keiko, Buzzkill, Maximillian 301X, Buddy-boy, Lil Scooper, and Putz. They walk, talk, compliment you, wipe your mouth (or your ass), tell you the time, and cook supper. One copulates with you on command.

139

From section 105

You don't push the red button, deciding it's better to leave the unknown alone. Who knows what it might do, probably flood the room you're standing in with corrosive acid or open the sealed door of some vault filled with flesh-eating zombies.

In fact, you decide not to even tell Aidan about it. Mr. Machine-Loving Gadget-Testing Monkey Man will want to see it for himself, and you just know he won't be able to resist temptation. You make your way back to the pantry and put the bottle of paprika back in its slot. The door *whooshes* shut. You move a heavy set of shelves in front of it, too, and load it up with canned goods so you'll never be tempted to touch it again.

Life goes on in the bunker. On and on and on and on. Your daily routines become more specific and intricate. Deviations from protocol irritate your nerves. Aidan is constantly disrupting the flow of things and sometimes you wish you were here alone—but whenever he leaves the bunker to run errands, you feel panicked until he gets back. The world above scares you. It seems noisy and out of control. Sometimes you wish it would all vanish, but then who would deliver your calligraphy ink? Who would make it? Not to mention your bonsais, which require exacting tools to sculpt them into miniature majestic oaks, and the copious amounts of high-end cookware and exotic groceries you have shipped in from around the world. Four ounces of fresh Iranian Imperial caviar sells for about eight hundred dollars, but it's worth every morsel. As time goes by your underground bunker becomes your whole world. Occasionally you think of the red button, but not often and not for very long.

140

From section 67

The trailhead for the north side of Mount Everest is in Tibet. Your group journeys by four-wheel convoy to the remote location and starts unloading gear. Everybody's excited and nervous and horsing around with each other. Then someone says, "Who's that?" as a military jeep followed by a canvas-covered truck comes bouncing down the road.

An angry Chinese officer in a dark green uniform arrives with a military escort. He starts pointing his finger and shouting at Kitchell, who in turn digs out some documents and tries to hand them over, but they're pushed roughly away. Then the officer goes apoplectic, his face the color of red prawns as he throws a wrinkled wad of cash on the ground. Kitchell apparently tried to bribe him, and he's not taking it.

Meanwhile, two soldiers struggle to lock the rusty chain link gate, while another uses an ancient staple gun to tack up an official-looking document on the wind-battered message board. The document is covered with large red Chinese characters and one of the guides who speaks Mandarin says the mountain is closed.

Can they do that?

Apparently they can—and they have. The officer says anyone who tries climbing China's mountain will be arrested. That's when someone is stupid enough to snicker, and it's like the wind dies down and the birds stop singing so the officer can figure out who it was. Finally he spits at the ground and gets back in his jeep.

Before you know what's happening, the expedition is over. You will not be climbing Mount Everest. Silence drops over all of you at this realization, which is heavier and harder to pick up than the unwieldy gear that must now all be loaded back onto the bus.

The group works quickly, without speaking. The next thing you know, the tour bus arrives in Lhasa and the group gets dumped off at a little café in Barkhor Square.

There's Kate and Faye, the Australian cancer survivors; Ed and Nick, the Canadian grandfather and grandson; Marcus, the electrical engineer; Daniel, the corporate trial lawyer, and his quiet wife, who has a name but no one can ever remember it. Last, there's Paulo and Valeria, the Brazilians. It should just be a general life rule to go wherever Brazilians go. They're fun and sexy, even in goggles, but not much can spice up this sad scene.

Kitchell buys everyone a round of weak barley beer before going outside to scream at someone on his cell phone. "So, it's all over now?" someone asks, but nobody answers. Everyone just stares into their beer. Kitchell finally storms back in and says the bus will take everyone to the airport in the morning. One of the Australian ladies asks if they'll be getting their money back and Kitchell says military intervention is considered *an act of God*, so sorry—no refunds, no discounts, and hopefully, come to think of it, no future treks whatsoever, because he doesn't even want to do this anymore. Why he ever thought dragging fat public television subscribers up the side of a mountain would be a good way to make a living, he doesn't know. He must have been crazy.

Then he storms out.

So there you are, grim little clods of disappointment sitting in a lousy little bar drinking warm beer in the middle of the day. All this time, all this money, and nothing to show for it? Is everyone really going home? You all commiserate as you drink and someone orders another round, probably the Australians. Then there are shots, then more beer.

Suddenly Nick, the youngest in the group, sits up and shouts, "Bikes!"

He pitches the idea so fast it's hard to catch everything. He thinks everyone should stick together and plan a new adventure. He knows exactly what adventure, too. You should ride across Tibet on bicycles. The Friendship Highway starts right here in Lhasa and runs the entire length of the country, through mountains and valleys, through villages and towns, all the way to Nepal. He has friends who took this route in college and they said it was the best blast ever. It's over six hundred miles, takes about twenty days, and covers some of the most severe terrain in the world, so, let's go! What the hell? You were ready to climb Mount Everest!

There's a moment of silence and then a huge cheer. People laugh and bottles clink as you celebrate the stupidest idea ever. Stupid only because while your group already owns some of the best camping gear money can buy, there's one thing nobody has for this grand bike trek across the mountains.

Bikes.

Not a bother! Within the hour you've all set about buying up a motley collection of ancient bikes from locals. These bikes! Some have no brakes and others are heavier than motorcycles. You wouldn't want to pedal them across the street, let alone the country, but nobody cares. It's not about that anymore. With a little elbow grease and ingenious repair work, they'll do.

The group embarks on its new quest two days later. There's a glorious sunrise, and as you leave town, squirrelly, mischievous Tibetan children line up by the side of the road and high-five each of you as you chug past. Some of them hit *really* hard. Outside the city limits the group slowly pedals its way up the steep, winding roads. The views around you are vast. Sweeping mountains rise up and acres of rocky plateaus are cut by deep river gorges.

As your bikes spit and weave along the gravel road, big, boxy Land Cruisers occasionally tear past and tourists snap pictures before disappearing in a cloud of billowing dust. How can they even see anything as they race through this incredible countryside? They're missing all the good stuff. The tiny villages along the road, the tin houses, and wind-whipped tangles of prayer flags. Certainly they're missing the smell of the sheep. You actually enjoy that smell. Everything smells good when mixed with mountain air. You are glad to be alive. You always knew money couldn't buy you happiness, but maybe sometimes it can, if you know what to do with it. This tremendous blue all around you, these white chalk mountains, these strangers who are now friends, all of it was possible because you had money. Now that you're here, though, it seems like a hot cup of coffee and a warm campfire is all you really need.

When you arrive at the first checkpoint, which is one of many military stops on the road, a stern woman in a dark uniform takes your papers. She frowns and yells at one of your friends for sitting on a nearby rock. You all wait around nervously; no one likes having their passport studied.

Finally, your troupe is allowed to pass. The landscape changes into pastoral farmland and the weather shifts from freezing to steaming hot. The road changes, too. It's rutted and then it's smooth, hard-packed one minute and sloppy with rocks the next. You stop struggling at some point and start living in the ecosystem of the moment.

At dusk, you make camp in a farmer's field. He brings you milk tea and yak skewered on bamboo kabobs, which you roast over your little cook stoves and devour like wolves. It's funny, you've had some of the finest food, but this unsalted yak meat is the best meal you've ever had.

As everyone packs up the next morning, a group of children appears and they surround you. (One thing you've learned about Tibetan children is they're anything but shy.)

They ask you for help and lead you to a nearby field, into a thicket of stunted trees, and a small clearing where a large statue of Buddha sits in an old wooden cart. He's big and mossy. Maybe twelve feet tall. The children try to explain in broken sentences and strange gestures that they need to *hide* the statue but they can't move it. It's too heavy. They want you to use your bicycles to pull the cart somewhere. You think that's what they say, anyway. They might've been trying to sell it.

Now it's always a good instinct to help children, but these kids are alone, unsupervised, and who knows what their parents would think of a group of foreigners wandering off with them into the woods. Plus, you have no idea why the children seem so agitated and worried, but it's possibly because they're asking you to do something illegal.

If you help hide the statue, go to section 74 (p. 235).
If you go on to Nepal, go to section 91 (p. 287).

1 4 1

From section 71

You become a Connector. You complete a course in conflict resolution and get sent to Israel. Good God in heaven. *That's* the conflict they want you to resolve? You're stationed in Jerusalem, where you live in a tiny stone dormitory. You share it with Ephraim, a Jewish kid from Toledo. He's in a permanently foul temper because he just made *aliyah*, or tried to. There are organizations that give Jewish people free tickets to return to the Holy Land, and they gave one to Ephraim, but when he arrived he was told that not only was his paperwork wrong, he wasn't technically a Jew. The Ministry of Absorption denied him citizenship, refused to give him a ticket home, and retracted the allowance they'd promised. So Ephraim, who came because he was "broke as shit," found himself broke, jobless, and homeless. He started volunteering for the Peacefighters, or as he calls it, "this King-Crap Circus," so he could sleep in a bed.

Ephraim gives you pointers on living in Israel, things *he* had to learn the hard way. You should never carry a milk shake into a butcher shop, because of the whole milk-and-meat problem. Also, he says, never leave your bag unattended in a public place. He set his gym bag down to answer his cell phone once and thirty seconds later he was under citizen's arrest. He also warns against talking to anyone of the opposite sex in public. "You can try," he says, "but I chatted up this girl on the bus once and it made me about as popular as a Christmas tree."

Your first Peacefighter assignment is going with Ephraim to the synagogue, where you study the concept of *tikkun olam*. It's a Hebrew phrase meaning "to repair the world," and it's a concept with many interpretations, but generally refers to an act that makes the world a better place, like volunteering and social work. It's closely related to *tzedakah*, financial support of the poor, and *g'milut hasadim*, acts of loving-kindness.

Ephraim's not a very good student. He's easily distracted and likes to bump heads with people, often asking the rabbis difficult, sometimes rude questions.

"Well, I say you're selling a wagon with no wheels," he argues, "because the most obvious *tikkun olam* would be to let anyone live in Jerusalem who wanted to. *Including* Palestinians. Especially Palestinians, because as far as I can tell God's message is about loving your enemies, not shooting at them through chicken wire."

That's around the time you both get kicked out of the study program. The rabbi calls the Peacefighters coordinator and tells her you're both hostile. *Both of you?* You hardly got a word in edgewise! The coordinator doesn't care. You're reassigned to the other side of the fence. Now every day you and Ephraim have to make the long, arduous, checkpoint-riddled journey to the West Bank, where you work afternoon shifts at Starbucks. (First Starbucks in Palestine.) You're told this mission is to familiarize yourself with Palestinian culture. You converse with people as they come in for their daily cup of coffee and try to understand the culture better.

Ephraim's just as diplomatic on this side of the fence. He argues with everyone. He asks Yara, the manager, if Allah made the *whole* world. Yara goes red in the face and shouts, "Of course Allah made the whole world!" Ephraim eggs him on. "You're sure? Because some people say he only made *parts*. Certain mountains, some oceans, a few lakes." Yara starts shouting and spouts a lengthy list of all that Allah has created. "Allah created every flower that blooms! Every animal that breathes! Every drop of water in the oceans! Every grain of sand in the deserts! Every single stone on Earth!"

He goes on and on until he's nearly out of breath and afterward the whole coffee shop applauds. Ephraim shrugs. "Okay then, if Allah made every stone on Earth, isn't it wrong to say one stone is more holy than another? Doesn't it defy God to call Palestine the Holy Land? If Allah made everything, then it's all holy."

The crowd falls into a hushed state of shock, trying to comprehend his blasphemous words. Yara points a finger at Ephraim and says he better sleep with one eye open from now on.

Sure enough, a week later to the day, you're cleaning off tables outside when you notice a backpack on the ground. It explodes before you even touch it. You're instantly blown to hamburger chunks and the blast can be seen from five blocks away.

That night on the news they show grainy video footage sent in by a local militant group who's taking responsibility for the bomb. Their leader is red-faced as he screams, "Wherever lies are found, so too our bombs will be found! Let it be a warning to all infidels! We are coming!" Then he holds up a photocopied picture of your face, taken from your Peacefighter ID badge. He calls a jihad on your family. You, apparently, are the infidel. Ephraim is not mentioned.

In heaven, God goes fishing. He doesn't like to be bothered, so you wait for just the right moment to ask him the one thing you want to know. You sit down beside him on the riverbank one day and ask who rightfully belongs in Jerusalem.

That makes him plenty mad.

"Can you comprehend the heartbreak of creating millions of damned idiots?" he booms. Then he spits. "Nothing is supposed to sit still! Everything I ever created—the birds, the fish, even the frickin' tectonic plates—it's all supposed to move around! Breathe! Grow! How many more examples could I have given you damn people?"

You stare blankly, and he finally answers.

"You all belonged there," he sighs. "You all belonged everywhere."

142

From section 67

The trail for the south side of Mount Everest begins in Nepal. The Chinese government has tried to shut this trail down before, especially around religious holidays, but their jurisdiction is limited. The guides say you're lucky, there's a rumor going around that the Chinese trail may be closed.

Not you, though! Your group is going forward as planned and the first step of the journey is to get to base camp. Calling it base camp seems strange, because that sounds like a jolly starting point with hot showers and jam donuts. Not so. It's one hell of a hike just to reach the starting point. There are only five other mountains *in the world* that are higher than Everest's base camp and there are certainly no hot showers. By the time you arrive at base camp, you're already considering an emergency airlift home. You're completely exhausted. There are mystery bruises all over your body. Feet blistered, legs aching, face burning, arms so heavy they hang like limp yak sausages. The guides say it's normal; you'll feel better after you're used to the thin air. *Oh, right.* You know when you'll feel better, and that's after you're checked into the Hong Kong Ritz.

This is a far cry from the Ritz. The communist-era wind-tattered tents are pitched at thirty-five-degree angles, which is the only angle available when you're clinging to the side of a mountain. There are no flat surfaces anywhere. The whole place is on a tilt, requiring you to bring an ice axe to pee, in case you lose your balance and tumble ten thousand feet down the steep, ice-coated scree before being jettisoned onto Rongbuk Glacier. Just the word "scree" makes you uneasy. It's like the mountain is letting you know what sound you'll be making should you fall.

Screeeeeeeeeeeeeeeeeeeeeeeeeeeeeeeeeeeeeeeeeeeeee!

Base camp does have some unexpected comforts, though, like a cheerful little wooden teahouse. A friendly place with benches and a wood-burning stove in the center of the room where trekkers gather to warm their hands while sipping tea and eating curry. The woman who owns the teahouse lives in a tent out back; her supplies come up by way of Sherpa, so she's on the mountain nearly year-round, which systematically makes her tougher than every other climber put together.

Your group spends downtime hanging out in the mess tent, eating, drinking, playing cards, and calling loved ones on the satellite phone. You call home once, but your parents sound so small and far away, you just want to dive into the receiver and swim up current till you're home. Grandpa Joe yells at you. "Who told you to climb Mount Everest?" he barks. "Oprah?"

"Grandpa, I just wanted to see if I could do it!"

"Yeah? You wanna see if my boot can survive inside your keister, too?"

"It's a test of courage."

"It's proof your damn biscuit ain't baked! Any jackass with hiking boots can climb a mountain. Some blind kids climbed up Rainier last month and everyone was hysterical, they were so happy! Know what I say? I say if you're blind, you're already enough trouble without throwing yourself up the side of a mountain!"

"I gotta go, Grandpa."

"Now listen, kid, I don't know how you got this idea in your head or why no one had enough sense to clip you with a car to stop you, but you're there now, so if you get into a jam, just remember all it took was one dumb decision to get you there and all it'll probably take is one dumb decision to get back. Just do what you gotta do to get yourself home. Got it?"

"Got it."

You hang up and go lie down in your tent and listen to the wind. You feel very, very alone. If there's one thing you've realized on this trip it's that people are all that matter. Living things matter, not houses or cars or titanium trekking poles. They're inanimate objects that can't breathe or grow or love you or call the marines to come get you in a helicopter. Only people can do that. People and some dogs.

Then the guides tell everyone that the other trekking group, the one going up the north side of the mountain, got turned back by the Chinese police. They're not on the mountain, they're not meeting you at the top, they're not even meeting you back at training camp, because the whole group got sent home. Man. Are you lucky, or what? Just knowing you picked the right group makes you feel better. Sometimes things do go your way.

Finally it's time for the real ascent. There'll be no more teahouses or wood-burning stoves. From here to the summit it's just you, your fellow climbers, and the thin rope that ties you all together. The Sherpas wake you up at three a.m. and you have a hasty breakfast of muesli and biscuits with strong tea. Then you take a deep breath and start.

Despite ugly weather and overcast skies, the group heads out, one climber in front of the other. It's cold and dark, but you must get going early, so you can cover the Khumbu Ice Falls before the high noon sun causes any ice to shift. Strong northerly gusts howl across the thick sheets of snow, and even with your goggles, once the sun comes up everything is blinding white. The only place to rest your eyes is on your own feet as you trudge through the snow. When you reach the falls it's surreal and beautiful, like a cathedral of jumbled ice. A booming sound crashes behind you as an icy serac smashes on a snowbank and avalanches down the side of the mountain. Everyone looks nervously at the guide. He just tells everyone to watch their step and *run* if wet snow starts dropping on you. *Watch your step? Run?* This is the plan? You're in a giant valley of ice chunks and gaping crevasses. There *is* nowhere to run.

The group presses on and breathing becomes a challenge. A competition between you and the atmosphere. It feels like you're trying to climb a ladder with a plastic bag over your head. You just . . . can't . . . get . . . air. This must be what it's like to drown, to have emphysema, to feel fluid fill your lungs, slowly. You feel so tiny, so insignificant. It's humbling and terrifying and causes your tiny mouse heart to hammer in your chest.

When the group comes to the first crevasse, it's the moment of truth. You can prepare for it, study for it, but nothing is like staring down a sheer thirty-story drop that plummets straight down into blackness. A guide lays a flimsy aluminum ladder across the chasm and anchors it on both sides. He crosses with no problem and then helps everyone else one by one to the other side. You casually inch to the back of the line so you're the last person to cross, giving you just a few more minutes of safety. Finally everyone is over except you. They're waiting. Okay, breathe. This is what you trained for; this is why you took four months to prepare.

You lock your crampon on the narrow rungs. It makes a flimsy *click* sound and you realize there's just a twenty-dollar aluminum ladder lying between you and death. You take another step. The ladder bows and vertigo pulls. Hang on to yourself now. Pray. Do *not* shut your eyes. Another step. Okay, halfway there now. The ladder creaks, the wind pushes you from behind. Someone is shouting a word of encouragement, but it's snapped away in the wind. A few more steps and you'll have made it across your first crevasse. Click . . . click . . . click. Finally you reach the icy lip of the other side and you plant your spiked foot down hard.

Relief. *Breathe.* What a miracle to be alive. Your climbing partner is there with a camera to snap your picture. The first time you make it across an ice ladder is an important moment. You just popped the cherry of your crevasse. Still, there are many more to come. You set your pack down and take your water bottle out. Then . . . *Boom!*

An explosion behind you, like a 747 crashed into the side of the mountain. *"Avalanche!"* You turn to see a thundering tsunami of ice chunks crashing down on you. You're frozen, staring at the horror of it. Besides, there is no time and nowhere to run. Then it hits like an ice locomotive, cracking your chest and sending you midair. The sensation of motion increases and then you're falling. Then it all goes black.

You wake up in total darkness, with a thousand wet hands holding you down. You can't breathe. You're packed solid in snow and don't know if you're lying faceup or facedown, so you achingly wag your head, making a small hollow space inside the snow. Then you spit, and when your saliva glops back onto your face, you know you're lying on your back. Gravity's the one thing that works in all situations. Now you know to dig up. You wriggle your arms until they break through and frantically claw the snow off your face before you suffocate.

Sitting up, you focus your attention on your new location, which is, judging from the dim light overhead, at the bottom of a crevasse about forty feet below the surface. Disoriented and aching, you stand. Your body feels like a sack of broken glass. Pain knifes through your left knee. Possibly shattered. *Sonofabitch!* Definitely shattered. Warm fluid drips over your right eye. There's a big gash on your head. Your helmet's thirty yards away, split in half like a broken walnut shell.

You feel your way around in the shadows. *Don't panic. Breathe.* You have no idea if anyone else is alive, but there doesn't appear to be anyone else down here with you and you certainly don't hear anyone calling your name. Just the steady sound of dripping water and the echoes of your own feeble movements. Is rescue coming? *Unknown.* Should you stay put? *Unsure.* Do you need to rescue yourself? *Inconclusive!* You settle for screaming, but your voice gets hoarse and no one answers. As time passes and you get your bearings, you try to calmly collect your options.

They are slim and shitty.

You could try climbing up. All your gear is gone, except for the crampons and the ice axe tied to your hand. You could also climb down. You find a small tunnel that drops steeply down into the crevasse, like a slide at the water park. It emanates a light blue glow, so you know it gets close to the light at some point, but where? If you get stuck in that tunnel, there's no one to pull you back out.

"This is not happening!" you suddenly scream. "I won the motherfucking lottery!"

As soon as the words leave your lips, you're all too aware of how meaningless they are. In the end, it's the same for everyone. No amount of money can save you, you have to save yourself. All it took was one dumb decision to get you here and now all it'll take is one dumb decision to get back. Just do what you gotta do.

Get yourself home.

Got it?

If you crawl down, go to section 45 (p. 156).
If you climb up, go to section 90 (p. 281).

143

From section 71

You train to become a Liberator, learning advanced life coach skills and empowering techniques to teach underprivileged people. You're hoping to get sent to Haiti or Guam, but you wind up in Utah. Your assignment is to liberate the sister-wives from a polygamist compound called Freedom from Life. It's a splinter sect of fundamentalist Mormons, another wackaloon group sponsored by the Church of Jesus Christ of Latter-day Saints (FLDS).

Great.

The Peacefighter director tells you they've been working for years to expose this group and you'll have to go in undercover. This means checking yourself into a Salt Lake City women's shelter and waiting for the sharks to circle.

Luckily, you don't have to wait long. One week in the shelter and a ruddy-faced pastor in a brown suit comes around. Pastor Bob. He says his congregation at the Freedom from Life Church offers free relocation housing to all eligible women in need. (Eligible means any woman of childbearing years with strong shoulders and an inexplicably submissive nature that allows her to wear floor-length plaid dresses.) You accept Pastor Bob's invitation to his church service and community fish fry. You go with three other women from the shelter, being taken by a creepy brown van up through the Utah hills.

The van finally turns down a long gravel road, driving past an odd assortment of old trailers and rusty outbuildings. You arrive at a large Quonset hut, which has been freshly painted turquoise blue. It's the church sanctuary and it's filled with parishioners sitting quietly on long narrow benches. You notice right away the majority of the congregation is made up of young females wearing pastel prairie-style dresses. Their hair is braided and pinned up neatly behind their ears and their faces are fresh and soft, no trace of makeup or jewelry of any kind.

Not even a cross.

Pastor Bob enthusiastically welcomes the newcomers in the crowd and asks them to stand. He promises you that you're not a stranger in God's house. You've all been assigned a family to show you around. Sure enough, after the sermon (long, tedious, and chockablock with freaky hymns), a young woman with soft brown eyes named Laila comes and introduces herself and says you'll be sitting with her family at dinner.

Laila tells you polygamy is not about sex. It's about raising a family together and serving God. Sure, sometimes people get jealous, want more time with their husband, pee on a sister-wife's toothbrush for revenge, but whatever. Everyone has those problems. She's in a marriage with two other women, and between them they have twenty-two children. Sure, it's not easy feeding twenty-two kids; they can go through five dozen eggs at breakfast and at least three loaves of bread a day. The laundry is 24/7.

She says no one here believes in underage marriage or coercing weddings. They just believe in living the way Abraham, Isaac, Jacob, and Joseph lived in the Bible. It's a holy lifestyle. One that promotes self-sacrifice, honesty, and community. You're always taken care of here, always watched over, always loved, and never left alone. Plural marriage means you'll never be lonely again.

She seems so damn happy, you half start to believe Pastor Bob's got a good thing going here with "the Principle." Then you watch the children on the compound. They're not as loud as children in the city. Polite, yes, but something else, too. Wary. Alert. Waiting for . . . something to happen. It makes you wonder what goes on when visitors aren't here watching. Laila invites you to come stay with her and her family at their home anytime, just to see if compound life might be for you.

Fast-forward six months and it's your wedding day. You are marrying Laila's husband, Rulon. He's a nice guy, a little chubby, but too exhausted from working so hard to be much threat. You had to get married in order to be initiated into the church and you have to get initiated into the church to get access to the really incriminating documents in the church office. Plus, the director at Peacefighters assures you the wedding is absolutely nonbinding and "consummating the marriage" only happens when a new wife wants it to. Rulon will be fine waiting as long as you like.

So you stand nervously on the well-vacuumed carpet in your new family's living room, a hundred or so people crammed in the room with you as Pastor Bob reads wedding vows, sealing you to Rulon for eternity. Everything about it is so creepy, the room is so hot, you feel faint. Nauseous. You just want to get out. As soon as the ceremony is done everyone claps and you walk decorously out of the living room together.

Then you eat cake.

Well, you were told you'd eat cake, but as soon as Rulon has you around the corner he pulls you roughly into the laundry room and pushes you down hard on the washing machine. What the hell? You start to say something and he takes a clean pair of sweat socks and stuffs it in your mouth. He's got your arm bent up behind your back and your dress pulled up around your waist. You can hear him grunting around as the piano starts playing in the next room and your guests all start singing, "Come lambs and gather round thy father." Rulon's ripped off your underwear and is trying to get inside you but you're completely dry, so he knocks over a bottle of Tide, causing a pool of viscous blue liquid to spill out onto the dryer, which he swipes up with three fingers and smears on your vulva. Then he's in like a piston.

"*I knew you'd be good,*" he croaks and the pounding gets harder. He's really in you now as you're pinned against the rattling washing machine. Someone knocks on the laundry room door. It's Laila.

"You two almost finished?" She giggles.

Rulon grunts and Laila goes away. He's finished a few moments later, pushing off of you and zipping his pants before spitting in the sink. "Welcome home, hon," he says and slams out the door. You just lie there a few moments before slowly, painfully disentangling yourself from your torn underpants. You run them under cold water and mop up in between your legs, having to dig deep to reach all the detergent, which is starting to sting.

A week later you still haven't gotten up from bed. You can't. You're tired. Exhausted. The world seems heavy. The air too dense to move through. Laila brings you tea and toast in bed and tells you it's all right. She didn't get up for a week after Rulon welcomed her home, either. "It's a shock at first," she says, "but you'll get used to it."

Meanwhile the directors at Peacefighters are worried. You haven't checked in and none of the other operatives in the field can find you. When someone finally reports that you went through with the wedding *and* the consummation, they decide to take immediate action, sending in the San Juan Platoon—a mercenary military group for hire comprised of thirty-two Puerto Rican women with guerrilla training and stiletto heels. Their convoy of Humvees and panel vans shows up one night when Rulon's at a church meeting. The commanding officer, Martina "La Abusadora" Martinez, lights up her electric nicotine-free cigarette and steps out of the truck with an AK-47 slung over her pale pink halter top.

She saunters up to your house and kicks the front door in, even though it was unlocked. Then she uses the nose of her gun to flip on a row of light switches along the wall, throwing the whole place up in lights. The sound brings Laila around the corner first, who shrieks, "What do you want! What do you want!" until Martina dreamily says what she really wants is a real cigarette, but she'll settle for taking her new sister-wife home instead.

Laila shrieks again as Jebediah, her youngest, peeks around the corner. "Jeb!" she hisses. "Get back to your room!" But Martina calls the little redheaded boy over. "Come here to your Auntie Martina," she says, waving the boy over with her gun. He hypnotically follows her command, walking over to the couch and sitting down. "You sit right there. Good boy. Your mami's going to get my friend. Right, Mami? *Mami!* What you waiting for, bitch! Go get my friend!" Laila screams and tears down the hallway to your bedroom, where she shakes you awake. She tugs you out of bed, whispering, "They've come for you, but you don't have to leave, Rulon will be here soon. No one's taking you anywhere!"

In the living room Martina is standing there smoking with one black stiletto anchored up on the coffee table. The rest of Laila's various sister-wives and children have all gathered on the couches and sit patiently, as though waiting for Mother Goose story hour.

Martina smiles when she sees you. "*¿Qué pasa, Mami?*" She casually points her gun at Jebediah, like it was a spatula or a pen, and says, "This redhead boy is coming, too."

Laila goes white. "Jebediah! You're not leaving!"

"*Oh jes* he is, Mami," Martina says. "He knows you gonna abandon his little white ass at a gas station in the city soon. Okay. Let's go now. We gotta ride." Martina strides over and takes your arm. When Laila refuses to let go, Martina says, "Bitch, I don't like wasting bullets!" but Laila hangs on, so Martina casually chucks the butt of her machine gun into Laila's throat, sending her sputtering to the floor.

Just then Pastor Bob barrels through the door. "What the hell is going on here!" He charges at Martina, who shoots him once in the leg. He collapses on the floor, shouting in pain. "They tole me not to kill anyone." She sighs regretfully and spits on the pastor as she helps you outside to the van, little Jebediah obediently in tow. The van screeches out just as Rulon and the rest of the church leaders show up. They give chase for a short while, but then Martina radios the last van and orders the cobras to be thrown down, and the troops toss out wicked-looking coils of barbed wire with blast charges attached. They send the first three cars into the ditch and cause the rest to pile up in a nasty wreck.

Back at Peacefighters Headquarters you apologize for your failed mission but the director says you were part of a team that succeeded. They finally got the incriminating evidence they needed. Plus, you can be a witness when the case goes to trial.

You go home, where you're pretty sure you'll never testify against Pastor Bob. It's not enough. The only way to fight fire is with fire. You buy a big piece of land in a remote part of the Utah mountains and name it the THPH Ranch. You have a ramshackle cabin moved onto the property, and behind the cabin you blast out a series of underground bunkers and tunnels, which connect to comfortable living quarters and thoroughly stocked ammunition stores. Inside the cabin, right beside the bed, you install an industrial metal hatch, which drops open at the flick of a hidden switch and shoots down to the subterranean holding cells.

Then you start writing letters to church leaders and tacking index cards up on grocery store bulletin boards. You put ads in the *PennySaver* and post messages on Craigslist. You're looking for any men in the area who can "help a poor girl get back up on her feet." You claim to be a recently orphaned fifteen-year-old with four younger sisters to look after. You're searching for a new life and a safe place to call home. You've been abandoned up in the hills of Utah, and in exchange for your rescue, you promise that you and all your waiflike sisters will be loving, obedient girls.

They come alone and in groups. All men. Pastors, plural husbands, pedophiles. They come to "rescue" little girls and eagerly accept invitations inside the ramshackle cabin. They have to pass a series of tests, of course, and make it all the way to the bedroom with express intent to commit lascivious acts with a minor. But there aren't many who fail the test. None, in fact. Lord, you can hardly dispatch them down the tunnels fast enough! They come in the front door grinning and get dropped down the bedroom hatch screaming. Certainly there's an adjustment period for these men, who've spent whole lifetimes manipulating and abusing women and believing all the while it was God's will. The deprogramming and reprogramming takes time. But you think eventually they really enjoy getting to know your staff of deprogrammers.

The amazing women of the San Juan Platoon run this place and they never cease to impress or amaze you with their tenacity, dedication, and creativity. Their ranks have grown considerably from the original thirty-two. The head officer, Martina "La Abusadora" Martinez, who was once prisoner number 648645 at the California Department of Corrections and Rehabilitation, is now in charge of over a hundred soldiers at the ranch. All women. Her connections at the penitentiary helped build a pipeline of new employees. After all, it's not easy starting a new life as a convict. You too have a new life, as chief in command. Imagine what a lovely fit it is, all that violence in your heart, which you have yet to work out, and all these men who need correction and who have nowhere else to go.

144

From section 106

You decide to fund the "adorable little indie film," which turns out to be a low-budget horror flick called *Virgin Slut Zombies Attack*.

It's a film about a group of vibrant young virgin Catholic schoolgirls who are gruesomely murdered en masse one summer day while waiting for the subway in Union Square. They're on their way to perform with a visiting choir from Haiti and they're all dressed up in their Catholic schoolgirl uniforms—pleated blue-plaid skirts, crisp white oxford shirts, and those mandatory insouciant cherry-red cardigans. The director *loves* these, because they *really pop* during the killing spree.

Just before the train arrives, though, and the choir breaks out into spontaneous song, a deranged serial killer known only as "the Pusher" barrels out of the darkness riding a bloody John Deere lawnmower and shovels them all off the subway platform and onto the Brooklyn-bound Q train tracks. The slaughter is horrific.

You drop eight hundred thousand on the movie, which is almost all the money they needed to shoot the damn thing. You don't care; you just like watching the insanity. Every moment on set sponsors a new, ridiculous drama. The director, Dick Sommerville, won't shoot until his vegan wheatgrass protein shake shows up. The special effects guy rages at the makeup stylist because the actors' fake facial blood doesn't match the fake blood sprayed all over the set. The sound guy threatens to quit because the set's fake subway walls are overdamping the Virgin Slut screams and the art department won't fix it. Virgin Slut #6 refuses to go on camera because the fake blood is giving her an incurable rash. Virgin Slut #3 has a zit on her forehead so big it looks ready to hatch a quail egg.

As an "executive producer," it's your job to stay uninvolved. You're allowed on set but your opinion is neither needed nor wanted, which is fine by you. It means no one's ever yelling at you, which makes you a statistical anomaly. Dick, the director, is notoriously difficult. He's already gone through three assistant directors, two dolly grips, and a camera loader. He's also caused a handful of executive producers to leave. He shouts at everyone, but mostly at the screenwriter. Dick hates the script and says so often. "What happens now, retard?" Dick shouts as the screenwriter cowers by the craft service table next to the emergency exit. "You got a herd of elephants coming next? How about singing cocks?"

The casting director, Barbara, says the actresses were difficult to find. "It was a nightmare and I knew it would be. When Dick said he needed twenty virginal-looking girls who were legal age and who spoke English and could act and dance *and* sing? Please! I dug out my passport, because I knew they weren't all here! He was looking for genetic anomalies! These girls are models from all over the place. That one I pulled off the street in Sweden and that one came from a modeling agency in Bulgaria!"

You had no idea farm-fresh girls were so rare.

"It's not easy to find *any* girls who look virginal these days," she says. "Kids get Botox before they're nine. I'm not kidding; they don't want lines to set in. Ever seen a nine-year-old whose face doesn't move when she smiles? Well, don't. It's enough to make you work with dogs. I start my first all-animal movie next week. I'm casting chickens."

As the shoot rolls on, Dick makes everyone's life hell. Two more producers quit. He seems to have a good sense of humor, laughs at jokes and cracks quite a few himself, but he runs a tight ship. When two of the younger grips started horsing around by the equipment area, they knocked into one of those big spotlights. Those things are huge and heavy, but they must have really bumped it because the head of the lamp wobbled. The light obviously wasn't on or even plugged in, and as soon as the guys realized they hit it, they both instinctively let go of each other and hopped up on the metal base like human sandbags to steady it.

The rest of the crew, the grips and electricians in particular, had all noticed what was happening by now, because knocking into a spotlight and wobbling it on a soundstage is a lot like standing in a china shop and juggling Ming vases. Luckily the grips caught their error in time and a wave of relief went through the room. Everyone else smiled, but not Dick. He screamed at a decibel that made everyone freeze. Then he stormed off the set toward the staging area, which was an unusual, if not unheard of, place for him to go.

Dick stood, arms akimbo, boxing the grips inside the small bay of equipment. He stared at them. They waited awkwardly for him to say something, shifting their weight from foot to foot. Dick, though, said nothing. He just stood there, rhythmically clenching and unclenching his jaw.

By this time both the grips, normally big, strong, jovial guys, looked ready to cry. Past the point of misery. Wishing he'd say something, and then he did.

"But you are!" he shouted. "You're exactly those kinds of men! You're the kind of men who get others killed."

Dick told them they were no longer grips. They were going to get jobs fit for them. From now on, they were sandbags.

He bellowed for Macready, the assistant director and the only one smart enough not to come over until now, and told him he'd hired two new sandbags. And these sandbags were to sit on the sandbag pile until someone came for them. They could not cross the room on their own. They could not speak or eat or use their thumbs at any time. They had to stay on the sandbag pile while wearing their work gloves backward. Any deviation from those rules would result in the immediate dismissal of the sandbags. Then Dick pivoted on his foot and the storm was over. He yelled for a roast beef on rye. He was starving.

The crew hurried back to the set, but Macready stayed behind, explaining to them that if they wanted to leave, he'd process the paperwork right away, but he promised them on his children's lives that from now on they would have to be sandbags; they wouldn't exist for Dick anymore, not as people.

The grips left with a nice severance bonus from the HR department.

Eight months later, when *Virgin Slut Zombies Attack* is finally released, it's a masterpiece of kitschy schlock. So bad, it's awesome. People line up for the premier dressed as zombie girls and maniacal farmers. The painful singing numbers and clumsy dance moves inspire audience members to get up in their seats and mimic the actors on-screen, creating a dance sensation called the Zombie Slut Two-Step that pairs perfectly with the new redubbed soundtrack, which creates its own musical category, "zombie-slut-slam."

A cult following springs up. *Virgin Slut Zombies Attack* suddenly finds itself at the epicenter of a viral publicity tsunami.

Your investment quadruples. Suddenly you're getting requests to produce every cheesy, campy bizarre movie ever conceived by a veritable army of pale, friendless Mountain Dew–fueled scriptwriting degenerates. You love it. It's like discovering you had a superpower this whole time. The ability to pick utterly awful movie scripts. You start production on three more films right away. *Vengeful Space Prostitutes*, a sci-fi thriller about mechanical women who can satisfy themselves while protecting their planet; *Killer Crabs*, featuring a race of mutant sewer crabs that start coming up through people's drains and toilets after an evil seafood restaurant owner releases them into the sewer; and, of course, *Virgin Slut Zombies Attack II*.

All three movies are hits. You're even starting to get A-list celebrities asking to be in your movies. The one and only Julia Roberts is interested in playing the lead for *Easter Bunny Kill-Kill-Kill* and Greg Kinnear has all but confirmed his availability for your upcoming production of *Lady Giant*.

Suddenly you have more money than you even know what to do with. You buy houses, boats, vacation homes, trips, jewelry, cars, furs made of anything except fur . . . and you know what? It's all a little boring compared to reading a new script and figuring out how to make it come off the page and dance on-screen. The movie bug has bitten plenty of people who had more than enough money, but nothing could quite satiate their burning desire to make something new. Lucas, Spielberg, Hitchcock, Scorsese, just to name a few. These guys have enough money to buy anything, except for the one thing they really want.

The next greatest movie of all time.

So you pursue your passion, your obsession, to its natural conclusion. After a decade of producing truly excellent crap, you fall victim to a script. That is, you're on set one day when the giant razor-sharp claws of Slicer the Clown malfunction, a short in the wiring somewhere, and he lurches forward, accidentally severing both your femoral and iliac arteries.

You're dead before anyone can even get you a towel.

145

From section 105

You push the red button and nothing happens. You listen carefully for any sound at all, a click or shuffle or scurry, any indication a mechanism has been triggered or set in motion, but there's none. You inspect the tunnels, look for any new secret passages that have opened up, but everything seems the same. The main breaker panels and junction boxes look normal.

The mystery of the red button remains. You resign yourself to the idea you'll never know what it was for. Then Aidan hollers at you from the master suite and says all the lights just blinked out a few minutes ago. "I was in the shower," he says, "and the water went ice cold for a second. Then it got hot again." You show him the red button and he seems weirded out, but after he inspects everything himself, he agrees with you, it must be broken or maybe just some unfinished project. He'll call Luxe Properties in the morning and ask if they know anything about it.

The next day, however, he can't get through. The phones are down and so is the Internet. Tuesday comes and Jamil never turns up with your groceries. It's no big deal, you have plenty of food, enough for a year if you needed it, but there's not a single head of fresh lettuce, and how exactly are you going to make a club sandwich without a fresh head of lettuce?

Fine. You'll go up.

Aidan presses the elevator button, but nothing happens. What's wrong with it now? You're going to scream bloody murder at the repair company. They've been out twice to fix it. Great, you both haul yourself up the long, steep spiral staircase. You need the exercise anyway; you're falling way behind on your exercise routine—why, you can barely lift the hatch! It's heavy. As you shove the door open a smell breaks in that makes your nostrils wince with its odor. Good God, did a raccoon die in the air duct again?

When you manage to wedge the door open and step through, you find yourself lost in yellow smog so thick you can hardly see the hand in front of your face. A gruesome, foaming blood-covered dog comes charging at you from the smoke, and Aidan pulls you back in the hatch just in time.

The button had a purpose, all right.

You've blown up the United Kingdom. At last there'll be peace and quiet. Now there will, however, be no fresh lettuce.

You and Aidan head to the bedroom. You have work to do. The fate of all humanity lies between the sheets and whether or not Aidan can freaking get it up.

146

From section 80

You choose Port-au-Prince, which is the capital city of Haiti and possibly an easier place to escape from. The pirates say fine and lock Aidan inside the barn. What? *No! Aidan has to come with you!* You shout and scream, threatening them with all kinds of horrible international retribution, but the smugglers drag you off to their waiting jeep anyway.

They drive you ten hours south, to the edge of a crowded open-air market. Exhausted and dehydrated, you sit back and stare out the dirty windows, which are rolled up despite the stifling heat. The market is a chaotic quilt of mismatched patches, all sorts of vendors selling their goods on top of one another. Tables of coconut, sugar cane, and sardines next to wooden cages filled with live chickens and cookstoves steaming conch shells. The shells heat up until the pale, fleshy creatures inside come out, whereupon they are neatly seared and eaten.

Women wearing bold-print dresses balance plastic buckets and laundry tubs on their heads. Wheelbarrows rattle over the rough, unpaved streets, and a donkey passes by, followed by a little boy and a black pig on a rope. There are a *lot* of children wandering around. One buck-naked toddler waddles down the road completely on his own. No one pays him the slightest attention. Dumas calls them *restaveks. Garbage. Orphans nobody wants.* God, this place is a hellhole. You've got to get out.

A woman comes up to the car and speaks French to your captors, who in turn say, *"Oui, oui,"* and tell you to get out of the car.

The woman says her name is Solange. She and her burly driver take you to a large Colonial house owned by a wealthy man named "Le Patron." He's away on business, but he'll be back in two weeks. Just enough time to get you ready. Ready for what? "The intercoursing," Solange says. She starts your "instructions" on how Le Patron likes his "sexing." He likes you to wear this and lie like this and say this and not that and here's the proper soap to use and here's the door where you leave right after he's done with you. Then she gives you some of her old clothes to wear. Among the pile is a sheer dark blue scarf that's so big it could be used as a tablecloth.

You break out of the house that night, which is surprisingly easy to do. You just unlock the front door and sneak out. There's no alarm system, and by creeping low along the bushes, you avoid being seen by the guard in his box at the end of the drive. You flee down the busy street to a nearby grocery store, a little market with half-empty shelves. You look around frantically for a phone, aware everyone in the store is staring at you. "Excuse me, do you know how I . . . Pardon me, do you think you could . . ." They all turn away as though you don't exist. No one will help you.

Then some tough-looking teens walk in and one whistles at you, making the hair on your neck stand up. These boys are bad, bad news. Black eyes, bruised faces. They come cruising down the aisle like a pack of hungry dogs and you bolt out of the store, running all the way back to the house, where you're beyond relieved to see the guard.

In the morning Solange sends you to the market to buy eggs. While you're buying a crate, a peculiar thing happens. The sun begins to burn your skin—not uncommon at this time of day—you can feel that tight, tender sensation on your forearms, face, and neck, so you take the dark-blue scarf Solange gave you and drape it over your head like a bridal veil. It's so sheer you can easily see through it, but the Haitians who see you drifting through the market like a blue apparition are unsettled by your appearance and make way for you. Silence follows. You look like a witch walking down the street. Only a woman with bad magic would dress like this, and your new name rises like floodwater. *Yon Bleu Mambo*. The Blue Witch.

That night when you sneak out again, this time wearing your blue veil, you find no one whistles at you or turns away. In fact, one woman rushes up to you and begs you to bless her—which you do by speaking in a fake language and crossing yourself several times—in exchange for a place to sleep that night. She takes you to her dirty, unlit room deep in the heart of a sprawling slum. It's the perfect place to hide, and to practice your new witchy skills, which allow you to procure food, medicine, and a phone card to call home.

After contacting the authorities and your family, you learn the shocking news that Aidan is dead. His body was found in a swampy river a few miles from where you were held, and ever since then the police have been searching everywhere for you. Your parents are offshore in a Coast Guard boat, combing the ocean floor in case you were dumped overboard. Aidan's dead? It hits you like a fist. He's dead because you brought him here, because of all that money that made you so happy. He never would have been exposed to drug runners or Haitians if it weren't for you.

Your parents are on their way to meet you; meanwhile, the Secretary of the National Assembly asks you to come to the presidential residence at once, by decree of the president himself. Twenty minutes later a black car delivers you to René Préval's ranch, headquarters for Haitian government ever since the 2010 earthquake, which made the presidential palace collapse like a wedding cake. After a medical examination and a short debriefing, you meet with the president.

Préval is a dignified-looking man with square shoulders. His easy smile and peppered beard cultivates an avuncular countenance, but his alert, ever-roving eyes belong to a man who has seen many things happen. In one long, near-breathless rush you tell him the whole story—how you and Aidan were kidnapped and your family had no idea where you were. The president assures you Aidan's body will be safely transported home and your family will be escorted to the ranch shortly. In the meantime, he has a proposition for you. He wants to know if you'd consider staying in Haiti. He explains word of Yon Bleu Mambo has spread not only to the government but to provinces far beyond, including Cité Soleil, one of the most dangerous villages in Haiti. Yon Bleu Mambo has triggered a widespread superstition, and "Superstition is fear," he says. "Fear, of course, is power."

He wants you, the Blue Witch, to become a paid member of the Haitian government. A covert emissary of good will. Someone the people fear and listen to, who tells them rape is evil and *restaveks* are holy. With your mysterious reputation and his power, much can be accomplished. Not everyone in Haiti is superstitious or believes in magic, but many do. He'll let you think about it and promises that your parents will be at the ranch by morning. You consider his offer while staring out the window at the wide green lawn. You could help the *restaveks*? You *hate* that word. That's the first thing you're changing.

And this is how you officially became Yon Bleu Mambo, one of the most loved and feared witches in Haiti. Aidan of course could not join you now or ever, because he got sick right after you were taken away and died a few days later. Sexy Star and Dumas are put in jail after confessing they dumped his body in the ocean just off the shore of Navassa Island.

After returning home to visit friends and family, you decide to take up the president's offer and return to Haiti. You move to Port-au-Prince, not far from the presidential palace and your favorite open-air market, where you buy eggs and watch cockfights and dodge children rolling bicycle tires through the stalls. Where Catholic schoolgirls flock in their starched blue-and-white pinafores and tired women in faded dresses line up to fill plastic jugs with water from the public spigot. Where pigs sleep. Where bleating baby goats wander through the crowds and old men sit on folding chairs and talk.

When you drift through the market in your navy-blue veil, people make way for you. They cross themselves, spit over their shoulder, or shout words of thanks, depending on their personal opinion of you, and safe to say, opinions vary. In general, men hate you, women love you, and children worship you. You live in Haiti until you're one hundred and twenty-one.

That's what the legends say.

In heaven, Jesus goes by "Papa Joc." It's pronounced like "Papa doc," but the similarity ends there. Mostly. He's a rapper and he's got a stage show all worked out with the angels up there in rhinestone baseball caps. You take a seat at his nightly gig and have a listen while a fallen angel gets you a cocktail. The crowd gets quiet when Jesus takes the mic. The beat is low and steady.

JC: Say! Who is me?

Angels: You the big JC!

JC: Who is me?

Angels: You the big JC!

JC: I made the animals! Without no manuals!

And Aboriginals, cause I'm originals!

Say! Who is me?

Angels: You the big JC!

JC: Who is me?

Angels: You the big JC!

JC: I say it's time to meet your creator!

A hirsute Capricorn and not no hater!

I'm the big tuna in every story and fable,

I'm the guy you want on the surg-e-ry table!

Say! Who is me?

*Angels:*You the big JC!

JC: Who is me?

Angels: You the big JC!

JC: I like Barack Obama and Taco Lasagna,

When peeps come to my house and sing, "Hosanna!"

It's not my fault I know what's next,

I like tornados and thunder—I gotta God complex!

Say! Who is me?

Angels: You the big JC!

JC: Who is me?

Angels: You the big JC!

You get up and leave the club. The song sort of gets old.

147

From section 58

You put the whole twenty grand on the last race. Then, just like the dream you've been playing on a running loop in your mind's eye, all four of your horses sail across the finish line in exact order. Rebel Springs comes in first, followed by Strange Candy. Next it's London Calling, and finally, a little filly named Double-Down-Domino. You just fucking won four hundred thousand bucks.

You can't even hear the screaming crowd around you. Your heart is pounding, your legs feel weak. A surging wave of strength is rising up in you, and a queer sensation of telepathic omnipotence. Right now, right here, you are standing in a narrow window of space where you know what will happen next. You know which horse will win. There's another race coming up and a voice in your head tells you to bet again. Bet big. Bet everything.

When you tell Rick you're going back to the betting window and plan to put all your winnings down, he looks pale. "Don't expect lightning to strike twice, kid. Never happens." He kneels down on the dirty stadium floor and begs you not to. He's sweet, but hell, you're lucky.

If you place another superfecta on the last race,
go to section 121 (p. 377).
If you take your money and go home, go to section 151 (p. 488).

148

From section 114

You decide to manufacture weapons. At least armaments can be used for protection as well as destruction, so you can mass-produce them with the full intention that people will choose to use them for good instead of, say . . . um, evil.

Mica is pleased. He was hoping you'd go with this industry; he already has a business plan ready to go and it's for the hottest category of weapons. Disguised weapons.

Mica says any kid with cash can buy a gun or an antiaircraft weapon. The problem isn't obtaining weapons; it's transporting them. You get your weapon at point A, but you have to move it to point B in order for it to be of any use. Whether you're trying to get a handgun on an airplane or a tank across a foreign border, disguised weapons is what people want. What they need.

He not only has the business plan ready to go, he's already picked out a cherry management team, located the perfect factory, secured a distribution center, and picked the company's name. Soixante-Six, French for the number sixty-six, which is exactly how many different types of disguised weapons you'll make. House keys hiding Asp blades. Crucifixes concealing hunting knives. Credit cards made of G10 laminate with edges sharp enough to cut a man's finger off. Cell phones that are also .22-caliber pistols. Flashlights that flip into fully functioning submachine guns. Hollow belt buckles made from melamine fiber to transport explosives. Visine bottles made with corrosion-proof plastic to transport chemical weapons.

Those are just "Accessories." In the "Heavy Artillery" department are guitars that become flamethrowers, crates of apples that are actually grenades, torpedoes that look like piles of rubble, and tanks disguised as farm buildings. You look at Mica and ask if these devices can all actually be made. He gives you his infamous big-boy grin and hands you a silver pinkie ring, which is actually a pistol capable of shooting three live rounds without being taken off the wearer's hand.

"They can all be made," he says, "most already are. We just need a visionary like you who'll manufacture them en masse."

So it is.

An old munitions factory in Munich is bought, new machinery installed, old machinery retrofitted, a management team procured, and an army of skilled workers hired. The doors open, the conveyer belts turn, and your disguised weapons plant is open for business. Mica arranges monthly payments for local government officials, easing the restrictive zoning laws and export taxes, putting Soixante-Six into full effect.

Part of your new life as an industry titan is to look the part, and so you purchase a giant castle outside Munich. You also get a private jet, a fleet of armor-plated limousines, a "safety assistant" who tastes your meals before you eat in case anything's poisoned. All this is to give the illusion that you have enemies, which is good for any arms dealer. Everything about your dress and demeanor in public implies something sinister. (Your signature outfit is a perfectly tailored handmade black suit with black calfskin gloves. You always wear those gloves, even indoors, and you often carry a crowbar. Nothing you've seen is quite as discomforting as someone wearing a nice suit and black gloves while carrying a crowbar.)

Since your products are particularly good for covert assassinations, a large part of your client base are government officials. In any one day you might have representatives from the defense departments of Israel, Afghanistan, Taiwan, South Africa, Greenland (ever wary of Iceland), the United States, and/or Canada (ever wary of America). Leaders from rival countries, ethnic groups, and gangs who visit the factory must be kept apart as you're making deals or the wars they're planning will start early. This necessitates a series of bulletproof meeting rooms with separate entrances, as well as a battalion of interpreters, some of whom can speak over twenty languages.

Your favorite interpreter is Hans, a tall lanky lad from Sweden, who calls the Soixante-Six delivery crew "the Yakuza," since they're all ex-military and led by Captain Black, who has a strict no-nonsense policy when it comes to delivering weapons. Any sign of trouble and he brings out "the drum," a device that uses sonic technology to deafen, literally and sometimes permanently, his target. (The best part of the drum is it's disguised as a hubcap.) Mica assures you in the weapons trade, ugly transactions are par for the course. At least for now none of your people have been hurt.

Your reputation, however, is hurt when some idiot kid in Iowa City accidentally takes off his own hand with a Soixante-Six "Frisbee-axe." Now everyone says *you* are the bad guy. The *New York Times* runs a nasty story about you. The article is a smear job, a character assassination, and your mother cries over the phone. They make you out to be a ruthless warmonger, a wayward evildoer "unencumbered by the burden of conscience." This histrionic editorial sparks the Associated Press to list "the top ten worst companies," in which you make number six, just beneath a sewage treatment plant that was caught dumping crap in the Mississippi River, and just above a company that manufactures chemical abortion kits in Malaysia.

You're splashed across the headlines as one of "The Terrible Ten." Publicly hated and regarded as everything that's wrong with society, you retreat into the company of your new band of brothers, the other nine sinners, which is an elite group, to be sure. You meet for the first time at the behest of your lawyers, and once you're finished it's like you're new best friends.

There's a CEO who siphoned millions from retirement funds when his billion-dollar company verged on bankruptcy, a hedge fund tycoon who had clients invest in a pyramid scheme of phantom mutual funds so he could live like King Farouk, a fuel industry titan who bought pristine Alaskan territory under the guise of a Native American tribe so he could drill for oil, the CFO of a software company who did cocaine off his secretary's ass and then framed her for drug possession and racketeering when she threatened to talk, and so on and so forth. It's an energetic group. Sure, you wouldn't leave any of them alone in a room with your dog, but they're great conversationalists and the hedge fund tycoon still has a yacht, which is actually a decomissioned battleship that he had retrofitted with a nine-hole golf course. It's true. Sinister has its sexy side. You buy your own yacht, which you stock with hookers, guns, and blow. You sail anywhere you want, buying drugs, jewels, and endangered animals. (You thought you'd enjoy having ponies onboard, so you could play polo topside, but the horse crap is just too messy.) Nobody stops you. Nobody interferes. Everyone knows who you are and what you're capable of.

Sinister has a costly side, too. One week before your court date, Hans shows up at your door with a big grinning smile. He has flowers. Yellow carnations. An odd choice for flowers in almost every situation you can think of in the 16.3 seconds you're still conscious. Hans steps inside your house, hands you the flowers, and they immediately start hissing. You start to cough and black out.

Apparently Hans grabbed Soixante-Six's newest inventory, the "chemical shower flower," a bunch of yellow carnations that emits a strong, caustic spray of Agent 15, otherwise known as 3-quinuclidinyl benzilate. (You had asked them to be made with yellow daisies. Daisies! But that's what you get when you work with all men.) When you wake up the next day you're plagued with hallucinations, disorientation, slurred speech, and impaired memory. The doctors explain over the course of the next few days (it takes awhile for you to understand anything now) that these effects are permanent.

Hans was hired by people who want to take over your company. (Read one Mr. Mica Baum.) He needed you incapacitated and unable to testify or return to work. Naturally as your business manager and the next in line at the company, he valiantly steps in. You're never able to explain any of these thoughts to the outside world, of course, as you're slow as a smelly baby elephant on Benadryl now. Everyone in your ward knows when you're coming at least fifteen paces before you arrive. You're like the rotten broccoli of mental patients. Agent 15 has a nasty effect on glands.

In purgatory you're practically a celebrity. The meaty little hobgoblins who carry out God's orders shriek with glee when they read your dossier out loud. Not only did you build an empire of weapons, which were all used to hurt, maim, and kill people, you built that empire with *Christian sex magazines*. This is what they call a pretty big "get" for God.

A high-pitched wail goes up among them and they smolder in various shades of viscous green and bilious yellow, screaming and sizzling with rage at each other, arguing over who gets to deliver which punishment. They finally draw tabs for assignments.

Boilpot will pluck out your eyeballs and replace them with white-hot coals of smoking sulfur, while Sludgeon will peel off your skin with a glass potato peeler, and Grimesore-Goil will turn your bones into swarming logs of blind worms. The hobgoblins whistle as they work. They're so happy you're finally here.

149

From section 58

You decide to take your money and go home. Rick's relieved and proud of you for not giving in to temptation. He walks you to your car and hugs you.

Then out steps Glue Bucket.

You're confused. Why is Glue Bucket here? Is he trying to give you another T-shirt? You tell him *no thanks*, but he holds out his big clompy hoof, which is holding a gun. He shoots you and you fall down onto the asphalt.

The men work quickly, Rick shoving you into your car, while Glue Bucket steals all your money. You bleed out before anyone finds you.

150

From section 57

You're not going to Rome. You tell Aidan you just can't take it anymore, so he loads every one of the group's complaining fat asses back into the bus and tells the driver to go without you. The feeling you get as the bus pulls away is fantastic. You're free and you're going to stay that way. Life is too short and you've got too much money to be spending your time with idiots.

Unfortunately, the bus breaks down on the outskirts of Rome in a particularly notorious neighborhood, which your group thought looked "interesting" and so while the driver (who did not speak English) radioed for help, the tourists insisted on getting off the bus and wandered aimlessly around in the dark, looking for an "authentic" trattoria or wine bar. They were like sheep to slaughter.

Luggage was stolen, wallets were pickpocketed, and ankles were twisted as they tried to hurry their self-entitled asses away. Your reputation is ruined though, and the lawsuits, thirty-four in total, bankrupt you. You receive scathing letters—hostile threats from the lawyers—and angry letters from the tourists. They're all delivered by the postman, a smiling-eyed man named Giuseppe, who stuffs them neatly in the small wicker basket outside your door.

You and Aidan never left Positano. You let the whole thing drift by on an Adriatic blue current.

You're home. Living in a small apartment on a back alley, wotking at a local bar, going to the sea on Sundays with crusty bread and cheap Chianti, making love in a nearby olive field, and watching sunsets with Aidan every night with a glass of limocello. It's true. You're poor and you've never been happier.

151

From section 147

You decide to call it quits and go home with four hundred thousand dollars. Of course when there's a payout that big, security walks you to your car. Track policy. Good thing, too, because you learn later there was a string of muggings in the track parking lot that very same day. You take your money and go to the biggest race track of them all.

The stock market.

After studying biotechs for a few months, you place a few bets on— rather, *buy a few shares of*—Instaconnexed (INXS), a tiny company that's launching an instant gene-mapping therapy, which will enable doctors to map their patients' genetic medical risks with a simple blood test. You also buy Zupacken-Groß (ZUG), a German conglomerate specializing in the hostile takeover of small pharmaceutical companies, and Meddie-Dins (DINRX), a company that makes medically enhanced frozen dinners for children.

You turn your four hundred thousand dollars into four million within a few years' time. Then you double that and double it again. You buy Grandpa Joe his own fishing camp in Montana, where all his buddies can come live, too. You stock the place with nurses, doctors, and a canteen filled with enough whiskey to drown the *Lusitania*. Your parents move out there, too, as do some of your cousins. Even good old Lanie, who recovered from her coma and is now fit as a horse, lives in her own yurt and makes molasses.

You like having a big compound for your family. Mostly because you know where they all are, and you can be somewhere else . . . namely on the prowl, sleeping with all manner of young men and having a grand old time spending money and traveling all over the world. You start a winery in Napa, open a restaurant in Berkeley, and launch a nightclub in New York.

Then you sell it all and start over again. Not because you love rebuilding businesses, but because you're tired of it. You're still pissed off Aidan got married and you never do. It just irks you. Itches at you late at night. None of your sexual conquests really matter, because none of them last. You go to therapy, hypnosis, nothing helps you set your sadness down.

You settle for having Aidan and his new wife killed. No blood, nothing like that, you just pay a man ten thousand dollars for each hit and then it's done. Poison in their Starbucks. Easy as pie. Like they were never here, and even if they were, there'll be no cute Christmas cards, no news of his promotion or her pregnancy, just a nice, long silence. You thought you might feel bad about it later, but you don't. Life just seems a tidier and more pleasant place.

152

From section 119

You choose to die naturally. You're not sure you're down with all that *Twilight / True Blood* sexy-undead stuff. Sure, actors and makeup artists can make vampires look good, but actual people? Just how many decades would you really want to cruise around hunting for blood while wearing complicated lingerie? Even the high-end stuff chafes. Lace is the worst.

So you die and then you're dead.

You come back as a mushroom in the Pacific Northwest. A *Cortinarius rubellus*, or deadly webcap, growing deep in the Hells Canyon National Recreation Area, right in the great state of Washington. You're very poisonous and very close to a walking path. You spend days coiled in muscular preparedness and nights tending your vibrant dreams. Every morning you reach out just a little closer to that walking path, hoping that some innocent hiker will finally pick you up and eat you. Angry little mushroom.

153

From section 119

You'll take being undead. You expect truth in advertising here, in that being undead must mean you are *not* dead. Not completely. Of course, you're not completely alive, either, which is across the board preferable. Being undead must be like the wine cooler of life-force options. Not exactly what you wanted, but better than milk.

Dottie breathes into your mouth with her black, smokelike breath, until you're sure you're going to suffocate. When you come to, you're asleep under a train trestle.

How typical.

You get up, dust yourself off, and wander around. No idea where you're supposed to go or what you're supposed to do. Are there meetings? Subscription fees? A Burlington Northern comes barreling down the track, and without any concern for your confused, muddled state, smacks right into you and in one inconsiderate wallop splinters you into meat mist. *What the hell!* What happened to floating through walls and objects passing through you? You settle on the gravel and iron rails like gristly raspberry jelly. Then you slowly start to ooze and pool together again, which feels like sluicing naked through a big vat of bloody chicken parts. It's cold, goose-pimple flesh and clammy. Like touching a dead animal.

Only this time, you are the dead animal.

You are what's gross.

Finally you've congealed up into a damp meat-loaf consistency and you're able to wobble up and stand. Your legs feel solid as pepperoni sticks. God! Is this what it's like to be undead? This is nasty! Where are all the svelte vampires with European haircuts? Why don't you have stunning, piercing eyes that command obedience from mere mortals? Your eyes look like small, scuffed-up eight balls.

The following weeks will introduce you to a whole variety of other unpleasant and humiliating facts about being undead. Birds, for instance, can chase you off. Even pigeons. Ever seen a pigeon suddenly start flapping its wings and scooting along the ground for no reason? It's shooing off the undead. Works, too; you're terrified of them. You're also easily seen by small dogs and perceptive children. Whenever a toy poodle goes ballistic yapping at thin air or a baby launches a loaded spoon of oatmeal across the room? You guessed it.

Shooing off the undead.

The main problem is your senses are for shit. All this talk about hearing more keenly or having the vision of a bald eagle is crap. You're constantly bumping into things, tripping over curbs, and walking right into backyards with dogs or babies or birds in them. Sometimes all three. They shouldn't call you undead, they should call you mostly practically senile or mostly useless. You couldn't scare someone if your leaky, squishy life depended on it.

Then you meet a frickin' vampire, who are like the most retarded assholes on the planet. Super show-offy. This one vamp-boy, Lichen, starts picking on you and chucking shit at you, which you can't dodge because you can't frickin' *see* anything. He threatens to tell COVICA about you, that's the Council of Vampyric International Community Affairs. You tell him to slap some Gyne-Lotrimin on his stupid vampire council and then he'll have a soothing ointment for the hot rash on his vagina. He whips a hubcap at you and it slices you right between the eyes. *"Fuck! Quit already!* This shit takes forever to close up again!"

He calls you *Rotty-retard meat puppet* and sails off laughing.

God, you hate vampires.

ACKNOWLEDGMENTS

Humble and endless thanks to Jeanette Perez, whose ferocious editing skills are both swift and serene. Ongoing chunks of gratitude are hurled at Carrie Kania's well-adorned feet, who waits and possibly wonders, but for some reason never walks away. Love and apologies to the entire editorial and production staff at HarperCollins, who sigh and shake their heads when assigned these books but always do the heavy lifting, especially Kolt Beringer.

Much gratitude to my family and friends for loving me despite the odds. Also to Minnesota Public Radio, Ira Glass, Billy Collins, and Joyce Carol Oates for egging this pale writer on. So to Elizabeth Sheinkman for getting the ball rolling.

Thompat helped me sneak whiskey-jack onto a New Orleans streetcar, Black Marcy supplied smart soothingness in the face of true weirdness, Thornswood sent spectacular oddities and Nils knows what swiftlet soup tastes like. Many thanks to Colin Bolton for Tibet, to Alex for Nicoya, to Adam "2B" Brooks for Hemingway, and to Angela and Jean-Christian for Haiti. Also to Wiebe for drogenbrot, the Favellis for Key West housing, Romeo for the hotels, Andrew, David, Bart, and Tim for levity, and to little Walter, who beat all the odds.

ALSO BY HEATHER McELHATTON

PRETTY LITTLE MISTAKES
A Do-Over Novel

ISBN 978-0-06-113322-0 (paperback)

In Heather McElhatton's interactive do-over novel, new choices wait around every corner. You can become a millionaire and retreat to Ireland, join a strange religious cult in your hometown, or end up a piece of sushi served to the King of Japan. Your fate is in your own hands!

"A chick lit–meets–noir [novel] where the choices are tougher, the stakes higher, and the characters sexier and far more disturbed." —*Curve* magazine

JENNIFER JOHNSON IS SICK OF BEING SINGLE
A Novel

ISBN 978-0-06-146136-1 (paperback)

Darkly funny and outrageously honest, McElhatton's wicked wit shines in this no-holds-barred cautionary tale about getting what you want—and how it can be the worst thing for you.

"You might think this is just chick lit, but keep reading. This brash and funny novel plays with the form, with a dark, intelligent and wholly unexpected conclusion."
—*Minneapolis Star Tribune*

MILLION LITTLE MISTAKES

ISBN 978-0-06-113326-8 (paperback)

You've just won $22 million in the BIG MONEY SUCKA! lottery. Will you keep your job or quit? If you're a tidy, goody-two-shoes rule-follower in real life, you can break the mold and make decisions you'd normally never make in this follow-up to McElhatton's first do-over novel.